An
Exaltation
of
Larks

An Exaltation of Larks

of

Larks

a novel

SUANNE LAQUEUR

CATHEDRAL ROCK PRESS | NEW YORK | 2016

Suanne Laqueur/Cathedral Rock Press
Somers, New York
WWW.SUANNELAQUEURWRITES.COM

Publisher's Note: This is a work of fiction. Names, characters, places, and incidents are a product of the author's imagination. Locales and public names are sometimes used for atmospheric purposes. Any resemblance to actual people, living or dead, or to busi-nesses, companies, events, institutions, or locales is completely coincidental.

Book Design by Ampersand Bookey
Cover design by Tracy Kopsachilis

An Exaltation of Larks/ Suanne Laqueur. — 1st ed.

ISBN 978-1539178743 (paperback)
ISBN 978-1-7379814-3-5 (hardcover)

Author's Note

THE USE OF HISTORICAL events and places in this novel are a respectful mix of fact and poetic license. The village of Guelisten does not exist in Dutchess County, and I feel it necessary to point out there is no Calle Isabella, Calle Trinidad or Plaza San Margarita in Santiago, Chile.

Augusto Pinochet's military forces took control of Chile on September 11, 1973, ousting Salvador Allende and bombing the presidential palace. Plans for the coup called for the arrest of any man, woman or child on the streets that day. Tens of thousands were detained, hundreds tortured and in some cases, murdered. The Caravan of Death—an army death squad—flew by helicopter from south to north, ordering and carrying out executions.

In the wake of the coup came Operation Condor, a campaign of political repression, state terror and forced disappearance. The number of deaths attributable to Condor remains disputed. Some estimates are that at least 60,000 Chileans died in the operation. Some estimate more. Victims included dissidents and leftists, union and peasant leaders, priests and nuns, students and teachers and intellectuals.

Thousands of Chileans remain disappeared to this day. *Los Desaparecidos* and the victims of America's 9/11 were never far from my thoughts during the writing of this book.

—SLQR
October 2016
Somers, New York

To Camille, who watched me strike the first matches;
Emma, who told me to burn the house down;
and Brian, who helped me sort the bones.

EXALTATION

Noun: ex·al·ta·tion\ ˌeg-ˌzȯl-ˈtā-shən

The act of raising someone or something in importance;
The state of being exalted;
A strong sense of happiness, power, or importance;

(**Astrology**) the sign or part of the zodiac in which the influence of a planet is most positive;

(**Zoology**) a flight of larks.

"Second chances are given or made."
—Rafael Gil de Soto

"You should be able to look your income in the face."
—Gloria Landes

"Pinochet shut down parliament, suffocated political life, banned trade unions, and made Chile his sultanate... His name will forever be linked to Los Desaparecidos, the Caravan of Death, and institutionalized torture."
—Thor Halvorssen,
president of the Human Rights Foundation,
National Review

"Hey, Mr. Pinochet, you sowed a bitter crop."
—Sting,
"They Dance Alone (Cueca Solo)"

Part One

DOORBELLS

FOREIGN ENEMIES

*T*HE DOORBELL RANG at three in the morning.

Alejandro Penda was awake immediately, sitting up in the double bed in his parents' room. Clementina, his mother, was slower to rise, her silhouette big and round in the moonlight.

The bell rang again. Alejo moved as close as he could to Clementina, his arm creeping across her pregnant belly.

"Cálmate, hijo," she whispered.

"It's a friend."

"Shh."

"Papi said friends ring the doorbell," Alejo whispered. "Soldiers and police bang with their fists."

"Get up," Clementina said, throwing the covers aside. "Come." She pulled on a robe, tied it above her stomach and stretched hands to her son. "Ahora, Alejito."

She pulled him toward her closet and pushed him inside.

"Stay here," she whispered as the doorbell rang again. "Just to be safe. It's me they want, anyway."

She shut the door. It was pitch dark within, a pillowy, inky blackness Alejo could sink his fingers into. It stopped up his ears, making the sound of his own heartbeat enormous, like an angry fist pounding on a door.

Friends ring the doorbell.

The bell rang one last time. Then silence, except for the blood rushing in Alejo's ears.

He was not quite eleven years old and didn't understand what was happening in the world. Only that Chile was heaving and bucking, caught up tight in a fist of change that squeezed harder and harder every passing day. The fist belonged to a man named Pinochet, who was the arm of something called the Right. Alejo tried to fathom his parents' frantic whispering, but he couldn't make sense of what was right and left, only what was *us* and *them.*

Back in September, *they* bombed La Moneda, the presidential palace, where *our* president Allende lived. Allende was dead now. *They* filled the streets with soldiers and crammed the skies over Santiago with low-flying airplanes and helicopters. *They* showered the streets with leaflets. The daily bomb blasts and dynamite explosions were *their* doing. But if *they* were the Right and the Right was right, it meant *we* were the Left. Which meant the left was...wrong?

Huddled under dresses and jackets, Alejo pulled his kneecaps tight to his mouth. The fear burned like a hard fire, pressing him from all sides, as if the walls of the closet were moving together. His mind chattered like teeth and silent tears leaked through his squeezed eyes, wetting the thin fabric of his pajamas.

Cálmate, hijo.

Four days ago, his father didn't come home from work. A doorbell rang that night too, but at the respectable hour of eight. It was Eduardo's assistant, Milagros. Her clothes were scorched, her eyes reddened with smoke, burns on her arms and hands and legs. The soldiers had torched the librería and arrested Eduardo.

"Alejo, go to your room," Clementina said. He ducked only halfway down the hall and hid behind a bookcase, listening. Clementina kept the front door half-closed and he could only catch scattered words.

"Leftist sympathy... Dissident literature... Student uprisings... A threat... Arresting foreign enemies."

Alejo's mind juggled the words around, trying to extract his father from them. Eduardo Penda was a tall, slender man. Handsome, almost pretty, with dark wavy hair and green eyes behind wire-rimmed glasses. He was left-handed, as was Alejo—was that what Milagros meant by *leftist*?

Dissident. Did that mean absent-minded? Eduardo's gaze was either fixed down in a book or up at the sky. He was always late, forgot important dates and often walked out of the apartment wearing two different shoes. But he knew everything about books and history and the magic inside stories. He owned a wonderful shop on the Calle Trinidad, filled with the smell of ink and paper and coffee, and the hum of students debating beneath tall, crammed bookshelves.

The librería was a threat? Eduardo was an enemy of the people? Eduardo loved people. The students loved him.

Clementina was crying now, which drew Alejo back toward the door. He was man of the house when Eduardo wasn't home. He crouched down, peering around the edge of the door, avoiding Clementina's foot that tried to shoo him. In the hall, other apartment doors were cracking open, tips of noses inching out, sniffing for news. The air was heavy with suspicion and fear.

Foreign enemies, Alejo thought, remembering the words on the leaflets showered over the city, calling for Santiguans to denounce all foreigners. He knew Eduardo was the son of Italian immigrants. Clementina came to Chile from Spain when she was sixteen. Were Spanish and Italians Right? Or Wrong?

"My guess is he's in the Estadio," Milagros said. "Or the Villa Grimaldi. I heard they're detaining people there as well."

Alejo couldn't imagine what his father would be doing in the Stadium. Playing soccer? For a moment he pictured Eduardo kicking a ball around with some other men, passing the time with a friendly game while all this nonsense got sorted out.

Maybe it's not so bad, he thought.

"Go home, Mila," Clementina said, her hand sliding along her curved belly. "It's not safe here."

"You should get out of Santiago," Milagros said. "Go to the American embassy at least. I know one of the attachés. Tell him your brother-in-law is a U.S. citizen and he can help with VISAs." Her hand reached for Clementina's and their fingers laced, knuckles clenched white on Clementina's stomach. "Tina, get out while you still can."

"I can't. Not without Eduardo. He needs me."

The women kissed cheeks. Milagros slipped away and Clementina shut the door. For hours she paced the apartment, her lovely curved brow twisted up with worry. Every so often she looked wild-eyed at Alejo, as if expecting him to make the decision whether to stay for Eduardo or flee without him. He avoided her eyes and went into the kitchen to make them some eggs.

On the wall by the phone hung the calendar, still showing September's page. Alejo had been crossing out the days in anticipation of their upcoming trip to Portillo—their last ski trip of the season. But the Xs stopped on September 11, 1973. The day Pinochet came to town, froze the calendar and put the country's plans on hold.

Clementina and Alejo ate their eggs in silence, an unspoken decision to stay. They should have gone.

⌒

ALEJO, NOW MAN of the house, shook in the dark of the closet, reaching up to hold the sleeves and hems of his parents' clothing. Worn out by fear, his young nerves shredded, the ball of his body tipped sideways until his head came to rest against the closet wall, cushioned by his mother's winter coat.

He began to play the game his father made up: Alejo named an animal, Eduardo gave the group term.

Lions.

"Pride."

Bears.

"Sleuth."

Zebras.

"Dazzle."

Giraffes.

"Tower."

Pandas.

"Embarrassment."

Alejo went on quizzing himself, his eyes dipping and drooping. When he woke with a start, dawn was evident in the thin crack of light beneath the closet door.

He snuck out once—to use the toilet and load his arms with things from the kitchen. He returned to his hiding place and waited.

The doorbell didn't ring. Nor the phone. The outside din of helicopters, guns, explosions and screams slipped into the open bedroom window and through the crack of the closet door.

Toads.

"Knot."

Camels.

"Caravan."

Rhinoceros.

"Crash."

Crows.

Murder, Alejo thought.

He never saw his mother again.

ALBACETE

BULLFINCH.
Bellowing.
Moles.
Labor.
Swans.
Lamentation.
Hedgehogs.
Array.
Crows.
"Murder," Alejo said.

He hid in the apartment closet for five days, venturing out only to the bathroom or the kitchen for food. Every hour on the hour, he thought about yelling for help from the window. Once or twice he pressed his ear to the front door, but heard nothing in the hallway. The building was eerily and sickly silent. The normal cacophony of music, voices, water in pipes and footsteps on ceilings seemed to be hiding as well. Or it had been silenced.

On the sixth day, the childish fear was replaced by a resigned acceptance. The helpless parts of his brain were spent. Other parts wired for survival began to wake up. Alejo opened the closet door and inched on hands and knees to the bedroom window, which looked out over Calle Isabella. Leaflets had drifted inside like large snowflakes. Alejo collected them in a neat pile. His mother liked things to be neat.

Outside, the rhythmic hum of helicopter rotors chopped across the sky. The rattling burst of a machine gun echoed off building walls. Boots marched on the pavement. Around corners and in alleys, Alejo heard voices raised in anger and despair. Scuffles with the soldiers. Scuffles among the starving people of the campamentos who were scavenging the streets for food. And layered over all, incessant barking and howling.

Carefully, Alejo peered over the windowsill. Santiago's streets were home to over a million stray dogs. Like the cats of Rome, this secondary canine population was taken for daily granted, neither culled nor coddled. But now the soldiers, bored and itching for action, were taking pot shots at the dogs. Alejo flinched as bullets ricocheted off brick and stone. His stomach sank in a sickening dread. He loved the street dogs. They were his personal pets.

I should go.

The thought tugged at his shirt tails. He'd been ignoring it for days now but the plight of the dogs galvanized him into action. He found the rucksack Eduardo wore when they went skiing in Portillo. He began to pack.

Papers first. Until this spring, it wouldn't have occurred to him he had papers. Then La Moneda went up in flames and Eduardo made a call to his brother, Felipe, in the United States. They began to discuss getting out.

Alejo found the stiff little folder containing birth certificates and passports and separated his own. The Hispanic custom of giving children both parents' surnames made filling out forms a challenge. He read his full name, crammed in tiny type across the allotted space: *Alejandro Gabriel Eduardo Penda Vilaró.*

"We gave you lots of names," Eduardo once said. "So you can be anyone you want."

Alejo put the envelope back where he found it on his father's desk, pausing, as he always did, to pick up the knife his father used as a paperweight.

It was an Albacete dagger, given as a gift to Eduardo from a student he tutored through university. Twenty-four centimeters long with a handsome bone-and-brass handle. The sheath was covered in buff velour with a pointed brass end, and the dagger slid from it with barely a sound. The double-edged blade had a ridge from the guard to the tip and if Alejo looked close, he could see faint floral designs etched in the metal. It felt light yet solid in his hand. And now, alone in the apartment, it felt like a needed friend.

He collected clothes, remembering it was the start of spring in Chile, but in New York, where Tío Felipe lived, it was autumn. He'd need long-sleeved shirts and a sweater. And the socks he wore for skiing would be a good idea. From a top dresser drawer he collected six handkerchiefs. His mother was always after him to remember a handkerchief. When he went to bed at night, she tucked one under his pillow. After these practicalities, he packed some books, a toothbrush, a few possessions he couldn't bear to part with. Last, he picked up the dagger.

"Albacete," he said, hefting it a few times in his hand. He put it in the pack. Just in case.

He set the small sack outside the closet door. Then decided it would be better off inside with him. He was about to shut himself in for the night when he heard a volley of gunshots in the Calle Isabella.

Then a dog screamed.

Alejo almost pissed himself. His blood solidified in his heart and stomach in a stupefied horror. He'd never heard a dog make that kind of noise. It sounded like a woman keening for a murdered husband.

"Murder of crows," he whispered.

He crept to the window. Plastering himself flat to the wall, he craned his head around and looked. He saw a group of soldiers, one of them with his rifle raised. The dog let out three high-pitched yelps, followed by another terrible moan. Alejo's hands clamped to his ears and pressed hard. Sandwiched between the ocean roar of his palms, he saw the soldiers amble away, guns slung on backs and arms around shoulders.

He let go his ears. From under the window, the dog cried and cried. Alejo slid down the wall, gathered himself into a ball once more and rocked furiously, willing the animal to die.

He watched the little clock on the bedside table lose twenty minutes.

The dog was still alive and crying. Alejo's face was covered in a fine mist of sweat. The tenderest part of his heart and the survival parts of his brain knew what he had to do.

He got his father's dagger out of the backpack.

Albacete, he thought. He didn't know it was a region in Spain. He thought it was the knife's name.

Albacete, help me.

He unlocked the front door, checked carefully up and down the hall, then went down the three flights of stairs, his back pressed to the wall.

He surveyed the block carefully, then stepped into the Calle Isabella.

It was dark. Only a single streetlight at the corner was lit, making a weak cone of light.

The dog cried, huddled against the building in a pool of blood. It was female. Her stomach was shot open and her dead pups scattered. She foamed at the mouth and panted between cries. Her glazed eyes looked up as Alejo approached.

Albacete, you're here. Help me.

The smell of the gutshot dog was appalling. The sound was worse. Alejo looked anywhere but the bloody sidewalk.

"Cálmate, hija," Alejo whispered, crouching down as his awareness floated up and out of his head. It watched as his bodily self lovingly took the dog's muzzle and pulled the head tenderly against his chest. Albacete made a firm, swift and merciful slice.

The street sighed into silence.

It's done. It's quiet now. Don't think about it anymore.

Alejo wiped the blade on his jeans and slipped back inside. He washed his hands, cleaned off the dagger and sheathed it. He went into the bathroom and threw up with an odd detachment. Then he went into the closet.

You mustn't think about this.

He ran a hand over the thick line of hangers, finding a thin cardigan belonging to Clementina, and a heavier one belonging to Eduardo. He thrust his mother's sleeves inside the sleeves of his father, then put on the doubled garment.

Do not think about it. Forget it.

Safe in a contrived embrace, Albacete tight in one hand, he fell quickly asleep.

He woke to the sound of the front door opening. His chest seized, flipping his heart backward as he scrambled to sit up in the dark.

Friends ring the bell. Soldiers bang on the door. Who walks in?

He pressed back against the wall of the closet, Albacete at the ready.

I'll fight, he thought. *I'll cut your throat. I've done it before.*

The closet door opened. Alejo saw ragged, bloodstained pant cuffs above two different, but equally dirty shoes. The forest of hanging clothes was thrust apart with a squeal of wire on wood. Alejo held up the dagger in a barely shaking hand, death behind his eyeballs as he looked up at the intruder.

I have many names. I can be anyone. Now I am a crow and I will murder you.

The man had blackened eyes and a deep cut along one cheekbone. A swollen, split lip protruded from a thick brown beard.

"Alejito?"

Albacete clattered to the floor as Alejo scrambled from the depths of the closet and into his father's arms.

⟞⟞⟞

EDUARDO SCOOPED UP the backpack, praising his son for the foresight to pack. They left the apartment for the last time and stole furtively across Santiago to the American embassy. They kept to the shadows and back streets and the stray dogs followed them, a protective escort. A few nuzzled Alejo's hands. One fell into step alongside him for two blocks, sniffing at the doubled-up cardigans that flapped around his legs.

You were merciful to our sister. We will be merciful to you.

"Milagros is good friends with an attaché at the embassy," Eduardo whispered, hustling his son along. "They've gotten you a VISA."

"What about you?"

"I can't come with you. Not right now."

Clementina was being detained in the Villa Grimaldi, Eduardo said. as they neared the embassy. "You have a VISA and a plane ticket. And Tío Felipe is waiting for you. I must stay and find your mother. You must go find our new home. Be the man of the house until I come with Mami."

The dim street blurred before Alejo's eyes. "I want to stay with you."

"You must do this for me, Alejito. Felipe is waiting. He'll help you."

The embassy gates were closed and barricaded and two American soldiers stood guard. A quiet conversation. Papers were shown. Then Eduardo's warm palms lingered on Alejo's face. His beard scratched when he kissed his son's cheeks. Tears in the mad, blackened eyes.

"You must do this."

Alejo tried to speak, to beg his father to keep him. But his throat was fused shut. One last rough hug and a kiss on the top of Alejo's head before the gates closed between him and his father. Their hands clasped between the wrought iron bars.

"You can do it, Alejito."

"Papi, wait. I have your dagger." Surely Eduardo would need it.

For the first time that evening, Eduardo smiled. "Keep it for me. And take good care of it."

"Papi…"

But Eduardo was moving away down the street.

"Eagles, Papi," Alejo called.

Eduardo looked back. "Convocation."

"Jellyfish?"

"Fluther."

"Raccoons."

A last word reached Alejo's ears.

"Gaze."

He turned his head against the narrow bars, watching as his father rounded the corner and disappeared.

No Dogs Allowed

OCTOBER 1973
GUELISTEN, NEW YORK

*V*ALERIE LARK RANG the doorbell of Dr. Penda's house on Stroock Lane. It bonged a Big Ben chime from within, followed by the din of barking dogs.

Beatriz, Dr. Penda's housekeeper, answered. "Good morning," she said. "Chilly out, no? Look at your pretty pink cheeks."

It was cold today, with a brisk wind off the river. Inside was warm, with the smell of a fire and a cake in the oven. In the front hall, three dogs circled Val's legs, barking and sniffing her hands. A fourth was missing—the Rottweiler.

"Where's Violeta?" Val asked.

Beatriz smiled, tripling the number of wrinkles in her face "Dr. Penda's nephew arrived yesterday. Violeta's taken a shine to him and hasn't left his side. Come. They're all in the study."

Val tried not to let her reluctance show as she followed Beatriz through the living room. She wasn't in the mood to meet people and make chit-chat. She wanted to walk the dogs quickly, then get home to finish her chores and collect her allowance so she could go to the movies. The cinema in Hudson Bluffs was having a double-feature matinee of *Charlotte's Web* and *Robin Hood*. Dr. Penda was not the man to encounter when you were in a hurry.

Dr. Penda was a professor at Marist College and everything that came out of his mouth sounded like a lesson. He didn't talk about the weather. He *informed* about the weather. Val's little sister, Trelawney, was a voracious reader and got along well with Dr. Penda. Val read only when she had to. The sheer number of books in this house intimidated her, as did the paintings, the sculptures, the grand piano and the sumptuous furnishings. She always feared she might break a priceless treasure or be forced to read some boring classic. Her brother Roger felt the same—he never ventured further than Dr. Penda's porch. He couldn't get through a day without breaking something.

"Miss Valerie is here," Beatriz said as she waddled into Dr. Penda's study.

This room smelled like a museum—old and dusty and full of knowledge. The walls were floor to ceiling bookshelves. Val got dizzy looking at them so her eyes focused instead on Dr. Penda, who sat reading in his leather chair. A boy lay on the Oriental rug in front of the fire, feet crossed in socks, his head pillowed on Violeta's back and a book hiding his face.

"Hello, Val," Dr. Penda said, getting to his feet. Val studied his appearance: she didn't like his conversation, but she liked the way he looked. Her mother said he was Latin American, which Val thought meant he spoke Latin, until Trelawney explained he came from Chile. (Which Roger took to mean the food, and then Trelawney declared she couldn't live in the same house as him anymore.)

Latin or American, Val sure liked the way Dr. Penda dressed. His light blue sweater was cashmere and he had the most gorgeous wingtip shoes. The sun coming in the windows sparkled off the silver in his hair as he leaned and spoke Spanish to the boy on the rug.

The book slowly lowered and the boy looked up at Val.

Oh, she thought. *He's beautiful.*

Confusion swept through her. She'd never thought of a boy as beautiful. She didn't think much of boys at all, other than they were obnoxious when they weren't being stupid. All the boys in fifth grade—whom she'd known since nursery school—used to be cute. Now they were lumpy and gangly, their adult teeth growing in weird or already shrouded in braces. One or two had serious BO issues. A few had pimples, some had down on their upper lips. They were too tall or too short and their voices skittered from squeaks to growls in one sentence. If they could put together a sentence at all.

Dr. Penda's nephew got up from the rug. Standing, he was Val's height and his skin was smooth and looked suntanned. His eyes were circled, but they were the green of a dollar bill and their gaze on Val was curious.

"This is my nephew, Alejandro," Dr. Penda said. "We call him Alejo or Alejito, which is Alex in English. Alejo, ella es Valerie. Ella pasea a los perros por mí."

Alejo, or Alex, or whatever his name was, lifted his hand in a wave and a corner of his mouth smiled. He looked a little like Robbie Benson, with dark hair falling across long, smooth eyebrows. He wore jeans and a T-shirt, no different than what Roger would wear. But Roger was sloppy and smelled like feet. Alex looked and smelled clean, rumpled and crisp. Like his clothes had been hung out in the sun to dry before he pulled them on. Val's heartbeat slowed. A strange heat pressed her cheeks at the thought of this boy putting his clothes on. She swallowed against her dry throat, feeling she was on the verge of crying.

"He doesn't have much English," Dr. Penda said. "And he's exhausted from the trip." His handsome face filled with sadness as he put a hand on Alex's shoulder and spoke again in Spanish. Alex chewed on his bottom lip and his fingertips pulled at one eyebrow as he answered. Only a few words, but his voice stayed steady on the same middle note. Val found herself tilting her chin, trying to hear more. Trying to understand.

Beatriz crossed her arms and tilted her own chin, laughing. She was as wide as she was tall, with pure white hair pulled back in a wispy bun. A mole on her chin, another beneath one eye. Soft jiggly arms and a bust that looked like one giant boob instead of two separate ones. She took Alejo's chin in her hand and said something kind, but firm.

"He'll go with you," Dr. Penda said. "Violeta likes to be near him and he could use some fresh air. Walk him down to Main Street and show him around."

Val was filled with panic. How was she supposed to play tour guide to someone who didn't speak English? And why hadn't she brushed her hair before she left the house, and worn her nice pea coat instead of her crappy windbreaker? She didn't even have a Lip Smacker on her.

She clipped leashes onto the three corgis while Alex pulled on a sweater and sneakers. He put Violeta on her lead and opened the front door, standing back so Val could go first. She felt her face heat up again. Holding the door for ladies was a courtesy Val's father was trying to instill in Roger. Not successfully.

A whirlwind of dried leaves greeted them on the porch as they stepped outside. As they walked down Stroock Lane and turned onto Bemelman Street, she opened and closed her mouth six times, not knowing whether to talk or shut up. The awkwardness tangled up in her legs like another dog on a leash. By the time they turned onto Main Street, she couldn't stand it anymore and began to babble.

"That's the train station," she said, pointing. "And see, there you can cross over the tracks and go to the park. It has a ball field and basketball hoops. We have concerts and stuff in summer. It's the best place to watch fireworks. That's the Mid-Hudson bridge down there."

Alex's gaze followed wherever her finger pointed. He nodded, his eyebrows wrinkling. Whether he actually understood or was only being polite, he was being attentive and Val relaxed a little.

"This is Scott's Variety," she said. "They have the best candy and on Thursdays it's all a nickel. They have good comics, too. This is Murphy's, their ice cream is the best. On Sundays it's buy-one-get-one-free. This is the liquor store. That's a barber shop. My dad gets his hair cut there."

Alex stopped and backtracked a few steps, looking first in the barber shop window, then further on to the liquor store.

"¿Qué son estas pequeñas casas?" he said. He glanced over at Val, shaking his head and snapping his fingers. "Little houses. ¿Por qué?"

"Oh those," she said, walking toward him. She leaned to look in the window of the liquor store and the tiny scale model on display. It was the shop perfectly rendered in miniature, down to the lettering on the window, the bricks, the awning and the flower boxes. Inside, its wooden shelves were stocked with dozens of tiny bottles, meticulously labeled and corked. Across the back of the little room ran a long counter with a cash register.

"My mother made it," Val said. "Every store on Main Street has one." She put her hand on her heart, wanting to convey this information properly. "My mother. Mommy."

"¿Mami?"

She patted her chest. "Yes, my mommy. Made. Them." She pointed to the miniature liquor store. "She makes doll houses."

Alex shook his head, his eyes apologetic. Val fidgeted in frustration, trying to think of a way to communicate. The only way was to show him. She gestured for him to follow and she showed how in the windows of Scott's and Murphy's, in the barber shop and the deli, stood a scale model. A second, miniature Main Street.

"¿Todas?" Alex said, pointing up, down and across the street. "Mami make all?"

"All."

His eyes widened and his grin broadened. He said something in Spanish that Val understood to be amazement.

"Come on," she said, beckoning him across the street. "This is the Lark Building. My great-great-grandfather built it. This is my grandmother's dress shop. See, she has her little house too. Pequeña casa? Did I say that right?"

"Little house," Alex said.

Val hesitated, wondering if she should take him inside. A boy might not like it. It smelled of lavender and glue and ironed fabric. Mannequins stood about, beautifully dressed and posed, as if at a party. The walls were bright with color: bolts of cotton, tulle, satin and lace. Tucked in a back alcove was Val's own sewing machine and her little work table. She had shelves for her remnants and swatches, jars for her collections of buttons, beads, sequins and ribbons. Her mannequins were Barbie dolls, all their hand-made clothing meticulously catalogued and organized. A single lost shoe could ruin Val's sleep.

The dress shop was both Val's playground and her schoolroom. She had a different name within its walls: her grandmother called her Valentine.

"I want to have a shop like this someday," she said softly. "It'll have a black awning with *Valentine* in white letters."

"Valentine?" Alex said. "¿Quieres decir como un Valentín?" With the end of Violeta's leash, he drew a heart in the faint film of dust on the window. "¿Así?"

"Yes." She looked at him, then looked down, smiling through warm cheeks. "Come on," she said. "Here's the drugstore, my grandfather owns this. It has a real soda fountain inside, it's one of the oldest in the country. Upstairs is my mother's dollhouse gallery. I can't take you up now, no dogs allowed." She pointed to their four charges, shaking her head with an exaggerated expression of regret. "No dogs."

"No se permiten perros," he said.

"Perros. Dogs?"

"Dogs," he said happily. "Perros." His hand lifted, an index finger reaching toward her face. Val's breath stopped in her throat, her eyes swiveling as his fingertip pressed her cheekbone. He drew it back and showed her the eyelash pressed there.

"Pide un deseo." He smiled and happiness splashed Val's chest.

"Make a wish?" she said. "You know make a wish on an eyelash? They do that in Chile?"

His shoulders shrugged. "Pestaña." His fingertip beckoned. Her mind fished around for a desire but couldn't think of one. Not when she was standing on Main Street with this beautiful boy who couldn't understand her, yet wanted to make her wishes come true.

She blew the tiny hair away, her chores and her allowance and her plans forgotten.

"Let's go to Celeste's," Val said. "My great-aunt's store. She allows dogs."

They ran in a laughing, barking, twenty-legged pack down the sidewalk. The bell on the jamb swung merrily as they burst into Celeste's Bookshop & Café.

This was Dr. Penda's study but on a larger, friendlier scale. The books were used, piled up helter-skelter, battered and loved and approachable. Aunt Celeste had children's books. Magazines and board games, too. She served coffee and tea and hot chocolate. Alex would *love* this place.

Except he didn't.

He stopped short, gazing around the high-ceilinged space with its exposed brick and scuffed wooden floors. The color drained out of his face and Violeta's leash dropped from his hand.

"What's wrong?" Val said.

"Hello, darling," Aunt Celeste said, coming out from behind the coffee counter. "Who's your friend?"

Alex looked at Val with eyes hard and hurt. Slowly he backed away, turned and left the shop.

Val stared after him, her wishes dashed to pieces on the floor. She ran to the window, pressed her palms and cheek flat against the glass, her tear-filled eyes straining to follow. Her bewilderment gave way to a helpless anger. She thought he was different, but he was just another stupid boy.

"Goodness," Aunt Celeste said. "What came over him?"

⸻

AUNT CELESTE TURNED the shop over to her partner, Martha, and gathered up the dogs' leashes.

"Come," she said to Val. "We'll go to his house. I'm sure there's an explanation."

Val, hurt and humiliated, didn't care to know. She went back home and moped through her chores. To spread the misery around, she teased Trelawney, picked on Roger and talked back to her father, who docked her allowance and sent her to her room.

Aunt Celeste came for dinner. She said nothing about the morning's events, only slipped a Spanish-English dictionary out of her handbag and gave it to Val.

Over meatloaf and baked potatoes, the conversation was all about Dr. Penda's nephew.

"That boy arrived in time to see a hell of a show," Val's father said. "I read in the *Times* Bork's naming a new prosecutor. No way they won't impeach Nixon."

"He's already seen a president ousted," Celeste said. "Terrible things are happening in Chile, Roland. When was the last time you saw it in the headlines?"

Roland shrugged. "Not since September."

"I read the CIA knew about it but chose to do nothing," Meredith Lark said, putting more green beans on Val's plate.

"You ask me, the CIA was behind it," Celeste said. "Minimal amount of refugees came here. Most went to Europe."

"What's a refugee?" Roger asked.

"Someone who seeks refuge," Trelawney said.

Val pushed her beans around her plate, not sure what refuge was but not wanting to be schooled by her know-it-all sister.

"So where are his parents?" Roger asked.

"Still in Chile," Celeste said. "Felipe said the mother was arrested. The father as well, but they released him. He got Alejandro out and stayed to look for his wife."

Val looked up. "Why were they arrested?"

"Their government was taken over," Celeste said.

"Like a revolution?" Roger asked.

"Not the good kind," Roland said. "His parents were arrested for being against the new regime."

"Where are they?" Val said.

Celeste shook her head. "Detained? Jail?"

"Then how did he get here?" Roger said.

"They got him out through the embassy. Dr. Penda was already here so it was easier to get a VISA."

"What's a VISA?"

"When will his parents come?" Trelawney asked.

None of the adults answered.

Val put her fork down. "Will he ever see them again?"

"Nobody's sure, honey," Meredith said, running a hand down Val's hair.

"His father owned a bookstore," Celeste said. "Just like mine, apparently. They burned it down." She patted Val's hand. "I can understand why he became upset."

"Wait, who burned it down?" Roger said.

"The new government."

"They burned *books*?" Trelawney said. "Why?"

Silence but for the clink of silverware on china.

"He'll start school next week," Celeste said. "Fourth grade, so he might be in your class, Roger."

"He doesn't speak English," Val said. "He only knows little words. Little houses." Her throat burned and ached. She wanted to run to her room and weep. Then she wanted to gather up every book she could find and bring them to Alex. Where was their copy of *Alexander and the Horrible, Terrible, No Good, Very Bad Day*? She could read it to him. He'd love it.

"I'm sure he'll have an aide," Meredith said. "And you have Spanish-speaking kids in your class."

"The Lopez twins," Trelawney said.

"And Maria Santoro," Roger said.

The thought of Maria Santoro made Val even more miserable. All the boys liked Maria. She had long shiny hair and beautiful dark eyes. She could speak Spanish. Alex would like her. Alex would want to follow her everywhere.

"You guys be nice to him," Roland said. "Even if you can't communicate, you can include him. Think how you'd feel if you were alone in another country where nobody spoke English."

"And you didn't know where your family was," Celeste said.

"I wonder if he skis," Roger said, drumming his fingers.

"Coming from Chile, it's a good chance he does," Roland said.

"Can we invite him to Stowe?"

Roland ruffled his son's hair. "That's not a half-bad, idea, Rog. I bet he'd love it. Remind me to ask his uncle."

"Can I be excused?" Val said. "Actually, can I go somewhere?"

All eyes turned toward her.

"Where?" Roland said.

She took a deep breath. "Back to Dr. Penda's. See if Alex wants to get ice cream or something."

"I'll go too," Roger said. "We'll all three of us go."

Meredith smiled. "Clear the table first."

"Take the dictionary," Celeste said to Val.

It took some coaxing from Dr. Penda and Beatriz, but Alex came out of the house and walked into town with them. He glanced once at Val, and slowly blinked his eyes with a shrug of one shoulder. She shook her head with a "don't worry about it" smile.

At their little table at Murphy's, Roger paged through the Spanish-English dictionary. "Ess...skewee...ar," he said, frowning. "Am I saying that right?" He pointed to the word for Alex, whose eyes and smile widened.

"Esquiar," he said. "Sí. ¿Tú también?" His finger went around the table.

"Si, yes," Roger said. "All of us ski. We have a house in Stowe. You can come with us."

Alex let loose a stream of excited Spanish, accompanied by high gestures of one hand—obviously mountain peaks—followed by downhill slices—talking about the steep trails.

So the evening passed, and between the dictionary and sign language and a dozen little pictures sketched on napkins, Alex and the Larks hammered out a foundation of bilingual, beginner phrases and a rudimentary lean-to of friendship.

Val learned a valuable lesson that night:

Ice cream needed no translation.

MUCH FRIENDLY

*A*LEJO BECAME ALEX and Guelisten became his home.

Certain things unnerved him all his life. Helicopters. The pitch dark. Enclosed spaces. Uniforms. Interrupted sleep in the middle of the night.

Certain things comforted him all his life. Skiing. Dogs. The group terms for animals. His two cardigans, lovingly folded in a drawer. And a handkerchief under his pillow. He curled his hand around it on the nights when his imagination drummed up horrific ways for his family to die and filled him with the immeasurable weight of a survivor's guilt.

Where are you? What became of you?

I'm waiting for you.

For a few precious months, Milagros Martínez was in touch. Via sporadic letters and telephone calls on faulty lines, she conveyed news. A woman released from the Villa Grimaldi said she saw Clementina Penda there. Someone else thought they saw Eduardo on the street. Another eyewitness placed him back at the Estadio.

Then the calls stopped. One last letter arrived, to convey nothing new had been learned. Then Milagros went silent.

All over Chile, tens of thousands of people fell silent, victims to the country's new intransitive verb: they were disappeared.

Every night Alex placed Albacete in the center of his desk blotter, sure if his father were truly dead, his spirit would come and move the knife a little to let Alex know. Every night he tucked a handkerchief under his pillow, sure his mischievous mother's ghost would take it away as a joke.

They would give him a sign. They would let him know.

They couldn't just *disappear.*

"They didn't disappear," Felipe said softly, turning Albacete over in his hands. "They *were* disappeared."

He gave Alex all the photos Eduardo and Clementina had sent over the years. Alex put them around his bedroom, clustered in small shrines. The first thing he saw when he opened his eyes in the morning. The last before he fell into troubled dreams at night.

Where are you? What did they do to you? What became of you?

Why am I alive and you are disappeared?

Felipe was a benevolent, but abstracted guardian. He gently shook Alex out of the bad dreams and soothed him back to sleep. He understood his nephew's need to have nightlights in his room and in all the upstairs hallways. Alex was clothed, fed and sheltered, and Felipe never missed an opportunity to further Alex's education or widen his cultural horizon. But when it came to practicalities, Felipe was more hopeless than Eduardo.

He didn't seem to know boys outgrew their shoes in an hour. Boys needed vaccinations and dentist appointments. Boys wanted to sign up for soccer or join the junior ski team. Boys needed permission slips signed, homework checked, boundaries set and odd jobs to make pocket money. Boys needed to be driven here and there, or at least organized into a car pool.

Some of the details Beatriz handled, but Beatriz was seventy-five and used to keeping house for an independent bachelor. She didn't have the energy to rear a child, let alone an almost-teenaged boy. Gradually, the raising of Alex Penda fell into the hands of Roland and Meredith Lark, who willingly and cheerfully took on the task. Their house was large and their hearts larger. One more fledgling in their nest wasn't an imposition. Besides, Alex and Roger were becoming inseparable, and Alex was a calming, grounding influence on the Larks' rambunctious middle child.

As images of Chile faded and curled at the edges, the photo album in Alex's heart began to fill with new family snapshots, all with his sleek, dark physique set like a black iris in the Lark bouquet of daffodils.

❧

THE LARKS LOVED to joke how the first complete English sentence Alex learned was "knock three times on the ceiling if you want me."

Roland Lark had a weakness for Tony Orlando's hit song, and a habit of interrupting quiet interludes by belting the refrain, "*Whoa,* my darling..." His family would groan, but join in with the rest of the chorus.

On his first trip to Vermont with the Larks, Alex—lounging in the back of the station wagon with Roger—listened, groaned and eventually sang as well.

Knock three times on the ceiling if you want me...

Roger's two sisters sat in the middle seat. Trelawney was in third grade, winter pale with nearly-white hair cut short. Val was golden blonde, like Roger. All three siblings had grey eyes. Trelawney's were pale slate. Roger's had a hint of blue. Alex thought Val's eyes tended toward green, like his, but he couldn't look at them long enough to tell.

All through the five-hour trip, he was keenly aware of her presence in the car. Something about the proximity of her hair and skin and scent made his stomach feel weird. In fact, since the day he met her, Alex had a hard time looking at Valerie Lark with both eyes. Worse, whenever he felt her gaze turn in his direction, a plug pulled in his mind and all the English he mastered swirled away.

He liked her. He didn't like that he liked her. He hated how it made him feel she didn't like him.

It was confusing as shit.

Roger taught him to say that.

At school, Alex worked with an ESL aide and spent much of his time in remedial language classes. After dismissal, his education belonged to Roger. On the playground or the ball field, one faltering conversation at a time, Roger filled the gaps in Alex's English. He made casual corrections if Alex forgot to use *I*, *he* or *it*, or mixed up *his* and *hers*. He laughed when Alex referred to Dr. Lark as a *beterinarian*, then laughed harder when Alex told him to shut the fuck up, asshole.

"You never make mistakes when you curse," Roger said.

Riding up the chair lift at Stowe Resort, in their bizarre mixed language, they talked and laughed about the world.

"So?" Roger said, gesturing to the mountainous landscape around them. "Different from Chile?"

Alex nodded, frustrated at expressing how. To his eye, the heights of Ojos de Agua and Mount Mansfield were approximately the same. But the mountains in Chile punched out of the ground like fists. They loomed up sharp and sinister, the continent's armored spine. Here, the eye's path to the summit was softened by pine trees and scrub. The earth yawned and stretched toward the sky, rather than assaulting it. The peaks were mighty, but gentle.

"Friendly," Alex finally said. "Is much friendly here."

During that first ski trip, Alex fell in love with the Larks. The soulful, forever love that comes when you find your tribe. Up and down the slopes, in and out of the house, he and the three Lark children piled on each other like puppies.

Playing Trouble and Monopoly and Sorry. Laughing loud, sleeping deep and eating nonstop. Learning each other's language as they read comics and *Mad* Magazine. Belting, "*Whoa*, my darling," whenever silence descended.

They slept in one room with two sets of pine bunk beds pushed head-to-head. Roger and Trelawney took the bottom bunks. Alex lay in the bed above Roger's, close to the ceiling with the crown of his head staring at the crown of Val's. The unique fatigue that belonged solely to skiing held him in soft arms as the Larks quizzed him on animal groups, trying to stump him and failing.

Finches.

"Charm."

Peacocks.

"Ostentation."

Hyenas.

"Cackle."

He was happy. Too happy to feel guilty about being happy.

Val sat up on her elbows and looked over the headboards between them. "Larks," she said.

Alex glanced at her with one eye. Then with both eyes. His toes curled tight in his wool socks as he answered, "Exaltation."

ALEX AT FOURTEEN. Dressed in his first suit and standing with Beatriz in Guelisten Cemetery, as the coffin of Felipe Penda was lowered into the earth.

Four days ago, the professor cancelled his evening classes and came home complaining of a headache. Beatriz told him to sit down, put his feet up and she'd make him some tea. When she brought the cup out to the living room, Felipe was slumped in his chair.

An aneurysm, the hospital guessed. Or a cerebral hemorrhage.

It was only in death that Alex grasped Felipe's influence in Dutchess County. His uncle had collected people the same way he collected books and art. The phone rang off the hook, flowers crowded every horizontal surface. The cards and letters collected into baskets and boxes until Alex and Beatriz gave up trying to open them all. The day of the wake, an endless line of callers came through the funeral home. Grown men weeping as they paid their respects. Countless women telling Alex what a treasure Felipe was.

Alex became the curator of all this grief, staggering under the inventory until it slipped through his arms and crashed to the floor in pieces.

What do I do now? Where do I go?

Felipe might not have been a second father to Alex, but Felipe was all the family Alex had in the world. Felipe had been a haven and harbor. He was kind and caring. He never claimed ownership of his nephew, rather he was always generous. Constantly encouraging Alex, "Go. Of course you can go. Go with your friends. Yes, bring them here, absolutely. Be with your friends. Bring a friend."

Now he was dead. And the enormity of Alex's situation towered above him like a tsunami wave about to break.

What's going to happen to me?

After the funeral service, Felipe's attorney requested a meeting with Alex, and asked the Larks be present. Seated around the massive walnut table in the dining room, the attorney read aloud Felipe's will. Bequests were made to Marist College, Columbia University, Guelisten Historical Society and the Latin American Cultural Center of Queens. Beatriz received a cash legacy that made her drop into a chair. The rest went to Alex, to be placed in trust until he was twenty-five.

"Why twenty-five?" Alex asked.

The lawyer smiled. "Knowing your uncle, he probably wanted you to go to graduate school," he said. "Dr. Lark tells me you have an interest in becoming a vet?"

Alex's nod was wary, not wanting to chisel any of his interests in stone.

Roland touched Alex's shoulder. "I don't want you to worry. We'll be here to guide you."

Dr. Lark and Felipe's attorney were named executors of the trust. Dr. and Mrs. Lark were named as legal guardians.

"Would you like to come live with us?" Meredith asked, holding both Alex's hands. She freed one and brushed his hair back from his forehead, then put her warm palm on his face.

He set his jaw, the emotion writhing between his throat and teeth. He wanted to go. He wanted the haven of Meredith's house, the safety of her arms and the protection of Dr. Lark. But to go with them meant becoming part of a new family, when he was supposed to be making a home for the family he already had.

"I'm supposed to wait," he said. "My father gave me a job to do."

"I know," she said. "You can still do it. We'll help you."

Dr. Lark and the attorney tactfully left the room as Alex wept in Meredith's arms.

"You come stay with us," she said, rocking him. "We won't hide you, Alex. You'll always be their boy, I promise. We'll keep you safe for them."

Alex crossed over the railroad tracks and walked to the Hudson that night. The evening air was soft and celebratory: it was Fourth of July weekend and pleasure boats were thick on the river. Alex sat on a bench, dry-eyed and scraped hollow inside, not feeling much of anything.

He thought about Felipe's grand life, now reduced to a single flower-heaped mound in the cemetery. At least Alex knew where his uncle was resting in peace. He wasn't disappeared. Erased from the record.

Where are you? What became of you?

He had to be careful with these thoughts. They lived like dragons in his heart, chained in a cave and hibernating, exhaling benign wisps of smoke. They were easily awoken, though. The chains could break and then they would be on Alex. Tearing him open as fire screamed from their throats: *My mother, my mother, what did you do, where is she, my mother, what did you do to her, my mother...*

Through the smoke and flame, Alex saw Clementina's magnificent belly, curved like a bell, ready to ring with a new life. She'd been due in November. Did she have her baby? Where? In one of the stadiums? At the Villa Grimaldi? Some other prison?

At all?

Of course, Alex thought, throwing a little gauntlet into the dragons' teeth. *Of course she did. They wouldn't hurt a pregnant woman or a newborn ba—*

He flinched in his skin as the dragons belched a fiery despair. Through the roaring heat came a cacophony of infant wailing that threatened to rip Alex's chest apart: *My mother, what did they do to her baby, my sister, my brother, where are you, I have to find you, the baby, what happened to the baby what do I do where do I look what happened to the baby what—*

He pulled within and slammed an imaginary closet door, closing out the horrible inferno and the crying newborns.

You mustn't think about this.

After a while, Roger came to sit by him, slinging an arm across Alex's shoulders. Val settled on his other side, looping her arm through his. Trelawney sat at Alex's feet, her elbows draped on his knees.

Nobody spoke. Alex, at the middle of the puppy pile, leaned into his friends. Roger and Val both smelled like summer: sunshine, cut grass, barbecue smoke and watermelon. Trelawney was scentless, clean and purposeful as a knife.

"You can have my room," Val finally said. "Trelawney's is big enough for two."

"Don't be stupid," Roger said. "He's coming in with me."

"Let him pick what room he wants," Trelawney said.

"You want to come back to the house?" Rog asked.

"I just want to stay here," Alex said.

Val and Roger pressed tighter to his sides. Trelawney wiggled back further between his feet.

"You're with us," Roger said. "Nosotros cuatro."

Us four.

A small smile touched Alex's mouth as fireworks began to explode in bright zinnias over the river.

HER GRANDMOTHER'S FAVORITE

*A*S THE LEGAL details of fostering Alex and sorting out his inheritance were worked through, he and Val were like a German and French soldier meeting in No Man's Land to have a smoke and sing *Silent Night*. Once Alex was moved in and established as one of the Lark family, he and Val shook hands and parted ways to separate trenches.

The war lasted three long years.

Their fights became the stuff of family legend. Every Thanksgiving, they'd tell the tale how Alex, fed up with Val playing her Linda Ronstadt album incessantly, swiped it off the turntable and locked himself in the bathroom to gloat. Val kicked the bathroom door down to get it back. When the slugfest was over, Alex had to pay for the broken record and Val had to pay for a new door. They didn't speak to each other for the month they were grounded.

Gone was the idealistic infatuation Alex felt for Val when he first came to the States. He swore he'd never known a bigger pain in the ass in his life. He couldn't wait for his foster sister to graduate high school and get the fuck out of his hair.

Practically the day after commencement she was gone. A summer internship with a bridal company in Philadelphia, then barely home for a week before she left for the Rhode Island School of Design. It was heaven. Alex felt the entire house collapse into a chair, close its eyes and sigh. Peace and quiet at last.

Then he got depressed.

He went about his social business as usual—he co-captained the ski team and had a wide circle of friends, but he was lonely in a way he couldn't articulate. He got into relationships with girls, then grew bored with them. He wandered around the house constantly *looking* for something. Restless in his own skin.

Itching for some inexplicable action. The only thing that brought satisfaction was working after school at Roland Lark's vet practice. Animals were the only company he could tolerate.

Or perhaps the only company that could tolerate him.

"Is something wrong with that boy?" Roland asked his wife.

"What in the world is wrong with you?" Meredith asked her foster son.

Alex had no idea. His mood worsened when Val didn't come home for Thanksgiving. Or Christmas. The latter left the whole family depressed, and they abandoned Guelisten for the house in Stowe. But even skiing didn't bring Alex its usual joy.

"Dude, what crawled up your ass and died?" Roger said.

"He misses Val," Trelawney said, which made the entire family burst out laughing. Everyone except Alex, who chewed on a thumbnail and narrowed his eyes.

Val spent her second semester abroad in Paris. Then did another internship in Milan. When she finally came home, it had been nearly a year since Alex had seen her.

Oh shit, he thought as she came screaming up the porch steps.

"Look at *you*," she cried. "You're gorgeous." She dropped her bag and jumped on him. Arms and legs and perfume and…

Oh shit, Alex thought.

"You grew up," she said, patting his shoulders and arms. "And *out.*"

His hands touched her back and her hair and wanted to die.

"Miss me?" she said.

He couldn't answer. Seeing her was a key turned in a rusty lock and now all his gears were churning. *She'd* been the missing link around here. Hers was the action he craved, the fight his nails wanted to dig into. He couldn't wait to talk and tell stories, to laugh and tease, to bash the bathroom door down and push every button. Val was home, and it was *on,* baby.

It was on, all right. By dinner, when his knee kept bumping Val's under the table, he knew exactly what was wrong with him.

Oh shit, he thought.

He thought it when Val stared at him over pancakes the next morning, the air swirling between them, thicker than butter and sweeter than syrup. He thought it every time he and Val brushed past each other in the hall or walked into the same room. As each teasing remark or joke smoldered at the edges. When their eyes met and couldn't look away.

Oh shit…

Running around getting ready for college kept them busy and separated. But now all ends were tied up, all bags packed and all cars loaded. Val was going back to Rhode Island in the morning, Alex was heading to his freshman year at Columbia. Out of time and excuses, they were cornered in a classmate's living room, closed up in a fist of music and buzzing voices and cigarette smoke.

"This is so weird," Val said, walking her fingers up the placket of Alex's button-down shirt. Her chin came up slightly, and he saw how the tendons in her neck fluttered around the hollow at the base of her throat. His thumb moved across her skin and settled into that warm, enticing notch. It fit him perfectly, the depression in her flesh adhering to the arc of his fingertip as if one had been created expressly for the other.

"I want to kiss you," he said. His thumb moved out of the hollow of her throat, and then back in. "Badly."

Her eyes closed and her brows hunched over them a moment. Then her forehead smoothed, as if she had worked out the solution to a problem. "No," she said. "You want to kiss me well. You just want it badly."

She drank the last of her beer and set the cup down on the floor. "Let's get out of here."

"Where?"

Guelisten was kind to children and drunks, but mean to randy teenagers. Cops knew all the good parking places. Roland and Meredith were home. But Val dug in her purse and pulled out a silver fob shaped like a bird. Off it hung a single key, which she shook at Alex.

"Who's her grandmother's favorite?"

"Oh my God." It was the key to Muriel's dress shop. And in the back of Muriel's dress shop was a little room with a day bed, where Muriel sometimes took little rests during lunch.

Val's eyes were wicked, a triumphant smile wrinkling her nose. "*Now* how bad do you want me?"

They skulked through the throng and down the street, turning onto Bemelman and practically running toward town. They slipped through the parking lot behind the Lark Building and into the dress shop.

"Please don't be a good kisser," Val said, backing Alex up against the door, winding her arms up around his neck.

"I'll try," he said. The first touch of his mouth to hers was tentative. She'd probably kissed a bunch of French and Italian boys during her semesters abroad, what the hell did Alex have on them? But as he sank a little more conviction into the kiss, his heated blood rose up, with a nationalistic certainty they didn't call his people Latin lovers for *nothing*.

"Try harder," Val whispered, her breath trembling against Alex's mouth as she pulled him in again.

He'd never known kissing like this. He plunged all ten fingers into her hair, held her head and turned her mouth around his, fitting it into him, melting into it. The buzz of the alcohol was gone and he was high on her taste, drunk on the soft slide of her tongue and the hard edge of her teeth.

"Where have you been?" she whispered. "Why didn't you *tell* me?"

"I didn't *know*," he said, laughing against her face. She tilted her head back, letting him kiss and lick down her neck.

"Do you have a condom?"

They both froze up, breathing hard.

"Shit," he said with a groan.

"Oh well," she said, drawing his shirt over his head. "We have other options."

"Right," he said. "Wait, what?"

A long, hot kiss. Then she slid down his body, falling to her knees.

"Oh, Christ," he said. She was unbuckling him, unbuttoning and unzipping. Sliding one hand into his boxers and pulling his jeans down with the other. His fingers closed in her hair and he cried out her name as she took him in, took him down. Warm and wet, soft and ferocious. With every groan he let loose, she matched it in her chest, sighing around him, licking along the length of him, catching the tiny sweet spot beneath the ridge and then pulling him into her throat again.

He had both hands in her hair now. He'd never come in a girl's mouth but she was pushing him along, pulling him along, sucking him hard and not letting up. His toes squeezed tight inside his sneakers, his eyes squeezed to slits, all of him squeezed into a pure hard core of want. Like a coin slipped into a payphone.

Do you accept the charges?

"Yes," Alex whispered. The dime dropped and he exploded on her tongue. His fists hammered the door behind him, his head writhed side to side against the wood. She was laughing around him, her hands moving up and down his body in long, loving strokes. He twitched under her, coming down, shivering. He shook his head hard, blew his breath out and looked down at her. From her knees she gazed up at him in the dim light, licking her lips, her eyes bright with desire.

"Was that one of your college courses?" he said, gasping.

She touched the corner of her mouth. "I got an A."

"Come here," he said, pulling her to stand. "Let me show you the new curriculum at Guelisten High."

Alex had gone down on a couple of girls, and it hadn't been the greatest of experiences. Both girls had been so skittish about how they'd look and smell and taste, Alex couldn't relax and figure out what he was doing. The sole impression left was confusion and Alex came away from oral sex feeling he'd been the victim of false advertising. But now his mouth grew damp as his hands moved sure and strong, unzipping Val's jeans, slowly sliding them down over her hips. He knew *exactly* what to do this time.

"You better not be good at this," she said.

"I'm terrible at it," he said, finding her mouth again. Little sounds sighed in her throat and chest as they kissed. He caught them up and swallowed them down, powerful and sexy and confident. His fingers slid between her legs. She was slick and wet outside while within was hot and pulsing.

"Alejandro," she whispered.

He pulled her kiss into his, sucking on the absurd rightness of it all. This was the girl he fought with about toothpaste caps left off and towels not hung up. The girl who listened in on his phone conversations and blabbed about his crushes. The girl who borrowed his sweaters and didn't return them. Swiped his good ski gloves and lost them. Broke the spines and dog-eared the pages of his books. Left a hundred IOUs in the mason jar where he kept his money. If she clogged the toilet, she asked Alex to plunge it. If Alex was going to Rite-Aid, she begged him to buy her tampons. She played her crappy music too loud, wouldn't surrender the TV clicker and used up all the fucking hot water.

He didn't know until now he loved it. Loved every fight and argument and annoyance. Every theft and inconvenience and favor. Because on the flip side, she never teased him about his fear of the dark. She knew the difference between his passive sighs for attention and his aggressive sighs from heartache. She understood how hard it was to keep the flame of hope alive for his parents. She knew his eyes remembered dead dogs and his hands remembered the big curve of his mother's belly. Only Val knew his mind couldn't free itself from wondering what happened to Clementina's unborn baby, because Val was the only person he'd told.

"Figures you'd turn out to be my best friend," he said, backing her up toward the day bed.

"We're ruining everything," she said. "Aren't we?"

"I don't give a shit." He eased her down, took her pants off and knelt between her shaking thighs. He was shaking all over as he peeled her open. He couldn't see a damn thing but he knew she was soft pink within blonde curls, glistening and quivering, waiting for his tongue. And when he got up close to that sweet, anxious heat, he wanted to literally *eat* her. Drink her, swallow and consume her.

He learned three valuable lessons that night:

Val tasted amazing.

"Alejandro" sounded really good when it was cried in the dark.

And going down on girls was the fucking greatest thing ever.

MAMAJUANA

THE MONEY

JULY 1979
CORONA, QUEENS, NEW YORK

*T*HE DOORBELL RANG at three in the afternoon.

This was an oddity in a building occupied by one extended family. Nobody rang. Doors were rarely even closed. At most you gave a cursory rap of knuckles before barging in.

In the Dominican enclave of Corona, doorbells were only rung by police and priests. Or, God forbid, immigration.

Javier Gil deSoto looked up from his composition notebook, wrinkling eyebrows at his cousin, Ernesto. Nesto shrugged and changed the cross of his ankles in Javi's lap.

"Which of you boys is in trouble?" Javi's mother said, wiping her hands on a dish towel.

Each cousin pointed to the other.

Rosa threw the towel at them and smoothed her hair. Before she could leave the kitchen, her daughter Naroba came in, followed by Javi's English teacher.

"Señor Durante," Rosa said, smoothing her hair again.

Javi stood up, knocking Nesto's feet away and running a quick hand over his own head.

Even casual and unshaven, dressed in street clothes and sneakers, Ramón Durante exuded authority. Six-five, silver-haired and movie star handsome (Rosa said he looked like Fernando Lamas), he was easily the toughest and most beloved teacher at Newtown High. All the girls crushed on him. Boys respected him, which was the macho way of crushing.

Javi ran a hand through his hair again. While something about Durante inspired Javi to pour words onto paper, something else made his voice hide shyly at the back of his throat.

"Sorry to interrupt," Mr. Durante said, regarding the array of glass bottles on the kitchen table. "Are you conducting a chemistry experiment?"

Rosa laughed. A little flirtatiously, Javi thought, which was unlike her. Then again, she was making mamajuana, the beloved elixir and (it was said) aphrodisiac of the Dominican Republic. The process always threw a cloak of magic happiness over everything.

He glanced down at his notebook, where he had been jotting this exact observation: *The kitchen giggled when Rosa Gil deSoto was making mamajuana.*

He closed the cover, wondering what was behind this visit. Durante had some papers in his hand, rolled in a tube which he tapped against his side. Arms crossed, expression attentive, he listened as Rosa explained what went into mamajuana. She began a new batch every New Year's, curing sticks, leaves and roots in gin. In July, she poured off the gin and replaced it with rum, adding cinnamon, molasses and Dominican herbs.

"For you," Rosa said, tightening the cork in one of the stuffed bottles and handing it to Durante. "But let it alone another three weeks. Put it in a dark place and let it brew."

The high humidity threw a fine sheen of sweat across Rosa's forehead and made the damp tendrils of hair stick to her neck. A slice of sun came through the kitchen window, lighting up her face and making it almost pretty. Her normal scowling expression was dreamy. Javi's eyes narrowed at this rare, soft version of his prickly mother and his fingers itched to pin the moment to a page.

"Writing?" Mr. Durante said, tapping Javi's head with the rolled-up tube. "I hope?"

"He never stops," Nesto said.

"It's either a pen or a fork in that one's hand," Rosa said.

Javi smiled, putting a knee on the seat of his chair and finally finding his voice. "What's going on?"

Durante unrolled the tube. "This came across my desk this morning. I thought of you right away. It's a fiction contest for a new literary magazine coming out this fall. First prize is five hundred dollars."

"Five hundred *smacks*," Nesto cried, standing up.

"And publication in their December issue," Durante said.

"Five hundred dollars," Naroba said. She looked at Javi with wide eyes and Javi tugged her ponytail.

"What's five hundred dollars?" Uncle Miguel came into the kitchen and as usual, everything stiffened in his presence. "We don't have that kind of money."

"We might," Nesto said.

Miguel's mustache bristled as he looked the papers over. He was Javi's father's eldest brother. He owned the building. And to a degree, he owned all the Gil deSotos.

He'd been the first to immigrate to New York and never let anyone forget it. Miguel came first. Miguel sweated in a factory in the garment district. Miguel waited tables. Miguel drove a cab. Miguel sent the money home and Miguel made it possible for his younger brothers Enrique and Rafael to come to New York. Because of Miguel, they didn't have to toil at unskilled labor jobs, but had the dignity of owning a small business. And when Rafael—Javi's father—wanted to open a restaurant on the ground floor of the building, Miguel lent him the money.

The Money. It was Miguel's favorite topic. The Gil deSoto apartments rocked and reeled with constant fights about The Money. Who earned the most, who sacrificed the most, who spent the most. With Money, Miguel dominated and controlled his brothers and sisters-in-law. The adults in Javi's life were constantly angry about Money, worrying over Money, or frightened they'd end up with no Money.

"Do you have something to enter?" Mr. Durante asked Javi.

"He's got a ton," Nesto said. "What about the baseball story?"

"No, that's no good," Javi said, running fingers down the filing cabinet in his head.

"I liked the one about the three grandmothers on the stoop," Durante said.

Miguel snorted. "Why don't you write a crime drama or mystery," he said. "Like a real man. Not this emotional sissy crap about what you see walking down the street."

"He has a gift," Durante said quietly.

"What about mine?" Naroba said. She had her hands behind her back and her back to the wall. Shy under normal circumstances, she went invisible when Miguel was around.

Javi studied his sister. She was older than him, but so diminutive and meek, everyone saw her as the baby. The story Javi wrote for her was, he thought, his best work. It was nothing he saw on the street. Rather, he'd taken Naroba's timidity and turned it inside-out, making an alter-ego called Naria Nyland.

A warrior queen who ruled alone, defending ancient lands conquered by her grandmothers.

"You'll lose if you submit a stupid fairy tale," Miguel said.

Nesto put his chin on Javi's shoulder. "You'll win."

"Well anyway," Mr. Durante said, "the deadline is the end of July. Read over the guidelines and submit something. Good luck with your alchemy," he said to Rosa. He gave a dry nod to Miguel, then looked at Javi. "Walk me out?"

Nesto followed them. Wherever Javi went, Nesto followed. Without his cousin's shadowing presence, Javi felt like he was missing a sock.

"I want you to enter," Durante said on the street. "Don't chicken out on this."

"He won't," Nesto said, an arm around Javi's shoulders, sounding like a sports manager.

"You doing your summer reading?" Durante asked.

"Yes, sir."

"It's a big year coming up, Javier."

"I know." Javi felt his spine straighten. That he could be the first Gil deSoto to go to college wasn't lost on him. If his writing could get him there, so much the better.

"¿Qué lo qué?" The men turned to see Javi's father coming out the side door of his restaurant, lighting a cigarette. "Señor Durante, it's July. My boy in trouble at school already?"

His hand rested wide on Javi's crown and his smoky mouth bussed above his son's ear. His expression was serious as he looked over the submission papers, his finger scratching his bushy eyebrows while keeping the cigarette out of the way.

"Javito tells a good story," Rafael said.

"That he does," Mr. Durante said. "So let's get him in front of a wider audience." He shook hands around and headed off down the street.

Rafael looked at his watch and frowned at the boys. "Who's working delivery tonight?"

Each cousin pointed at the other.

Rafael exhaled a ribbon of smoke. "Nesto, you deliver. Javi, I'm short a dishwasher tonight. Get in the back, it's already piled up to the ceiling."

"Maldita madre," Javi muttered, which got him a hard but loving whack on the ass.

"Go," Rafael said. "Do a good job."

Of all the adults, Rafael fretted the least about Money. Like a sunbeam through Miguel's perpetual clouds, he measured success in contentment, not dollars. He believed it was important to have something to show for the long hours spent working, besides cash under the mattress.

"Do a good job," he always said to Javi. "No matter what you do, be excellent at it."

Rafael believed the goal of excellence was achievable by a strong work ethic. Still, he always bought a lottery ticket on Fridays.

"I'd like to be excellent at having no job," he said, ruffling Javi's hair.

In the hellish, humid kitchen, up to his elbows in hot water and soap, Javi decided he would submit the Naria story. It was his best job so far. Scrubbing pots and lids, his head played with words and his heart swelled with excellence, wanting to work harder at his gift. His words were the ingredients for mamajuana and his stories were the bottles. He could open them and slice through Miguel's thunderstorm like a ray of July sunshine, making his home calm and magical and almost pretty.

⟶

"IT TASTES LIKE cologne," Nesto said, passing the squat bottle choked with leaves and twigs to Javi. "Cheap cologne."

Javi couldn't disagree. Naroba wore a cloying perfume called Violetta di Parma and he imagined a swig from that bottle wouldn't be much different than mamajuana.

He was disappointed. He and Nesto had contrived quite the commando mission to swipe a bottle out of the kitchen cabinet and steal away with it to the roof. For all that trouble, the least the mythical drink could do was taste good.

He took another chug, wincing at the burning sweetness and passing the bottle back to his cousin. Leaning elbows on the brick parapet, he closed his eyes and let his sweating skin become one with the thick night.

"What are you going to do with the prize money?" Nesto asked.

"I haven't won yet."

"You will. Durante likes you."

"It's not like he's judging the contest."

"You're cute when you get all bashful around him."

"Shut up. I just respect the guy."

"Yeah, the kind of respect that makes you *blush*." Nesto knocked Javi's arm and gave him the bottle. Javi gave it a vigorous swirl before taking a drink. It helped: less sweet this time. He could taste more things going on and it didn't burn as bad.

Nesto belched. "Mets play San Diego tonight?"

Javi grunted, squinting toward the northeast. They were on the edge of Corona with not much obstruction from taller buildings. On a clear night you could look across the diamond artery of Grand Central Parkway and make out the blue-and-orange blob of Shea Stadium. To the east were the World's Fairgrounds, the silvery globe of the Unisphere lit up like Venus.

"She's sad," Javi said.

"Who?"

"The sphere."

"What are you talking about, she's the queen of Queens."

"Yeah, but she's out there all alone. It's like the fairgrounds are haunted."

Nesto's hand curled around the back of Javi's neck, giving him a little shake and a squeeze. "I love you. You're so weird."

They talked baseball a while, passing the booze. Nino Espinosa had been traded to Philadelphia in the off-season. With no Dominicans on the mound at Shea, the Gil deSotos pledged their loyalty to the Panamanian relief pitcher Juan Berenguer. With his long hair, mustache and ninety-mile-an-hour fastball, the man was *badass*.

Their speech got looser. Sloppier. Broken up by fits of laughter. Baseball being a metaphor for sex, they started talking girls and the humid night got a lot juicier.

"Cristina Cardenal let me touch her tits," Nesto said.

"Bullshit. Her blouse doesn't unbutton below her collarbones."

"Had 'em right in my hands." Nesto ran a palm up Javi's chest, squeezing an imaginary breast.

"You're full of it. Nobody gets past Cristina's brothers anyway."

"Oh man, those guys kill me. They're so fucking hot."

"Who?"

"The Cardenal brothers. It hurts to look at them. Hurts *not* to look at them. It's so fucking unfair."

"You're weird."

"I'm drunk," Nesto said, his head lolling on Javi's shoulder.

Javi rolled his lips in, chewing around their numbness. "Me too." The tarred rooftop swayed beneath his feet and the streets below rippled. "Mamajuana," he said, giggling.

Nesto hiccuped loudly. His hand was still on Javi's chest. Born days apart, he and Javi shared a crib and were incarcerated in the same playpen. Javi's earliest sense memory was napping with his cousin to the rumbling whine of a box fan in summer. Chubby Nesto jammed tight into Javi's side, slack-limbed and sweaty.

As they got older, Nesto shed his baby fat and became lean and bold. By adolescence he was brash and tough, swaggering around Queens with a posse, making himself known. But alone with Javi, his plate armor of arrogance dropped away and he drifted back into Javi's side, leaning on his shoulders, soft and tactile. Putting his feet in Javi's lap. Always wanting to be touched.

"Scratch my back," he said now.

Javi ran his fingernails along the unreachable edges of Nesto's shoulder blades.

"You been over to see Leni?" Nesto asked. Leni Rivera owned a beauty shop a few blocks away and Javi sometimes unloaded boxes for her. Among other things.

"Last Tuesday," Javi said, smiling.

"You fuck her yet?"

"No, she won't let me until I'm eighteen."

"What the hell happens on your eighteenth birthday that makes you fuck-able?"

Javi laughed. "Maybe it's being able to vote?"

"That's bullshit. What does she do in the meantime?"

"Everything else."

"She jerks you off?"

"All the time."

Nesto grabbed his wrist. "She blow you, too?"

"Mm."

"Goddamn." Nesto laughed then. "Shit, look what you did…" His hand slid down and squeezed the tent pitched in his shorts.

"What *I* did?" Javi felt the words coming out of his mouth but it seemed to be someone else talking. His brain was split down the center—one half trying to keep up with the conversation, the other wandering around the stockroom of Leni's shop, where he'd gotten his first blow job. Like a movie he watched her sink onto her knees, unzip his jeans and pull them down. He stopped the movie and ran it backward, watched her pull his pants up, zip them and stand again. Then he started over.

Leni went up and down like a marionette, reliving that one delicious moment. Knees. Zipper. The pulling. *She's not. She is. She's actually going to…* He'd stop, rewind and play it again.

Now he had an erection, too. A giant one, sinking down roots that coiled up his spine. The hot night writhed in frustration around him. It was the worst kind of horniness. An unreachable itch, exacerbated by wanting something he didn't quite have a name for yet.

"Mine's bigger," Nesto said.

"The hell it is."

"Oh yeah?" And then he had it out.

Javi barely blinked. Nesto had been making jokes about the size of his dick since he learned what an inch was. He didn't need being drunk as an excuse to whip it out at Javi. It was practically a greeting.

"Put that away, asshole," Javi said, laughing. "Before you hurt someone." He made a backhanded motion, as if to... Well, he guessed as if to swat it away. But Nesto stepped into the swat.

And then it was in his hand.

How'd that happen?

The night threw back its head and laughed, flung delighted arms around Javi and enveloped him in violet-scented rum. It drew him close, intent on brewing his soul from twigs and leaves into magic.

"¿Qué lo qué?" he heard himself say as fingers slowly opened.

"No te muevas." Nesto's hand slipped under the hem of Javi's T-shirt and inside his shorts. A warm hand on his cock then. A strong hand. Better than a woman's hand because it was a *knowledgeable* hand. One that knew exactly what to do here.

A thought tapped his shoulder. *Maybe not a good idea.*

His dick, thinking it was an excellent idea, told his thoughts to fuck off.

"Holy shit," Nesto said. "Yours is huge."

"Tengo un suape," Javi said, just to get it on the record. To make sure the night knew he was shit-faced and had nothing to do with this. Mamajuana was entirely to blame.

Nesto chuckled low in his chest, his hand moving. "Yo también..."

His breath whispered strong and sweet on Javi's face. Javi licked his lips, aware of his teeth and tongue and the damp desire in his mouth. He was a piece of the night, soft like velvet and hard like glass. A curtained window. Skin dripping with a heated certainty yet drawn up tight with goosebumped trepidation because maybe, really, this wasn't such a good...

"It's only me, man," Nesto said. "We're blood. This is nothing."

"Nothing," Javi said. Then Nesto kissed him and it wasn't nothing. Javi felt their blood boil up and overflow in his mouth and behind his closed eyes and beyond his pounding eardrums. The last shreds of the night dissolved and Javi was left only wanting *something*, wanting what had no name, wanting this hot sweet in Nesto's mouth and the burning grip of his fingers.

"You won't forget about me when you get famous," Nesto said. "Will you?"

Javi shook his head, breathing hard as he stared at the curve of Nesto's bottom lip. Thinking it would feel good between his teeth. His hand pushed aside air to slide in the hair at the back of Nesto's head, damp and soft through his fingers. Nesto groaned and moved in closer.

"Touch me," he whispered, his lip caught in Javi's gentle bite. Pulsing steel filled Javi's other hand and his fingers closed up tight and began moving, knowing exactly what to do.

Then an iron crash sliced the rooftop in two. The night screamed and fled cringing into a corner as the dragon presence of Tío Miguel filled the doorway to the stairwell. He unfolded, tall and terrible as he took in the sight of his kissing nephews, each with the other's parao in his hand.

Javi was instantly sober.

And he knew after tonight, it would no longer be about The Money.

THE TIGER'S TRIBE

*M*R. DURANTE WAS pale as he lifted the ice pack off Javi's forehead, inspected the egg underneath, and replaced it. "You can stay here," he said. "We'll figure something out."

"Lo siento, Javito," Mrs. Durante said, swabbing Javi's cheek with peroxide. "You poor thing."

Javi winced as his cuts and bruises were tended, but he pressed his lips tight and made no sound. The slightest loosening of his jaw and he would start crying like a fucking baby. He focused on the Durantes' Christmas tree, staring hard until the twinkles from the colored bulbs blurred together.

"We should call CPS," Mr. Durante said. "This is unacceptable."

"No," Javi said behind the wall of his teeth. "I don't want anyone knowing about this."

"It's all right. I'm sure it will blow over," Mrs. Durante said. Her fingertip was gentle as it dabbed Bacitracin on his lip.

Javi shook his aching head. "No it won't."

His teacher exchanged a glance with his wife, who got Javi two aspirin, then led him to the spare room where he could lie down. Alone, Javi still made no sound, but the tears spilled out of his eyes and he made no attempt to stop them.

Nothing could have prepared him.

He wondered how he could have been so naive about his own people.

The one-upmanship talks about sex and girls. Racking up conquests. Bragging about the size of your cojones. Whipping them out if you had to prove a point. Javi thought nothing more of it than an aspect of being male.

He didn't know it was a central tenant of being a Dominican male.

Five months had passed since the night on the rooftop. In that time, Javi learned a lot about tiguerismo: the Dominicans' standard of masculinity. Men were raised to be tigers. Predators of love. In matters of the heart, the ideal man was passionate but strong. Sexually commanding and confident. Above all, *macho.*

Pájaro, or bird, was an endearment for a girl. It was the worst kind of slur on a man. To be gay or even perceived as gay not only went against the laws of God and man, but went against everything it meant to be *Dominican.*

The tiger did not suffer weakness.

The tiger's tribe did not tolerate outsiders.

It was nothing, Javi kept insisting that night on the roof. They were *drunk,* it was stupid, harmless fooling around. It didn't mean any—

That was when Tío Miguel threw him down the stairwell. Javi was lucky he didn't break his neck. He guessed being drunk made him loose enough to absorb the shock.

He looked to his father for help but Rafael was comforting Rosa, who was wailing into her hands. Tío Enrique and Tía Mercedes were dragging Nesto away and Nesto wouldn't meet Javi's eyes.

He never spoke to or touched Javi again.

Javi wondered how he could've been so wrong about his cousin.

Nesto had the harder heart, the faster reflexes and better survival skills. He seized the high ground of the battlefield with a three-word opening salvo: *Javi started it.* By throwing the first words, he gave Javi no chance at the last words. He brought in the cavalry of his friends, who joined the campaign of taking down a pájaro with macho glee.

Stunned by his cousin's betrayal, Javi could only stumble through the bombardment, zigzagging to avoid fire as the family, his friends and the entire Dominican community in Corona rose up and shunned him as a foreign abomination.

It had to be a joke. He kept waiting for the punch line. Kept waiting for the law to be laid down, this was *never* to happen again, don't *ever* let us catch you again…

"It won't happen again," he said to Rosa, who ignored him.

"I'm sorry," he said to Rafael, who didn't answer for a long time. Javi watched his father twist his hands together, fingers callused, nicked from knife cuts and spotted with burn scars. His smile had deserted him. He was smoking more and his soft voice had splintered into a rasp. His disappointment in Javi hung about the apartment like toxic clouds, worse than Miguel's cuffs and punches.

"Second chances are given or made," Rafael finally said. Javi put his head in his hands and wished he were dead. Then his father touched his back, broke through the pain in a slender lifeline of hope.

"You make this one, Javito," Rafael said.

Javi was sure he could. Sure he would make it right. He just had to tough it out. He'd be told to go to confession and do penance for his sins. He'd get the silent treatment a couple weeks at home. He'd endure the fights and bullying at school until something bigger came along to divert everyone's attention. He'd ride it out. This too would pass.

Long, abusive weeks passed.

Then his father passed. One October day, he clutched his chest and went down in an avalanche of pots and pans in the restaurant's kitchen. Nobody failed to see the metaphor: Rafael Gil deSoto died of a broken heart, leaving a grieving wife and daughter, a disgrace of a son and a mountain of debt still owed to Miguel.

Javi was utterly alone. Naroba loved him, but she was easily dominated and totally under Rosa's control. Rosa in turn was falling further under Miguel's control, and Miguel continued to poison the well of the apartment building until this morning, when a manila envelope arrived from *Cricket* magazine. Inside was the December issue with Javi's winning story and a check for $500.

The victory was bitter. Rosa demanded he sign the money over to Miguel. Javi refused and for once, Naroba displayed a backbone and took his side. The warrior queen Naria had won the prize, and it was Naria who seized the check out of her mother's hands and made a run for it.

Then it was war. Miguel beat up Javi, which he could've handled if Rosa weren't beating Naroba at the same time. Not the typical open-handed swats of their youth, or the sterner blows of the *chancla*. Rosa had one of Rafael's belts doubled up in her hand. Naroba was screaming under the blows, curled in a ball with the *Cricket* check clutched in her fist. The coffee table fell over. Kitchen chairs toppled. The Christmas tree swayed dangerously back and forth. Through a bloody fog, Javi looked at the destruction of his life and knew he would never win back what had belonged to him. He surrendered.

"Stop," he cried, curled in his own ball against the kitchen cabinets, bottles of mamajuana rattling within. "You can have it. You can have all of it. Just stop."

He crawled to Naroba, his fallen queen, and pried the check out of her fingers. He signed the back, *Paid to the order of Miguel Gil deSoto*. He threw clothes and notebooks into a backpack and he left.

THE DURANTES MADE a haven for Javi until the end of February, when Mrs. Durante's mother had a stroke. She had to come live with them, filling the spare room with her hospital bed, visiting nurses, medications and equipment. Javi assured his teacher he could find digs elsewhere.

"Finish school," Mr. Durante said, a stern finger by Javi's face. "A little less than four months left. Tough it out and finish. Promise me."

Javi promised and thanked the Durantes from the scraped bottom of his heart's barrel. He packed up and went to the one other person who hadn't turned a back on his plight.

Leni Rivera had been kicked out of her own house when she got pregnant at sixteen. She built her beauty supply business on guts and unsentimental determination, writing off her family's estrangement as pure laziness.

"So much easier to blame the slut," Leni said. "Throw it away like garbage and pretend it never happened."

"What happened to your baby?" Javi asked.

"None of your business."

Leni was tough but decent. She let him sleep in the storeroom of her beauty shop and cooked him a meal or two. When she heard of jobs in Flushing or Elmhurst, she sent them Javi's way. He lugged boxes, stocked inventory, made deliveries and got paid in cash, which he socked away in a empty coffee can. Counting it comforted him. Work soothed him. He went into a job knowing exactly what was expected and what he'd get in return: *I will do this. You will give me that. We have an agreement.*

Unlike the made and broken promises of love, the transactions of employment were absolute.

"Love's dangerous," Leni said. "It destroys more than it creates. I've seen more people use love to be manipulative than be supportive. Fuck it, Javi. Sex and money, those are your constants."

True to her word, she took Javi to bed on his eighteenth birthday. His life shifted into a triangle of school, work and sex. He laid low at school. He worked hard—no matter the task, he gave it his best.

Do a good job.

Whatever you do, be excellent at it.

Instead of his father's pride, he was rewarded with sex. Leni didn't love him, but that was all right.

Love was no friend of his.

⌒

HE HEARD ROSA sold the restaurant. He heard she paid back some of the money owed to Miguel, but not all. He heard these things from Miguel and a few buddies, who cornered him at a loading dock, informing him the outstanding debt was now Javi's responsibility.

"Coward," Leni said, laying a steak on Javi's blackened eye that night. "He can't deliver the message himself, has to bring a posse along. Some men can't do anything unless there's an audience."

"What am I going to do?" Javi said.

"Soon as you graduate, you get out of here."

"And go where?"

"Let me think."

She had a friend who had a friend who knew a family with a spare room in their Washington Heights apartment. Javi packed up his things once more. Leni drove him over the Triborough Bridge, along 125th Street through Harlem, then up Broadway to the building on West 172nd Street.

"Don't come back to Queens," she said.

"With pleasure," he said.

She kissed him goodbye and drove away. Javi stared after, imagining an umbilical cord attached to him and her bumper. Stretching out long, then snapping.

He had to breathe on his own now.

His room was tiny, but out its single window he could see the George Washington Bridge. The family was cordial to him. He came and went invisibly, leaving his bed made and no trace of himself in the kitchen or bathroom.

He made one phone call a week to the apartment in Queens. He was still too hurt and angry to speak to his mother, but he made the gamble in case Naroba picked up. She never did. He took one entire Sunday to go to Corona and skulk in the shadows of his neighborhood, searching for a glimpse of the Queen. She didn't appear.

Fight them, Naria, he thought, heading home on the subway. *Fight them hard. You're a queen, not a pawn.*

He found work waiting tables at a popular place on the Upper West Side. He was an excellent waiter without having to try: bilingual, charming with the customers, deferentially flirtatious with the women. His coffee can bulged with the money he made in tips. You could bartend in New York at eighteen, and the manager gave him a couple brunch shifts.

"Goddamn, I thought the building was going to tilt off the foundation," the manager bragged to the closing staff. "You should've seen the women crowding his end of the bar. How many phone numbers you get, kid?"

Javi got a ton, but he didn't dare bring a woman back to his little room. Hook-ups had to be done at her place. Problem was, it was usually married women slipping him their digits.

And his heart had rules about things like that.

He came home late one night and Tío Miguel was waiting outside his building. To his credit, he came alone.

"Time you started paying me back," he said.

"Hello to you, too," Javi said, shouldering past. He was hitting the gym in his free time, finding physical strength comforted him as much as cash. But he was tired tonight. Taken off-guard by Miguel's appearance. And he was young, still harboring a shred of stubborn belief your family would do you no harm.

Miguel seized the back of Javi's jacket and yanked him back off the stoop. "Don't fuck around with me, bugarrón," he said. "I will fucking *bury* you."

"You and who else," Javi said. Then he was thrown down to the pavement.

"You're gonna pay, you cocksucking pájaro."

"I don't owe you shit," Javi said. A kick to the balls immobilized him. He curled up tight, enveloped in pain and nausea.

"You move up here looking for more of your papi chulos, huh? You looking for Nesto? Is that it? You won't find him here anymore."

The words and blows blurred together. Javi curled tighter, sucking wind through more kicks to his back and ribs. Finally they stopped, and he felt Miguel's hands rifle through his jacket and pants pockets. He found the wad of cash, nearly three hundred in tips. He put one more kick in his nephew's side, then walked away down the sidewalk.

"I'll be back," he said. "Better suck enough dick to make the next payment."

Javi missed two days of work from the beating. He went back the third day, wincing and limping, and told the manager he'd been mugged. He was put behind the bar where he didn't have to lift trays or hustle too much. After the brunch rush, the restaurant took a siesta. Only a couple tables were occupied. Two customers nursed drinks at the stools.

Javi was inventorying bottles when in the mirrored wall behind the shelves he saw a man take a seat. He turned and looked into the face of Nesto's father, Enrique Gil deSoto.

"I've been looking for you," Enrique said.

Javi stared back, secure with the wall of the bar between them.

Enrique's eyes narrowed. "Can I get a beer?"

In silence, Javi set down a coaster, then drew a beer. He slid the heavy glass in front of the man he used to call Tío Kiko. Then he set both his hands on the bar top and waited. Ready. The bar's owner kept a sawed-off pool cue under the deck. If Kiko was looking for some shit, Javi would give it.

Enrique took a single, almost prim sip. "Where's your sister?"

"What do you mean, where's my sister? How would I know where she is?"

"She ran away."

Javi's heart lurched but he kept his face neutral. "Good for her," he said, while his mind filled with visions of his big little sister on the streets somewhere. Easy prey. A delectable morsel to feed New York's underbelly.

Fight them, Naria. Remember, you're a queen.

"Your mother's heartbroken," Kiko said.

"My mother has no heart."

Uncle and nephew stared at each other. Finally Enrique looked away, clearing his throat.

"Something else you want?" Javi said. "Miguel already shook me down, I got nothing to give you. Beer's on the house, all right? I'll buy you a fucking beer. That's all I can do."

"I paid off Miguel," Enrique said. He took a drink as Javi stared, then put the glass down and rubbed his hands together in a gesture so reminiscent of Rafael, Javi's eyes misted.

"You paid…?"

"I paid it off. I'd rather you owe me the money than him."

Now Javi's eyes burned. "Oh, so I'm being refinanced? Am I supposed to be grateful? Why am I the one who has to pay for what happened? What the fuck has Nesto done to make amends after he ruined my life, huh?"

"Nesto's dead."

Javi stepped back. The duckboards behind the bar were slippery and he almost went down on his ass. The world wobbled on its axis as he looked into Enrique's eyes, suddenly remembering Miguel's words.

You looking for Nesto? You won't find him here anymore.

"¿Qué?" he whispered.

"He's dead."

"He… How?"

"Jumped off the GWB." Enrique took another sip of beer, his eyes never leaving Javi's.

Cool, hop-infused air rushed into Javi's open mouth. The majestic George Washington Bridge was the backdrop of his tiny world. He saw it every day from his little bedroom window. It was the gateway out of Manhattan. Not the end of the road.

"I… Kiko, I'm sorry…"

Like a cobra strike, Enrique's hand shot out and grabbed the front of Javi's shirt. "You sorry little faggot," he said in a hiss. "You killed my brother and you killed my son."

The world stopped and abruptly began spinning the other way as Enrique released his fingers and took the ballpoint pen in Javi's shirt pocket. He wrote something down on a napkin and pushed it across. "That's my address. You pay me back. All of it. Or I'll leave a hole in your ass so big, you can fuck two men at once."

Javi ducked as the pen was pegged at his head.

"Pay me back and then this is over," Enrique said. "I don't ever want to see your face again."

As he left, he tipped the beer glass over, spilling it onto his nephew's clothes.

THE NECKLINE OF THE COMPLIMENT

*T*HE BRIDE'S FATHER must have spent a fortune.

It struck Javi as obscene, the amount of dough people were willing to wantonly throw around to prove it couldn't buy love. Still, he couldn't complain—a lot of that thrown money ended up in his tip jar. He'd emptied it twice already.

He enjoyed tending at parties and events more than he did at the restaurant. He could laugh and joke with the guests and pretend he wasn't a worker, but a family friend who good-naturedly tossed off his dinner jacket and stepped behind the bar to lend a hand. Catching sight of himself in the mirrored wall behind the bottles, he thought his appearance agreed. He hated looking seedy and polyester at these kinds of venues. His shirt was crisp, the sleeves fastened at his wrist with silver cufflinks. His belt was tight and trim at his waist. The bowtie *tied* not clipped.

Two women had been loitering at the bar all evening. One was about sixteen, buxom and fidgety in a strapless dress she kept fussing with, hauling it up her breasts. She was the only one in her age bracket here and clearly didn't know what to do with herself. Stuck in the demilitarized zone of adolescent misery, either too young to do one thing or too old to do another. She reminded Javi of Naroba, who apologized to the oxygen in the room for breathing.

Javi wished he could give her something to do. Nothing like a useful task to make you feel you belonged somewhere. Instead he made her beautiful Shirley

Temples and coaxed her out in conversation. He bit his tongue from telling her to quit yanking at her neckline and relax. When she held still, she was lovely.

At the other end of the bar was an older woman. Javi guessed mid-forties although she could've been well-maintained fifties (he wasn't good with age estimation and with women, he'd learned to avoid the subject). In stark contrast to the teenager, this lady would've been serene in a wind storm. Her back was straight on the barstool, yet she looked as comfortable as if lounging on a chaise. She was all elegant economy: not a word or gesture wasted. The oxygen thanked her for the privilege of being breathed and hoped she had enough. She didn't go to the bride and groom to convey her best wishes. They came to *her*.

Javi served her two glasses of Bordeaux as she held court. All evening, her eyes followed him, with an interest he couldn't quite put his finger on. Attraction, definitely. But something more. She studied him when he interacted with guests, her analytical gaze caressing the back of his neck. The caress turned to a press when he talked with the young teenage girl.

It wasn't unpleasant.

Through the toasts and the bouts of dancing and the cake, Javi was kept busy. Then it was last call and last dance and the floor filled up with couples swaying to "Unchained Melody." The busboy delivered racks of clean glasses. Javi dried them, deftly spinning them with one hand against a white towel in his other, holding them up to the light and then lining them up on the bar.

"One for the road?" he asked the woman.

She crooked her finger at him. When he came closer, she offered her hand. "Gloria."

He shook it. "Javi."

She frowned. "Short for?"

"Javier."

"No. You should be just Jav. One syllable is best. And it suits you."

He smiled, rolling the new name around his mind a few times and thinking she might be right.

"You're an extremely handsome man," she said.

He didn't yank at the neckline of the compliment, only continued drying a glass and letting her look at him.

"Tell me your troubles," she finally said.

He laughed. "Shouldn't you be telling me yours?"

"I have none. And you sigh a lot when nobody's looking."

Which was true. His worries tended to store in his lungs.

"Money problems?" she asked.

"Are there other kinds of problems?"

"What if I paid you to come home with me tonight?"

Jav almost dropped the glass. "Why would you pay me?"

She put her cheek on her hand. "If I don't pay you, it's about you. If I do pay you, it's about me. Understand the difference? Because with your looks and the way you behave with women, you could make…" She leaned toward him on her forearms and her voice turned confidential. "A *lot* of money."

⌒

ON THE CAB ride to the Riverdale address, Jav felt a twinge of taboo guilt. He hadn't been to church since leaving home, but the inherent Catholicism in his blood knew God wasn't smiling at him right now. You didn't get off for this kind of sin with ten Hail Marys. A pilgrimage to Lourdes on your knees more likely.

Get paid for sex.

This woman was going to *pay* him to sleep with her.

Technically he could be called a prostitute. Or gigolo? Was that the word? *She's going to pay me to fuck her.*

Could he do it?

It wasn't a question of ability. He was twenty-one years old. He could fuck a fire hydrant and get something out of it.

Why not money? A business transaction.

I will do this, and you will give me that.

Staring out the window, a montage of Richard Gere and Blondie's "Call Me" in his head, Jav thought about the hand-to-mouth existence of the past three years. He worked hard, was excellent at what he did and every Friday night, he bought a lottery ticket.

Second chances are given or made.

Six months ago, his numbers came up lucky.

It wasn't the windfall of a lifetime. He wouldn't be excellent at having no job. But to a cast-off boy living in one room in Manhattan, the lottery win was a miracle. He'd entered into a business agreement with fate:

You give me a second chance and I will make the most of it.

He paid off Tío Enrique and cut ties with the family for good. He found an apartment on St. Nicholas Avenue, miniscule and Spartan, but *his*. He opened a bank account and put a grand away, a stash not to be touched unless in emergency.

He relaxed a little and started meeting his own eyes in the mirror. After a late, but welcome growth spurt, he stood up straight at six foot two. His debts were paid and he was allowed to breathe again. He enrolled in a few courses at Hostos Community College and started thinking about some actual goals. Like getting a degree. Getting a job that could lead to a career. Getting a life.

"You getting out, man?"

Jav shook his head back to the present. He paid the cabbie and stood in front of the house a moment. And it was a house, not an apartment building. A mansion in a leafy green neighborhood that bore no resemblance or affiliation with New York City.

What the fuck are you doing?

He exhaled. Best case, they'd have a good time and he'd walk out with some cash. Worst case, he wouldn't be able to get it up for her, he'd say an embarrassed good evening and run like hell. It wasn't like anyone would know either way. Not like Miguel would bust in and throw him down the stairs.

He rang the bell and Gloria opened the door. She was still wearing her black silk dress but she had taken her hair out its bun. "How lovely you came," she said, beckoning him.

Inside was golden warm, sleek and expensive. She hung his coat away and then crossed her arms, her expression stern.

"Does anyone know where you are?"

"My mother."

"Don't be fresh," she said. "Rule number one, always tell someone where you're going. Even if you write it down and tape it to your mirror."

"All right," Jav said, wondering what she meant by always. Always in general? Or always when he was going to a strange woman's house to get laid? He got the feeling she had done this before.

But who says I'm doing this again?

"Rule number two," Gloria said, "trust your gut. If you get where you're going and your gut tells you to leave, put down the money and get out."

She handed him an envelope. "Rule number three, the money is given up front. And the money is for your time. This is for the next three hours and what happens in those hours is between two consenting adults. Rule number four, it's about me. Got all that?"

Jav nodded.

"Can you handle one more rule? Put that away, please, the less we *see* of the money, the better."

Jav nodded again, slipping the envelope in his pocket.

"Slow is better than fast. Less is better than more. Be confident. And if you're not feeling confident, fake it."

"That was four more rules."

"Spoken with confidence." She turned around and drew her hair aside, revealing the long zipper down the back of her dress. "Now let's see what you can do."

How about let's see me not have a heart attack?

He was, all at once, nervous as hell. He set his hands on Gloria's shoulders and let them rest there *(less is more)*. He took a deep breath, calling on his excellence and understanding he was being paid to pay attention, not get his rocks off. As he picked the tab of the zipper out and slid it down *(slow is better than fast)*, he gathered together his sexual resume and put it with what he'd read in books and seen in the movies.

He let his fingers linger on her skin as he undressed her, then turned her around and took her face in his hands. He kissed her, letting his consciousness sink deep into the embrace and look at her from all angles. Under his hands and in his arms, Gloria's body was straight and proud. Then, little by little, it began to soften. Like a pillar candle that had been burning so long, you could press your fingers into the warm wax and reshape it.

"I love when I'm right," she whispered.

"You strike me as always being right."

Her lips glistened in the lamplight. "Often wrong. Never in doubt."

He took her hand and confidently headed down a hall that looked like it led to a bedroom. It did, and there she stretched out on the bed, on her side, holding up a soft palm to indicate he shouldn't join her yet.

"I'm still seeing what you can do," she said.

He undressed slowly. He didn't camp or tease, didn't smile or crack nervous jokes. He held her eyes and unpeeled his layers. Only then did Gloria's composed face melt into mischief, as she sank lower on her side and put her cheek on the heel of her hand.

"Oh my," she said around a throaty laugh. "Honey, with a cock like that, you'll have to work *really* hard to suck in bed."

He crawled up her body, nudging her down on her back. "I don't suck," he said, filled with a power he didn't know he possessed. "I lick…"

He did an excellent job and walked out three hundred dollars richer.

Plus cab fare home.

A PROFESSIONAL LOVER

"**T**AKE MY COAT first and give it to the girl," Gloria said. "Then yours. You tip at the end of the evening."

Gloria Landes had the uncanny ability to speak through her smile in a voice meant only for Jav's ears. And he was becoming adept at listening to it while keeping the other ear on the world. This five-star Manhattan restaurant was definitely a foreign galaxy.

"The maître d' will hold out my chair for me," she said as they were led to their table. "Don't sit until I'm seated. He'll ask if you want to see the wine list. Say yes. Don't stare at the room. Act confident."

Table manners were nothing more than common sense, Jav thought. But projecting confidence was an unpredictable struggle. He made mistakes, which Gloria always covered effortlessly.

"You're young," she said. "You'll get the hang of it. You never make the same mistake twice, which is refreshing."

Her eyes swept the wine list and then she handed it across the table. "You'll order a bottle of Penfolds Grange Hermitage. It's Australian."

"Is it good?"

She smiled. "It's easy to pronounce."

"Thank you."

"You're welcome. And it's a lovely wine. Say it back to me."

"Penfolds Grange Hermitage."

"Good. Don't point to it when you order. In fact, put the list down."

Jav opened the dinner menu and was about to ask what was good to eat here, before remembering tonight was about Gloria. "What would you like to eat?"

She had put on her reading glasses and her gaze was slower over the entrées. "I'm not sure yet. Some women like the man to order for them, but I don't. Always find out what your date is having and when the waiter arrives, simply ask, 'Would you like me to order?'"

"Have you done this before?"

"Done what, darling?"

His mouth started to say "hired a man" before instinct kicked his ankle, warning the word would be ugly in this setting. He flailed for an elegant substitute. "Groomed a man," he said.

Her eyes lifted and her smile was pleased. "No," she said. "So take heart I'm learning just as much as you are."

"Why are you doing this?"

"Why are *you* doing this?"

"I want to make money."

She closed the menu. "I was married to an alcoholic for fifteen years and endured abuse I won't speak of at the table. I sacrificed my publishing career for him. Sacrificed money and pride and things you can't imagine. Although…" Her hand dropped on top of his and her thumb rubbed his wrist. "Maybe you can. When I was finally free, I never wanted to get involved again. I focused on rebuilding my career. But the human heart craves connection, Jav. Many people like being alone, but nobody likes to be lonely. I became lonely, and I decided if I was going to have male company, it would be company on my terms."

"What made you pick me?"

"Besides being easy on the eyes? It was the way you treated every guest at the wedding like a family member. How you handled that teenaged girl took my breath away. You didn't just treat her as a princess, you *made* her a princess. I thought, *This boy has a gift for women and he doesn't even know it.*"

She took her hand back and folded it with the other on the table. "I want to hone that gift of yours, Jav. Both for my own needs and for yours. I want company and you want money. We can serve each other beautifully. But you aren't my prisoner. Or my possession. And none of what I'm teaching you comes at a price."

The room swam for a minute. Jav bit the inside of his lip hard until it held still again. "You promise?"

"I promise. And you may order me the sole meunière with pommes château. Say it back to me."

"Sole meunière with pommes château."

"EVERY DATE YOU have will be an opportunity to learn something," Gloria said. "Never stop learning. You already like to read, which is an advantage. Read *everything*. Newspapers, magazines, books. Be informed. Be up-to-date. Be both interesting and interested in others. Everyone has something fascinating about them, Jav. Your job is to find it. *Then* you can fuck it."

At first his only dates were with Gloria. She called him at least once a week. Sometimes twice. Under her tutelage, he began to invest in himself as a marketable product.

"Your body and your looks are assets," she said. "Take exceedingly good care of them, darling, and always show them to their best advantage."

She took him shopping and showed him how to build the foundation of a wardrobe. She taught him about the importance of good shoes, an impeccably-cut suit and a well-fitting sport coat. Where to get the best haircut and where to rent the best tux. He took a few ballroom dancing classes. Audited French and Italian classes at Hostos. Even took a course in massage therapy. He learned how to choose wine and negotiate the place-settings of a ten-course meal. Social niceties, table manners and all the tiny, essential details of being the perfect gentleman.

The phone began to ring at his place. "I'm a friend of Gloria's. I'd like you to take me out."

"Gloria Landes told me to call you. I need a date to the opera next week."

"Gloria gave me your number. I have a wedding coming up."

He had a post-mortem with Gloria after each date. No names or personal details, only what went wrong and how to fix it, or what went right and how to make it better next time.

"Are you my pimp now?" he blurted out during one such meeting.

Gloria winced. "Mentor, darling. And do you see me taking a cut of your earnings?"

His face burned. "No."

"Pimp is an ugly word. I don't want to hear it again."

"You won't."

"Apologize."

"I'm sorry."

She gave a prim sniff.

"It was thoughtless," he said.

"You *must* think, Javier. Always think before you speak."

"I will. It's just… I'm not used to people helping me. For nothing in return."

Her eyes remained resolutely across the room. The fear he'd disappointed her twisted in his stomach. His eyes blinked fast as he tried to explain himself. "I guess I still don't understand why you're doing all this for me."

She looked at him then and her face softened. "Because you remind me so much of myself, Jav," she said. "Nobody helped me. And I couldn't help myself."

She schooled him in safety, both for him and his client. He knew CPR and basic first aid. Along with his daily gym workouts, he took a self-defense course. He never drank or drugged on a date. His client could get as plowed as she wanted but Jav stayed straight and sober. He never, absolutely never, went into a woman without a condom. He'd leave money on the table before he rode bareback. Every three months, without exception, he was screened at a walk-in clinic for STDs.

"Do not trifle with your health," Gloria said. "It wouldn't do not to be around to enjoy the money you make."

And he was making good money. $100 an hour. Then $125. $200. He kept raising his price, and clients kept paying. He got hired for a weekend in Montauk and when he returned home to his apartment, he gleefully ran around strewing $1500 in cash, the most dough he'd ever held in his hands at one time.

By 1986, he was almost finished with his associate degree in liberal arts from Hostos. He made up his mind to escort the next two years to save enough for tuition at City College, where he could get a BA in creative writing.

He liked living in northern Manhattan, but his dates took him frequently into Midtown and the Village so he migrated south down St. Nicholas Avenue to an apartment in Hamilton Heights, where he had a second phone line installed for clients only.

One day he got a call from a woman wanting him as a date for her and her husband. It was the first time he'd been hired by a couple.

"It will happen," Gloria said long ago. "And it's good money."

"I don't fuck men," he said.

Her hand soothed the back of his neck. "You don't have to," she said. "And often, darling, the man isn't interested in you anyway. Be professional. Ask what the expectation is and then decide if you can meet it."

"He doesn't want to join in," the caller said. "He just wants to watch."

Jav took the job, but it ended up being an unsettling experience. He'd never deluded himself that some of his clients were married. He'd fucked other men's wives, but not with those men right there watching him. For the first time, he felt *hired,* and discovered it was distinctly different from feeling *paid.*

As the woman moaned through his kiss and writhed against his thrusts, Jav was hyper-aware of the money and the transaction and of sex being a service. His back squirmed under the husband's scrutinizing and possessive gaze. The longer the sex went on, the more Jav was convinced the husband *didn't* want to be there. Something else was at play. The dynamic of this marriage comprised a fourth party in the bedroom. The money made a fifth witness. All the additional presences left Jav slimy.

This agreement didn't agree with him.

He tried it once more to be sure. This time the husband joined in, but by unspoken agreement, he and Jav stayed out of each other's way. Jav relaxed into being an extra mouth, dick and pair of hands. A little story curled around the edges of his mind: he imagined the husband was an apprentice, making a first solo run. Jav was just there to assist.

He was deep in the narrative and thinking couple work wasn't so slimy after all, when the husband's hand slid around Jav's waist and took hold of his penis. His mouth ran up Jav's spine and touched the nape of his neck with the tip of a tongue.

"Damn, you got a great cock," he said, squeezing and stroking with a knowledgable grip.

Jav froze, balanced on the edge. He liked the feel of that hand. A melting moment of intense pleasure. A remembered taste of sugar and rum. The burn of cinnamon at the back of his throat and the feel of Nesto's bottom lip between his teeth.

"Turn around," the husband whispered, a palm wide between Jav's shoulder blades.

Now Jav was paralyzed with an intense, instinctive fear. The sweet in his mouth went sour. The caress on his back readied to shove him down a flight of stairs. A hole opened in his soul and sucked out his excellence. He deflated in the husband's hand and pulled away. Without a word of explanation, he put his clothes on, left the money in its envelope and got the hell out of there.

"So take it off your resume," Gloria said. "You should be able to look your income in the face."

His business card read *Javier Soto* with a phone number. He was a straight male escort, with or without sex. No pay-to-gay, no couples. No violence, no drugs, no urine, shit or blood. Nothing ugly or degrading. He was a professional lover. A champion date who specialized in attention, both in and out of the bedroom.

Word of mouth spread to the ears of women who wanted what he was giving. He began to amass regulars. Those regulars told their friends. His bank balance climbed. His clothes grew more expensive. His passport collected stamps. Gloria assured him he was on the way to becoming one of the top-paid escorts in Manhattan. He was a self-made success.

But he ran into Tío Enrique and Tía Mercedes on the street one day and his confidence stumbled. He stared like a jackass, his hand lifting in a shy wave and qué lo qué on his lips. Thinking, like a fool, that with time passed and debts cleared came forgiveness. Or at least cordiality.

They walked by. Not a word. Not a look. No acknowledgment. Jav stood on the sidewalk staring after them, feeling freshly seventeen and abandoned, as deeply wounded as if it had been a kick from Miguel's boot.

Some things couldn't be repaid.

WALKERS
AND NEPHEWS

LE HANDSOME

1986
NEW YORK CITY

"**H**E'S HERE."

"He is?" Hands reached for compacts and lipsticks. Fingers smoothed hair. Mints were popped and teeth checked in reflective surfaces.

"He just walked in. Usual booth. Who's got a quarter? I call heads."

The arrival of *him* was the highlight of the graveyard shift at Morelli's Diner on Ninth Avenue, off Columbus Circle. *He* had been coming in for three weeks now. Always after midnight, always dressed to kill and taking the same back booth. The waitresses flipped a coin to take his order (egg white omelet, dry toast, coffee). They called him Le Handsome.

"Why don't you ask his name?" Alex Penda said.

"Shh." He was swatted by six sisterly hands. "Oh my God, look, he's putting his glasses on. Look."

"He's gorgeous."

"I swear, I just got wet."

Pushing his own glasses up his nose, Alex turned his head from the exploding panties and put it back into his textbook, trying to get some discreet studying done while the diner was in a lull.

Stuck in the pages were two envelopes from today's mail. One from Roger Lark, who had been kicked out of the University of Chicago for a fraternity prank that went south. Roland and Meredith were *furious* and immediately pulled the plug on financing Roger's future if he were going to show this utter lack of common sense.

Undeterred, Roger hit the road with a couple of his buddies and turned their collegiate disgrace into a life experience, working and couch-surfing their way across the country. The postmark on today's letter was from Seattle, where Roger was working in a fishery by day, bartending by night, and spending weekends with a girlfriend in Vancouver.

"Living the dream, man," he wrote.

The other letter was from Trelawney, now in her junior year at Brown, majoring in Gender and Sexuality Studies. Since Trelawney was the most sexless person Alex knew, he couldn't figure out if her degree made no sense or perfect sense.

He didn't get letters from Val. She was here in the city. After graduating from RISD, she was hired by designer Theoni Aldredge to work on the costumes for *La Cage Aux Folles*. She ran wardrobe for *La Cage* another year while freelancing costume design on the side. Six months ago she entered and won a design contest for American Ballet Theater's Jazz Age production of *Cinderella*. Now she and her production team were working their asses off in a garment district warehouse.

Alex saw her every now and then, usually when she needed a last-minute date to a thing.

"Be my thing for a thing?" she'd ask.

"What am I, your favorite fallback position?"

"Yes."

"Pick you up at eight."

Now in his second year of vet school, Alex didn't get out much. He and Amanda—his steady girlfriend at Columbia—had finally broken up for good, after a year of torturous on-again-off-again negotiations. Swamped with course-work and lab work and the swing shifts at Morelli's, he had little time for socializing. But if Val called, he answered.

He was kind of her bitch that way.

The glorious hookup in the back room of Muriel's shop—referred to as The Oral Dissertation—remained a one-off event. Rather than ruin their friendship, the encounter cemented the deal and they parted the best of pals. Their relationship wasn't without its flirtatious teasing, but they only carried on to a point. When apart, they genuinely missed each other. When together, they wore each other's company like a favorite pair of jeans. The ones that fit perfect, made your ass look great and didn't bind in the crotch.

Val never wandered far from Alex's thoughts, but he had a feeling about her he wasn't in a hurry to dissect. An instinctive hunch they were treating each other like a pleasure saved for a rainy day. The bit of expensive chocolate stashed away. The dessert saved for last, but not least.

One day, he often thought. *Not today, but one day…*

"How's it going?"

Alex looked up. Le Handsome was at the register.

"Hey," Alex said, taking the check and the $20 and ringing it up. He noticed Handsome had a textbook under his arm. Noticing Alex noticing, Handsome turned the cover out a little.

"Human Behavior in the Social Environment," he said.

Alex turned his own book slightly. "Parasitology."

"Hopefully in four years, I'll be able to analyze how you behave."

"And I'll be able to check you for worms."

Their eyes held as the joke crashed on the floor in a million pieces.

"That sounded better in my head," Alex said, handing over the change.

"If I were you, I'd keep it in my head."

Alex nodded, having a hard time meeting the guy's eyes. "Right."

"Call me if you plan to hit the bars any time. You're in serious need of a wingman."

"Something tells me you'd be the worst wingman I could take to a bar."

Chuckling, Handsome took a mint and left.

Alex fought off a weird embarrassment the rest of the shift, feeling like a freshman who'd split his pants in front of the senior jocks. The next time Handsome came in, Alex avoided him.

As he cleared one of his booths, he overheard one of the girls attempting to draw the guy out.

"Do you always dress up to study?"

"I dress this way for work," Handsome said, not unfriendly but not looking up from his reading.

"What do you do?"

"I'm a hired assassin."

Alex was passing by with his bus tub then. He stopped and half turned. "You got a card?"

Handsome looked up. "Why? You got a problem?"

"Big problem."

Handsome took out a card and leaned out of the booth and around the waitress to stick it in Alex's fingertips. Alex milked the conquest in the girls' faces for an hour afterward. They weren't amused. One offered him half her tips in exchange for the card.

Alex chuckled all the way home on the subway. He gave the card one last look—*Javier Soto* with a phone number beneath.

Then he chucked it.

Between Vendettas

"**B**E MY THING for a thing?" Val asked.

"What kind of thing?" Alex said.

"Fashion Week benefit thing."

"I haven't a thing to wear."

"Wear your best suit and your cute little dimples."

Alex only owned one suit and Val had picked it out for him. It cost a sock of money but she said it would last forever.

"Who stood you up this time?" he asked.

"Nobody," she said. "I miss you."

"Bullshit. What happened to Matthew?"

"You mean Jason."

"Sorry, I can't keep up."

"He can't come. And missing you is bullshit. We live in the same city. I shouldn't have to miss you. Come on, be my thing?"

The event was in Chelsea and attended by the glitterati of Manhattan society. Not Alex's world, but Val was in her element. And she looked beautiful: shoulders rising soft and creamy above a strapless dress. Blonde hair in a sleek chignon. Providing a fascinating, murmured commentary through her teeth, half professional observation and half juicy gossip.

"A lot of these society matrons have strangely hot dates," Alex said.

"Walkers and nephews," Val said, spearing a stuffed mushroom from a passing waiter.

Alex raised his eyebrows.

"A walker is a young gay man who escorts ladies of society. If it's a young straight man being paid to screw said lady, then he's tactfully referred to as a nephew."

"Even if the lady is an only child."

"Exactly."

As if on cue, a smoky female voice shrieked from behind them, "Cynthia! Cynthia, come meet my nephew!"

Val's eyes went wide. Alex turned to see a maven in satin and diamonds, shouldering her way through the crowd, leading a tall man in a tux by the hand. Alex blinked and peered closer.

It was Le Handsome.

"Holy shit," he said. "I know him."

"Who?"

Alex took a finger off his glass and pointed. "The nephew. He's a regular at the diner. I see him all the time."

"Introducez-moi," Val said. "Good lord, he's like illegally gorgeous."

"He's hot," Alex said. "Not that I judge a guy by his looks. But I will say, that guy is hot."

Val pushed her elbow against his arm. "You *securely* say."

"Straight observation."

Standing at the fringe of his aunt's circle, hands behind his back, Javier Soto caught Alex's gaze. He looked away, as if annoyed, and then quickly back. A smile unfolded. He set his hand at the small of his auntie's back, murmuring at her ear as he took the empty glass from her hand. She waved ringed fingers at him, dismissing. Still smiling, he made his way over to Val and Alex.

"You dress up nice for a worm checker," he said.

Alex gestured to the room at large. "Who's the target tonight?"

"You." He turned to Val. "I'm Javier."

"Valentine," she said, using the name she preferred professionally instead of her real one, Valerie.

"I still don't know your name," Javier said to Alex.

"Isn't that preferred in your line of work?"

"For some. Me, I like to have a name when I make a kill."

"I'm Alex."

"Your date is glaring at you," Val said, touching Javier's arm and nudging her head across the room.

"She's thirsty." Javier gestured with his empty wineglass and with a last smile and a wink, insinuated himself through the sparkling crowd toward the bar.

"Walker," Val said.

"Nephew," Alex said, although he was trying to work out if the parting wink was for Val or for him.

The encounter kept them thoroughly entertained for the rest of the evening. They ogled away, fascinated by Javier, making outrageous speculations while he barely threw a glance their way.

Later on, though, emerging from the men's room, Alex saw Javier and Val standing together. Javier had his hands behind his back—it seemed to be his parade rest position. Val looked up at him, poised and confident in Javier's intent stare. Her clutch purse under an arm, holding her drink easily as she talked.

Val turned her head and looked at Alex. A corner of her mouth went up and her eyes crinkled. Javier turned and looked as well. And smiled.

A bubble of self-consciousness swelled around Alex's head. As if he were coming downstairs in prom finery, and all parental eyes turned to gape and coo at their not-so-little boy. The kind of attention that made you want to throw up or kill yourself.

Alex did neither, but his dress shoe caught on the carpet and he stumbled as he reached them.

Why does this guy make me act like such a dork?

"Could you move that dead body?" he said to Javier. "Nearly killed me."

Javier hadn't stopped smiling at him. "You're going to be harder to bump off than I thought."

AN HONEST LIVING

"**1**'LL SEE MYSELF out," Jav said.

Kristina reached behind her and handed him the ice pack. "Get me a new one before you go?"

"Of course."

He switched out the packs, wrapping the fresh, cold one in a dish towel and laying it on her bum.

"Thanks, baby," she said. Breezy, confident, good-natured. No resemblance to the school-uniformed woman over his knee a couple hours ago, cotton panties down around her penny loafers. Getting her ass handed to her until she apologized to Daddy and sucked his cock to show what a good girl she could be.

People were weird.

"Call me," he said, leaning to kiss her forehead. "Be good."

She laughed. "Get out of here."

He collected his jacket and bag from the living room and the envelope from the hall table. The lobby doorman gave him a nod and touched the bill of his cap. Jav nodded back, pulling on his sunglasses and catching sight of himself in the gilt-frame mirror over the front desk. He looked good.

He felt good. Well, his hand was a little numb from spanking Kristina for twenty minutes, but one had to make certain sacrifices while making an honest living.

Jav smiled at New York as he strode into the perfect spring twilight, the air soft around him. He could walk a bit uptown before catching the subway to Harlem. A disco nap, a shower and off to his once-monthly dinner with Gloria. Thank God. No baggage, no bullshit, no daddy issues or self-punishment by proxy. A leisurely meal with good wine and excellent conversation, then back to her place for relaxed, unscripted sex.

I will do this, and you will give me that.

The day's net intake of *that*: $1800.

Cha-ching.

While his mind was on money and the evening ahead, his feet had their own agenda, and he looked up to see the red neon sign of Morelli's Diner.

What, this again?

This again.

He did a walk-by, scanning the interior through the windows. He paused and looked at his watch, casually shuffled through his messenger bag. Then walked by the other way, scanning again.

He's not there.

Alex hadn't been there in weeks. Jav tried different days, different shifts, everything except flat-out asking one of the staff.

Disappointment curled up in his gut. Where did Alex go? Heading up Broadway once more, his pace was heavy and the evening leaned on him as if it were exhausted.

"Son of a bitch," he mumbled.

Then he laughed under his breath. He was an idiot, but it was fun while it lasted. Something to feel dumb about yet look forward to. And it didn't suck looking at it.

Especially his smile.

FROM DAY ONE, before even knowing the guy's name, the smile nudged Jav in the ribs. *Hey*, it said, *I got a story for you*. Sitting in a back booth at Morelli's, Jav strained eyes and ears, his fingers itching around a pen poised over a notebook.

He wrote about the way the smile flew up the waiter's face like a window shade, his cheekbones rising to the bottoms of his glasses. The two bullet-hole dimples on either side of white, straight teeth.

The story unfolded to include the way the waiter took off his glasses and rubbed at the indentations on his nose. Clowning around with the waitresses during a rush, he'd tilt the frames off-kilter and mess up his hair, crying, "Mother of *God*," as they all ran here and there.

Chapters detailed the waiter's natural, athletic grace and dexterity: he could hold a loaded tray one-handed, or balance five hot dishes on his bare arm while pouring coffee for six people. He had a social grace, too. His regulars laughed and joked with him. Parents handed him their babies to hold while they took younger children to the restroom. Girls checked out his ass when he walked by, then giggled behind their menus.

Charming, Jav thought, while his fingers turned a page in his notebook and picked up a pen. *His looks had an old world, pagan charm. Some invisible promise of luck, long life and good fortune clung to him like gold dust. His smile was a gift from the gods and you wanted it to shine on you, include you and keep you in the warm, rough palm of his hand. "Hold the baby," women said, not because they needed a favor, but because they wanted a blessing.*

Weeks of heady, covert observation passed. The staff at Morelli's didn't wear name tags, and the waitresses called everyone honey and sweetheart and love. Jav had no name to go with the smile until the night at the Chelsea event.

When their eyes met across a crowded room.

Like hell. Jav almost looked straight past the guy. Who could blame him? The waiter was completely out of context: slicked up and sharp in a well-cut suit and really good shoes. Looking Jav dead in the eye, he was Rob Lowe with glasses, a cool, gorgeous blonde at his side. A predatory edge in his grin that made Jav look away a moment, annoyed and defensive.

Wait a minute…

He looked back. Gold dust swirled in the chandelier light. The waiter raised a hand. Jav felt it close around his heart and gently pull him forward, into the story.

Finally he had a name. Alex. Great name. A heroic name. You bit it out of the air and let the X puff up against the roof of your mouth, then melt out with a little hiss.

When Alex introduced his date, Valentine, Jav's interest made a swift pendulum swing in the other direction. His mind turned a page and picked up a pen. Valentine was hot from across the room but close up, she was stunning. A sunshine blonde with wintergreen eyes. Slender, but real solid flesh and muscle under the strapless dress, beautiful shoulders and breasts. While making small talk, he admired her cool composure and the serenity of her hands: she never once touched her hair or her clothes. She reminded him of Gloria. No apology to the air for breathing, the same economy of movement and the ease in her own skin. Friendly, but sexy as hell. She'd listen to your troubles, give sound, practical advice and then fuck you senseless.

Is he fucking her?

Jav glanced back at Alex, whose head and shoulders lined up with Jav's six-two frame. Behind the lenses, his eyes were green as well. His hands also stayed to himself. He didn't touch Valentine, not casually, not territorially. Still, a chemistry crackled between them. A complicity. Or a weighted history. A relationship.

For a moment, the three of them stood in a tableau. The golden flame of Valentine posed between the dark pillars of Jav and Alex. For the single, shining, gold-dusted moment, Jav felt part of the charm. They were in his story and he was in theirs.

Later in the evening, he saw Val standing alone, gazing over the rim of her martini glass at an invisible horizon. Jav supposed his professional side drew him over to chat with her: a woman standing alone was a potential client.

"Do you have a card?" Val asked.

He never went anywhere without a card. He gave her one.

I will give you this, and you will give me...

He glanced through the crowd at Alex, returning from the men's room.

That.

⌒

FOUR DAYS AFTER the fashion event, Jav was back at Morelli's, but Alex worked tables in another section, not even glancing in Jav's direction. Jav tried not to take it personally, though he wondered if Alex knew Jav had given Valentine his card and was pissed about it.

"Dude, you were in the men's room," he mumbled. "I went over to make a little chit-chat and she asked me for it." He drained the last of his coffee. "I'm not the morality police. Just trying to make a living."

Maybe what Jav did for a living was the reason Alex was avoiding him.

"Hey, don't knock it until you try it," Jav said under his breath. "Actually, don't. Good-looking guy like you could put me out of business."

"Private conversation?"

Alex stood by his booth with a carafe.

Jav gave a weak laugh. "Was I talking out loud again?"

"Mm." Alex reached and topped up Jav's cup.

Jav uncapped his highlighter and started marking text. "You never called me."

"Pardon?"

"I gave you my card. You didn't call."

Alex smiled around a chuckle. "I'm afraid I lost it."

"Ah."

"And I'm between vendettas at the moment."

"Glad to hear it," Jav said, taking a sip of coffee.

"¿Dónde estuviste trabajando esta noche?" Alex asked, putting down some creamers.

Where were you working tonight?

Jav looked at him. Alex stared back a moment, until the carafe in his hand tilted and splashed on the linoleum. Then he shrugged and ran his foot across the drips.

"Actually, don't tell me," he said. "You'll kill me and if I miss my lab practical tomorrow, I'm screwed."

Alex's Spanish was melodic, with a slightly mushy accent Jav couldn't place. He decided to take the inquiry at face value.

"I was at the Plaza," he said. "New York Historical Society was having their History Makers Gala." He accelerated his already-rapid lingo, challenging Alex's ability to dissect the string of words.

Alex's face didn't move. "¿Como caminante o sobrino?"

Walker or nephew?

Jav stared, the gauntlet at his feet and the blood crawling up from his collar. He felt a corner of his mouth lift as Alex's eyebrows slowly raised over the top of his glasses.

"Your pants are smart," Jav said.

"When they fit right."

"How'd you figure it out?"

"Your date was far too hot for you."

Both the crack and the language leaned on Jav's ears like a brother's loving, playful hands. He wanted more, wanted Alex to keep talking, wanted to point to the bench opposite in the booth and say, *Sit the fuck down, you. Stay awhile.*

Alex raised a palm in farewell and went back to his tables. Jav went back to reading, sure something significant had happened but unable to say what.

Alex rung him up at the register. Taking his change and receipt, Jav noticed the tattoo on Alex's forearm: it was the Unisphere of the World's Fair.

"You from Queens?" Jav asked, pointing at it.

Alex looked down and gave a half-laugh. "No," he said. "I… It's kind of a story."

"I love stories."

Alex turned his arm in, regarding the inked globe. "I came to the States from Chile when I was eleven. My uncle picked me up at JFK." A corner of his mouth grinned. "In a nineteen sixty-six Ford Thunderbird convertible."

"Nice," Jav said, nodding.

"We drove through Queens and he took me by the fairgrounds. I looked up to see this globe. This big silver planet Earth, the side with South America facing dead-on. It was like a welcome sign, you know? It always meant something to me. My first memory of America. That and the World Trade Center. I remember going across a bridge and my uncle pointed down Manhattan to the two towers. It was nineteen seventy-three, they'd just been finished…"

He trailed off and leaned his forearms on the counter. Jav was tempted to trace a finger around the fine detail of the tattoo but held himself in check.

"That's a good story," he said. "I grew up in Corona. I could see the fairgrounds from my rooftop. I always thought something was so awesome about the structures, but sad at the same time. A giant's abandoned playthings."

"Yeah." Alex's eyes were wide as he looked up, nodding slowly. "It's kind of a haunted place. Everything about it is crying, *Don't you love me anymore?*"

Jav nodded as well. Words piled up on the tip of his tongue: *You want to hang out some night?*

Instead he slid another card across the counter. "Don't lose it this time," he said in Spanish.

Alex put two fingers on the card but didn't pick it up. "You must be Dominican."

"Wow." Jav took a mint. "What's an astute guy like you doing in a place like this?"

"Dominicans speak the fastest."

"Don't let a Puerto Rican hear you say that," Jav said, smiling as he bumped the diner door open with his back.

He took only a couple steps on the sidewalk before looking back. Craning his neck, he saw Alex pick up the card, gaze at it a moment, then put it away in his wallet.

Jav rode the subway home with triumph in his veins. The satisfaction of an agreement made. Jav would do this and Alex would give him that.

Or wait. Wasn't it the other way around?

It turned out not to matter because Jav hadn't seen Alex since then. He was gone. Two months now. Disappeared like last night's dream, taking all the dopey fun and leaving the bereft confusion. Reducing Jav to pathetic walk-bys that invariably ended in disappointment and a bummed-out subway ride home.

An abandoned toy lamenting, *Don't you love me anymore?*

ONE-HANDED

1987

NEW YORK CITY

"*L*IFE HAS RULES," Val Lark said through her teeth. "You don't break up with your girlfriend four days before she is making her design debut with American Ballet Theater. That is a *rule*."

Unfortunately, the egregious breaker of this rule was now over the Atlantic Ocean, on his way to Europe with his new girlfriend. Leaving Val to show up at the Metropolitan Opera House with no date.

"Come on, honey," Alex said. "Think. You know tons of guys. Someone can be a Plan B."

"*You're* my Plan B," she said, clutching the phone in a white-knuckled fist, as if to wring Alex's presence from it. He was two thousand miles in the other direction, doing an internship in Colorado.

"I'm sorry," he said. "I'd be there if I could."

"No," she said, drawing a deep breath. "No, I'm sorry. I'm just…"

"Tired," Alex said. "You've been working your ass off for six months. You're exhausted, you're nervous, this is your big night. Jason could've waited four fucking days. It sucks."

"Sucks," she said, dropping onto her couch.

"We'll work it out," he said. "We'll get through this. Try to think…"

She couldn't. She spun the mental rolodex of her people but it was one dizzying blur of names. The thought of calling men up to get a date was too exhausting. And humiliating, goddammit.

"Where's Roger?" Alex said. "Is he home?"

"Last I heard, he was in New Mexico."

"Well, that does us no good."

Val smiled. Among a thousand other things, she loved Alex for his easy use of *we*. His willing, unconscious way of taking an oar at the galley of your problem, even if it was just to listen. Even if both of you knew he couldn't do anything to help, he made it about *us* and made you feel less alone.

"I could take my grandmother," she said slowly. After all, Val's career had been born in Muriel Deane Lark's dress shop in Guelisten. It would be a fitting tribute. But Muriel was getting on in years. Having her come to the gala would mean arranging transportation and a wheelchair and a dozen other details. Val would be too busy fretting over her grandmother's comfort to enjoy the performance. With not a little guilt, she scrapped the idea.

"I suppose it wouldn't be terrible going alone," she said, sighing.

No answer.

"Hello?"

A giggle on the other end of the line, then something scraping against the phone.

"Alex."

"I'm sorry, what?" His voice was tight with suppressed laughter and a hint of…

"Jesus Christ, you're naked, aren't you," Val said. "Who's the lucky girl?"

"Katie," he said. "Val, Katie. Katie, Val."

"Hello," a girl's voice called. "I've heard a lot about you."

Val rolled her eyes. "Put your dick back in her mouth," she said.

"Shh," Alex hissed.

"I'm going to find a date. Wish me luck."

"You don't need luck."

"Love you."

The fucker hung up without replying. Val didn't grudge him his girlfriends, but getting laid while she was in the lurch added insult to injury.

Fucker.

"Think," she said under her breath, pacing. "Think. Think. Think."

She could go alone but she didn't want to. She didn't need a romantic date, she just needed a hand to hold in the dark. A supportive and attentive presence to make sure she didn't barf. Someone to walk beside her and…

She stopped short. A smile began to curve up her mouth. She bit down on it, but it broke through as a terrible, horrible, no good, very bad idea unspooled in her belly.

She went into her closet, stood on tiptoe and pulled down her black clutch purse. Her fingers fished in the inside zip pocket and drew out a business card. Pure white, heavy stock. Black lettering. A name and a number.

Javier Soto.

❧

HE WAS ONE of the nephews escorting society dames at the Chelsea Film & Fashion event.

And he was gorgeous.

When he first shook her hand, Javier didn't give her an up-down. Didn't put his other hand on top of the shake or hold onto her fingers. Yet Val felt swallowed up in his gaze. His manner was easy and relaxed, but no doubt he could pounce at any given second.

He and Alex were trading cracks, laughing about the random encounter. Alex inched slightly closer to Val, rattling the loose change in his trouser pocket. He was nervous, but an excited kind of nervous, beading on him like condensation on a cold glass.

Val's eyes moved between him and Javier. They were the same height and build, both dark-haired, good-looking Latinos. But any woman would look at Alex and deduce she could spend the night with him and get breakfast the next morning. Whereas with *that* guy, she'd be nothing but a smoking pile of ash with her jewelry resting on top.

Javier excused himself and both Alex and Val exhaled. They giggled and whispered. Two teeny-boppers who'd gotten their idol's autograph.

"Well, this turned out to be a great thing," Alex said. "Remind me to thank Jason for slacking off."

Val screwed a fingertip into one of his dimples, then ran it down his lapel and picked off a bit of lint. She glanced across the room at Javier, watching his mouth as he talked. What would it be like to kiss him?

A hand waved in front of her eyes. "Hello?"

Val blinked. "Sorry, I'm in the middle of a train wreck."

Alex laughed. "I'm hitting the head. If you run off with him, leave me a note."

Alone, Val sipped her drink and shifted into her at-a-party-solo stance—eyes fixed slightly above the horizon, chin tilted as if she were studying something across the room intently.

A hand touched her back.

"Don't move," Javier said. "The hook of your dress is undone."

"Already? You just got here."

He laughed softly. "I couldn't help it." A half-inch tug of her zipper tab. Then a deft twist of his fingers. "Secure now."

"You did that one-handed, Javier."

"Most people call me Jav."

"Call me impressed," she said. "I work as a dresser on Broadway. Hooks and eyes one-handed is a gift."

He made a modest little bow with his head. "With a background in pick-pocketing, it comes naturally."

The man had to know what a lethal weapon he was, yet his demeanor was utterly casual. He wore a tux like it was a bathrobe. Hell, he probably could stand there in a bathrobe and own it.

I wonder what he costs?

"What show do you work on?" he asked.

"*La Cage.*"

"You must have amazing stories."

She pinched her fingers and drew them across her lips. "Breaking my silence is expensive."

"As it should be."

She could smell his skin. She didn't know if it was soap or cologne or simply him, but it was warm like leather and clean like winter air, with a top note sweet like fruit but smoky—like the fruit were suspended in brandy.

"Do you have a card?" she heard herself ask.

He gave her one. No smirk, no wink, no joke or knowing glance. He could've been flicking a lighter or passing her a napkin. She put it in her purse without looking at it, then tucked the purse under her arm as she spied Alex coming back.

⁓

SHE LOOKED AT the card now.

Javier Soto.

She could hire him to walk her. A professional date.

Why not?

He'll walk you? Is that all?

She tapped the card against her teeth. Yes. A pure escort. Nothing more.

You're sure?

She was sure. What the hell. Chance of a lifetime, and it would be a *gas*. A great story to tell backstage. She chewed her bottom lip two more seconds, then dialed the number. It rang four times before going to voicemail.

"Hi, my name's Valentine." She almost added her last name but bit it off, sensing it wasn't necessary. "We met last year at the Chelsea Fashion and Film benefit. Would you give me a call please?"

He called an hour later. "This is Javier Soto."

"I don't know if you remember me, I was—"

"Hooks and eyes," he said.

"You remember," she said, laughing.

"It was kind of unforgettable. How are you?"

Her gut said the best way to do this was purely business, with no apologies or giggling. "I'm in need of an escort."

A pause. "Are you asking me or hiring me?"

"Hiring."

"When do you need me?"

It was ridiculously simple. Almost clinical in its setup. "Just so we're clear," she said after giving him the date and time. "I'm hiring you for a fabulous, attentive date to the ballet and a hand to clutch. Possibly a drink afterward. And a cab ride home."

"I'm your guy."

"Excellent. It's black tie." She was tempted to put on a British accent and told herself to behave.

"Not a problem."

"Can I ask your fee?"

"One hundred an hour."

Val blinked. She knew massage therapists who charged more. Perhaps Jav was giving a discount based on their previous encounter. Or maybe it was lower because no sex was involved. She could easily afford this.

"When do I pay you?" she asked.

"At the start of the evening. I'll pick you up. At your apartment if you like. Or in the lobby if you prefer. Or at the Met. You tell me."

"My apartment is fine." She gave him the address. "I'll let the doorman know. Do you prefer cash?"

"Yes."

A mental post-it to go to the bank. "Excellent."

"I'm looking forward to it."

A sunshiny feeling of reckless happiness splashed her chest. The thrill of the outrageous. Almost taboo. "So am I."

DOOR TO DOOR

*I*T WAS FANTASTIC.

No offense to Alex, who was a terrific last-minute date, but Jav was a fucking *professional.*

"I'm so glad I did this," Val said as they walked into the lobby of the Met.

"So am I," he said. And sounded like he meant it.

Jav made it easy to believe in the charade. Everything he did was natural, spontaneous and imbued with pleasure. He was delighted to be on her arm. During the pre-show cocktail hour, his manners were perfect and his conversation seamless. He asked a hundred wonderful questions about the costume design process, another hundred questions about her. He made effortless small talk with anyone Val introduced him to, all the while keeping an eye on her wine glass and occasionally touching the small of her back. He looped Val's arm through his as they filed into the theater. When the lights dimmed and Val let out a measured, anxious breath, he took her hand and held it tight. No romance in his touch. Only support.

The first half of the first act wasn't anything to be nervous about. Cinderella was in rags and the stepmother and stepsisters were meant to look ridiculous. The entrance of the Fairy Godmother was the first test. Disguised as a beggar woman at her entrance, she suddenly threw off her grey cloak and the audience gave a collective gasp. Applause burst open like a champagne bottle as the Godmother stood motionless in her floor-length, white fur coat. She wore a bobbed wig of red hair with thick bangs. Her head floated like a single rosebud over her collar. With barely a motion, she shrugged the cloak to the floor, revealing a bias-cut, silver satin dress. Now she looked like a glinting sword that had drawn a single drop of blood and the applause rose up a level.

"Holy shit," Jav whispered. He held her hand in both his now, gently rolling it between his palms.

"Mean it?" Val said.

"Mean it."

The second act ballroom scene, with Cinderella in a white, beaded flapper gown and gold toe shoes, nearly brought the house down.

"Her headdress," Jav said softly. "She's Mia Farrow. This whole thing is *The Great Gatsby*."

"Yes," Val said, squeezing his hand. Dancing against the guests' shimmying palette of blacks, reds and golds, the ballerina was a phoenix, exactly as Val had envisioned.

"It's brilliant," Jav said.

"Really?" she whispered.

He looked at her, slowly nodding his head. "You nailed it."

Six months of adrenaline cascaded out of her body, replaced by a triumphant exhaustion. Her eyes welled up and she had to reach in her clutch for Kleenex. A glass of champagne at intermission made her eyes droop in the third act. She tilted her head until it rested on Jav's warm, solid shoulder. He laced his fingers with hers and kissed her hair.

"You should eat something," he said afterward, helping her on with her coat.

They went to a late-night cafe and ate French onion soup, bread and cheese. Jav lounged like a comfortable cat on the other side of the booth, the ends of his bow tie open and his collar unbuttoned. Val's eyes ate him up between bites: strong jaw, high cheekbones, deep brown eyes under straight brows. Dark brown hair that was starting to look the slightest bit tousled.

He was sexy as all hell, yet she found that sex already negotiated out of the evening was liberating. She had no need to impress him—he came pre-impressed. She could eat onions and cheese and drink coffee without worrying if her breath would knock him out later. She didn't ask him anything about himself, and he was fine with it.

It was all about her.

I could get used to this.

He accompanied her in the cab to her apartment. "You don't have to," she said.

"The service is door-to-door."

She nestled against his chest, sleepy, her hand at home in his. He told the cabbie to wait and walked her to the door of her building, where he enfolded her in an enormous hug.

"I can't remember when I had a better time," he said.

"Bet you say that to all your clients."

He sighed. "None of them believe me."

Laughing, she pulled back in his embrace. "This was a treat."

"Well, if you ever find yourself stood up again, you know where to find me."

"I do."

He leaned and kissed her mouth, warm and quick and neutral. Then he let go of her and opened the door. "Goodnight, funny Valentine."

"Goodnight, Jav."

MONEY ON THE TABLE

"**O**H," VAL SAID. "Hello."

From his place in line at the deli, Jav turned around. His eyes widened. Something in his expression was on the wrong side of surprised. He looked almost horrified.

Shit, Val thought. *Am I not supposed to acknowledge him?*

Then Jav's face opened up in such a grin of pleasure, Val's own smile had no choice but to match it.

"How are you?" he said.

"Good. What are you up to?"

"Just getting a cold drink."

"Same. It's hellacious out today." They doctored their iced coffees and walked out into the blistering, muggy afternoon, both of them drawing on sunglasses.

"God, I hate New York in summer on trash day," Jav said.

"I know. The way the garbage bakes on the street."

"You know, I don't see Alex at Morelli's anymore. Did he get another job?"

"He's doing an internship in Colorado," Val said. "And doing some chick named Katie as well."

"Oh?" Jav glanced over the tops of his sunglasses. "A little bitterness there?"

"None. He and I are practically siblings."

What's a little oral sex between siblings, she thought, smiling around her straw. Jav smiled back. Their feet fell into step, the conversation following like a friendly companion, as if they were picking up where they left off an hour ago, instead of three weeks ago. All at once they both stopped, looking around and back at each other.

"Wait, where were you going?" Val asked.

"Nowhere, I'm following you. Where are you going?"

"Nowhere."

They laughed. He hadn't touched her at all, yet this whole time it felt like his arm was around her. His presence was an embrace.

"It's so good to see you," he said.

"Listen," she said. "I just finished a gig with a small ballet company. They premiere tonight at City Center and they gave me two free tickets. No gala, no cocktails, no black tie. Just casual, low-key culture. Do you want to come with me?"

"Are you asking or hiring?"

She felt her eyebrows dig down. "Asking," she said, a little put out.

He thought about it, his mouth closing around the straw of his drink in a way that made her flushed skin shiver all over.

"Sure," he said. "I'll pick you up?"

"No, no," she said, still thinking about his mouth. "Meet me there."

The ballet was called *Well, Silently Overflowing,* set to music by Philip Glass. The choreographer wanted costumes with a streetwear look. Val rampaged a dozen thrift stores to get the effect she wanted.

"How do the guys' shirts not come untucked?" Jav asked at intermission.

"Because it's all one piece. Pants and shirt attached, they step into it like a unitard and it zips up the back."

"Isn't that difficult to dance in?"

"You have to put lycra in all the right places. The dresses are easy but the men needed about four fittings each. You want it to move with them, not against them. And every man's range of motion is different so it's extremely customized."

"I see."

"The shirt is sewn with an extra fold so it starts out neat and trim, but during the course of the ballet, it blouses out a touch at the back or side. Gives it realism."

"How about the way the female soloist's dress kept coming more and more unbuttoned?" he asked. "That was hot, and it looked totally uncontrolled."

"It's controlled," Val said. "It has little snaps and undoing them is worked into the choreography."

After the performance, without much thought, she invited him over for a little supper.

"Asking or hiring?"

She swatted him as if he were Roger. "Asking," she said, laughing. "Good God, who hires a guy for supper?"

He smiled without answering.

"I love supper," she said. "It's such a great word."

"Supper always sounds like it should be eaten on a tray."

In her blissfully cool apartment, she poured wine into two jelly jars and showed Jav her copy of Marion Cunningham's *The Supper Book*. They pored through it together and decided on Idaho Sunrise, which was a twice-baked potato with an egg broken on top before the second baking. Val threw together a salad, then they took their plates and the wine to eat cross-legged on the living room floor.

"So of course, I have a thousand questions," Val said.

"About?"

"You."

He smiled, a bit of egg yolk in the corner of his mouth. "Fire away."

"You don't mind?"

"You seem like a non-judgmental person. And you asked me to supper."

"How long have you been an escort?"

"Four years."

"How did you get into the business?"

"I needed the money. My family cut me off and—"

"Cut you off? Why?"

He closed his eyes and his smile wobbled a little. "Story for another day, all right?"

She held up her palm. "Fair enough."

"I owed someone money. Also another story. I waited tables and tended bar. Noble work, but it doesn't pay much. Original long story short, I was working at a wedding and a woman offered to pay me to come home with her. She became my mentor."

"Your pimp?" The word was out of her mouth before she knew it and it hit the opposite wall with a thud, like a thrown tomato, oozing seeds and jelly. "God, that sounds terrible out loud."

"I said it to her once, too," he said. "Once. She made it clear it was mentor. She didn't take a cut of anything I earned."

Val took their plates into the kitchen and came back with a pint of ice cream and two spoons. As they shared the dessert, Val started and stopped a half-dozen questions.

"Don't be shy," Jav said.

"I can barely formulate what I want to ask," she said, laughing. "Do you enjoy what you do?"

He nodded, mouth closed around his spoon.

"What if your client is…unattractive? Do you just have a hell of an imagination?"

"I actually do," he said. "I'm the kind of person who always has a story going on in his head. If I can't get into a date as myself, I make up something else. And I take acting classes, which helps a lot."

"How?"

"Ever been on a really boring date?"

She laughed. "Too many."

"So what do you do? You convey with your body language he's losing your interest. You change the subject. You fake an excuse and go home. I don't have any of those options. I can't show I'm bored out of my mind. I have to figure out a way to get interested or act interested."

"Which is easier?"

He tapped his spoon against his teeth. He had killer teeth. "Neither, really. Like any other skill in the world, it takes practice."

"Do you look at it as a skill?"

"I don't get paid three fifty an hour to be bad at it."

"Three fifty? You gave me quite the discount then."

He smiled, holding her eyes. "I would've done it for free."

Val stared, at a loss. "Oh."

Jav set his spoon carefully in the lid of the carton. "I'll ask a question now. Why do you think women hire escorts?"

"To get laid."

"But you didn't hire me for that."

She nodded. "Touché."

"Men call an escort, they want sex. Ninety-five percent of the time, they blow a load and the escort hits the road."

"It's a purely physical exchange."

"They want to get off. Or sometimes get someone else off or watch someone else get off. But once the off is got, the job is done.

"Women call an escort for company. For connection. For attention. They want to be looked at, listened to and appreciated. They want the perfect date, the perfect boyfriend. A guy who makes them feel gorgeous. They pay me for my time. And if sex is part of it, great. If they want to make out a little, fine. They want to shake hands and say good evening, it makes no difference to me. I get paid either way."

"Are most of your clients single?"

"Yeah. And the single ones almost always have an ulterior motive going on. Like they want me as a date to stick it to an ex-boyfriend. Or show the lover who dumped them that they're just fine without him. Or to get their nosy family off their backs by showing up with me to a wedding. That kind of thing."

"But you do have married clients?"

"Quite a few. They're typically in a loveless marriage or neglected. Or revenging their husband's affair. Then I have my outliers."

"Who are they?"

"I have one regular client who's going through chemo. Her body is a mess. She's lost her hair, she's skin and bones. And she's alone. She's got no one. She's starving. She hired me to come sleep next to her and hold her. It's all she wants."

"I never thought of escorting in that context," Val said.

"Neither did I until it called me one day."

"So... You're always playing a part."

Jav nodded.

"What about it turns you on enough to have sex?"

"I like sex," he said and something about the simplicity of the answer and its earnest delivery made Val crack up. Jav joined in, rolling his eyes and raising his shoulders to his ears.

"What do you want from my life," he said, laughing. "I mean, come on, who doesn't like sex?"

"My sister, actually," Val said. "She rarely has sex. It's not a driving force with her."

"Really?"

Val nodded. "She's been to bed with both men and women and neither turns her on. And you'd think it would make her seem cold or unfeeling, but she's one of the most loving, affectionate and tactile people I know. She loves to be touched and held, but nothing more. I have a lot of trouble getting my mind wrapped around it. Then again, I'm kind of a sexed-up individual."

"Which brings up a good point. When you think of a male escort, you think of some over-sexed guy who loves fucking, right?"

"Right."

"Those types make lousy escorts. Because it's all about them. And the slightest little thing gives them performance issues because they have no psychological backup."

"Huh."

"Don't get me wrong, I like fucking women but…" He ran a hand through his hair. "It gets kind of murky here. I mean it's really hard to put into words."

Val ventured a guess. "You like paying attention to women?"

"There's something genuinely exciting about seeing them bloom. Sink into their own skin a little more and feel sexy. And even if she's not physically attractive to my eyes, part of my job is seeing around that. Gloria, my mentor, says everyone has something fascinating in them. It's my job to find it."

They were quiet a moment. Through a lull in the air conditioner's hum, Val heard New York singing its theme song: revving engines, honking horns, clattering manhole covers. She stretched out on her side. Jav sat with his back against the couch, arms crossed and one hand fiddling with his earlobe.

"What you said before," he said. "What if a client is unattractive? I have less of a problem if she's visually unappealing than I do if she's an unpleasant person. If she's boring, or racist, or bigoted. Or mean-spirited. Those are really hard dates."

"Have you ever walked away from a client?"

"You mean bail? Yeah. I've left money on the table. I know my limits. Gloria says you should be able to look your income in the face."

"You should write a book someday," Val said. "It'll be called *Gloria Says*."

He laughed. "Honestly, I don't get paid because I'm good at fucking. I get paid because I'm good at finding. And when I find a woman's fascination and have it in my hands, it's really not all that difficult to get aroused for it. Let me rephrase that. Getting aroused for it is rarely the problem. Getting off on it is not a guarantee."

"You don't always come?"

"No. But it's not about me anyway."

Val nodded slowly, wondering what he looked like when he came.

"I won't lie," Jav said. "I have times when I can't get hard for a client. But tell me if I'm wrong: you can satisfy a woman without your dick being involved. If you're any good, that is."

Val laughed. "True. But what about love?"

He didn't move a muscle yet his skin seemed to harden like a shell. "What about it?"

"Who loves you?"

"You mean, romantically?" He shook his head. "Nobody."

"No girlfriend?"

"What for?"

"To love," she said, laughing.

"I love what I do. I get loved at an hourly rate and I don't have to deal with any hassles."

"Sounds so cynical." She stretched out on her back, hands laced behind her head. "Who was your first love? Like in high school, I mean."

He shrugged. "Nobody."

"You've never made love."

"Have you?"

She opened her mouth, then closed it, filled with a troubling confusion. "Of course," she said to the ceiling, which raised its eyebrows at her.

Really? With whom?

"Love and I aren't friends," Jav said. "I get my fill of sex and companionship and when I'm not working, I like being by myself."

"You've never met anyone you wanted to open your heart to?"

"No. Well… Yes. Once."

"Who was she?"

Jav smiled, his eyes fixed on the opposite wall. "He."

Val lifted her head. "You're bisexual?"

"I don't know." He glanced at her. "I've never told this to anyone."

She gestured around. "Doesn't leave these walls. Believe me, I worked as a dresser on Broadway. I know how to keep secrets."

Jav ran a hand through his hair. "He was just someone I saw. Saw at the same place all the time. I started going out of my way to be in that place. I couldn't explain why I kept wanting to see him. It's not like we interacted or talked that much, but I kept going back. One night I gave him my card but he never called."

"Called to do what? I mean, what did you want from it?"

"I don't know," he said softly. In that moment, he was intensely vulnerable and painfully sexy. "I think about him. And I do think about guys sometimes."

The way the words fell out made Val think it was the first time he'd ever spoken them. She made her voice as soft and neutral as possible when she asked, "Have you ever been hired by a man?"

"Once I was working with a couple and the guy started touching me. I got turned on, and then I freaked out."

"Why?"

He shrugged. "I don't know. Maybe I'm bisexual but only in my thoughts. Those thoughts feel fine in my head but they're clumsy in practice. Maybe I'm just curious."

"Bi-curious," Val said.

"And bi-cautious."

A long interlude of silence. Val glanced at her watch. It was nearly one in the morning. Her heart thumped steadily behind her breasts. Her eyes roamed over Jav's far-away expression and superb body. Her thoughts folded over and over, like a ribbon of cake batter poured into a bowl. She wanted to take him into her bedroom. Correction, she wanted to *pay* him to come in her bedroom.

A single, wicked chuckle in her chest.

"What?" Jav said, smiling. His mouth was delicious. Those full lips and straight teeth.

She rolled on an elbow. "I have three hundred cash in my dresser drawer. Will you stay a couple hours? Or however long the amount gets me?"

She couldn't fathom his expression as he gazed at her. Finally he said, "You shouldn't keep that much bread around."

"I don't usually. I would've gone to the bank today but I bumped into you."

He blinked a few times. "Why did you say hello?"

"Why wouldn't I?"

More staring. "You're not lonely. Or neglected."

"I'm curious and horny."

His eyes narrowed slightly. "You don't want to go to bed with me for me? Because we had a spontaneous date and a good time and you're interested in me?"

"I'm extremely interested in you. I also know you're not interested in being loved. So paying you keeps me from getting too emotional about this."

"This wasn't where I was expecting the evening to go."

"Me neither."

"And I don't have any condoms with me."

"I have some."

He looked away from her. A single index finger lifted off his wrist. "You have to give me a few minutes," he said. "I have to be in a certain frame of mind to work. It doesn't switch on and off."

"Take your time." She got up and gathered the ice cream carton and the spoons, dumped them in the sink. She went into her bedroom, counted out three hundred and put it in an envelope. Back in the living room, she set the envelope on top of the fake fireplace mantel.

"I'm going to take a shower," she said. "Which I usually do before bed anyway. You can see yourself out and I will have absolutely no hard feelings. I had a fantastic time tonight and it can end perfectly right here. If I come out of the shower and you're gone, then goodnight and sleep well. If I turn around in the shower and see you there…"

He tilted his chin. "How do you know I won't take the money and split?"

"Because I have one of your secrets."

Soaping up in a soufflé of bubbles, she was immensely pleased with herself. And turned on. She leaned a shoulder against the cool tiles and slid fingers between her legs, her bottom lip tucked under a tooth. God, she was practically inside-out. What a wild night.

Then she heard the jingle of a belt buckle on the other side of the curtain. The dull tinkle of loose change spilling from a pocket onto a bathmat and the soft drop of clothing.

Her mouth formed a clichéd crack. *Is that you, dear?* But she swallowed it back. Talk would only ruin this. She waited patiently.

The scrape of the curtain rings on the rod. A cool breeze through the steam.

His dry body slid up against her sleek, wet skin. His hands found her breasts and his mouth slid along the curve of her neck, drinking her.

She was beautiful and soft.

And he was so fucking hard.

BUY THE TIME BACK

"**I**'LL SEE MYSELF out," Jav whispered.

"All right," Val said, her voice indolent and slushy.

He leaned down to brush his nose along her cheekbone. "I can't think when I had a better time."

She smiled behind closed eyes. "Bet you say that to all your clients."

"How come none of them believe me?"

Her smile grew wider and she pulled the sheet tighter around her breasts, burrowing down into the warm nest their bodies had made.

He kissed her softly. "Goodnight, funny Valentine."

"'Night, Jav. Be careful going home."

"I will." He'd stayed an extra hour for free—weird things happened at four in the morning in New York and cabs were easier to hail when the sun was up. Of course, that was the professional reason. The real excuse was he'd fallen asleep. Something he rarely did with a client.

He walked softly into the living room and took the envelope off the mantel. Usually he slipped it into an inside pocket of a suit jacket or sport coat. Now he had to fold and cram it into his shorts pocket where it stuck, awkward and obvious.

All his movements were clumsy and reluctant. His fingers balked at tying his sneakers. Turned locks the wrong way while opening the door. He stumbled going down the hall and the elevator door banged him on the elbow as it was closing.

He didn't want to go.

After the date to the *Cinderella* premiere, Jav figured he'd seen the last of Valentine. She'd obviously hired him as a last resort. A personal dare, just so she could tell the story later. A gorgeous, confident chick like that didn't need to buy what Jav was selling.

When he saw her in line at the deli yesterday, he'd pulled his shades down, turned his back and went invisible. It was the code of escorting. He'd learned early on not to say hello to clients he saw outside of dates. One embarrassing gaffe drove the point home like a spike. He was hired for certain services during certain hours. When the hours were up, the relationship ceased to exist. At least in public.

He got used to it. After a while he stopped questioning it. So he kept his back to Valentine and if she recognized him, he expected she'd look straight through him. Instead, she said hello.

It was the first time a client acknowledged him outside a date.

She wanted to spend time with him for him, and he couldn't say why it touched him so much.

Then the ask turned into a hire, and he couldn't say why it disappointed him so much. She put the envelope out and it took him quite a while to switch into work mode. He couldn't find a story. He wasn't sure one could be written. Or needed to be.

He went into her bathroom feeling strangely vulnerable. Feeling only like himself. He pulled off his shirt and looked a moment at his chest and arms and shoulders. *This is me.* Both in and out of his experience, he undid his belt and slid his shorts down, looking at his legs. *Me.*

Hot steam filled in his lungs, but his skin rose up in goosebumps, his nipples two tight hard beads in his chest. His hand closed around his penis. He was hard, aching and ready to do an excellent job. Yet he hesitated.

Me, he decided. *I will do this as me. And you will give me that which is you.*

He held her from behind a long, breathing moment. Then, soaped up and slippery, Val turned in his arms and drew him into the spray of water, holding his face in her hands.

"Now what are you going to do," she murmured.

He set his thumb in the center of her bottom lip and trailed it down beneath her chin, tilting it up for his kiss. "I'm going to ruin you," he said.

They tore up the next three hours. He had an autobiography in his head and a fire in his belly. He fucked her into an incoherent heap between the sheets, then he crashed down next to her, an arm and a leg flung over her body, his fist in her blonde hair. Her juice on his tongue and her perfume in his pores. Feeling like one single, eight-limbed body.

Excellent job, he thought before sleep took him.

⌒

SHE HIRED HIM six more times in 1987. Always to accompany her to some short party or event, then back to her apartment for sex. She always put three hundred in an envelope on the fake mantel. He took just one hundred and left the rest. They never discussed it.

"Is there something you want me to be?" he asked.

"What do you mean?"

"I told you, most clients have an ulterior motive going on. A role they want the escort to play."

She thought about it a moment. "I want you to be a lover who can't wait to get his hands on me."

The pattern and flavor of the dates quickly fell into place. At events, Jav was attentive and deferential, following Val's lead, taking silent direction and being precisely where she needed him to be. They didn't hold hands or steal kisses, and when asked, they said they were simply friends. But every now and then Jav broke the rules, leaned in and smoothed a bit of her hair, or moved her necklace clasp from front to back. Whispered, "I can't wait to get my hands on you."

With each date, the whisper grew bolder.

"I can't wait to get my tongue on you."

He'd move a bit closer to her, leaning a moment and letting her feel his impatience against her hip.

"See what you do to me?"

She never blushed. Only a rapid blink of her eyelashes above the cool nod of her chin showed her arousal.

"I can't wait to put it in you," he said, stepping away again.

"You're going to have to."

She called the shots in public. Once her apartment door locked behind them, she wanted Jav to take complete control. Unhook her bra one-handed and put all his gifts to use.

He always enjoyed it. She was good in bed. A pleasure to fuck. No neurotic quirks or insecurities. She relaxed completely during sex. She knew what she wanted, knew how to communicate that want in whispered words or a guided hand. Picking up her cues took no effort. Jav found from the first kiss, he could read her like a map, instantly knowing if they'd be sweet and tender, smoldering and silent, or lewd and loud. No matter the mood during sex, they always lay around afterward, talking like old friends.

He liked the talking even more than the sex. With little prompting, he told her about his childhood in Queens. About the bitter estrangement from his family and the years of scraping by until he met Gloria.

"Is Javier Soto your real name?" she asked.

"Maybe." His finger traced her eyebrows. "Is your real name Valentine?"

"Maybe." She turned in the circle of his arms and put her back against him. "Let's keep it maybe."

Their chests rose and fell in deep, contented breaths.

"Tell me about Alex," he said.

"What do you want to know?"

Everything, Jav thought. "How did you meet?"

The story captivated him. "Alex fled Pinochet's coup in Chile in nineteen seventy-three," Val said, "and came to live with his uncle. Dr. Penda lived a few streets over from us, he and my father were good friends. My brother Roger was Alex's age. They hit it off, so Alex was always around, hanging out, sleeping over. I think every Sunday morning of my childhood, he was at our breakfast table. Then his uncle died when he was fourteen and my parents took him in."

"Adopted him?"

"No. They couldn't. They had no proof his parents were dead and there are international refugee laws about such things. If his uncle hadn't specifically named my parents in his will, it could've turned into a real complicated legal matter. But it worked out as a foster situation, and he came to live with us."

"So he's like a brother to you."

"Yes," she said, shifting in Jav's arms. "But...no."

"No?"

She sighed. A heavy dark one, like the worried huff Jav often expelled from his own lungs. "I've always been attracted to him," she said. A hesitation Jav had never heard filled her voice. "But I don't mean sexual attraction. It went deeper, but... I was only twelve when we met."

"Your brain doesn't have language for it at twelve."

"He made me so confused. The air felt different when he was around. Like it was trying to grab me by the shoulders and shake me. *Do you see? Look at him. Do you understand? Look...*

"I did the only thing a twelve-year-old girl could, which was to either joke everything away or ignore him. Treat him like Roger. Nothing but a brother."

"What about when he came to live with you?"

"Oh, I was fifteen and impossible by then," she said. "Sophomore in high school and wouldn't be caught dead crushing on a freshman. Please. I ignored him at school, and at home, we bickered constantly. Fighting over everything and driving my mother insane.

"I still felt strange around him. Instinctively drawn to him, able to tell him anything, but scared of him at the same time. Scared of how I could tell him anything. So I fought him instead. He's such a transparent guy, it's easy to push his buttons."

"How do you feel about him now?"

"Funny, whenever my thoughts start to dig into how I feel about him, it's like a voice inside says *No, dear, you're not old enough yet.* I'm twenty-fucking-six years old, what does that even mean?"

She let out another dark sigh. "We were both on the ski team in high school. My senior year, we were on an overnight meet in Lake Placid, and Alex hooked up with one of my girlfriends. I'm telling you, I thought I was losing my mind.

"I saw him kissing her in the hallway in the hotel. I stared, literally with my mouth open, as she stepped backward inside her room and pulled him along by the lapels of his shirt. Into her room and the door closed. Not with a slam but this little *click* that slapped my face. I thought I was going to throw up."

"From jealousy."

"The kind of jealousy that makes you want to commit murder," she said. "The thought of her kissing him and running her hands all over him? I felt rabid about it. Foaming at the mouth and territorial. Like she'd robbed my house."

"Robbed your cradle."

"Then on the bus ride home, when she and I were sitting together? Out of the blue, no context whatsoever, she casually turns the page of her magazine and says, 'Alex has a really big dick.'"

Jav laughed and Val joined in, hands over her face. "I wanted to *kill* her. I hadn't even *seen* a guy's dick at that point in my life and not only had she seen one but it was Alex's."

"She must've seen more than one. You can't say a guys' dick is really big unless you have something to compare it to." Jav was starting to get hard, either from Val's gorgeous body in his arms, or all this talk about Alex's dick.

Possibly both.

"So nothing happened between you and Alex?" he asked. "Ever?"

She rolled over and pulled Jav into a deep kiss. "Story for another day, as you're so fond of saying." Her hand closed over his erection. "Right now I've got another hour of this big dick."

"Bigger than his?"

But then she was kissing him and a voice inside answered, *No, dear, you're not old enough yet...*

BE A LOVER *who can't wait to get his hands on me.*

Jav kept collecting the materials to build his story.

"Where did you and Alex grow up?" he asked.

"Little town upstate," Val said. "By Poughkeepsie."

"What did your parents do?"

"My dad's a veterinarian. My mother…" She laughed softly. "My mother makes dollhouses."

"Really?"

"She was once a curator at the Chicago Museum of Science and Industry. Which displays one of the greatest dollhouses ever built. A silent film actress commissioned it. My mother's father was one of the craftsmen who worked on it. He was in charge when the house went on tour in the thirties. Breaking it down, transporting, setting it up. Breaking it down again. My mother learned on the road, and when the house came to the museum for permanent display, she took charge of it. And in her leisure time, she built dollhouses."

"Well, that's a profession you don't come across too often."

"Her houses are displayed in a gallery in our town. Brings in a lot of tourists. We have this iconic Main Street, the heart of the business district. Every shop has a scale model, made by my mother, displayed in their front window. So it's like we have two Main Streets: one big, one small."

Between dates, he found himself wanting her. Not just to fuck her but to be near her. To talk to her. To hear the stories of her family, anecdotes about growing up with Alex. In a weird twist on the Scheherazade tale, her stories about him were Jav's reward for excellence.

By the fourth date, it became hard to leave.

"I'll see myself out," he whispered, as he always did.

"All right," Val said.

He pulled the covers around her, tucking in. "I can't think when I had a better time."

She smiled. "Am I your favorite?"

"Yes," he said, telling the truth. He kissed her.

A little hum of pleasure curled in her throat.

"Open your mouth," he whispered. She did and he went deep, as if starting things, not finishing them.

"You're worse than a used car salesman," she mumbled against his lips.

He laughed and wormed his hand under the sheet, ran it down her stomach and between her thighs. She sighed as he slid fingers inside, then she crossed her legs around his hand, stopping and trapping him.

"I can't afford this," she said.

"It's a gift," he said.

"No," she said. "You start giving me gifts and then I start giving you my heart. Then I ask you to stop working and be faithful to me and then it's over."

And the shitty thing was, he couldn't argue with her. He gently took his hand away, tucked her in tighter and kissed her forehead. He dressed, retrieved his envelope off the mantel and left.

Their sixth and last date, before Christmas of 1987, he almost went into her without a condom. Her hands stopped him, reached for one and rolled it on.

"You're getting sloppy," she said softly.

I want to feel you, he thought.

When the three hours were over, he asked to stay.

"I can't pay you," she said. "The budget is spent."

"I don't want to be paid."

"Jav…"

"I'll pay you," he said in a desperate impulse. "Another three hours, I buy the time back and it's a wash."

Her fingers ran through his hair. "What's the matter?" she whispered. "This isn't you."

"I know," he said, setting his forehead on hers. "I don't know what it is, I only know I don't want to leave. I want to stay and sleep with you."

"Jav." Her arms crossed over his back. A hand settled warm and firm on the back of his head. "It won't work."

"How do you know?"

"Because whatever drove you to become an escort is part of you."

"I do it for money."

"You do it because you're good at it. You like being good at it." She kissed his temple. "You're crushing me."

He rolled off her, staying on his side to face her. Their bodies mirrored: cheek resting on a bent arm, kneecaps touching.

"You're a beautiful lover," she said, stroking his cheek. "Best I've ever had."

"Mean it?"

"Mean it."

"Being with you feels like home."

"I shouldn't have to be your home." Her eyes were bright and liquid in the dying candlelight of her bedroom. "The people who should've kept you safe put you in danger. The ones who should've known and loved you best threw you away. I don't understand how, because you're so good."

"Am I?"

"Of course."

He only had about twenty minutes left. He ran his hands all along her body, pressing the moment into memory. "Are you going home for Christmas?"

"Yes."

He imagined a multi-leaved table laden with food, surrounded by generations of silver- and golden-haired people. "Will Alex be home?"

"Mm-hm." The wordless affirmation was suffused with affection. It left Jav standing in a hotel hallway, watching Val be drawn into a room, a faint *click* slapping his face.

"Tell me more about him," he said.

"Why?"

"I love stories."

She blinked slowly. "Alex is like bread."

"Bread?"

"Not Wonder bread. I mean like a well-crafted, artisanal loaf of really fucking good bread. You know? He's simple, but he's finely made. His experiences have crafted him. He has a moral compass that only points one way." Her laugh was soft in the dark. "He's a lousy liar. No poker face whatsoever. But he's good to have in a crisis. He does we."

"We?"

"He always says things like, 'We'll get through it.' Even if he knows he can't do a damn thing, he's there at your side. 'We'll work it out.'"

"I sensed that," Jav said, now hearing his voice from far away. "He was the guy I was telling you about. The night we had supper. I'd been going to Morelli's for weeks. All those nights hanging around when he was working. Going out of my way to be where he was. The way he worked with the other waitresses, like he was the heart and soul of the night shift. I'd sit there wanting to belong. Wanting to be part of his we."

Val was slowly nodding, no shock in her face, only a satisfied revelation of pieces falling into place. "I see," she whispered.

Now Jav could smile at himself, an actor telling secrets to his dresser. "Giving him my card even though I figured it would end up in the garbage."

"I don't know what else he'd do with it," she said. "Maybe I don't know everything about Alex, but I know he's straight."

"And I'm bi-cautious," he said. "It stays in my head, anyway. And now that you've described the dimensions of his manhood, I have a lot to think about."

She whacked him with a pillow. They wrestled a bit before he pulled her into his chest and held her still. "Let me stay. Just this once."

"I can't," she said. "I'm sorry, Jav."

"I know." He kissed her, then slid out of bed and got dressed. "I'll see myself out," he said, as he always did.

"All right."

"I can't think when I had a better time."

"Bet you say that to all your clients."

He put his face against her hair and inhaled deep. "You're the only one who believes me."

"Goodnight, Jav."

"Goodnight, funny Valentine."

He took no money from the envelope on the mantel this time.

And she never called him again.

SOBREPASARLO

MAIN STREET

JULY 1988
GUELISTEN, NEW YORK

*W*HEN THE DOORBELL rang, Val ignored it. Her aching head turned on the pillow and her dry eyes swept over the low eaves and gable windows of what had been her childhood bedroom. A guest room now, her twin bed long gone, replaced by this queen-sized one. Only a few of her mementos and possessions were on the walls and shelves.

The doorbell rang again.

The chime echoed away through the Lark home on Courtenay Avenue. The house was quiet but full: Val was in her room, Trelawney in hers, and the boys bunked up together in their old lair. All of them home for Fourth of July and hung way the hell over. They'd closed down McKierney's Pub last night and then took a few six-packs down to the riverfront. Val fumbled on the bedside table for the water glass she'd wisely set there a few hours ago. It was empty. She winced as the doorbell rang yet again.

A stumbling thump, followed by Roger crying, "God*dammit.*"

He sounded exactly like their mother. It was her favorite oath. Enjoyable to hear if it wasn't directed at you. You didn't want to be on the receiving end of Meredith Lark's damnation.

Groaning, Val got up and stumbled toward her door.

"Who rings the bell at the fucking crack of noon," Roger said. He wore nothing but briefs and five o'clock shadow. One arm was in a cast—he fell out of a tree two weeks ago and broke it.

"Put some pants on," Alex said, slapping a pair of shorts into Roger's chest.

"Where's Mom and Dad?" Roger said, yawning as he stepped into them.

"They took Grandma to brunch, remember?" Val said.

Trelawney came out of her room, pale as milk. "A cop car is parked out front."

A vague nausea squeezed the back of Val's throat.

Roger led them down the stairs. Until he was sixteen, he never used the bottom four when descending, preferring to get a hand on the banister and hurdle the newel post. Sixteen was the year of the growth spurt, however, and he jumped the post one day, clonked his head on the front hall chandelier, broke three of its expensive bulbs and earned a "God*dammit*, Roger" from Meredith that lost him the car keys for a week.

Rog turned the locks on the heavy front door and opened it slowly, a waft of oven-hot air coming through the screen. Two officers were on the porch. This was Guelisten, so of course the Larks had gone to high school with one of them and been pulled over by the other.

"Hey, Mark," Roger said. "What's going on?"

Mark Ritofsky. Once GHS's basketball king and top chick magnet. Now one of Guelisten's finest. Twenty pounds heavier and his hair starting to recede. "Hey, Rog," he said quietly.

Val's stomach tightened and the walls of her chest lurched inward. Trelawney moved closer, her hand creeping into Val's.

Sgt. Bradshaw, the other officer, crossed his arms. "Can we come in?"

No, you can't, Val thought. Her breath trembled in and out. Trelawney's fingers were ice cold in hers. Alex hadn't come off the stairs and his knuckles were white around the banister. He didn't like doorbells and he didn't like uniforms.

"Come in," Roger said, gently stepping past Val, putting himself between her and whatever was now entering their house. "Mark, what is this?"

"Rog," Sgt. Bradshaw said, stepping inside. "Son… There's been an accident."

Roger backed up a step. Val put both arms around Trelawney. Alex came down a tread. The front door closed, slicing off the sunlight.

"It's bad, Rog," Mark said, putting a hand on Roger's arm.

The Adam's apple in Roger's throat bobbed as he swallowed. "My folks?"

"I'm so sorry," Bradshaw said. "Maybe you should sit down."

The Larks sat. Val and Trelawney on the floor, Alex on a step. Roger backed up until his heels hit the bottom of the stairs and he sat, pressed between Alex's knee and the newel post.

The driver of the pick-up truck wasn't drunk, Bradshaw told them.

"They think it might've been a seizure," Mark said. Whatever the cause, the driver had flown unconscious through the intersection, T-boning Roland Lark's car and essentially cutting it in half. They found Muriel twenty yards from the impact. Paramedics were quick to agree she'd died instantly. Roland was dead on the scene. Meredith had a faint pulse and one EMT had contorted himself into the wreckage to do chest compressions while the fire department worked with the Jaws of Life to pry her out. She died in the ambulance on the way to Hudson Bluffs Trauma Center.

Trelawney was sobbing in Val's arms. Val stared open-mouthed over her sister's head, unable to comprehend what was happening. Her dry eyes flicked around the foyer, lost and looking for landmarks. This was her home. The pegs where she hung her jackets, the table where Alex and Trelawney stacked their library books. The banister Roger jumped and the chandelier he once broke. The front door they went in and out of tens of thousands of times, to the hello and goodbye of their parents.

She looked back over her shoulder to the dining room. They'd all sat there last night, laughing over dinner. The siblings had cleared the table and cleaned up the kitchen before they went out for the night.

Had she kissed her mother goodbye? Did she hug her father last night?

I didn't know, she thought. *How was I supposed to know? Nobody* told *me...*

Bradshaw made a gesture toward the door. "We need you to come to the hospital. So you can identify..."

Roger stood. He'd gone down a boy but now rose up a man. Tall and shirtless on the step, his broad shoulders straight, his casted arm like a mighty weapon.

"Let me get some shoes," he said.

Alex stood, too, and put his hands on Roger's shoulders. "I'll come with."

VAL COULDN'T CRY. She kept waiting for the breakdown, the flood of tears and a long, hard jag. Her parents were dead. Her beloved grandmother gone. Trelawney cried. Alex cried. Even Roger crumpled and wept.

Val's throat ached and an intense, dizzying pressure buzzed behind her eyes, but the tears wouldn't let down. Like a sulking teenager, the grief dug in its heels and refused to come out of its room.

Trelawney came in to sleep with Val almost every night. "They're together forever," she said. "They'll never be parted. Never have to see each other decline. One will never have to live without the other. Oh my God, I'm so fucking selfish. I really mean I'll never have to *see* one of them miss the other."

"You're not selfish," Val whispered in the dark. "It's the truth. We'll never see Mom miss her mother, either."

But we'll never see her again, she thought. *She and Dad won't see us married. They won't see their grandchildren. We won't see their faces seeing us in our adult lives.*

"I wish I'd accomplished something before he went," Roger said, forcing words through a tight jaw. "I hate that Dad went when he was still so fucking disappointed in me."

"Rog, he adored you." Val got arms around her brother but he held himself stiff and unyielding, holed up in a private fortress of shamed misery.

"I couldn't even give him a college graduation," he said, his voice thick and hoarse. "I had a life handed to me and I either broke it or pissed it away. I can't even build a fucking playhouse without breaking an arm." He pulled from Val's embrace and slammed out of the house, heading for town, for the river, for Lark House, for anywhere he could find answers.

"Stand with Roger," Val said to Alex at the wake. "Stay close to him, he needs you."

In what had become a familiar gesture, Alex stroked her cheek, then brought her forehead against his. "What about you?"

She pressed her lips together hard and drew in a powerful breath. "I'll be all right."

He hugged her to him. "You're so strong."

His praise gave her courage. Alex was no stranger to tragedy. He'd always been transparent and wide-open, his cards played at arm's length from his chest, yet he had the uncanny ability to reduce in a crisis. He squared off tight into a thick solid brick for Roger to lean on. They all leaned on Alex those first few days and under their combined weight he didn't budge.

The intense week of mourning gave way to a mountain of logistical and legal matters to sort out. Roland's vet practice. The house on Courtenay Avenue. Muriel's house on Tulip Street. And the Lark Building in town, with Lark's Pharmacy, Meredith's dollhouse gallery and Muriel's tailor shop.

"Burn it," Roger frequently mumbled. "Burn it all."

Alex came to every meeting. He couldn't make final decisions on the estate, but he was always there, taking notes, making lists, remembering the details while reminding them to keep their eye on the big picture.

"We'll get through it," he said.

"Will we?" Trelawney said. She was completely drained of what little color she had. Beneath the bangs of her nearly-white hair, the swollen red-rimmed eyes made her look like an albino.

Val didn't have to look in a mirror to know her own eyes were cut beneath with deep circles. The accident had come smack in the middle of production—she was designing costumes for the revival of *An American in Paris*. This was her Broadway debut and the stakes were triple what they'd been for *Cinderella*. This could mean a Tony Award nomination. In between lawyer meetings, she was calling her team to field questions and handle emergencies, or jumping the train back into the city to do what only she could do.

"I'm exhausted," Val said one evening. "I cannot make one more decision."

"Dad would say to take a bank holiday," Roger said, getting a finger underneath the edge of his cast to scratch. "And I'm speaking for Dad. All Larks will take a Valium and go to bed. Tomorrow we're doing nothing estate-related. Everyone go play."

The next day, after twelve hours of sleep, Val put on shorts and sneakers and pulled her hair back in a ponytail. She went out the front door and stretched a few minutes on the porch before heading up Bemelman Street at a brisk pace. She passed houses she knew by heart, noting—despite years of absence—a tree had been cut, or a fresh paint job finished. A new fence, a new gazebo, a new roof.

The grade grew steeper. Val leaned into the incline, breaking a sweat, arriving at the cul-de-sac winded. Here the terrain leveled out in a magnificent vista and revealed the former estate of Val's great-grandparents. Great-aunt Billie Lark converted it to a private group home in the 1930s. On paper it was the Mid-Hudson Juvenile Resident Facility. In conversation, it was Lark House.

Val wandered down to the grove where the new multi-level tree fort was being built. Roger waved to her from the middle of construction. Shirtless, a bandanna tied around his head, he was supervising a small gang as they built a spiral staircase up to the main deck anchored between three big oaks. An octagon structure and safety railings had been roughed out here, along with a stepped ramp to a smaller house on an adjacent maple. When finished, the fort would be more like a village in the trees. Swinging walkway bridges and platforms connecting the grove in a lofty, mystical universe. The kids chattered from the bases of trunks and up in the branches, amidst hammering, sawing, drilling and a background of music from someone's boom box.

"It's going to be magnificent," Val called to her brother.

"I know," he yelled back, and Val took an extra moment to study him. He was a happy creature by nature, but something about this work at Lark House had set him afire.

"Goddammit, Roger, you carry on as if your home were in a tree," Meredith always said when she was exasperated with her son's restlessness.

Maybe, Val thought, heading off the grounds and back down Bemelman Street, Roger carried on because he *wanted* his home to be in a tree.

❧

GUELISTEN JEALOUSLY GUARDED its Main Street culture. Zoning laws were strict in this little town. The populace would burn the business district to the ground before any golden arches were allowed. When a gas station just outside the village limits added a Dunkin Donuts franchise, it was as if a local chapter of the KKK had hung out its shingle.

With the keys she'd been given as a teenager, Val unlocked the door of Deane Fine Tailoring—Muriel Lark's dress shop.

Muriel taught Val how to sew, how to build the foundation pieces of a wardrobe and how to recognize good workmanship in thrift store garments. In her teens, well-schooled in her grandmother's knowledge, Val took over the meager costume room of Guelisten High's drama club and transformed it into a department.

Her shoestring budget stretched through flea market stalls, vintage shops, fabric warehouses and the Salvation Army. She let out seams, took in jackets, turned fabrics inside out for interest and cut it on the bias to make it drape like a dream. She could make an eighteen-gored skirt or construct an authentic whale-boned bodice with a set of hoops. She worked miracles with trimming and buttons and knew how to boost the confidence of the most awkward freshman boy in the back row by making him look like a six-foot superstar.

When she wasn't sewing for others, Val was ripping her thrift store finds apart and altering them. No seam was safe. No button permanent. Clothes were power. Clothes were in her blood. Clothes made the woman and a woman's best friend wasn't a diamond. It was her tailor.

A frantic knock on the shop window broke Val out of her reverie. A woman with hands cupped around the glass peered in. Looking for her tailor.

"We're closed," Val mouthed.

The woman clasped her hands together in a gesture of begging. Val sighed and unlocked the door. The woman came in, apologetic and distraught. The zipper on her best skirt was broken. She had a job interview in an hour.

"Give," Val said. "I'll fix it."

"Oh, thank you. I'm Nadine, I've been coming here forever and I'm so sorry for your loss. The town is just devastated."

"Thank you." Val found a pincushion, threaded a needle and sat in the wingback chair by the front window. She had the zipper anchored and was about to take the first stitch when she stopped and peered closer at the skirt.

"This is a Christian Dior," she said.

"Yes," Nadine said happily. "It's my lucky skirt."

"But this is an original." Val turned the garment in her hands, examining the seams and the lining. "Where on earth did you get it?"

"It was my grandmother's. It was part of a suit. She got married in it."

"Christ," Val said softly. "Where's the jacket?"

Nadine made a face. "My sister got it."

"Between you and me, you got the better deal," Val said. "You can do anything and everything with the skirt. The jacket only looks good when it's with the skirt."

"That's exactly what your grandmother said. She was so knowledgeable."

"I'm sorry," Val said, putting down the skirt. All at once, her family history and the combined wisdom of her ancestors was pressing her from all sides. The Lark Building put arms around her and breathed. Its heart beat in her veins.

I want to go home, she thought.

"I'm sorry," she said again.

Nadine pressed a tissue into Val's hand. "Don't be."

"It's so much."

"Yes," Nadine said. "I know."

A balloon was swelling in Val's throat and she squeezed her lips and teeth tight against the storm. Her eyes and the inside of her nose began to smolder. She finished the zipper and once Nadine was gone, Val locked the shop and went running home. Her lungs dissolved along the incline of Bemelman Street. By the time she turned onto Courtenay Avenue, she was sobbing.

Inside, Alex sat on the steps, tying his sneakers, Walkman at his side as if he were about to go for a run. As Val burst through the door, his green eyes widened in alarm, then immediately downshifted into understanding. He opened his arms and Val threw herself on the step between his feet.

"It's all right," he said against her hair. "You don't have to be strong anymore."

She pressed her face into his chest, crying her heart inside-out. An ocean of loss flooding the foyer, lapping at her ankles. Alex rocked her in his arms, his body warm and solid under her cheek. He stroked her hair, caressed her head, then let go just long enough to fish his handkerchief out of his pocket and tuck it in her hand.

"Poor baby," he whispered. Something she normally would've found cloying, but from Alex it fell soft on her shoulders. A bittersweet truth: she wasn't anyone's baby anymore. She'd been left bereft. Her value diminished. She was poor.

Alex led her upstairs and got her a cold washcloth for her face. She lay down on one side of her bed and Alex stacked the pillows high on its other side, leaning back with a book.

"Go to sleep," he said, resting his palm on her head. "I'll be right here."

And I'll be home, Val thought, slipping away beneath his touch.

ANOTHER YEAR

THE LARK CHILDREN took the pieces left to them—the dining set, the leather chairs, the walnut credenza. China, crystal and silver. The heirlooms and bequests went into storage. The auction company had come and gone. Now all that was left was stuff.

Jesus Christ, the *stuff*.

The possessions, the objects, the things, the junk, the clutter and the *paper*, good God, the amount of paper a house accumulated over a lifetime was enough to make you scream. Val did scream. Privately. Into a pillow. Several times.

"Burn it," Roger kept saying. "Let's torch the place like a Viking funeral ship. We'll take the insurance money and build a community garden on the lot."

"Do it," Val said.

"Make it so," Trelawney said.

"Who's got a match?" Alex asked.

They sighed together, then turned around and went back to the desks, dressers, shelves, closets, boxes, folders and drawers.

They expected their grandmother's house to be a nightmare, having had more years to collect minutiae. Instead, Muriel had put her affairs in immaculate order ("This attic is *empty*," Val cried. "Whoever heard of an empty attic?"). They had her house sorted out in two days. Roland and Meredith turned out to be the secret hoarders.

At first, they systematically picked through the items, stopping often to sigh over a memory, or scream over a class picture. Belly-laugh at the nursery school drawings and the elementary school book reports. But as the days went on and little dent was made in the mountain, they grew increasingly ruthless and unsentimental.

"Do you want this?"

"No."

"You didn't even look—"

"No."

"You think maybe the Smiths would—"

"No."

"Burn it."

"Get rid of it."

"Give it to Goodwill."

The garbage bags bulged. The siblings started jettisoning things from second story windows into the dumpster in the driveway, hooting and laughing.

"Keep the memory, let go of the thing," Trelawney kept saying.

Clothes were cruel in their resistance, grabbing onto the closet doorframe as they were dragged from the rod. Val, who typically went over a garment like she was undressing it for sex, culled the wardrobes blindly, ignoring the screams for mercy from beloved cardigans and wool sweaters and slippers.

Keep the memory, let go of the thing.

They weren't entirely heartless. "I'm saving Mom's cashmere for us," Val called to Trelawney.

"Duh," her sister said, laughing as she separated the books she wanted.

"Rog, I put Dad's Harris tweed jacket aside for you."

"I don't want it," Rog said, going through Roland's vinyl collection.

"You want it. You just don't know you do. Trey, you should take Mom's camel swing coat."

"That old thing?"

"That old thing is a *Halston,*" Val said.

"Oh my God," Roger said, pulling out an album. "Tony Orlando and Dawn."

"You put that on and I will kill you," Trelawney said.

He put it on, and they sang "Knock Three Times on the Ceiling" as they hauled and stuffed and chucked and tossed.

Worst were bathrooms. All the prescriptions and toiletries, the cures and remedies for the ailments, aches and pains of an aging body. So intimate. So *personal.* Val averted her eyes as she swept bare the medicine cabinet and vanity drawers ("Keep the Valium," Trelawney yelled.). For a wild, hysterical moment, she wanted to take hairs out of father's comb. Have something to touch. To set on a shrine and revere. She unscrewed a bottle of his aftershave and waved it under her nose.

Then she had to stop, sit on the closed lid of the toilet and weep.

Finally, she and Alex were down to the last two drawers in the master bedroom: the ones in the bedside tables. To Val, this was a subcategory of intimate. Your bedside table drawer was beyond private. Sacrosanct. Secrets lived there.

"On count of three, dump them out," Alex said, patting the stripped mattress. "Ready?"

They grabbed and tossed items, clearing the drawers quickly.

Alex tossed three issues of *Playboy* on the recycle pile. They had a good laugh over the dated illustrations in Meredith's copy of *The Joy of Sex*. They piled up more prescription bottles, tissues, pens and pencils, KY Jelly, eyeglasses, lozenges. Clipped newspaper articles and recipes ripped from magazines. A set of silver Ben Wa balls that chimed.

Holy shit, Mom, Val thought, eyes wide.

Postcards. Letters. A Rosamunde Pilcher paperback in Meredith's drawer. A hardcover copy of *Sho-Gun* in Roland's.

And then, from each side drawer, a rubber-banded stack of cards.

"What are these?" Val said, sliding off the rubber band and fanning them out. Across the bed, Alex was doing the same. The cards were three-by-three squares of heavy paper, each handwritten on one side. Val's eyes flicked from one to the next, seeing the same sentence over and over.

September 7, 1962. I'd like to be faithful to you another year. Roland.

September 7, 1963. I'd like to be faithful to you another year. Roland.

September 7, 1964. I'd like to be faithful to you another year. Roland.

"'September seventh, nineteen sixty-four,'" Alex said, reading from one of his cards. "'I'd like to be faithful to you another year. Meredith.' I don't understand... These all say the same thing."

"These, too," Val said. "September seventh is their anniversary. They'd be married twenty-seven years this fall." She counted twenty-six cards. Of course. It was July. This year's card hadn't been made yet.

I'd like to be faithful to you another year.

"What does it mean?" She looked at Alex, who looked back, slowly shaking his head.

"I don't know," he said. "But I think you should keep them."

Speechless and bewildered, she nodded. Her mind raced with thoughts as she put the cards in order in two piles and rubber-banded them.

"Let's get a beer," Alex said.

They put four Rolling Rocks in a bucket of ice and grabbed a bag of potato chips. They sat on the back porch steps, looking out at the small yard. Meredith and Roland had planted sensible, evergreen shrubs and low-maintenance perennials. No pots and urns of annuals, no vines that required pruning and tying and training. This was a garden that could take care of itself. It only needed an occasional day's weeding, a day one chose to spend in the garden as a treat, not a chore. Val remembered days when she'd see her parents out in the little yard together, tidying things up. Then collapsing, tired and dirty, into chairs with beers. Holding grubby hands and admiring their work.

I'd like to be faithful to you another year.

"They weren't each other's first spouses, were they?" Alex said.

"No," Val said. "Second marriage for each. Both divorced the first time. I wonder..."

"Yeah."

Her eyes filled up. "I wish I'd found the cards sooner," she said, her voice trembling. "I wish I'd known about them. Mom and Dad should've been buried with them."

Alex's forearm was warm across her shoulders, the hand on her neck icy-cold from holding his beer. "It's all right," he said while she wept.

"They're *gone*. It makes no sense. I have no family anymore. I mean, I *have*, but... Christ, what am I saying? You know what I mean. Shit..." She broke down again and Alex rocked her.

"I know what you mean," he said. "Trust me. I know."

"Jesus, do you do this every day?"

He laughed in her hair. "Not every day. Well. No. I do think about them every day. Wonder what became of them. But you have a place where you can go see them. Go visit. And you have the things of theirs you'll keep forever. Just like I do."

He laid his handkerchief on the ice in the bucket a minute, then gave it to her.

"You and your little snot rags," she said softly.

"It's clean. And you love them."

"I do." She pressed the cool damp to her burning eyes, then opened her other beer and took a long, soothing pull. "God, the more I think about those cards, the more I'm in awe."

"Of what?"

"Well, how many couples treat fidelity as a given, and how many sit down before they marry and lay out the rules? This is what being faithful means to me. This is what I want, this is what I expect. This is what I consider cheating. This is forgivable. This isn't. You know?"

She wrapped her arms around her calves, chin on knees. As the idea in her head grew bigger, she felt the need to become smaller.

"And how many," she said slowly, "do it every year? Sit down and renew the terms. Take the pledge again."

"But the words," Alex said. "The words they used aren't a pledge. *I'd like to be faithful to you.* Not *I promise to be* or *I swear to be.* I'd *like* to be. I *want* to be. It doesn't guarantee success. Only the desire. It's a pledge of a desire to be something."

"They didn't promise forever," she said. "They took it year by year."

"I guess they knew marriage evolves over years." Alex had moved into the same position as she, arms around knees. Their hips, shoulders and beer bottles touched. "I guess they each learned a lot the first time around."

"Maybe fidelity was a problem with their first spouses."

"And when they got married, they decided to lay it all out from the get-go."

"I'd like to be faithful to you another year."

"We'll talk again next year."

Val turned her cheek and looked at him. He looked back, the wind ruffling his hair a little. His finger reached to trace her eyebrows, her nose, her mouth and along her jaw, tucking her hair behind her ear.

"A pledge to the desire," he said. "Not the act. I kind of like that."

"I'm so glad you were with me," she said, softening under his touch. "It feels like you were supposed to be here. We were supposed to find them together."

He nodded, looking deep in her eyes, his fingers continuing to outline her face. The moment shimmered hopefully between them, reaching out to touch as well.

You're old enough, dear, it said.

The kitchen door bounced open—"*Whoa,* my darling"—and Roger came out singing, "Knock three times on the ceiling if you want me..."

The moment yanked its hand out of the cookie jar and retreated.

"Rog has a brilliant idea," Trelawney said.

"Oh?" Val said, a pulsing desire curling up in her stomach.

"Road trip," Rog said. "We hop in the car tomorrow and drive to Stowe."

"Shotgun," Alex said.

"Let's go," Trelawney said. "Let's just do it. The four of us."

"And Tony Orlando," Roger said.

ONE DAY

*R*OGER LAID OUT a firm plan: "We leave at dawn, sisters."

They pulled out of the driveway around eleven-thirty.

"Dawn means anytime before noon," Roger said, passing around coffees.

They took turns at the wheel and made good time through the rolling farmlands of southeast Vermont. They'd talk and laugh for an hour, then lapse into thoughtful, sighing silence. Then Roger would belt out, "*Whoa,* my darling," and startle everyone into singing "Knock Three Times."

They pulled into the drive of the family's ski house, the trunk loaded with groceries and beer.

"This was a good idea," Val said, putting her arms around Roger as they grilled steaks on the little back deck.

"I'm full of good ideas," he said. "Full of shit, too. But good ideas."

Val examined his casted arm. "Still hurt?"

"Nah," he said. "Itches more than it hurts."

"Still. A compound fracture. Must've been gruesome."

"I puked when I saw the bone," he said. "All over Lark House's nurse."

"She must've been enchanted," Trelawney said. She'd braided a garland of dandelions and wore it around her head.

"Mm." Rog dug his finger underneath the cast, scratching. "I need to call her later."

"Oh," Val said. "This wasn't a one-time puke, I see."

Roger laughed. "No, we've been hanging out. Broken bones and barf: it's the newest thing in seduction."

They sat at the picnic table, eating, drinking and telling funny Lark stories into the night. For nostalgic laughs, they decided to cram into the downstairs bedroom with its two sets of bunk beds. Three larks and a cuckoo.

"No snoring," Val said, taking one bottom bunk.

"No farting," Alex said, taking the other.

"No jerking off," Rog said, climbing above Alex, who punched his leg. "Ow."

Silence as Trelawney clambered up to her bed over Val.

"Come on, Trey," Rog said. "Don't cry. Make a rule."

A loud sniff. "No leaving."

Val listened as the talk died away and silence filled the room. She knew the sounds her siblings made at rest—the deep cadence that marked Trelawney's slumber and the faint whistle that signaled Roger's. As soon as she heard both, she reached over the headboards separating her from Alex and caressed his head.

Hand in hand, they slipped upstairs to the master bedroom.

"It's time," she whispered as the door shut behind them. "Isn't it?"

"It's time." His arms closed tight around her. Her forehead fit to the base of his neck like a puzzle piece. He smelled like soap and water. His hands slid up the back of her tank top, so warm on her bare skin. His mouth drew up her throat, hands gliding around to cup her breasts.

"I knew one day we'd be here," he said.

She slid his shirt over his head. "I think I knew, too."

No more words as they took off their clothes and lay down. Val stretched out on her back on the bed, and he came crawling along her. His hands dug beneath her head like a cradle. Boxed in by his thighs at her sides, his weight soft and warm and heavy. His eyes even heavier in the moonlit room. Her palms slipped along his shoulders and back, feeling the lean, solid, adult mass of him. He was all man now.

Her man.

"I knew it," he said.

She touched his mouth. "Knew what?"

"This." His mouth brushed hers. "Us." His kiss went deeper. Then it went harder. Val cried into his mouth, arching up and opening wide. His legs pushed hers apart then he burst into her like a sunrise, like a ten-fingered chord on the piano. He slid deep, hot, golden and syrupy and she thought she would fly apart at her joints, splash in puddles of joy on the walls. He made some indescribable sound, and she made yet another. For ten seconds all was madness: they grappled wildly, twisting, writhing, trying to kiss, trying to breathe, trying to be everything.

Then he stopped. His hands took her wrists, pressed them against the mattress and the universe came to a slow halt with him.

"Wait," he whispered. He lay still within her, hard and huge, filling her up to her eyes. Up on his elbows like a cobra, cradled in her thighs, he rested his forehead on hers.

"Are you all right?" she said. He nodded but didn't speak, didn't open his eyes. She understood this wasn't the plunge. Not yet. He was still poised at some final edge and she knew him so well then, knew beneath his desire to do right by her was a fierce and sometimes uncontrollable passion. And he was about to unleash it on her. About to hold her down and fuck the top of her head out into space, or scoop her up and love her with glorious tenderness, or both—quite possibly all those things at the same time.

He was so fine at that moment. He was what she wanted. All she wanted.

"One day is today," she said.

Their eyebrows rubbed as he nodded and she felt their thoughts blur and blend. She knew he wanted to be all things to her, and he wanted all of her selves with him, or else none. Anything in between simply wouldn't work. Not with Alex. Not with this one day.

"I want to stay with you," he said.

She pushed against his grip and her hands flew free like birds, arcing up around the back of his neck.

"No leaving," she whispered. "It's the rule."

IN THE COOL, gray morning they woke and looked at each other, caressing without talking. Alex shifted sideways to lay his head on her heart. Val imagined its rhythm was erratic. Little stabs of anxiety kept piercing her at odd moments. A faint sense of unease, laced with the mountain of things that needed to be done in the wake of her parents' death. And glazed with the overwhelming loss…

"Remember the Oral Dissertation?" Alex said.

"No," Val said. "Was I there?"

His smile was patient.

"Yes, dumbass, I remember."

"Afterward when we fell asleep a little while," he said. "Squashed on the daybed. I was lying like this, with my head on your heart. I fell asleep listening to it. When I woke up, we were spooning. My head was against your back but I could still hear your heart beating. I remember thinking…"

"What?"

He put a finger on her lips. His eyes closed. He listened. "I love your heart."

Emotion welled up in her throat and eyes, spilling down soft and warm on her face.

"I haven't made love in…" Her voice fractured and she couldn't go on.

He pressed his lips to her sternum, then laid his cheek down again and smiled at her. "A long time?" he asked.

My whole life, she thought.

The last man she'd been with was Javier Soto, and she'd been so sad, so bewilderingly blue after her decision to stop hiring him. He was getting too close to her. And for all he was a good soul and a fantastic lover, something about his painful past and damaged psyche made Val recoil. It wouldn't work. If she didn't leave now and hurt a little, she would undoubtedly be left later and be destroyed. She'd always seen Jav as the kind of guy who left a woman in a smoldering pile of ashes.

She thought about him often though. The affair—could you call it that?—left her singed and smarting from brutal self-realization: *I've never made love.*

Jav made her reflect on the string of boyfriends in her wake. She felt no regret, but no warmth in the remembering either. It all seemed childish now. Cheap. Relationships chosen and arranged exactly to her needs. Dating men she could easily control. She nearly always got what she wanted and real life didn't work that way. Love didn't work that way.

She'd never made love.

No dear, you're not old enough yet.

After Jav, Val went without intimacy of any kind. A celibate interval of hard work and harder thinking as all her ideas of love were re-negotiated. Her body, sated on months of decadent sex, closed for renovations. Her heart put up a velvet rope and hired a bouncer. The next time she let anyone in, it would be for love. The kind you made, not bought.

"Don't cry," Alex said, his thumb moving across her lips.

"It's been a long time," she whispered. "And I feel like I'm home now."

Her eyes and fingertips wandered over him. He had beautiful skin—tanned golden warm in summertime, like melted caramel. Whenever she touched her tongue to it, she expected to find it sweet, bits of sugar clinging to him. On his right forearm was the inked Unisphere showing South America. Around his left upper arm was an intricate band of lines and letters. His parents' names in a beautiful script, encircling his bicep. Between them was a thicker, darker band, in stern block letters: ¿Dónde Están Los Desaparecidos?

Where are the disappeared ones?

"You're so beautiful," he said, caressing her face.

"Alejandro," she said, lost in his eyes, his name heavy and sweet in her mouth.

"I want to be your home." His lips ran soft across her brow. "I want to wake up every morning and listen to your heart. I want to be the last man you slept with. When you say it's been a long time since you made love, I want that time to be a matter of hours. Because I loved you last night. And I'm going to love you again tonight."

He pulled her tight into his arms. All the anxiety cracked like a brittle shell and fell away. Her chest filled as her hand slid along Alex's neck, fingertips finding the pulse beneath the curve of his jaw. Feeling it beat with her own.

She was small in his arms but love was a gigantic thing, spilling out her pores, a sparkle at every tip of every hair on her head. His kiss filled her mouth, all his passion and pain, all his strength and weaknesses, all his past and all their future.

"Lie back," he said, shifting to put his head on her heart again. "Rest now."

"So much to do," she said softly.

"We'll get through it," he said. As he always did when any of the Larks had a problem.

We'll get through it. We'll work it out.

Val's mind shuffled through her years of high school and college Spanish. "Vamos a sobrepasarlo," she said.

Alex lifted his head a little. "What?"

She bit her lip, sure she had it wrong. "Vamos a sobrepasarlo? We'll get through it?"

His sweet smile unfolded, the dimples creasing on either side. "Kind of. Sobrepasarlo… It's more like you'll avoid or evade something entirely. Get around it. Not through it."

"What should I say then?"

"Vamos a superarlo."

"Now say what I did before."

"Vamos a sobrepasarlo."

"See, that's sexier," she said. "The shape your mouth makes around it is hot."

"Well then, fuck it." He laid his head back down. "Who cares what it means as long as it looks good in your mouth?"

"Vamos a sobrepasarlo," she said.

The nudge of his cheek against her breast as he smiled. His lashes looked damp around his eyes. Her beating heart swelled beneath his head. Her breath lifted him up and down. She caressed his face, wondering how in hell she'd lived this long without touching him this way.

My heart beats with yours. Wake up to hear my heart one day. This day. Every day. Sobrepasarlo.

Civil Court of the City of Poughkeepsie
County of Dutchess
PETITION FOR INDIVIDUAL ADULT CHANGE OF NAME
In the Matter of the Application of
Alejandro Gabriel Eduardo Penda Vilaró

for Leave to Change His Name to
Alejandro Gabriel Eduardo Lark-Penda

By this petition, I allege:
I am twenty-eight (28) years old. I was born December 8,
1962 at Clínica Santa María, Santiago, Chile. My present
residence is 14 Tulip Street, Guelisten, New York.
I have not been convicted of a crime.
I have not been adjudicated as bankrupt.
There are no judgments or liens of record against me.
There are no actions or proceedings pending to which I am
a party.
I have one minor child: Deane Vilaró Lark-Penda.
I have no obligations for child support.
I have not made a previous application to change my name in
this or any other Court.

The reason for this application is:
to join my surname with that of my wife,
Valerie Meredith Lark.

WHEREFORE, your petitioner respectfully requests that
an order be granted permitting this change of name.
Alejandro G.E. Penda Vilaró
(Signature of petitioner)
August 1, 1991

TRUEBLOOD CAY

SAVANNA-LA-MAR

Hello,

A friend directed me to your website. She's used you before. Ugh, that sounds terrible. She's hired you before. That also sounds terrible. I'm sorry, I've never done anything like this. But I'm newly divorced, I feel like shit (sorry) and I'd like to learn more about having a date with you. I can be reached at this email. Sorry this is so disjointed.

> Thank you.
> —Susan (not my real name)

Jav's smile was sad. Half his email inquiries started or ended with the woman apologizing.

Hi Susan,

I'm so glad you got in touch. I can tell you're feeling bad, please don't be sorry for anything. I'd be glad to meet you somewhere public for a cup of coffee. No fee, no strings, no pressure. A half-hour to see how your heart feels about it. If you do hire me, it's simply for my time. What happens during that time is entirely up to you. No have to. Only want to. It goes where you wish and stops

*whenever you want. If it stops at coffee, I won't be offended. If it
stops after this email, I completely understand.*

Please hang in there. I know it hurts.

Best,
—Javier (my real name)

Standard operational reply. Acknowledge the emotion in the inquiry. Make
her feel comfortable. Lay out a simple, non-threatening plan, stressing how she'd
be in control at all times. Give an exit strategy. Sign off by showing you'd listened.

He hit send knowing he had her at least for coffee. Six inquiries usually
turned into four meets. Four meets typically yielded two dates. Ah, here was
one of his coffee clinches:

Javier,

*Thanks for meeting me yesterday. I thought it over and I'd like
to have a date. Are you available later this week, or early next?
Dinner?*

Let me know.
Eileen

Hi Eileen,

*I'd love to. I'm free this Thursday or next Tuesday. Tell me which
works and we'll go from there. Really looking forward to it.*

—Javier

At least one of his new dates would want a second, as the next email in his
inbox confirmed:

Hi Javier,

*I had such a good time last night. You made an old lady happy,
ha ha. Seriously, I feel so good about everything today and wanted
to let you know.*

I'd love to see you again soon.

—Natasha

Hi Natasha,

I had an amazing time last night. The work you're doing for your dissertation is incredible, and I admire how you're reinventing yourself with this dream you've put off for so long. Not a lot of people have the courage to step out of the comfort zone the way you are. It's a thrill to watch. And "old" my ass—other women can only wish they looked like you at 48.

Me, I look forward to seeing you again soon, too. You know where to find me.

—Javier

He hit send and took a sip of coffee. *Tell the lady what she wants to hear, guys,* he thought. *It's not difficult.*

Sometimes he had to deliver bad news. Which wasn't difficult either.

Hey Trevor,

Thanks for getting in touch. Of course I remember you—that Boston Marathon story was crazy. Unfortunately, I have to decline your offer as I only take female clients. I have a colleague you might like to meet, though. I'd be happy to pass along his info if you're interested.

Take care and good luck with the Iron Man. I bow down to that kind of feat.

—J

Rosemary,

Great to hear from you. I enjoyed meeting you in Montauk and talking with you and Dan that day on the boat. I'm flattered you approached me and I'm so sorry to have to decline. I don't work with couples—it's my personal preference and nothing to do with the invitation. I have a contact I could put you in touch with. I know you'd enjoy meeting him, and vice-versa.

I hope the summer's going well. Congrats on your son graduating Syracuse. A fantastic accomplishment for both you and him.

Cheers,
—Javier

He dealt with his regulars next—women who had their specific days and standing dates. His longtime, high-end clients, the women who wanted him for weekends or business trips, he handled by phone. They'd earned special attention.

"Our flight is at ten," Samantha said. "You'll meet me at JFK?"

"I'll be there."

"Will you wear the Armani?"

"Is there anything else?"

Her laugh caressed his ear. "Are you a member of the Mile-High Club?"

"Yes," he said. "And it's highly overrated. Trust me, we don't have to leave our seats to have a good time."

"You think?"

"Don't wear underwear."

"Do I ever?" she said.

"No," he said. "One of the many reasons I like you."

Sam's voice became a skeptical purr. "*Do* you like me?"

"Passionately."

"I'll see you at the airport."

"Can't wait."

Escort matters taken care of, he poured a second cup of coffee, switched computers and switched hats. No longer Javier Soto but J.G. deSoto.

As the sex trade business moved online in the 1990s, Jav was quick to jump onboard. Most male escorts quit the business by their thirties but Jav had the looks, talent and reputation to stay even with his younger competition. Plus he had a large, devoted clientele who weren't getting younger either, and wanted a date who ignored the unpleasant fact.

He hired a designer named Russel Fitzroy to build a personal website. Russ had a brilliant eye for design but his copy was shit. Jav wrote it all himself, easily, and soon after, Russ began funneling jobs his way.

Over time, Jav learned the ins and outs of web design and search engine optimization, but the task he loved best was getting clients to think about not *what* they did, but *why* they did it. And then making the website tell that story.

"I don't know how you do it, man," Russ said. "But I love watching you in the flow."

"Flow?"

"The perfect zone of challenge and passion. Say the word and I'll draw up a partnership agreement."

"Nah. I dig you too much to get in bed with you."

"I'm not even touching that."

After lying dormant so many years, Jav was a tree in early spring, the creative sap high in his veins. Mining people's stories made him want to go digging for his own. He started fictionalizing amusing anecdotes from his escorting career. Followed by some of the less amusing ones.

When he was thirty-four, his longtime client Lucy, who had hired him to hold her through chemo and radiation, finally lost her battle with breast cancer. Full of genuine grief, he wrote a short story about his relationship with her and called it "Bald."

Gloria pressed him to submit it to the New Yorker, which he did, but under the pen name Gil Rafael. It was published in their fiction issue, which won them the National Magazine Award. "Bald" was then nominated for an O. Henry award but didn't win—it missed third place, beaten by a little tale by Annie Proulx called "Brokeback Mountain."

Gloria was philosophical about it: "Between a cancer ordeal or gay cowboys, I'm afraid gay cowboys always win."

"Duly noted," Jav said. "Next time I'll write a dying ranch hand who turns tricks to pay for chemo."

When Universal Pictures called, Jav hung up, figuring Russ was fucking with him. They called back, used to such reactions, and asked if Jav had an agent.

"Do I have an agent?" Jav said, deftly juggling Gloria on another line.

"Have them call me."

"Isn't that a conflict of interest?"

"Javier, don't argue when you have a producer on hold."

"Yes, ma'am."

Universal Pictures bought the movie rights to "Bald" and Jav started publishing regular stories and articles in Esquire and GQ. Always as Gil Rafael. His experience as a sex worker was a bottomless well of material and it wouldn't do for his best clients to see his name next to the copy.

In 1999, "Bald" was published with five of Jav's other short stories. He often paused at his work and glanced up at the small shelf over his desk. The slim book with its emerald-and-black cover nodded back at him: Client Privilege.

He wrote as Gil Rafael. He escorted as Javier Soto. He did web design as J.G. deSoto. To his friends he was Jav, and he kept his gallery of buddies small and carefully-curated.

Sometimes he met a guy he liked. A guy who made him stop and remember a rooftop night in Queens, and the feel of Nesto hard in his hand. Jav would think it over, play with the imagery, admit it might possibly be something he could consider wanting to hypothetically do again. And then he did nothing.

Occasionally he met a woman he liked. Passionately. But these relationships never lasted long, possibly because he guarded his privacy so jealously, possibly because he was forthright in saying he'd never be sexually faithful.

"Never?" Russ asked, one summer evening in 2001. He and Jav were taking the subway up to a bar in the Bronx.

"I doubt it," Jav said. "Not everyone's wired for monogamy, you know."

Russ's fingers drummed on the guitar case he had propped between his feet. "I don't know anyone as down on love as you are."

"Not everyone's as lucky in love as you."

Russ was a hopeless dope for his girlfriend, Tina, and she thought the sun rose and set in his dreadlocks. Jav got a kick out of their romance, while both of them regarded Jav's escorting with a mixture of fascination and horror.

"At the risk of sounding like Grace Slick," Russ said, "don't you want somebody to love?"

"Plenty of people love me," Jav said.

"Name one."

"You."

At the top of the subway stairs, Russ checked the address he'd written down. "Bar should be along this way."

"How do you know this band again?"

"It's a buddy of mine from high school with his cousins. They invited me to jam."

Savanna-la-Mar served Jamaican fare and boasted an outdoor courtyard with a small wooden stage. The band was called Trueblood Cay and Jav dubbed their music techno reggae rap. Four guys—five with Russ sitting in—made up the ensemble, and Jav's attention kept getting drawn to the drummer, a black man perhaps in his late twenties. Or early thirties. Fit arms in a white T-shirt coaxing magic out of his kit. His chin was tucked down toward one shoulder, his expression pulled intensely inward, listening to a message within the rhythm. Jav recognized a man in the zone. One with the flow, at the intersection of challenge and passion.

The drummer's head swiveled in Jav's direction, ducked down again as if an entirely different message could be heard with the other ear.

His face could launch ships, Jav thought.

No.

His face could sail ships.

Jav's fingers itched to write but he had neither pen nor paper, nor a place to sit and jot things down. As he stared over his beer bottle, pinning impressions and feeling into the bulletin board of his brain, his body moved in time to the music. Purposefully. Attaching gross motor movement to an idea helped him remember it.

It was a mariner's proud face, he thought. *Set atop a neck stretched from long years looking out to sea, floating above shoulders broadened by rigging.*

Broadened by rigging, what the hell did that even mean? Jav tapped his foot, collecting ideas about arm strength and rope and rigging and boxing them up for later.

His hair was shaved close from the temples down, a corona of tiny dreadlocks above, like the mane of a young lion. His long brows curved high above his eyes, the ends nearly touching prominent cheekbones…

His veins crackled with a need to tell a story. It was a captain behind the drum kit. No. A pirate king. An island king.

Then the drummer lifted his chin and smiled. And it wasn't a king, but a prince. Not the captain, but perhaps the second-in-command. The beloved, trusted lieutenant. The navigator who steered past the shoals because he knew how to read the ocean. The sea was in his blood.

He's the heart of the band, Jav thought.

The other members turned around frequently to look at the drummer, and his expression changed for each musician. Steady encouragement for Russ, who was a guest here: *You're doing great, good to have you. Relax. I'm enjoying this.* For the second percussionist, the drummer's face was wreathed in pure collaborative joy. His smile stretched to fill his face, white teeth flashing in his dark skin, eyes squinting, nose wrinkling. They traded riffs like jokes, building layers of rhythm like setting up for a punch line.

Whenever the bassist turned back, the drummer gave a single, solemn nod, wearing a look of pure blood-love, reminding Jav the band was made up of cousins.

The set list was mostly original work, interspersed with covers of Bob Marley and UB40. Reggae's indolent heartbeat invited you to dance—to plant your feet in the earth and let your upper body sway like a sunflower. On the floor in front of the stage, the crowd shifted and morphed, shoulders and heads synchronized to the hypnotic offbeat.

A lithe redhead emerged from the crush, her shoulders making slow figure eights. She held out a hand to Jav. Caught on the wave of the mariner's drumbeat, he took it, let himself be swept up in the music and the atmosphere. The crowd swarmed lazily around him. Men moved in and out of his space, women moved through his hands. The sweet smell of pot hung like a cloud overhead. Fingers reached up, grabbing handfuls of the night.

The band took a break and hopped down from the stage. Sweaty and grinning, they pressed through the people, shaking hands, hugging, laughing and pointing. A flustered shyness hid behind Jav's back as Russ approached, an arm around the drummer.

"Jav, baby," Russ called. "What do you think?"

"Fucking incredible, man."

"This is Philip Trueblood."

Trueblood, Jav thought.

The drummer extended a hand, the wrist thick with beaded bracelets. "My friends call me Flip."

Trueblood. Jav saw it painted on the side of a ship. He heard men shout it as the ship came into port. He heard a woman sigh it in the velvet dark of the ship's cabin.

Trueblood.

"You enjoying yourself?" Flip said. He had a silver hoop in one ear.

"I'm loving it," Jav said.

"What else do you love?"

"Pardon?"

Russ laughed. "I had a feeling you two would get along," he said. "Jav never asks 'What do you do?' He asks, 'Why do you do it?' And Flip always asks, 'What do you love?'"

"It's a better question," Flip and Jav said at the same time. Then caught gazes and laughed.

"I gotta take a leak," Russ said. "Be right back."

"Known Russ long?" Flip asked, taking a pull of his beer. A dragonfly was tattooed on his forearm.

"Couple years. You guys were in high school together?"

"That's right. And I dated his sister a while. That kind of thing."

Jav crossed his arms. Uncrossed them and put his hands in his pockets. Took them out and crossed his arms again. He was acting like a client on her first date, what the hell was wrong with him?

"Are you named for the band or is the band named for you?" Jav asked.

"We're all Truebloods," Flip said. "The bass player, he's my brother. The other two are our cousins. Old Jamaican family. There's a bump of coral reef off the coast of my father's hometown, called Trueblood Cay."

Flip pointed out his brother, Talin, and the cousins, Simeon and Smoky. The Truebloods all lived in the same apartment building in the Wakefield section of the Bronx. Flip and Talin's mother died a few years before and their father went back to Jamaica shortly afterward.

"To Trueblood Cay?" Jav asked. The name felt good in his mouth and he wanted to write it down.

Flip laughed. "It's the size of the stage, you couldn't pitch a tent on Trueblood Cay."

The letters painted on the side of a ship morphed into letters on a book cover. *The Adventures of Trueblood Cay.*

No.

The Voyages of Trueblood Cay.

"What do you love?" Flip said.

"Stories."

"Reading them? Writing? Listening? Telling?"

"All of those. Careful what you say and do around me, I'll put it in a book."

"Be sure to change my name."

"Your name's the best part," Jav said.

"What?"

"Nothing. So what do you love?"

Flip waved a hand around the courtyard. "Music. Listening to. Playing. Performing. Teaching."

"You teach?"

"At the High School of Performing Arts."

"Why?"

"Because music makes good citizens and beautiful hearts." He smiled. "Shinichi Suzuki said that. He was a Japanese music teacher." He tilted the neck of his beer bottle in a salute and drained half of it.

During the second set, Jav didn't dance as much. The gorgeous redhead chatted him up but he was distracted by Flip's presence. Like the band members, Jav kept looking back to the drummer, not wanting to miss the moment when Flip's face burst into a smile. He had deep dimples in each cheek. So did Alex, whose smile had made Jav want to tell a story.

This has happened before.

The five musicians and Jav closed down Savanna-la-Mar that night, clustered tight at a table covered with Red Stripe bottles until the owner regretfully kicked them out.

"We should hang," Flip said. "I'll give you my card. You got one?"

Jav gave him one. When he got home, he took Flip's card out of his shirt pocket and pinned it to the board over his desk. He put a knee on the chair and reached for a pen. Across the back of a dry cleaning receipt, he scribbled:

Off the coast of Jamaica is a tiny sand island called Trueblood Cay. Its good citizens have beautiful hearts.

IN NICE COMPANY

*F*LIP CALLED THE following Friday, saying Trueblood Cay had a gig up in Port Chester the next night, if Jav wanted to come.

"Crap, I have a date," Jav said.

"Bring her," Flip said after a beat.

"I can't, we got a thing. But put me down for the next one."

"You don't have to be nice."

"I'm not. I want to see you."

Another pause.

"I mean I want to see you guys play," Jav said.

"A band I know is playing in Hoboken tonight. Want to come with?"

They went. It was a ska band with a souped-up horn section and a healthy number of groupies swarming the front of the stage.

"The horns are all my former students," Flip said. "Are they beautiful or what?" His eyes lit up white and wide and the crescent moon of his smile shone beneath. He wore a dark grey porkpie hat with a small feather in its black band.

"I love the trombone player," Jav said. "He's something else."

Flip laughed. "That's a *girl*."

Jav peered closer. "Shit, I'm drunk."

When the band took a break, he and Flip drifted outside to grab a table and cool off.

"So," Flip said. He used his beer bottle to push his hat up. "Russ tells me you're an escort."

Jav stared. "Oh, he does?"

"Mm."

Annoyed, Jav took a long slow pull of beer, giving him time to organize his inebriated thoughts. "I guess I'll have to put Russ in my next book and kill him."

"I don't think he blabbed to be a dick," Flip said. "We were rehearsing the other day and my cousins were asking if you were a mascot."

"A what?"

"Gay."

"Christ." Jav tried to laugh but it sounded like the bray of a jackass.

"Russ defended you. Said you get more pussy on a weeknight than any of us did in a month. And get paid for it."

"What's the Jamaican term for pussy?"

Flip's laugh curled around the humid air. "In nice company we'll say glamity."

"Dominicans have about six words. None of them nice."

"A mantel is what we call a guy who's a real player. Or a guy who's a gigolo."

"You mean because the money is usually left on the mantel?"

"Is it?"

"It's typically where I find it."

"Huh. Learn something new every day." He smiled, showing his dimples. "Teach me another trick of the trade."

"A date without sex is called a walk."

"What about a date with?"

"A run?"

"A crawl?"

They both laughed then. Jav's anger with Russ sulked into a corner, still pissed off but acknowledging this might be a better conversation now rather than later.

Later when? Jav thought. *Tonight?*

"I'm not judging you," Flip said. "You of all people know everyone has a story."

"You want my story?"

"Only if you're telling it." Flip leaned back in his chair, feet wide on the planks of the dock, elbows resting easy on the chair's arms. His fingers drummed an idle beat, making the dragonfly tattoo flutter. His T-shirt was tight across his chest and shoulders. Sweat glistened in the hollow of his throat.

He's hot, Jav thought, turning the fact over and over, as if looking for sharp edges. *Generally speaking, any human being would think so. He's a good-looking guy.*

The thought was smooth in his mind.

He looks good to me.

"Once upon a time?" Flip said.

"It's not an uncommon story in the industry," Jav said. "I got into escorting for the money. I've stayed because I'm good at it."

"And you like it."

"I do," he said. "And I like the life it lets me lead. I can write all day and love all night. Get paid for both."

Flip pushed the brim of his hat back and scratched his head. "How long they hire you for?"

"Typical date? Three, four hours."

Flip's grin was wicked. "And are you making love three, four times in a night?"

Making love hung in the air like two shimmering soap bubbles. The roll of Flip's lips around the M, the touch of his tongue to the roof of his mouth for the L.

Jav looked away. "When I was in my twenties, yeah," he said, forcing a laugh. "But now let's say the focus is on quality, not quantity."

"I figure you always have Viagra in a back pocket."

"It does the job but gives you a mean headache," Jav said. "I'd rather rely on my imagination and nature."

Flip drained his beer and set the bottle on the table. "Your clients are women?"

"Only women. No pay-to-gay, no couples."

"No girlfriend of your own?"

"No."

"So who loves you?"

Jav laced his hands behind his head. "People always ask me that."

"You seem lonely."

Jav looked at him. Flip gazed back, slowly blinking.

"I do what I do," Jav said. "So I can get loved a lot. Without anyone leaving me."

"That's fair," Flip said. "Who left you?"

From inside, the band kicked off a song and the crowd screamed its approval.

"Story for another day?" Jav said.

Flip smiled and stood up. "It's what you do."

THE POOL OF INDUSTRY

*R*EGGAE BECAME JAV'S soundtrack for the summer of 2001 as he worked on *The Voyages of Trueblood Cay.* At first he scoffed at the idea of writing an adventure story. But the tale begged to be written. It bloomed like a flower in his dreams. It ran alongside him as he did laps around Central Park. It sat down next to him on the subway. It made love to him when he was on dates. And it became real life whenever he saw Flip.

He could laugh it off, but he couldn't *not* write it.

"You're hanging a lot with Flip," Russ said.

"Yeah, he's cool. We get along."

"He likes guys."

"Man, Russ, you need to work on your subtlety. A fucking hippo has more finesse."

Russ shrugged. "He used to date my sister, Jade. So I think he goes both ways."

"You think or you know?"

"Do you know Jamaica's one of the most homophobic places on earth—"

"You're preaching to the choir, my friend."

"Personally, I think he dates girls to take the edge off. His brother and cousins tease him about being batty, but only within their circle. He's the baby of their bunch."

"He's the heart of the band," Jav murmured.

"The Truebloods are a fierce clan. They'll kill anyone who tries to give him shit."

"I'm not giving him shit about anything. We're just hanging out."

"Well they're teasing him about that, too."

Jav didn't say anything for a moment, then asked, "Batty is Jamaican slang for gay?"

Russ nodded. "You know I never asked you. About the escorting thing. You know."

"What? If I have male clients? No, I don't."

"Okay."

"Anything else you want to ask?"

"You have the copy for Banks and Levi ready?"

The summer slipped away in a blur of music and words. One early September day, Flip invited Jav to come with the band to Flushing-Corona Park.

"It's part of a summer music festival," Flip said. "They call it Playing in the Neighborhood. My mates say you can help out."

"Me?" Jav said. "You mean on cowbell? Say yes."

"They want you to stand around and hold the CDs. It'll make the girls stop. Where girls stop, guys stop. People who stop to listen buy. You're a marketing man's wet dream. And mine. But that's a story for another day."

"Wait, what?"

"Can I rope you in?" Flip said. "So to speak?"

"Jesus," Jav said, laughing. "I haven't been to Corona Park in years. You know it's my old hood."

"Come with then."

It was a glorious September day. Bright and crisp, a lusty wind kicking up hard yet blowing soft on skin. Not wanting to lug around drum kits, amplifiers and a generator, Trueblood Cay pared themselves down to acoustics: Flip and Smoky had a collection of bongos and hand-held percussion, and Talin had swapped his electric bass for an upright. Simeon thrust a box of CDs into Jav's hands. "Stand there and look gorgeous," he said. "We'll do the rest."

They busked a rigorous two hours, Flip's porkpie hat open on the sidewalk. They made $134 in tips and emptied one box of discs. The crowds after lunch were lazier, with a tighter hand on their money. Only coins lay in Flip's hat and two boxes of music were yet unopened.

Jav ripped a cardboard flap free, borrowed a magic marker and wrote FREE HUG WITH PURCHASE OF CD.

Flip laughed. "You? Giving it away for free?" He wore jeans and black converse sneakers today, and a mustard-gold T-shirt. When the sun hit him, it lined his face and body in bronze.

"Taking one for the team, my friend," Jav said, pulling off his shirt. Trueblood Cay let out a collective yell, peppered with wolf whistles. Jav tossed the shirt at Flip's face, then turned to the public with his sign.

In an hour, all the CDs were gone. The band howled laughing as Jav turned out his pockets, scraps of paper with phone numbers wafting to the pavement.

"What a fucking mantel," Simeon said, scooping them up. "Unbelievable."

"You're coming to all our gigs," Smoky said. "Hey, look, this is a guy's number. Flip, you want this one?"

Talin punched him in the arm and indicated the gear that needed to be packed up. Jav helped load it into the van and refused a cut of the tips. "No charge to stand and look gorgeous."

"Coming home with us?" Talin asked. "We can grab dinner at Savanna-la-Mar."

"No," Jav said, putting his shirt back on. "Think I'm going to take a walk and see my old battleground."

"I'll come with," Flip said. A look passed between him and his brother, then the members of Trueblood Cay waved and pulled out, heading back to the Bronx.

"Which way?" Flip asked.

They were quiet a few blocks, anticipation rising in Jav's chest the closer they got. The neighborhood seemed smaller. A diorama of days gone by. Then it loomed large overhead, memories lurking in alleys and skulking on rooftops. Sniper rifles poised. Jav in the crosshairs.

Relax, he told himself. *It's been more than twenty years. Nobody knows you. And if they do, they're old now. Miguel's an old man. He can't hurt you. Not with his fists, not with his words.*

The decades jumped on his shoulders like an unwanted piggy-backer. He felt old, too. Wordless and with no fight in him.

"Tell me why it's a battlefield," Flip said.

"Story for another day," Jav said.

"No." Flip put a hand on Jav's arm and stopped him. "No, it's for today. Make it a simple story and tell me now." His eyes flicked toward the intersection. "You have until the light changes. Go."

"My family threw me out when I was seventeen. My father died. My sister ran away. My mother… I don't know where she is. I haven't seen or talked to any of them since."

Flip's eyes twitched, not quite blinking. "What happened? Simple story."

"They thought I was something I wasn't. It got into a thing of someone's word against mine. And my word lost. I was young. Ganged-up on. I lost friends, I lost family, I lost my place around here. Then they took the last thing I could call my own. Prize money from a story contest I won. They beat it out of me. My sister tried to save it and they beat it out of her. So I left."

The light changed. They stood and stared, the crowds jostling past. Flip's hand still on Jav's arm. "Did anyone look for you?" he asked.

"My uncles. To squeeze more money out of me."

Flip's hand slid off. "Money seems to be the driving force in your life."

Jav smiled and shrugged. "I can't argue. Come on."

The restaurant had a different name. Jav didn't recognize anyone sitting on stoops or standing on corners. He looked close at the names next to buzzers but didn't see the name Gil deSoto among them.

"You want to go in?" Flip asked, indicating the restaurant.

"No. No, I just wanted to see. Look the tiger in the eye, you know?"

"Are you disappointed no one recognizes you?"

Jav nodded. "Weird how within the dread is hope." He made a visor of his hand over his brow, shielding the sun and squinting up at the rooftop. His tongue moved over the roof of his mouth, trying to remember a sweet taste. Before it all turned bitter.

"Up there," he said, pointing. "Fourth of July, nineteen seventy-nine. The last good night of my life. No, that's not true. It was the last night of my youth. I went up to the roof a boy, and got thrown down the stairs a man." He laughed. "Good opening line. I should write it down."

Flip's hand pressed wide and warm between Jav's shoulder blades. "I'm really sorry." His hand slid and gently closed around the back of Jav's neck. His thumb moved up and down once, then was still.

Jav closed his eyes. "Thanks."

"You want to go?"

"Yeah."

As they walked away, Flip's hand stayed on Jav's nape a minute, then slowly slid off.

They wandered back toward the park, the late afternoon air soft and warm. The Unisphere sparkled on her throne, majestic and melancholy.

"What do you have going on this week?" Jav asked. They were leaning on the wall of the Pool of Industry, the wind blowing a spray in their faces.

"I'm going to San Francisco on Tuesday," Flip said. "Buddy of mine is getting married."

"Ah."

"I was thinking. When I get back. Maybe you and I should have a talk?"

Jav looked at the noble face of Trueblood.

"Because I don't know how much longer I can do this," Flip said.

Jav slowly nodded, taking a long careful breath, as if trying out a new pair of lungs.

"I'm not out to force your hand or give an ultimatum or change you or…" Flip smiled. "I'm just confused what's going on. I've been bisexual all my life. My social antenna's pretty good but Jesus Christ, I can't get a bead on what you are."

Jav felt his own mouth unfold in a small grin. "It's…strange."

"Well that's one I haven't heard. Sexual orientation: *strange*. I like it. Can I steal that for our next album title?" He leaned on the wall of the pool, fingers laced, hips kicked back and ankles crossed. "Just a conversation," he said, tapping his thumbs together. "If you're open to it. Or hell, shoot me down now and we'll part as friends."

"I'm straight," Jav said.

Flip didn't look at him. Only closed his eyes and tilted his face into the sun. "I figured."

"I have zero interest in men."

Flip winced, then his chin rose and fell. "Gotcha."

"And I don't stop thinking about you," Jav said, closing his eyes and letting the sun color his lids orange and yellow within. "I dream about you. I wake up wondering when I'm going to talk to you. And I write about you. I don't even have the language for it but I'm writing…you."

"Will you show me?"

Jav opened his eyes. "Maybe."

"Change my name if you publish it."

"I can't. Your name is the whole point."

"Philip?"

"Trueblood."

Flip's chin tilted. "You like my name?"

The fountain spray blew cool on Jav's burning face as he answered, "I like you."

Flip exhaled. "If it makes you feel better, my heart's pounding right now. I've been feeling pretty idiotic since we met."

"Same here."

"Look. This is fragile, but it'll keep. Why don't we call it a day and split? I'm going to Cali on Tuesday. I'll be back Sunday. A week to process."

"All right."

But neither moved. The day was too beautiful. The moment too fragile to leave alone where it could slip and smash.

The sun glinted off the silver continents of the Unisphere. Jav's fingers itched.

Captain Trueblood leaned on the railing, staring out at the approaching storm. "*Within the dread is hope,*" he said.

Flip's elbow nudged his side. "You really write about me?"

Jav nodded. "I'm doing it right now."

"Shit." Flip's cheekbones rose as he smiled. His top teeth were perfectly straight, though the incisors were slightly longer than the others. His bottom teeth were a crooked mountain range. As if swapped from someone else's mouth.

Jav thought, *If you were a woman, I'd do and say a lot of stupid things to get you to smile like that. And I'd tell you I was acting like a clown to get you to smile. But you're not. And I can't. I can't say it. I can't write it. I barely know how to think it.*

EIGH' TOUSAND ONE TINGS

BY MONDAY AFTERNOON, Jav couldn't take it anymore.

"Come over," he told Flip on the phone. "I want to talk about it now."

"Fuck, man, I can't. I got eight thousand things to do…" Flip had no accent, no Jamaican mannerism. He never lapsed into patois unless he was mimicking someone anecdotally. But every now and then, when he was agitated or tired, his soft "th" hardened and his hard "t" disappeared: he had eigh' tousand tings to do.

Make it eigh' tousand one tings, Jav thought.

Flip sighed. "I'll… Let me think. Maybe I can later. All right? You'll be around?"

"I'm going nowhere. I'm writing."

"About me?"

"Yes."

"Hm. All right, let me do some shit and I'll call you."

But the evening went by and no call. Jav went to the store to get a few groceries. When he came back, Flip was sitting on his stoop.

"I knew the minute I left, you'd show up," Jav said, happiness doing cannonballs in his chest.

"Like a bad penny."

Jav put his hand down. Flip slapped his opposite palm against it and let Jav haul him to his feet. He followed upstairs, saying, "I can't stay long. Have to be up at asscrack of dawn."

"Where you flying out of?"

"Newark." Inside, he leaned on the kitchen counter, watching Jav put things away. The silence loitered like a third wheel. Now that he had Flip alone in his apartment, Jav didn't know what to do.

"I don't know what I'm doing," he said, fingers curled on two cabinet handles, holding the doors open as if searching for his life within.

"I'm kind of missing you already."

Jav shut the cabinets slowly and looked back over his shoulder. "I kind of wish you weren't going."

Flip hitched up to sit on the counter. He took off his porkpie hat and set it down beside him.

"Come here, Javier," he said, a hand reaching.

Jav went. He hesitated only a second before stepping between Flip's calves. He set his hands on the counter, one on either side, and with an exhale, let his head fall on Flip's shoulder. "I'm sorry."

"Shut up." Flip didn't hug him. Only set his palms at the sides of Jav's arms. Jav could feel all ten fingers pressing into his muscles. The scent coming off Flip's clothes was green and watery, salt-soaked at the edges.

"How old are you?" Flip asked.

"Thirty-eight. Why?"

"I couldn't tell. I can't get any kind of bead on you."

Head still down, Jav touched the mass of bracelets on Flip's wrist, wanting to take one and keep it.

Flip's hands moved up and down Jav's arms. "This feel all right?"

"Yes."

Flip shrugged his shoulder, caught Jav's head in his hands and brought their eyebrows together. Jav could feel him tremble as he asked, "This all right?"

Jav nodded.

They shared breath, poised on a shared edge, shaking all their separate pieces into one.

Flip brushed Jav's mouth with his. Pressed into him a little. Then a little more. Sitting on the counter, he was taller than Jav. Jav always looked down into his client's faces. He'd never looked up to be kissed.

Flip kissed him.

"All right?" he whispered.

"Yes," Jav said.

Jesus, yes.

He'd never turned inside-out like this when kissing his clients. Peeled apart, folded back and drifting in a thick sea of desire. Vulnerable, electric and wanting. Wide open to his bones, conscious of *himself*. A lovee instead of a lover. Thinking of his own pleasure in a way he never did when he was working. So selfish, it was selfless.

Don't you want somebody to love?

He leaned a little further into the attraction. Tested it with one foot. Then the other. Gingerly sat on it, then stretched out. Fingertips to toes. Taut and trusting. His mouth opened. His tongue reached. His hands pulled Flip down from the counter to stand. When Jav opened his eyes, they looked straight into Trueblood's.

Yes, he thought. *I do.*

"God, man," Flip said. "This is *large.*" His arms wound around Jav's waist and pulled him in tight.

"I take it large is good where you come from," Jav said. "Or are you just happy to see me?" He could feel Flip against him, turned on, shaking with excitement. Jav had never been so hard in his life. Never this dialed into a physical situation. Inside-out with craving because he wasn't doing an excellent job, he was simply being an excellent human.

"Jesus Christ." Flip put their foreheads together again. "We are definitely talking about this when I get back."

Through talking, Jav went after Flip's mouth again. Flip's palm slid down Jav's throat and ran in slow circles around his heart.

"Feels so good," Jav said, lolling in revelation: these huge, powerful, masculine hands on him made him feel just as huge and powerful. His masculinity mirrored. Twinned. Doubled in size.

Large.

"I'm telling you," Flip said. "I've never felt this way."

"Me neither."

"Man, you took your shirt off yesterday and I lost my mind."

Jav pulled his shirt off. Flip stared a long, smiling moment, shaking his head.

"Rude." He yanked his shirt off and pulled Jav against him. "Rude is good where I come from."

Skin on skin. Muscle and bone, hearts and mouths. Jav leaned into the immaculately beautiful moment. Everything was so strong and steady and immutable. And soft. It was the velvet embrace of a summer night. It was perfectly brewed mamajuana. A winning lottery ticket. A $500 check from *Cricket* magazine. A call from Universal Studios.

Hey. It's me.

I'm home.

A fire ignited in his veins. An aching desire to grab this with both hands and guard it. His palm made circles on Flip's hard chest, then glided down his stomach.

"Oh God," Flip said, looking up at the ceiling. His smile from this angle was an incredible thing.

Jav held his breath and slid his hand along the front of Flip's jeans. Felt what was there and wanted it.

Flip took Jav's head and kissed him. Harder this time, setting something in stone. "Open your pants for me, rude bwoy," he said, running his thumb along Jav's bottom lip.

Jav pulled at his button and zipper tab. Flip did the same but then he took Jav's wrists and made him set his hands down, flat to the counter on either side of Flip.

"Don't move," he said. "Stay still and feel this."

Shirtless, pants open, pressed against Flip, Jav held still and died.

"Right here," Flip said. "On the edge like this. The door open but not yet coming in. You feel it, Jav?"

"I feel everything."

"Feel it and want it."

"I want it so fucking bad."

"This is what we're talking about when I get back."

"No," Jav said, laughing softly. "No, don't. You can't do this to me."

Flip gently pushed him away. "It's going to be large." He zipped, buttoned and pulled his shirt on.

"You're killing me."

"Good." He kissed Jav, his teeth falling slow off Jav's bottom lip. "I'll see myself out."

"That's my line," Jav said.

"What?"

"Nothing. Have a good trip."

Flip laughed. "I'll try." From the door he looked back, touched a hand to his brow as if to say something.

"What?" Jav said.

Flip shook his head. "Nothing. I'll see you Sunday."

"Wait, you forgot your hat…"

The mariner smiled as the door to the apartment closed.

WAANT AAL, LOSE AAL

*F*LIP CALLED FROM Newark Airport at seven the next morning. "Did I wake you?"

"No, I'm up. Was about to go for a run."

"I needed to see if you were all right."

"I'm good. You?"

"Yeah. I feel good. I mean, whatever happens. You. Me. Whatever. I feel good about it so far."

Jav took a deep breath. "Me too."

"I was about to say something when I was leaving your place. Waant aal, lose aal."

"What does that mean?"

"Jamaican proverb. Basically means if you're greedy for everything, you have more to lose in the end."

"True."

"Anyway, I wanted... You know. But I left before I could get greedy."

"Funny how I appreciate that you did and hate your guts at the same time."

"Same. For the record, I can still taste you."

"For the record, your voice gives me a hard-on."

Flip chuckled and let his Jamaican accent off the leash. "Tanks, rude bwoy. My hard buddy real gwine be agony on the iron bird."

"What?"

"I'll tell you on Sunday. Show you, rather."

Jav ran his six miles, did his pushups and situps, showered and dressed. Filling his coffee cup in the kitchen, his eyes fell on Flip's porkpie hat still on the counter. He put it on.

By 8:30, he was sitting at his computer with his game face. The flow was good today, but only twenty minutes in, Russ called him.

"Dude, turn on the news. A plane fucking hit the World Trade Center or some shit."

One thing Jav didn't suffer gracefully was having the flow interrupted. Annoyance huffed out his lungs at being forced to *get up* and click on the TV.

He didn't return to his desk. Along with an entire nation, he watched, slack-jawed and horrified as the smoke rose from lower Manhattan. The morning slowed into timelessness as events unfolded with increasing horror and rapidity.

A little after nine, a second jet hit the World Trade Center. Another column of smoke rose above Battery Park and Jav rose as well, standing up and thinking it might be a good idea to get the hell off the island.

He sat down again. And watched. All over the country, flights were being grounded and diverted to other airports, clearing the skies. Jav kept glancing to his phone, expecting Flip would be calling him soon. Stranded somewhere ridiculous like Kansas.

Little by little, it emerged that one, no, two more jets had ceased transmitting, turned their flight paths around and were heading suspiciously off-course.

Jav's phone rang at 9:30. He heard a crackling whoosh of air, then the line disconnected.

His heart swelled larger in his chest and began to beat hard. The hand still closed around the receiver grew damp.

The phone rang again at 9:36. "Hello?"

"Jav."

"Flip?"

"Jav, listen to me. My flight's been hijacked—"

Jav was on his feet. "What?"

"Listen to me. Three men. They have knives. They say they have a bomb. One might have it strapped to him."

Jav strode to the window and looked out, as if he could see Flip's plane from here. "Holy fucking Christ…"

"We don't know the demands or what they… Wait… What?"

"Flip?"

"Hold on." A crunching scrape and Flip's voice muffled. "The pilot? Where? *Shit.*"

"Flip," Jav said. "Stay with me. What's happening?"

Ambiguous, muffled noise in Jav's ear as his breath squeezed through his throat and open mouth. On the TV, the towers burned. The ticker beneath was reporting a plane crash in Arlington County. The cemetery. No, the Pentagon.

From the open apartment window came the sound of sirens, a Doppler wail from north to south.

"Jav?"

"I'm right here."

"What are you hearing? They say other planes are—"

"Yes," Jav said. "Two hit the World Trade Center. Another just went down in DC. Jesus Christ, we're under attack."

"Oh fuck, man, this isn't a... This is a plan. There are no demands here. *Fuck.*"

A wave of nausea crashed into Jav's stomach, reached up to seize his throat.

He's going to die.

"Flip."

"Fuck god*dammit.*"

The room swayed. Jav crouched down, then rolled onto his kneecaps, breathing hard.

He's going to die. They're going to fly that plane into another building and...

"Jav... Jav, what do I do?"

Jump, Jav immediately thought, actually wondering for a wild moment if a seat flotation device could double as a parachute.

"Jav, are you there?"

Get out. Let him off. Please, God, get him off the plane.

"Jav?"

He had to yank the words out of his own throat. "I'm here. I'm right here. Talk to me, tell me what's happening."

"I don't know, I... Listen to me. I've been trying to call my brother but he won't pick up. My cousins aren't picking up either. I don't want to break this line, it's all I got."

"No, don't hang up, you stay with me."

"Listen to me. You tell them you talked to me. If this goes down—"

"Oh Christ."

Get him off that plane. He can't die. We're having a conversation on Sunday. He's coming back and we're talking about it.

"—You tell them I love them. Tell my brother I love him, do you understand? He's my soul mate, he is the truth of my blood. You tell him that."

"Yes." Calmed by having a job, Jav's hand grabbed for a pencil, then yanked a sheet of paper off a pad.

He loves you.

Talin: my soul mate. Truth of my blood.

"And tell my father... Oh God..."

"Tell me, Flip. Put it in my ear. Give it to me."

I can do this. I am excellent at this.

I will do this, and you will give him back to me.

"Tell my father," Flip said. "He is everything, *everything* to me. And I'm sorry I… No. No, don't say I'm sorry for anything. No regrets. You tell him I loved my life and he made me the man I am. And tell him I'll be with Mummy and it will be all right."

"I'll tell him," Jav said, writing as fast as he could. *Everything to me. No regrets, I loved my life. You made me the man I am. I'll be with Mummy. It will be all right.*

"My cousins. They are my life and my songs. You tell them."

"I will, Flip. I swear."

My cousins.

My life.

My songs.

Aunt Vonnie. Aunt Ramerra. Uncle Desmond. Jav wrote the names and the words. Captain Trueblood's last will and testament from the ocean above.

"And Jade," Flip said. "Tell her…I'm sorry. Just that. Tell Jade I'm sorry. She'll know."

"I have it, Flip. I have it all."

"All right. Oh Jesus God. All right. Wait… What? Hold on—"

The line went dead.

"No," Jav said, getting up. "Flip? *Flip?* No, don't. Don't…"

Clutching the phone and cursing, he paced to the window, back to the TV. He headed into his bedroom, forgot why, turned and went back to the living room. He looked at the TV and couldn't recognize the world. Couldn't make sense of the smoke and fire rising into the sky, knowing Flip was up there somewhere, part of it all.

He went to run a hand through his hair and knocked the porkpie hat to the floor. He picked it up, held it over his chest, as if shielding his heart or singing the national anthem. He went back to the window and looked up at the skies over northern Manhattan.

"Give him back to me," he said through the wall of his teeth. "You don't get any more. You took my youth. You took my father. You took my five-hundred dollar prize check. I let you have it all. Not this time. You *fucking* better give him back to me or I swear—"

The phone rang.

"Jav?"

"I'm here," he said, right as the tilted top of the south tower crumbled to dust and began to sink in a volcanic grey cloud. "Oh my God, there it fucking goes. Jesus *Christ.*"

"Jav, we got no more time."

"Flip, the fucking World Trade Center just fell down," Jav whispered. His eyes bulged so far from their sockets, his vision was beginning to tunnel.

"*Jav.* We think they got a plan to take this plane down somewhere big. The passengers are talking. We're going to try to do something. Jav, are you listening?"

He's going to die.

"I'm here," Jav said. "I'll do whatever you want."

"You tell my brother, all right? You tell all of them."

"I will. I swear I will. I promise."

"Jesus God. Listen to me, Jav. You're all I got now. You have to get me down from here."

Jav was on his knees now, an elbow on the coffee table with his head sunk into its crook, the phone pressed tight to his ear. Flip's hat upside-down before him. "I got you," he said, his throat choking him. "I got you in my hands."

I had him in my hands and I let him go. Why did I let him go?

"You have to get me down... Oh God, talk to me. Anything. Get me down."

"Hold onto me," Jav said. "Just hold on." His fists clenched tight, hating themselves for staying flat and obedient on the counter last night when he could've taken hold of Flip and not let go.

"My name," Flip said. "Say my name."

"Trueblood."

"Tell me what you wrote. Give me a story to get me down."

Jav didn't need to consult notebooks or screens to tell him. The words were burned in his heart. "First time I ever saw you I thought, *He was a man of the world. His was the face everyone loved to see come into harbor, and they'd call his name in joy. They'd shout it to the sea and the skies: Trueblood.*"

"Yes."

"*His was the face they cried to see leaving port and they'd wail his name as the silhouette of the masts and rigging disappeared from view: Trueblood.*"

"Yes."

"*His was the name in gold letters on the side of the ship, heralding his presence on the seas, shouting a warning: Trueblood. A desire-filled voice in the ship's cabin, calling his name softly to the velvet dark: Trueblood...*"

Flip was crying. "Write it. Write me. Tell the story and don't let it be forgotten."

"I will. I swear, Flip."

He's going to die he's going to die he's going to die…

"You hang onto me," Jav said, his teeth chattering. "I won't let go. I'm here until the end."

"It felt good, Jav. You felt good to me and I'm sorry it—"

"No, no don't give me sorry. I don't want your sorry. You *stay* with me. As long as you can. Just stay with me, Trueblood, I won't leave you."

Don't leave me. You said we'd talk about it. I want to talk about it when you get back.

"Wait," Flip said. "What? All right, they're going. We're going now."

Jav's face was numb. Fingertips ice cold. His shirt stuck to his back with sweat and every square inch of skin prickled and tingled. He could feel his heart breaking down, dropping off piece by piece into the rolling boil of his stomach. Every splash sending up clouds of toxic steam, choking his throat. He was sure the next words out would be inside a scream. Instead he heard a strong, calm voice—a seasoned captain taking over the helm.

"I'm with you," Jav said. "Fucking take their ship down. I'm here. Right until the end, I won't leave."

Flip's voice had changed as well. The shrill, hot edge of panic filed away, leaving it smooth. Dull. Cool to the touch.

"We're fucking doing this, Jav," he said. "I'm going to die on my feet, okay? Tell my father. Put it in the story."

"I will. Don't hang up. Leave the line open. Take me with you, all right? I'm with you. All the way."

"It felt good, Jav. Good enough to want and good enough to lose. Say you believe me."

"I believe you. I felt it."

"Call your mother. Find your sister. Don't die with it unfinished. Try one more time. Promise me."

"I promise."

"All right, I'm going. Jav, it felt so good. I'm taking it with me."

"True," Jav whispered. His voice fell apart. His fingers reached into the air, grabbed onto nothing.

"I'll talk to you later."

"True…"

No reply. A rattling thump, a rush of noise followed by a cacophony of screams.

"Trueblood."

The clock read 10:02 a.m. Smoke, debris and death filled the TV screen. The sirens grew louder outside.

Give him back to me.

He pressed his face harder against the phone, trying to sort out the layers of sound. "True…"

10:03.

Layers of sound became layers of silence.

"True?"

Ash and steel and paper and dust falling in layers over Manhattan.

"I'm with you," he said. "You go, I'm right behind. Listen to my voice. I'm here. I'll get you down."

One last click. Then dead air.

10:04.

"True," Jav said into the phone. "We'll talk about it when you get back."

Kneeling at his coffee table before the shrine of the news, he made his offering again and again into the phone.

"Trueblood."

10:27.

"True, I want it. I want all. And when you come back…"

The TV shrieked at him. He lifted his head as the north tower of the World Trade Center fell to its knees. The phone rolled out of his hand and clattered onto the tabletop.

He's gone.

At 10:37, the first reports began filtering out of Pennsylvania that a passenger plane had gone down in Somerset County.

Jav's mouth shaped a mariner's name.

COME HERE

"**C**OME HERE," GLORIA said. "Come here now."

"I can't."

"Come here *now*, Javier."

Mass transit was a mess and he was terrified of being underground or even confined to a bus. He needed to see the sky, needed to keep looking up through the smoke and haze in case some small part of Flip came floating down to find him. He walked the seven miles to Riverdale, numb and stunned, gazing upward as he put one foot in front of the other.

He paused at parked cars and cabs, their doors open and the radio on. A half-dozen strangers hugged him. Convenience stores and restaurants set out placards. *Food and drink free today. We are all Americans today. God Bless America. If you need help, come in.*

Jav needed help but he didn't go in. He made his way up Broadway, sometimes in a group, sometimes alone. One foot in front of the other.

Talin you are my soul mate, you are the truth of my blood. Simeon and Smoky you are my life and my songs. Father you are everything, everything to me. No regrets, I loved my life and you made me the man I am. I'll be with Mummy and it will be all right.

Through Inwood Hill Park and across the Henry Hudson Bridge and over Spuyten Duyvil. Under a wide blue sky layered with smoke and smelling of Trueblood.

Aunt Vonnie you were my mother when I needed you. Aunt Ramerra you fed me love and music and wisdom. Uncle Desmond your laughter filled my days. Jade, I'm sorry.

Church doors were open, people crowding the pews and spilling onto the sidewalks. Voices lifted in song and prayer and weeping.

He passed parks where people huddled in candlelit circles, holding each other and crying. He walked on by, into the wealthy green of Riverdale where Gloria was waiting.

"Turn that off," Jav said, pointing toward the TV. "No more."

She silenced the world. He sat down at her computer, opened a browser window and started searching New York phone listings.

He tried every combination he could think of: Naroba Gil deSoto, Naroba Soto, Naroba Gil, Naroba deSoto. He tried substituting Naria for Naroba. He even looked for Naria Nyland. He widened the net, searching everywhere. He called a Naroba Sota in New Mexico and a Naria Nylind in Texas. Neither was his sister.

The warrior queen had disappeared.

He opened a new window and looked for Rosa Gil deSotos. He found them in Queens, Haverstraw, South Providence, Philadelphia and Tampa. He began dialing.

Don't die with it unfinished.

I'll talk to you later.

For hours Jav sat, dialed and crossed names off, refusing offers of food or drink and shaking off any touch or caress Gloria attempted. Finally, at around six in the evening, the phone in Tampa was answered and the single "Hello" was all he needed.

"Mami, it's me," he said. "Javi."

Silence.

"Are you all right?" he whispered. "It's a terrible day."

The silence swelled, oozed noxious and decaying through the receiver. Like leaves and twigs of mamajuana left to rot.

"Mami," he said. "Please…"

"What do you want?" Rosa said, her voice a slurred hiss.

"I want to talk to Naroba," he said. "Do you know where she is?"

Peal after peal of laughter answered him.

Jesus, she's drunk, he thought.

"You think I'll tell you?" she said. "She hates you. She'd spit in your pretty face."

"Let me find that out," Jav said. "Give me her number. Please."

"So you can do to her what you did to Nesto? You'll never get it from me. You'll never find her. She doesn't want you."

Jav pushed his face into his hand, knuckles tightening white around the receiver. "Mami," he whispered. "Why are you doing this? I'm still your son. Your only son."

"You're nothing to me," she said. "You disgusting pájaro. You killed your father and you killed your cousin. You can rot in hell for all you're my son."

The line went dead.

Jav replaced the phone gently. Then he arm-swept everything off the desk and howled like a kicked dog. Gloria pulled him into her arms where he cried hard, bucking and twisting inside the grief.

"Give him back," he cried. "Give him back to me."

He went limp in her lap, nearly unconscious with exhaustion. She took him to her room, undressed him and eased him down into her bed. She held him into the night. And when he awoke, his sorrow and anger hard and demanding, she took him into herself. Let him unleash it until he collapsed spent and weeping in her arms again.

It was the last time they slept together.

Civil Court of the City of New York
County of New York
PETITION FOR INDIVIDUAL ADULT CHANGE OF NAME

In the Matter of the Application of
JAVIER RAFAEL GIL DESOTO

for Leave to Change His Name to
JAVIER RAFAEL LANDES

By this petition, I allege:
I am thirty-eight (38) years old. I was born May 6, 1963 at
Booth Memorial Hospital, Queens, NY.
My present residence is 556 W 149th St., Apt 7D, New York,
NY 10031.
I have not been convicted of a crime.
I have not been adjudicated as bankrupt.
There are no judgments or liens of record against me.
There are no actions or proceedings pending to which I am
a party.
I have no minor children.
I have no obligations for child support.
I have not made a previous application to change my name in
this or any other Court.

The reasons for this application is
to honor Gloria Landes, the woman who took me in
when my family cast me out.

WHEREFORE, your petitioner respectfully requests that
an order be granted permitting this change of name.

Javier Rafael Gil deSoto
(Signature of petitioner)
November 16, 2001

Part Two

FRIDAY

SOLOMON GUNDY

GLORIA OPENED THE front door of her home. "Jav, darling," she said. "How lovely you came."

Twenty-three years and she still acted like Jav chose to grace her with his presence, instead of responding to her summons.

She was sixty-four now. Slender, white-haired, elegant as ever. Still a powerhouse in the publishing industry, but not single anymore.

"Marriage agrees with you," Jav said, holding her at arm's length after he kissed each of her cheeks.

She rolled her eyes but her smile was pleased. "Frank Sinatra was right," she said. "It's better the second time around. And with a pre-nup."

"Is Harry home?"

"He's at a lunch. Come in, come sit down."

He followed her into her study, painted pale green with heavy cream drapes and a sweeping oak desk. All across the walls was a gallery of framed book covers. Gloria reached to straighten a pair of them. "What do you think?"

Jav smiled, peering close and stepping back. One cover was a black and white shot of a Manhattan neighborhood. Seedy and sinister and film noir, the underground underbelly. The title read *Client Privilege*. Underneath, *by Gil Rafael*. The other cover had a 1920s flapper with an eerie, genderless beauty to her. She stared out with enormous, kohl-rimmed eyes, smiling around a cigarette and daring the reader to guess what she was. *Gloria in the Highest, by Gil Rafael*.

"I thought they came out superb," Gloria said. "A vast improvement over the first editions."

Jav sat on the small sofa. Gloria sat kitty-corner on her favorite chaise. "I read the article in *Vanity Fair*," she said.

"What did you think?"

"You were articulate and eloquent as always. But you still won't show your face, will you?"

"Nope," Jav said, smiling. It remained a bone of contention between him on one side and his agent and publisher on the other. They were exasperated by Jav's insistence of hiding behind a pen name and remaining faceless. He did written interviews, radio interviews, phone interviews, but no pictures, no signings, no TV, no public appearances.

"But why not?" his agent said. "Look at you. Talk about the face that sold a thousand books."

"I manage the sale of my face," Jav said. "You get to manage my words."

It wasn't up for debate. He'd wanted all and lost all. After 9/11, he sealed his heart in cement, culling his circle to the handful he trusted: Gloria, Russ and the remaining members of Trueblood Cay.

He didn't write for six months, the first of which was spent at Gloria's house where he could barely get out of bed. But get up he did, to go to Wakefield and talk to the Truebloods.

He was drawn into apartments where Talin, the cousins, men and women with red-rimmed eyes and sing-song accents put their hands on him and begged for the story. They fed him rice and peas with coconut milk, oxtail with broad beans, "run down," pumpkin soup and Solomon Gundy. Then they asked for the story again. For Flip's words from the sky.

Talin you are my soul mate, you are the truth of my blood. Simeon and Smoky you are my life and my songs. Father you are everything, everything to me. No regrets, you made me the man I am. I'll be with Mummy and it will be all right. Aunt Vonnie you were my mother when I needed you. Aunt Ramerra you fed me love and music and wisdom. Uncle Desmond your laughter filled my days. Jade, I'm sorry.

"Who is Jade?" Jav asked.

"Jade Fitzroy," Talin said. "Russ's sister. She loved Flip awful, but he didn't feel the same."

Jav nodded.

"He liked you," Talin said, his voice a fragment of sandpaper. "Jav, he liked you so much…"

Jav tried to give the hat back—first to Flip's father, George, who wouldn't take it. Then to Talin, who said Jav should keep it. So did the cousins and the aunts and uncles. They only wanted the scrap of paper with Jav's scribbled transcript. They made copies and framed them under glass, displayed them on walls and tables and lit candles beneath.

Jav made his way back to his apartment, which reeked with spoiled food and rotting garbage. He cleaned up, then he moved the manuscript of *The Voyages of Trueblood Cay* off his hard drive and onto a flash drive. He put the flash drive in an envelope and the envelope in a drawer. He shut off his computer and would not write. He was too busy waiting for later.

I'll talk to you later.

Day after day, Jav set his hands flat on his kitchen counter, his forehead resting on an invisible shoulder. Wishing it were later. He knelt before the open well of Flip's hat, praying for later. He ran his hand in circles on his chest, touching his heart and remembering later. The phone rang and it was later, only it wasn't. It was now. And Flip wasn't coming back.

While grief dried the imagination of his soul to dust, it made the imagination of his body spurt up in enormous geysers of desire.

Open your pants for me, rude bwoy.

Night after night, Jav opened. He kissed pillows, humped the mattress and fucked the sheets, making his bed into Flip. Atoning for the years and months of only looking and not touching, Jav's angry, mourning hands seized and grabbed his invisible lover. He got Flip underneath him and pinned him down. Safe. Beautiful. And listening.

I have you here and I will talk to you now.

The ghost of Flip's laugh filled the bedroom as Jav took him again and again. He sunk his hands deep into Flip and didn't let go. The mariner's smile flashed in the dark as he navigated Jav past the shoals of inexperience and out into the open waters of love, where Jav put magic words in both their mouths.

Your voice gives me a hard-on, Captain Trueblood whispered.

"I can still taste you," Jav said.

Feel good?

"I feel like me." Through weeks and months, Jav hugged and kissed and made love to the space Flip was supposed to come back to. He strained his ears into the dark, waiting for the talk they were going to have later.

"Write it, Jav," Gloria said. The woman whose name he now shared stroked his hair and caressed his gaunt face. "He'd want you to."

Jav couldn't. His wasn't the only flow gone dry: without their heart, True-blood Cay quietly fell apart. No animosity, only an utter inability to rise above the destruction and create music, even though they knew Flip would've wanted them to. The fierce Trueblood clan had been brought low with mourning. All of New York was mourning. America donned a fiercely patriotic coat lined with fear and suspicion and sadness. All it wanted was lost in the ashes at Ground Zero.

Jav crammed his calendar full of dates. As many as he could fit in. Not for the money—although he raked it in—but to keep his thoughts focused elsewhere and to tire him out. He had no idea how he was getting aroused for these women when the rest of him felt so impotent, but apparently his dick was the sole part of him that still needed to be excellent at something.

C'mon, man, we have work *to do.*

He did an excellent job, but he rarely came with his clients. He fucked them limp then faked a convincing finish. With a condom, they didn't know the difference. And it wasn't about him anyway.

He asked Talin to find a picture of Flip that showed his dragonfly tattoo. He took it to a parlor and had it replicated on his forearm. On his other arm he had a ship's wheel inked.

He ran a lot. Running silenced the voices in his head. He doubled up on workouts, because physical strength was a small comfort. And he wanted to look good in case Flip came back later.

He took the long train ride to Corona sometimes, no longer afraid of ghosts or who might see him. Or not see him. He walked the fairgrounds, not giving away anything for free. He looked up at a giant's abandoned playthings and wondered, *Don't you love me anymore?*

He once took a long walk to the middle of the George Washington Bridge. Eyes watering from the icy gusts buffeting the span, he leaned on the rail and looked into the abyss. Gazed at the matrix of sparkles on the waters below. The siren who had lured Ernesto to his death. Jav listened hard, but heard no temptation for him in the river's call. No pull to swing a leg over the railing and end it all. He stared down the river a while longer, making sure. Then he went home.

He grew comfortable in the apathetic complacence. This was how things were now. If they changed, they changed. If they didn't, whatever.

Then he woke up one day with an idea.

Apropos of nothing, it wandered into his brain like a stray cat. He stared at it a minute, confused. He almost shooed it away but it stubbornly stayed.

Write me.

He took it in. Fed it a little. Let it sit in his lap and purr. A rain cloud appeared on the horizon of his dustbowl. It rumbled and billowed, pregnant with possibility. He put Flip's hat on, opened a new document, flexed his fingers and began to type.

The first rains hit the parched ground and rebounded, beading up in dirty droplets. Like him, the earth didn't know what to make of this sudden moisture. Then his story started to sink into the surface, saturating him. A swampy mess at first. No plot, no arc, no thread. For a month, he simply threw handfuls of mud and gunk at the screen. He began to find rocks, then bones. And finally, he hit the vein of gold at the intersection of challenge and passion. He heaved a novella called *Gloria in the Highest* to the surface. A dark tale of a dark woman, raised by a gangster father in the 1920s. She took his life, his name and his empire, becoming queen of Manhattan's underbelly.

"Darling, it's so twisted and despairing," Gloria said, reading the first proofs. "I'm afraid I love it."

"It's not you," he said. "Only your name. And the play on your name. The twisted despair is all me."

She gave him a long, thoughtful look over her glasses. "It's me, too," she said. "It's astonishing how well you know me."

Gloria was a New York Times bestseller, and long-listed for a New York City Book Award, though it didn't advance. Jav kept working, writing and escorting. He started relationships with women that ended quickly. He looked at men sometimes, but didn't dare touch. The want wasn't worth the loss.

This year, his publisher re-issued both *Client Privilege*—his short story collection—and *Gloria in the Highest* with the new covers now framed on Gloria's wall.

"So tell me what's next," she said.

"Well," he said. "I did have a little idea. Have you heard of Post Secret?"

Her eyebrows drew together as she twisted her earring. "It's a blog, isn't it? People submit anonymous postcards with their secrets?"

"Yes," Jav said, drawing a folded piece of paper out of his pocket. "I saw this one a few weeks ago. And I can't get it out of my mind."

He handed the printout to her. The postcard showed a pen and ink sketch of the tops of the Twin Towers, wreathed in billowing smoke. Along the top was written, *Everyone who knew me before 9/11 believes I'm dead.*

"Goodness," she said. "Here's a story."

"Right? I can't stop thinking about it. How one tragic day was the end for thousands, but perhaps for someone, it was the beginning."

"An out."

"A chance for a new life."

She handed the picture back to him. "You should go with it."

"I'm going to try." He glanced discreetly at his watch. When he looked back to Gloria her face was wreathed in an expression he couldn't fathom.

"Look at you," she said. "All grown up."

He laughed. "Not quite."

"Forty-three," she said. "Still gorgeous, fit, built and in-demand. You've done well. You're lonely, but you've done well."

Jav stood up and leaned down to kiss her. "Can't have everything."

Her hand caressed his cheek. "Call me if you need me."

"I always need you."

EVERYONE WHO KNEW ME

*H*E TOOK THE subway back to Manhattan. A woman got on at Marble Hill and sat across from him, crossing her arms over her purse and exhaling a ragged sigh. Jav lowered his eyes and looked at her through his lashes. *She was dressed neatly,* he thought, *but her hair hung limp and unwashed and her complexion was slightly grey, as if she'd been eating ash. Her eyes stared at nothing, with an intense purpose that saw everything. Her gaze broke through atoms and protons and neutrons, searching for the space between...*

He shook his head free of the purple prose, looked away, then looked back. The woman was staring down now, biting on her lower lip.

Maybe for someone it was a beginning. An out.

"Are you all right?" he heard his voice ask.

She looked up and he saw her eyes were dark blue. She blinked at him and he expected a terse nod or a simple "fine." Or even for her to get up and move away from this strange violation of subway etiquette.

Instead she sighed and said, "I will be."

She got off at the next stop. Jav shivered inside his pea coat after the train lurched into motion again, as if the woman took all the available heat with her.

Everyone who knew me believes I'm dead.

"I don't believe you're dead," Jav said under his breath. He reached behind his head, sliding fingers under his collar and along his backbones, until they touched the tender skin where a new tattoo was healing. His beloved mariner and the place where his ship went down five years ago:

TRUEBLOOD

39° 59′ 0″ N, 78° 51′ 59″ W

As he was walking up the subway steps at 168th Street, his personal cell phone rang. The screen showed an unidentified number with a 914 area code. "Javier Landes."

"Mr. Landes," a woman's voice said. "My name is Pearl Paradise."

I'll bet it is, Jav thought, ducking around some scaffolding outside the subway stop. "Yes?"

"I'm an attorney with the law firm of Lowenstein, Silver and Snow. I'm looking for Javier Rafael Gil deSoto. Have I reached the right person?"

Jav was crossing Broadway and nearly stopped short in traffic, tripping over his own name. "That's me," he said, his heart kicking up a few beats. "In another life, anyway."

"Mr. Landes, I'm calling about Naroba Seaver."

"Naroba?" Now Jav did stop short. Stood still in the middle of the sidewalk, the sea of pedestrians parting around him. "My sister, Naroba?"

Everyone who knew me believes I'm dead.

"Mr. Landes, would it be possible for you to come talk to me?"

"When?"

"As soon as possible."

"Where?"

"We're located in Poughkeepsie, but we have office space in White Plains as well if it's more convenient."

"And what is this regarding?"

"I'm not comfortable discussing this on the phone. It's critical I meet with you in person."

She's dead, Jav thought. What else could it be? He swallowed and began walking again. "Is she alive?"

"I can come to White Plains tomorrow. Are you available at nine thirty?"

"Can you at least tell me if my sister's alive?"

A pause. "No, Mr. Landes, I'm sorry. She passed away a few days ago."

The queen is dead.

"What happened?"

"Mr. Landes…"

"Fine," he said, shaking his head. "All right. Nine thirty. What's the address?"

She gave it to him. "It's a short walk from the train station. I will see you tomorrow then. And Mr. Landes?"

"Yes?"

"Bring some identification."

Jav got the feeling she didn't mean his library card. He took the train up the next morning, armed with proof of his existence. Driver's license, birth certificate and a copy of the court petition with his legal name change.

He'd chewed all night on the idea of Naroba being dead and couldn't connect with it. Sadness for the estrangement stirred his heart, then a small fistfight between defiance and guilt broke out. The schism wasn't his fault. He'd looked for her after 9/11. Occasionally, in the five years since, he looked again, searching combinations of Naroba and Naria and rearranging Gil deSoto.

Did he try hard enough?

His pride crossed its arms. She didn't look for him, either. She was no Queen Naria. She was Naroba the Weak. She'd always been a doormat.

Now she was dead.

I looked for her. I couldn't find her, she changed her name.

Naroba Seaver. So she'd gotten married. Thanks for the invitation.

You changed your name. How would she have even found you?

He looked out the window of the train with a small snort. They'd found him now, hadn't they? And what was this all about anyway, did she *leave* him something?

To my brother, Javier, I leave my deepest apologies...

"Bet she left me her debts," he mumbled. His eyes narrowed, remembering Rosa's drunken laughter over the phone.

Naroba hates you.

She championed him once. She grabbed the check from *Cricket* and held onto it while Rosa beat her with a belt.

She'd spit in your pretty face.

Naroba apologized to the air for breathing. The air turned its back on her.

The queen is dead.

Jav got off at White Plains with a headache, and walked the few blocks to the office building. Pearl Paradise was a good-looking woman in her forties, sleek and sharp with glasses. With her name, she needed that uncompromising appearance. Jav accepted a cup of coffee and kept the obvious remarks to himself.

"Thank you for coming in," Pearl said, closing the door. "Did you bring ID?"

Jav handed his papers over.

"Yes, the name change," she said, peering over the tops of her glasses. "It delayed us tracking you down."

"I'm not used to family looking for me."

"I'm sorry to know that. And despite the circumstances, I am sorry for your loss."

Jav gave a small nod. "Can you tell me what happened?"

She took off her glasses. "A tragic accident, I'm afraid. She fell down the stairs."

Jav's eyebrows came down. "At home?"

"Yes. Her son found her."

"Her son."

"Yes. Aaron Seaver, he's seventeen."

Jav's hands grew cold. "Jesus... What about her husband?"

"Mrs. Seaver was a widow."

"I see." His fingertips were prickling. "Where's her son now? Who's taking care of him?"

Pearl laced her fingers together. "This is why I've had you come in, Mr. Landes. In her will, Mrs. Seaver named you as legal guardian for Ari."

Jav felt his eyes bulge and blink rapidly. "Me?"

She nodded, then separated out a sheaf of papers, folded them back to a page and slid it across the table. Jav reached for his own glasses and leaned to look where Pearl's fingertip circled:

> *...If it is necessary to appoint a guardian, I appoint my brother, Javier Gil deSoto, as guardian of my child, Aaron Rafael Seaver (born Aaron Rafael Gil deSoto)...*

Jav flipped to the first page. "When did she make this?"

"It was last revised in two thousand, following the death of her husband."

Jav flipped back, reread the guardian paragraph and looked up. "Do you know if my mother is alive?"

"Our research found she passed in two thousand four."

"In Florida?"

"Yes."

Now I'm the only one left, Jav thought. "I still don't understand," he said. "Why weren't any of her husband's family named as guardian?"

Pearl opened her hands. "I'm afraid I don't have an answer. One possible reason is Ari wasn't Nick Seaver's biological child. But Nick legally adopted Ari in ninety-eight. That's why he's Seaver."

"Jesus Christ," Jav said, running a hand through his hair. "Where's my uncle now?"

"Pardon?"

Jav shook his head, confused. "My nephew, rather. I'm the uncle."

Pearl sat back, swinging her glasses by one earpiece. "He was just released from Hudson Bluffs Medical Center. He collapsed at the police station and we've learned he was extremely ill last year. An adrenal infection of some kind. It still affects his body's capability to cope with a severe shock such as this."

"But he's all right?"

"He's fine. Physically fine, that is. He's been transferred to a juvenile residential facility in Guelisten." She put up a hand, anticipating Jav's next question. "It's not a detention center. It's a private group home for adolescents. In fact it's one of the best in the state."

"You're telling me nobody... No friends, no one who could take him in? A priest or a teacher? A coach?"

Pearl pointed to the papers. "We start with the will, Mr. Landes. He's a minor and his mother made legal, binding instructions."

"I meant in the interim, instead of sticking him in a... Oh, never mind. Who am I kidding? I slept in a stockroom for three months." Jav drummed his fingers on the table. "I'm sorry, it's hard to get my head around this."

"I can only imagine. Please, whatever questions you have, ask them. We have to do what's best for everyone, so it's important you know your options."

"Suppose... Remove me from the equation. I mean, suppose I was dead as well. What would become of him?"

"Both the social worker at the hospital and the county social worker agree Lark House is the best place for him."

"Lark House is the...?"

"The group home, yes. It's structured toward transitional living for teens phasing out of foster care. Foster care for Ari is pointless because of his age. He's seventeen. He'd age out in a year anyway, it would be more disruptive than beneficial. Lark House is the ideal place for him to transition to independence. Second, the boy's been traumatized by a shock, which is the worst thing for someone with adrenal deficiencies. He needs to be somewhere where his physical and mental health can be monitored. He needs counseling. He needs an advocate. Lark House can do all this."

"I see."

"Plus he has a dog." Pearl sighed. "If you thought it couldn't get worse. When Mrs. Seaver fell down the stairs, her purse spilled out onto the floor. The dog got into it and chewed up a pack of gum. Apparently sugarless gum has a chemical that can be lethal to dogs. Poor thing almost died. He's at the Hudson Bluffs Animal Shelter."

"Christ," Jav said, exhaling heavily. "All right. So he's at this place, Lark House?"

"Yes."

"In Guelisten."

"Yes. North of Poughkeepsie. Pretty town."

"Where is my sister now? I mean, was there a funeral? Will there be?"

"Per the request in her will, she was cremated. The ashes will go to Ari."

"Poor kid," Jav said. "Seventeen?"

"Yes. He's a junior at Morgantown High School."

"Seventeen's when I got thrown out of the house."

"Mm."

Jav ran his thumb along the edges of the will's pages. "I'll be honest, I don't have a lot of good experience with uncles. One had a hobby of ambushing me on the streets, shaking me down for money. The other would pass me on the sidewalk without a word or a glance."

"I'm so sorry for everything that's happened."

"I'll go up tomorrow. I'll drive up in the morning and see him. And we'll... meet."

She smiled. "It's a start."

"Is Pearl Paradise your real name?"

"It is," she said. "Do you want to get a drink?"

He laughed. "Thanks, but at the moment I like you for your brains."

She squared off her papers, looking pleased behind her glasses.

IT HAPPENS

*J*AV WENT HOME and tried to write—he kept to a disciplined quota of a thousand words a day. Whether the words were good, bad or utter crap, the daily allotment kept the faucet open.

His attention kept wandering. To Gloria. To the woman on the subway. To the voice of Paradise on the phone. To memories that touched him on the shoulder, then ran away teasing when he turned his head.

Everyone who knew me believes I'm dead.

He went for a run, hoping it would either silence his thoughts or sharpen them. As he neared Central Park, a firm clear conviction settled in his mind: *Don't be them. Be different. Be what an uncle is supposed to be. Be what nobody was for you.*

He called Pearl Paradise in White Plains. He called Lark House in Guelisten. And he called Gloria and asked if he could borrow her car.

He threw some stuff in a bag, took the subway back to Riverdale, then headed up the Henry Hudson Parkway in Gloria's Range Rover. It was a grey, chilly day, the Hudson Valley painted in neutral shades of brown. Two hours after leaving Manhattan, Jav was turning off Route 9D and following the signs to Guelisten. As Pearl said, it was a pretty, quaint village perched above the river, charming with its streets of well-maintained Victorian houses.

Bemelman Street wound uphill through a residential area, petering out at a bluff with spectacular river views. A large, white farmhouse was set back from the cul de sac and further beyond was an immense barn converted into living space.

Jav parked in the small visitor's lot and headed up the front steps of the farmhouse. It was colder and more blustery up on this plateau. The wind chimes hung between the struts of the porch were singing their hearts out.

A plaque next to the door read *In Memory of Beatrice "Billie" Lark, 1905-1981. Who dedicated a life to service and made a home for the children of Dutchess County.*

The cheerful woman at the front desk had Jav sign in, making a copy of his driver's license. "Ari's in the library," she said. "I've put it on restriction tonight so you'll have privacy. Can I get you a cup of coffee?"

Jav declined, thanked her and headed in the direction she pointed. His heart was pounding. Even going on his first paid date didn't make his heart into a kettle drum like this.

He paused in the doorway.

It was Señor Gil deSoto in the library with a bottle of mamajuana.

The fire was lit and a dark-haired boy slouched in an easy chair in front of it, reading, one knee hooked over the chair's arm. The careless, sideways sprawl that looked uncomfortable to adult eyes but was second nature to adolescents.

"Ari?" Jav said.

The boy looked up.

Jav's first impression was Ari was sicker than Pearl let on. He was thin. Painfully thin. His face hollow, the jutting cheekbones fragile. But they were Jav's cheekbones. His eyes had the same shape as Jav's, the brows above following the exact same slant. As Jav walked closer, he found a bit of Rafael. And when Ari stood up, crossed his arms and lifted his chin, it was Nesto's cocky, defiant stance.

"So where've you been?" Ari said. The voice was surprisingly deep and strong, coming from such a skinny kid.

He's a kid, Jav reminded himself. *He's lost his mother. He's scared shitless. Hostility makes good armor.*

"I only found out this morning," Jav said. "And now I'm here."

They stood two feet apart now, uncle and nephew, looking each other over. Ari's eyes were nearly on a level with Jav's. Kid was at least six feet, but Christ, he'd fall over if you yawned in his direction.

"Mind if I sit down?" Jav asked.

Ari shrugged and flopped back into the easy chair. Jav sat in the one opposite, shrugging out of his jacket.

"I'm really sorry to meet you like this," he said. "And I'm sorry about your mother."

Ari put an ankle on one knee, his arms crossed again. "Are you?"

"Of course I am."

"When was the last time you saw her?"

Jav closed his eyes to do the mental math. "Coming up on twenty-six years. I left home in nineteen-eighty."

"And what, you never spoke again?"

Jav shook his head. "It was an ugly situation. Did you mother tell you about it?"

"Dude, I didn't even know you existed until yesterday."

"Then you can see how ugly it was. I didn't know about you until this morning."

"Twenty-six years," Ari said. "That's a long time to hold a grudge. What was all the bad blood about?"

"Did your mother tell you anything about her family?"

Ari shook his head. "When I asked, she said her parents were both dead."

Jav stared at the crossroads a moment. He could give a vague, sanitized version of events, but the kid was already reeling from his mother withholding information. It wasn't fair. Jav had to lob the truth out there and see if Ari wanted anything to do with it.

"The shortest version," he said slowly, "is a misunderstanding led my family to think I was gay. And they threw me out."

Ari blinked twice. "For real?"

Jav spread his hands out. "Twenty-six years, you ever hear my name?"

Ari's eyebrows pulled down to make a single thick line. "So they thought you were gay but you're not?"

I'm not sure, Jav thought. "No," he said.

"No one believed you?"

Jav shook his head.

"One strike, out on the street, slam the door and goodbye forever?"

"Pretty much."

"Dude, that's fucking harsh. Even my mother cut you off?"

Then Jav felt like shit, casting Naroba in this light when she'd been gone only a few days. Pouring brine on a bleeding heart. "Look," he said. "Out of all the animosity I've carried around for my family, my sister had the least of it. Let me be honest about what I know. I heard Naroba ran away after I left. But did she stay away? I'm inclined to think she went back."

"Why?"

"Because in a household full of tigers, she was a baby gazelle. My mother always said Naroba couldn't decide her way out of a burning building. She was a follower, not a leader, happy to do what someone else told her. So who knows how my mother bullied or brainwashed her into cutting me off, but it couldn't have been difficult."

"Yeah." Ari was nodding and picking at one of his shoelaces. "Mom didn't always make good decisions when it came to people," he said. "Which was weird. Because at work, she—"

"What did she do?"

"She was a nurse. A good one. Really competent and confident. Few times I saw her on the job, it was like looking at a completely different person. Soon as she was out of her scrubs, she became…afraid. She always needed someone telling her what to do. You're right about that."

"What happened to your father?"

"My real father?"

"Do you want to tell me about him?"

"No."

"Then what happened to Nick Seaver. The man who adopted you."

"He died. Six years ago. Heart attack."

"And he had no other family?"

One of Ari's shoulders rolled. "Only child. His parents were dead." The eyes that turned to Jav were far older than seventeen years, the smile below filled with irony. "Seems to be the story of my life. You sure you want to hang out with me?"

Jav nodded, unable to think of anything to say.

"Nick was a great guy," Ari said to the fireplace. "Nothing was the same after he went."

"Did you call him Dad?"

"I was starting to. He was good to Mom. Good *for* her. When she was with him, it was like she had her scrubs on all the time. And when he died…"

"All her confidence died, too?"

"Pretty much. She got involved with a real loser a few years ago. Tom Kingston. Started out fine, he seemed like a nice guy. But pretty soon it became obvious he was hooked on painkillers, and her being a nurse was convenient for him." Ari shook his head. "It got real ugly real fast. Talk about not being able to decide your way out of a burning building."

"Where is he now?"

"In jail. Arrested for dealing heroin. Huge drug ring got busted up. Ever have a police raid smash down your door? It's a gas. We were real popular in the neighborhood afterward. Not."

"I'm so sorry."

Ari stared at Jav a long time, his lower jaw moving back and forth. Then he freed a hand and reached across the space between them. "It's nice to meet you."

"Likewise," Jav said, shaking it. The kid had a good grip. "You feel all right staying here?"

Ari shrugged. "It's okay. People are nice."

Jav looked around the room. Tall windows with the beautiful views. A large sofa, a couple more easy chairs. Two tables with mismatched seating. A good place to chill out or study.

"You're a junior?" Jav asked.

Ari nodded.

"Play sports?"

"I wrestled. Then I got sick last year."

"Your lawyer told me. How are you feeling now? All things considered."

"Like shit."

Jav crossed his arms and ankles, feet stretched toward the fire. "That's fair."

Ari glanced at Jav. "So what do you do?"

"I'm a writer."

"Books?"

Jav nodded. "And some web copy and freelance journalism."

"You live in Manhattan?"

"Little bit north of Harlem."

Ari's gaze slid far away. Jav studied him out the side of his eye. The thinness of Ari's face couldn't support his strong nose and jaw. But when he gained some weight back, he'd be a good-looking kid.

"Do you have a girlfriend?" Jav asked.

"I got nobody," Ari said evenly, cracking his knuckles one at a time beneath his thumb. "I have my dog, Roman. And he almost died, too."

"What about your real father?"

A chuckle. "I have no idea who he is, where he is or if he even knows I'm alive."

Jav leaned forward. "What can I do to help you right now? Tonight. Or tomorrow."

The boy rubbed his face vigorously, raked his fingers through his hair. "I want to see Roman."

"Done," Jav said. "I'll stay the night somewhere. I'll come back first thing in the morning and take you to see him. He's at a shelter, right? Close by?"

Ari looked over, nodding, mouth pressed in a tight line.

"Okay. We'll go tomorrow."

"Thanks." A single thick syllable but half of it got stuck in Ari's throat and he looked away.

"Look," Jav said, not sure where he was going but feeling he had to say something reassuring.

Jesus, what the hell do I know about being an uncle? Only that an uncle's love comes at a price.

"Look," he said again. "I was cut off from the family, but none of the reasons have anything to do with your mother. Or with you. It was long before you were born. None of this is your fault. You're my sister's son and I'll help you. But I need to say…two things. One is you owe me nothing. None of my help comes at a price. Second, I might not be good at this. I've never taken care of anyone except myself."

And my clients.

Ari sunk further in the chair, looking gaunt, overwhelmed and helpless.

I can help him.

"I'm kind of a solitary and selfish individual, Ari," Jav said. "Maybe this can help me change."

"Don't change for me," Ari said dully. "I'll be out of your hair in a year."

"Have you eaten? You want to go get something in town?"

Ari shook his head. "I'm good. Thanks."

"All right. I'm going to find a place to stay tonight. And I'll be back in the morning."

"All right."

They both stood up. Jav hesitated, decided it was too soon and too weird for hugging. He went for a handshake and a back pat. He could feel the bumps of Ari's spine and the edge of a shoulder blade.

"It'll be all right," Jav said. "We'll figure something out."

"Sure," Ari said, reaching down for the book he dropped on the floor. "I'll see you tomorrow then."

"Vale, hasta mañana." Jav made to leave but turned back after a few steps. "Do you speak Spanish?"

"A little." Ari's head bobbled around. "I mean, I can understand a little. I don't speak much. Sorry."

"No, I was just curious. Goodnight."

Ari held up a palm. "Adiós."

DOING IT

*D*EANE LARK-PENDA THOUGHT sex was weird.

She and her boyfriend Casey started Doing It after New Year's and so far, after two months, sex felt superficial and phony to Deane. Somehow *required*. Perfunctory lines on a social resume instead of a conscious act of passionate expression.

"I thought sex would be bigger," Deane said to her best friend, Stella.

"Bigger?"

"More monumental."

"Casey's not a monumental kind of guy," Stella said. "Don't get me wrong. I mean, he's good to you."

"I know," Deane said. "But I don't feel changed by this. I thought sex made things more serious. And I thought being in a serious relationship would be more...*more*."

"Well, look at your parents," Stella said. "What in hell could measure up to what you see in front of your face every day? You were doomed to be disappointed in love."

"Thanks," Deane said.

"Sorry, Pooky," Stella said. "I guess it's better than if they fought all the time. Or maybe it's just as hard having parents who are painfully in love."

Deane's parents were *ridiculous*. Always hugging and kissing and grabbing each other's asses. Walking down Main Street arm-in-arm, holding hands at Deane's lacrosse games. Once Deane and Stella came back to the house to find Alex and Val wrestling in the back yard. Rolling around in the grass, laughing and roughhousing while the dog barked her head off and Stella stared in open-mouthed fascination.

"Jesus," she said. "Is this normal behavior for them?"

"Yes," Deane said. "It's fucking mortifying."

"It's epic," Stella said. "My mom and dad shake hands goodnight. I look at all my other friends' parents and feel sad and tired. I look at your parents and all I think about is sex."

"Ew," Deane said, caught in her own crossfire between fascination and embarrassment. She *knew* when her parents were making love. It was more than their bedroom door being shut and the dog kicked out. More than overhearing little noises and soft laughter. It was the way the air in the house vibrated. It changed color, like an aura. Deane would get up to pee or get water and it might be utterly, spookily silent. Still she knew they were Doing It.

"They Do It even when they're not Doing It," she said to Casey once.

Casey, who could be maddeningly literal sometimes, shook his head, not getting it. A star football player in fall and captain of the baseball team in spring, imagination wasn't in his DNA. He made love by the playbook, running the bases in order. Kissing. Touching above the waist. Touching below the waist. He'd put a condom on and then they Did It.

Deane held county records in three ski events and was co-captain of the lacrosse team, but this neat, structured passion wasn't her idea of lovemaking. She was starting to think Casey Bradshaw might be a bit of a prude.

"He wants it," Deane said. "But he never talks about it."

"Well, he's Catholic," Stella said. "Of course he wants it, but he's not supposed to."

Casey never said anything like, *Let's make love tonight.* Or, *I can't wait to make love tonight.* The school week went along with their time eaten up by homework and jobs and sports practice, and it was simply a given that the weekends were for sex.

Tonight was Friday and they were Doing It down in Casey's basement TV room.

Woo-hoo.

Deane didn't make any little noises when Casey was moving inside her. They didn't laugh softly together. The air didn't shimmer or vibrate. It stood around, wondering what it was supposed to do, like guests at a really lame party. Or the losers who arrived at the party on the wrong night.

She was missing something here. Or maybe she was doing something wrong. Her mother often left her phone lying around and Deane would see texts from her father:

Can't get shit done today, I keep thinking about last night.

And her mother's text back:

I fucking love being your wife.

The words bewildered Deane. Her parents' passion was an eternal flame, while Deane's inflated and deflated like a balloon. After sex, Casey said he loved her. She thought you couldn't help but love the person who made you come a minute ago. He never texted her the next day, saying he was still thinking about it. To distraction. He never said he loved being her boyfriend.

Tonight she'd tried a trick play. After they rounded third and before he reached for the condom. She stilled his hand and pushed him down on his back.

"Whoa," he said. "You want to be on top?"

"I just want to look at you."

"What?"

"Shh. Hold still." She lay on her elbow and ran her hand over his naked body, from his head to his feet, looking at everything close up in the flickering light from the soundless TV. Touching. Searching. Looking for what it was about him that worked with her. That turned her on and moved her.

He's sweet, she thought. *He isn't moody. You always know how he'll react and behave. He's loyal to his friends. He's decent. He doesn't target weakness or make fun of people who are different. These are all good things. He's good.*

Her hands moved over the planes and curves of his muscles. The hair on his chest and under his arms. The four-pack he was so obsessive over. The whorl of his belly button. Ignoring his erection, she ran her hand down his strong quads, the rough skin on his kneecaps and his calves. His feet jerked away from her touch, too ticklish. She turned around and headed up his body again, looking at his handsome face.

He wasn't returning her gaze with adoration or tender amusement, his face saying *I love being your boyfriend.*

He looked impatient. Almost…annoyed.

Like, *Are you done yet?*

"Sorry," she mumbled. She stopped her exploration and tore open the Trojan packet. He took it out of her fingers and rolled it on himself. Weird how he never let her do it.

"What," she said, leaning on her elbow and stroking his arm. "I can be trusted with a hand job but proper condom technique is beyond my skill?"

The pink crawled across his cheekbones as he shook his head. "You're so funny." He slid on top of her, they Did It and afterward he put his face in her neck and said he loved her.

Why? she thought.

She shouldn't be so cynical. He wasn't a bad guy.

She just wished he were more monumental.

They got dressed and she walked home. Casey always asked if she wanted him to come with and she always said no. It was two blocks on well-lit streets. This was Guelisten—people left keys in the ignition and parked napping babies in strollers outside stores. She didn't need an escort.

Besides, she wanted Casey not to ask to come, but *just come*. Because he couldn't stand her leaving.

She wanted him to be dire. To text, *Do you miss me?*

I love making love with you.

I can't stop thinking about it.

The house on Tulip Street was quiet and dark. Her parents liked to know when Deane was back, so she rattled soft knuckles on their bedroom door and pressed her mouth close to the jamb.

"I'm home," she called.

A shimmering pause.

"Thanks, honey," Val said.

"Duerme bien, cosita," Alex said.

Deane got into the shower, reaching for her Clarisonic facial brush, which she'd used on her face for a week until she discovered it had a much better purpose. With the spinning head on its lowest setting in one hand, and the detachable shower head in the other, she could come in twelve seconds.

Breathing hard, her head lolling with the release, she leaned into the warm spray, now limp and relaxed as a cat. Why was it so simple alone and so maddeningly difficult with Casey? How many times did you have to take a guy's hand and tell him, "Dude, it's right *here*." If he had that kind of learning disability in sports, he'd be a bench decoration.

She was inept at this game, something she wasn't used to. The rules kept changing.

Deane Lark-Penda hated not knowing the rules to a game.

She wrapped up in a towel and crept past her parents' room.

Behind the door, she heard them laughing softly.

SATURDAY

DOWN TO DEATH

*A*RI WOKE UP hungry.

He wasn't supposed to skip meals—the hospital warned against putting any undue stress on his body. But he found he thought better on an empty stomach. In a weird way, he liked waking up to a gnawing hollow in his belly.

Hunger became a funny little friend to him in his wrestling days, when he had to hold steady at 132 pounds, or drop down to the 126-pound weight class if his coach was short. He liked being able to rise above his stomach's needs, reducing bulk without reducing his strength, converting every bit of fat into muscle and keeping the muscle as compact as possible. He discovered when hunger curled up in his belly like a warm cat, his mind curled easier around things. He felt sharper. Keener. He was *faster* when he fasted.

The sun sliced through the thin curtains of his little room at Lark House. He sat up, twisting from one side to the other to get his back to crack, then he reached for the bottle of water on the nightstand. The mattress sucked and it was roasting in here. Pulling the curtain aside, he saw a cloudless, brilliant-blue sky. A walk and some air seemed a good idea. He dressed and made his quiet way downstairs, ignoring the salty, greasy smell of bacon wafting from the dining hall.

No luck slipping away, though. "Good morning," said his caseworker, Lauren, materializing like a pixie. "How about some breakfast?"

He knew it was pointless to refuse, so he sat at a little table with Lauren, nibbled on some bacon and had a cup of weak coffee.

"So, your uncle is coming back for you today," she said.

"Yeah. He's taking me to see Roman."

"Good, good. How did it go last night?"

"All right, I guess. I mean, for never meeting the guy before. He's okay."

"Excellent. How are you feeling?"

"Fine. I'd like to walk around, get some air?" He wasn't yet sure how much authority this place had over him, and if he were required to account for his whereabouts at all times.

"Sure," Lauren said. "Stop by the infirmary because they'll want vitals. Then sign out at the front desk. You can walk anywhere on the grounds, but I suggest going down to the grove to the treehouse."

"Treehouse," Ari said, pressing his finger on the last few bacon crumbs.

"The guy from HGTV built it. He's from Guelisten, you know, and now he's got that show. *Home in a Tree*."

"Oh yeah," Ari said, sucking on his finger. "My mom has a huge crush on him." A prickling upset went across his eyes and he looked down into his coffee cup. "I mean, she had."

Lauren touched his hand. "My father passed away three years ago," she said softly. "I still catch myself using present tense when I talk about him. And I still have his number in my cell phone."

Ari nodded, swirling the last bit of cold java around.

"Go take that walk," Lauren said. "If your uncle gets here before you're back, I'll send him your way."

❧

ARI PREPARED HIMSELF for something cool, but when he got to the grove he stopped short, his mouth falling open. It wasn't merely one house in one tree, but an entire, elevated compound built within the grove. As if a piece of Rivendell had been plucked from *Lord of the Rings* and transported.

"Holy shit," he said, going up the spiral staircase to the hub of the structure. He kept repeating "holy shit" under his breath as he walked around the octagonal hall with four trunks piercing its shingled roof. A rustic railing encircled the platform, off which led three swinging bridges to other trees with smaller houses, tinier crows' nests and more spiral staircases to the ground.

He explored the entire thing from tree to tree, then made his way up one more winding stairway to the highest level. Through the leafless branches, he could see the artery of the river stretching north and south. The pale blue Mid-Hudson bridge spanning the banks like a lady spreading her skirt. The geometric trusses and struts of the old railway bridge beyond.

Ari sat on the deck, putting his feet between two spindles and letting them dangle. Alone, hovering above the world, he dug his hands deep in his pockets, set his forehead against the railing and exhaled.

My mother is dead.

The words whirled non-stop around his mind. And his mind stood with the door half open, shaking its head with a blank stare. *I'm sorry, you are...?*

It wasn't supposed to be this way.

"You know what?" Naroba said to him on New Year's Eve, only five weeks ago. "It's our time now."

Having emerged alive from the black hole that was 2003 to 2005, they could make fun of the ordeal. After Ari's illness, the heroin bust, Tom Kingston's arrest and conviction and the fallout, Naroba looked as thin and exhausted as Ari. Yet something in her eyes was electric, galvanized for change. She had both her scrubs and her game face on.

"Second chances are given or made," she said. "That's what my father always said. You and me, we're going to make something happen this year. We've been to hell and back, but you wait, Ari. It's our time."

He shut his eyes. Naroba was etched behind his lids as he'd last seen her: sprawled on the floor, her head twisted and her eyes staring. Close by lay Roman, his eyes also fixed and glassy, barely breathing.

Ari thought it was a professional hit. It had to be Tom Kingston's doing. This was clearly a vendetta. He had screamed as much to the 911 dispatcher. But when it became clear it wasn't murder but an accident, Ari became angrier than he could ever recall feeling in his life. His brain flared up white hot behind his eyes. It was like staring into the sun. His mother was dead because she'd *tripped*. She skipped a step, stumbled, faltered, went for the handrail and missed. It was the stupidest thing he'd ever heard of.

"No," he kept saying at the precinct, telling the police, yelling at the social worker, shouting to anyone who would listen it was their time now. They'd made it through hell. They were going to make something happen and it was impossible Naroba *fell down* to death.

When he started throwing things, one of the cops got arms around him. Ari's wrestling instincts took hold and he was about to break out when the lock turned into more of a hug. The strong, solid grip pulled him close. Compassion like a blanket pulled up tight and a deep voice inside a barrel chest. "It's all right, son. Don't throw it out there, give it to me. Come on now..."

He collapsed in this stranger's embrace, his throat slashed apart with crying. Through the blinding glare he wept so hard, his nose started to bleed.

Then he passed out.

"Here you are."

Ari looked down from his perch. His uncle stared up at him. Jesus Christ, the guy said he was a writer but he could've been an actor. Or a model. He said he wasn't gay, but he could probably walk down the street and collect panties and boxer shorts in equal amounts.

"I'd have given my left nut to have this place when I was a kid," Jav said, coming up the stairway.

"They said the guy who built it is on TV. He goes all over the world building tree houses like this."

"Nice work if you can get it."

"No shit."

"You sleep all right?"

"Some," Ari said. He cried a good portion of the night but that was nothing Jav needed to know. "I think my mother used to work here."

"Really?"

"Yeah. She said she once worked as a private nurse at a group home. In some rich little town on the other side of the river. I think this was it."

"I called the shelter. They said Roman's doing all right. They open at ten so I'll take you over."

"Thanks."

"You hungry?"

"No."

"I am. Mind if we stop in town so I can grab a bite?"

Crunching across the gravel parking lot to the car, Ari asked, "Why did you change your name?"

"I didn't feel part of the old one anymore."

"Why Landes?"

"I usually save that story for the third or fourth date."

"Fair enough," Ari said. "What do you want me to call you?"

A moment of confused staring, then his uncle said, "Jav is fine."

PICTURESQUE AS FUCK

*A*S BEMELMAN STREET descended, it widened to a divided boulevard with majestic old houses on either side. Houses that would only be law offices or funeral homes in Morgantown. All the yards were clipped, groomed and ship-shape. No junk or clutter on porches. Curb appeal was a priority, and people put their names and addresses on their mailboxes like an artist would sign a canvas: *The John Smiths, 1928 Bemelman Street.*

Jav turned onto Main Street and parked by the railroad station. Beyond it stretched a waterfront park, the river sparkling under the sunshine.

"This place is picturesque as fuck," Ari said.

Jav laughed. "Right? Norman Rockwell's wet dream."

They crossed the street and walked past shops. A dressmaker's. A restaurant. Then a bookstore with a coffee bar one of the staff members at Lark House recommended. The sign hanging down from two chains read *Celeste's* and the door opened with a ring of the bell on its jamb.

The smell hit Ari first. He drew it in through his nose, filling up his chest. Wood. Leather. Paper. Ink. Coffee. Bread. Sugar. Chocolate.

His eyes widened at the floor-to-ceiling shelves behind couches and easy chairs and tables. A fireplace at the far end of the space, a long bar with a few stools along one side.

And books.

"Wow," Jav said.

"Yeah."

"I wouldn't mind being held hostage here."

They took stools at the bar. Ari stared. The man working behind the bar was… No, wait. It was a woman.

"What can I get you guys?" she said. Her voice sounded how Ari imagined bourbon would taste. She had white-blonde hair, buzzed short at the back and sides, long bangs falling over her forehead. Her body was arrow-straight under black leather pants and a tight denim shirt. Ari couldn't take his eyes off her. She looked like the offspring of David Bowie and Annie Lennox.

"Here you go," she said, sliding large, round cups to them. She had a ring in her nose and the smiling gaze she flicked toward Ari was icy grey.

The coffee was superb, a strong, rich shot, straight to the veins. Ari ate a croissant. Then another one. The lost sleep of the night before began to creep down the top of his head. Warm and full, he looked at one of the chairs by the fire, thinking he could drop down right there and crash.

The bell on the jamb rang out, then a blast of cold air. Someone darted through tables and chairs and slipped under the coffee bar. No trouble classifying this time, it was definitely a girl. Dressed for running in leggings, sneakers, a fleece top. Sculpted legs and a tight ass. Long blonde hair in a high ponytail. Cheeks pink with cold and exercise and above them, the same ice grey eyes as the barista.

A daughter? Ari wondered. Sister? She acted like she owned the place, taking a glass cloche off a cake stand and helping herself to a danish. She held it tight in her teeth as she replaced the dome, and her eyes caught Ari's.

His heart whipped around and his stomach sat up.

Hello…

Her eyebrows raised and a conspiratorial smile stretched around golden flaky pastry.

Don't tell, her eyes said.

Ari blinked twice. *To the grave.*

The barista capped a paper cup of coffee and handed it off to the runner as if it were a baton.

"Don't fall down," she called, as the girl ducked under the end of the bar and jogged back out of the store. The bell. The breeze. The thump of the door closing. Then silence. The air in the girl's wake swirled and sparkled. As if the bookstore were a snow globe that got shaken up and set down again.

Who was that? Ari thought.

"We have another half hour to kill," Jav said, finishing his coffee.

"The gallery is open upstairs," the barista said, taking their cups. "The door is on the other side of the restaurant. Right next to the dress shop."

The sign over the dress shop read *Deane Fine Tailoring.* Yet another gorgeous blonde woman was arranging the display in the front window.

"Is being blonde a residential requirement in Guelisten?" Ari said.

Jav laughed. "Think you can live here?"

"I'll take one for the team."

Just as Ari stepped inside the stairwell, he heard bells ring next door. He leaned back to see the runner emerge from the dress shop and head up the street, the turquoise soles of her sneakers flipping up behind her. Calves tight, ass tighter, ponytail bouncing. Ari stuffed his eyes with her, swallowed hard, then followed Jav up the stairs.

He was expecting an art gallery but instead, the open room was full of dollhouses.

Miniatures certainly weren't anything Ari would seek out on his own, but he couldn't help being charmed by the displays and impressed by the craftsmanship. Crouching down to peer in the rooms, shuttering his focus into a small, close pinpoint was strangely relaxing.

His mother would love this.

A whistle blast and hiss of brakes as a train pulled into the station across the street.

You mean she would've loved this. If she hadn't fallen down.

"I'm having the weirdest déjà vu," Jav said. "I feel like I've seen these houses. Or knew about them."

Ari looked through a tiny bedroom window and met his uncle's eyes.

"Ready to go?" Jav said.

⟡───

"YOU GO ON in," Jav said as he drove up to shelter's entrance. "I'll park."

The vet was waiting for Ari, a tall guy with glasses, dressed in green surgical scrubs. "I'm Alex Penda," he said, shaking hands. "I'm so sorry for your loss."

"Thanks."

"Come on, I'll take you to see Roman. He's doing great."

It was warm in the shelter. Ari shrugged off his jacket as he followed Dr. Penda down a hallway.

"Did you come alone?" the vet asked. His shoulders were broad and he had bands tattooed around each upper arm.

"My uncle brought me," Ari said, *uncle* still foreign and surreal in his mouth. "He's parking. So what was in the gum that made Roman so sick?"

"Xylitol," Penda said. "It's in a lot of sugarless gums and candy. But it's incredibly toxic to animals."

In one of the adoption rooms, a volunteer sat on the floor by a dog bed where Roman lay, still hooked up to an IV pole. He was a Nova Scotia Duck Tolling Retriever. Pure copper with a white chest and one white paw.

"He's been on dextrose and fluids all this time," Penda said. "We're doing glucose checks every six hours and we'll have to run the liver tox screens for another seventy-two hours. But his heart rate is excellent, blood pressure too. He's going to be all right."

"He's so chill," the volunteer said as Ari sank down on his knees.

"Hey, buddy," he said softly. "What's going on, huh?" Roman burrowed his muzzle beneath Ari's arm and made high, keening noises in his throat while his tail thumped hard.

"I'm between surgeries," Penda said. "But I wanted to say hi and bring you up to speed. Eve's here for you. Stay as long as you want." He raised a palm and then hurried out.

Eve dragged over another dog bed. "We don't have much in the way of chairs here," she said, but Ari wasn't listening. He put his face into Roman's neck and let the world disappear. Faintly he heard the click of a door closing and knew he was alone.

"Did you miss me?" he whispered, his voice falling to pieces. "Did you think I wasn't coming back? It's all right. I came back. You're going to stay with me, okay?"

He jammed the second dog bed tight up against the first and sank down onto it. Roman pushed up against him and his arms closed around the dog.

My mother's dead.

She left me, she lied, she kept secrets, she fell down. Now all I have left is in my arms.

Soft copper-colored hair. The smooth, domed forehead. The panting muzzle in his neck. The utter joy in his presence. The unquestioning love and loyalty and adoration.

My mother is dead.

Roman clasped tight to his chest, Ari cried himself into sleep.

THE EDGES OF ATTRACTION

*A*RI AWOKE, NOT knowing where he was until Roman licked his ear, tail thumping like a heartbeat. Ari sat up, rubbing his face. His head swam with a prickling fog. He'd slept so hard he broke a sweat.

The door opened a bit and Dr. Penda stuck his head in. "How you doing?"

"All right," Ari said, and cleared his sludgy throat.

"Your friend could probably use a walk." Penda opened the door further and behind him was the girl. The runner. Wearing jeans now, her hair still up in a ponytail. She took one hand out of her hoodie pocket and raised it at Ari, who stared back stupidly.

"This is Deane," Penda said. "Rhymes with mean."

The girl rolled her eyes. Ari got to his feet, conscious of his dry mouth and sweaty nape, wondering if his hair was messed up or if he smelled like a dog's bed. In Deane's steady gaze he felt thin and insignificant and he wished he'd put on more layers this morning.

"Deane, this is Aaron," Penda said.

"I go by Ari, actually."

"Ari." Penda smiled. He had deep dimples in both cheeks. "You and Deane can take Roman straight out that door into the run. He can walk on the paw with the IV, just keep the line out of the way." As he left the room, he gave Deane's ponytail a little tug and said something in Spanish. Ari's ears pricked up but couldn't grasp the words.

The other volunteer, Eve, stuck her head in. "Your uncle was here," she said. "But he saw you were asleep and didn't want to disturb you. He said he'd run some errands."

"Thanks." Ari pulled on his jacket. Deane put on a dark grey windbreaker with *Guelisten High School* in white letters on the back, encircling a grizzly bear's head. She took the IV bag off its pole and coiled the extra tubing up. "Come on, Roman," she said. The dog yawned and got up, stretched his front legs, then the rear and padded toward the outside door. "He's so beautiful. I love his color."

"I think I saw you this morning," Ari said as they let Roman into a small courtyard. "In the bookstore."

She smiled, showing her own dimples. "You did."

Roman stopped every fifth step to shake his needled paw out and sniff it. He took a lopsided pee, then walked around smelling everything, Ari following and holding the IV bag out of the way.

"The woman behind the coffee bar," he said. "Is she your mother?"

"My aunt. My mother owns the dress shop on that same block."

"I saw you in there, too."

And now here.

"Dr. Penda is my dad," she said.

This girl was a ribbon sewing together the events of the day.

Ari crouched down as Roman came to him and turned circles within his arms. Deane had her hands in her pockets and her face turned up to the sun. The light glinted off her different neutral tones. The dun-gold of her hair. The grey of her jacket and the washed-out blue of her jeans. Her pale but pearly skin and the ice storm of her eyes. All the colors Ari saw in winter along the river banks in Morgantown. Hues he associated with poverty and crime. Abandoned houses and crumbling rowboats. Dead fish and broken dreams. A palette turned around and made beautiful on this aloof, slightly sleepy-looking girl with her face in the sun.

"Are you a senior?" she asked.

"Junior."

"Same."

"Do you work here?" he asked.

"I volunteer," she said. "Gets me community service hours. And I like it. Sometimes it's easier dealing with animals than people."

"I know."

"But you also deal with a lot of people who treat animals like shit. That's the hard part."

Ari hummed as she knelt to pet Roman. The wind blew along the fine wisps at her hairline. The pink was rising up in her cheeks. Even through jeans he could see the definition of her quadriceps. Two silver bracelets jingled at her wrist as she scratched Roman under the chin.

Say something.

He swallowed. "You speak Spanish?"

She shrugged. "My dad's from Chile. Do you?"

"A little. Think you want to be a vet someday?"

She smiled and he saw she only had one dimple, not two like her father. "My science grades are shit," she said. "I love animals and I think about running a shelter or something. But I don't know if I could go the full-on veterinarian degree."

"You play sports?"

"I ski. Lacrosse in spring. You play anything?"

"I used to wrestle. Not anymore." As their hands stroked the dog in tandem, their fingers kept bumping, then parting.

"I'm really sorry about your mom," she said. "It must've been horrible."

He looked into the grey eyes. This close, he noticed flecks of gold close to the pupil. Her eyes weren't icy at all. They were warm. Friendly. "Thanks," he said. "It was pretty fucked up."

"I don't want to make you talk about it, I just…"

"I know," he said. "It's all right."

"What will happen to you now?"

"I'm not sure," he said. "I have this uncle. I didn't know I did, my mom never talked about him. But she named him my guardian in her will and he showed up yesterday and…" The rush of words trailed off as he worried he was coming off too pathetic. He shrugged with a careless chuckle. "Sounds like a Charles Dickens story."

"Only if he's rich," she said.

Ari laughed. His face felt stiff around it, as if it had forgotten how to handle a joke.

"Is he cool?" Deane asked. "What's your gut feeling about him?"

"He's all right, I guess. He's not treating me like a baby and he's…honest. I think he's just as thrown off by this as I am. He and my mother hadn't spoken in twenty-five years."

Her eyes widened. "Why?"

The story was on the tip of his tongue but he checked it, biting on the realization it was only half the story. Jav's half. And the other half was lost forever.

Deane shook her head. "Never mind, it's none of my biz," she said. "I'm glad you had someone who can help you. And man, I'm glad Roman's all right. My dad said he's never seen this kind of poisoning before. It was pretty hairy that first night."

"I know," Ari said. "And from gum. Who saw that coming?" Gum made him think of his mother's purse spilled across the floor, the strap laying across her open palm.

Did she see it coming? Did she die right away? Did it take a while? Was she scared? Was she sorry? Did she call out for me?

He squeezed his eyes, like hitting the power button on the TV remote. He put his face against Roman's head and let the dog's panting breath warm his ear.

Deane sat cross-legged now. "Do you think you'll stay at your school the rest of the year?"

"I guess. I'm right in the middle of my portfolio, it would suck having to switch schools now."

Her eyebrows raised. "Like an art portfolio?"

"Yeah. I'm in this fast track program for visual arts."

"I love art," she said. "I only do it for fun, though."

"What do you do?"

"Mostly paper collage. I'm obsessed with paper, it's really stupid. I collect it the way my mother collects fabric swatches. I like watercolors, too."

"I suck at watercolors," Ari said. "I can't control a brush to save my life. Give me pencils or markers any day."

"I'm obsessed with magic markers."

"I love a new pack," he said. "You know how you open a new thing of markers and they're all lined up in color order, and none of the tips are smashed or dry. It's like you've got the world at your fingertips."

"New box of Crayola crayons," she said. "Sixty-four colors. All the points are perfect and none of the labels are peeling."

"Don't touch them," Ari said. "You want to color, use the shoebox full of peeled, broken crayons. These are for display only."

She was laughing and nodding, her ponytail sliding across one temple. Ari's eyes picked out the different shades, remembering Crayola colors like tumbleweed, desert sand, raw sienna.

And beaver.

He swallowed and looked away. *Nice, dude.*

The outside door banged open then and they both turned. A blond boy stood there.

Jesus, what's with the blonds in this town, Ari thought.

This one was tall and husky and good-looking. An alpha aura filling the doorframe, wearing an identical jacket to Deane's.

"Hey, you," Deane said.

"Here you are. What's going on, baby?"

Ari had been expanding in Deane's friendly presence and just starting to touch the edges of attraction. Now he felt his bones shrink inside his clothes as he immediately guessed who had shown up.

Shit.

"I thought you were working at Celeste's today," the boy said, reaching a hand down to her.

"No, it's Saturday," Deane said, taking it and letting herself be pulled up. "I'm here."

"Damn, that's a cool-looking dog," the boy said. "What happened to him?"

"Case, this is Ari," Deane said.

"Hey," Ari said, transferring the IV bag into his left hand so he could shake the hand being offered.

"Casey," the boy said, holding the shake an extra moment, as if measuring, then letting go and sinking onto a knee. He held a hand out to Roman, who took an extra moment of his own to sniff it out. When he acquiesced to being petted, he looked sideways at Ari with a resigned expression.

Thanks, bud, Ari thought. *I feel the same.*

"Is he a retriever?" Casey asked. "I've never seen one this copper color."

"He's a Toller," Ari said. "It's a Canadian breed."

"Gotcha." Still scratching Roman's head, Casey looked up at Deane. "What time you get out?"

"Four."

"Can you get sprung any earlier?"

Deane blinked coolly. "No. Sorry. It's really busy today."

"What about tonight," Casey said. "Russ and Joey might get a keg from Joey's brother, tap it over at Grayson's Field."

"Kind of cold for an outdoor kegger," Deane said, her eyes glancing at Ari and moving away again.

"C'mon." Casey reached up and took Deane's hand, making her bracelets jingle.

"I'll see." She looked more directly at Ari now. "You need help taking Roman in?"

"Nah, I'm good," Ari said, arranging his face into a careless smile. "Nice meeting you. I'll see you around here, I guess."

He pulled up to the top of his six feet as he walked toward the building, imagining his shoulders pulling wide and the air getting the hell out of his way. He didn't look back to see if Deane was watching him go. He led Roman inside and caught the door with a foot before it could slam.

THE CLEAN PLATE CLUB

*W*HEN JAV CAME back to the shelter, Ari looked worn down to a thread. From the far end of the kennel, Jav stared as his nephew said goodnight to his dog. Deep in his bones he felt a strange tug. Something that felt like ownership, but at an instinctive level. Could it be the bond of blood?

I just met him, he thought. *Yesterday, I wouldn't turn my head if I passed him on the street. Today he feels like mine.*

"I talked to your lawyer and the police chief in Morgantown," Jav said as they headed outside. "I can take you over to your house. If there's anything you want to get from there."

"Yeah," Ari said. "Would you mind?"

"Not at all."

Ari fell asleep on the drive across the bridge, again in the boneless sprawl of the young, his head curled down against the window in a way that made Jav's neck ache. He exploded awake with a cry when Jav touched his arm.

"Disculpa, disculpa," Jav said softly, patting him. "I need you to navigate."

"Jesus," Ari said, rubbing his face. "I keep crashing."

"Sorry, I know you're tired."

Morgantown crouched like a rat beneath the span of the bridge. Ari directed him through a depressing business district into a run-down residential area. They turned onto a street that was slightly smarter looking, but still a far cry from Guelisten's handsome and healthy lanes high above the river. A police car was parked out front and a tatter of yellow ribbon fluttered from one of the front stoop railings.

"Do me a favor," Ari said, looking out the window as he unbuckled his seatbelt. "Wait here. I won't take long."

Jav detected a vein of embarrassment in the thickened voice and agreed. He wasn't sure himself if he wanted to go in anyway.

The cop let Ari in, then walked down to Jav's car. Jav got out and they chatted a while.

"Shame," the officer kept saying. His badge read Morales. "It's a goddamn shame. Tell you man, I can see the most fucked-up crime scenes—shootings, stabbings, babies thrown in the garbage, guys who set their wives on *fire*. And I'm numb to it. I can turn the feeling off, you know? But I see something like this? Hardworking single mother who never bothered nobody trips on the stairs and her boy is left alone in the world? It haunts me for weeks. I want to go home and cushion all my own stairwells. Tell my wife to go down the steps on her butt."

"It's crazy," Jav said.

Morales pulled at his ear as if it were bothering him. "He'll come live with you now?"

"I'll take care of him, but I've got a tiny place in Manhattan that doesn't take pets. Plus I have to think about his school and his health needs and a bunch of other things. I want him disrupted as little as possible, you know?"

Again, the odd, inherent sense of responsibility. Deep in his bones, as if coded into his DNA and awakened only when in the presence of similar DNA.

Ari came out with two duffle bags.

"Well, in the meantime, would you feed that kid's ass?" Morales said quietly. "Good lord, one good gust off the river and we'll be picking him up in Pough-keepsie."

"Got everything you need?" Jav called. "For now?"

"Yeah."

"Take it one day at a time, my friend," Morales said, and Jav thought he could hear the more anxious subtext: *one step at a time, and watch your step, go down on your butt if you need to.*

⸺

"I WANT YOU to eat something," Jav said, making his voice firm as he pulled into a diner. Ari made no objection, but only ordered some soup. The waitress set down a magnificent Mom-made-this-with-love bowl swimming with tender chicken and wide noodles. Bright orange carrots and slivers of onion and celery. Flecked with fresh parsley. Ari started with slow spoonfuls but accelerated as his stomach warmed up. He drank the last dregs and exhaled, showing the empty vessel to Jav.

"Proud member of the clean plate club."

Jav smiled. "How much you weigh?"

"None of your business," Ari said, puncturing the amiable balloon between them.

"Wow, you killed that quick," the waitress said, picking up the bowl.

"You want another?" Jav asked.

Ari nodded and the waitress put a fist on her hip, smiling around her gum. "How about a cup this time. And a grilled cheese with it, maybe?"

Ari ate it all. Plus a chocolate milkshake and a side of fries that Jav picked at.

"You're a junior, right?" Jav said. "Have you started looking at colleges yet?"

Ari nodded, wiping his mouth. "Mostly the SUNYs. Purchase and New Paltz have good visual art programs."

"That's what you want to pursue?"

"Yeah."

"What medium?"

Jav was expecting a shrug but Ari answered without hesitation. "Illustration and sequential art. Animation, too, and minor in creative writing."

Jav closed his eyes, letting the pieces fit together. "Sounds like you want to be a graphic novelist."

"I do."

"What drew you to that?"

Now the shrug, but justified, because it was never any one thing but an array of influences. "I always loved comics," Ari said. "I'd trace and color them when I was little. Then I started making my own. And I kind of have a reading disability. I can't process big chunks of text. My eyes freak out and start wandering all over the place. I have to use this card when I read: it has a two-inch wide window cut in it so I cover the page and only see a block of text at a time."

"That's smart."

"My remedial reading teacher thought of it. She was awesome, had a lot of cool and creative ideas. When my class started reading harder books, I was having a really tough time. She was the one who got me the graphic novel version of *Canterbury Tales*. When I'd read them side-by-side, it clicked all of a sudden. I could understand what I was reading and I *liked* what I was reading. For the first time in my life, I was reading on my own for pleasure. Graphic novels changed my life."

Ari was barely drawing a breath. It was the most animated Jav had seen him.

"I started collecting them," Ari said. "I convinced the school libraries to get copies because I couldn't be the only kid with this issue, right? Graphic novels can be a godsend for kids who struggle with reading comprehension. I did a whole exhibit on it for the freshman science fair."

"Tell me about it."

"Well, I had to get my English teacher on board. We divided the class into three groups. One read the straight text. The second read the text side-by-side with the graphic novel. And the third read only the graphic novel."

"What was this for, what book?"

"*Tale of Two Cities.*"

"Gotcha. And then you compared test scores at the end?"

Ari nodded around his straw. "Drilling down into short answer, reading comprehension and essay questions. The essays were where you could really see the difference. Kids who read the text side-by-side with the graphic novel blew the other groups away."

"No shit? And you took this study to the science fair?"

"Yeah. I won second place. Got beat by a kid who built a robot. Figures." He slumped back in his seat, as if the exchange drained him. "Did you go to college?"

"In fits and starts. I got an associate degree from Hostos. Then a bachelor's from CUNY. It took a bunch of years because I was working at the same time."

Ari chewed on a fry. "Must've been hard. Being on your own, I mean. What did you do for work?"

"Anything I could. I lived hand to mouth for a long time. Waiting tables, tending bar. I did a few things I'm not too proud of, but you do what you have to to survive."

The words were spilling out, starting a story he couldn't finish. Not with a seventeen-year-old kid. Under the table, he kicked his own ankle in a cue to rein it in. "Anyway," he said. "I met a woman who helped me get my act together and eventually, I got into writing."

Ari slurped at the last of his milkshake. Hungry, rattling bubbles from the bottom of the glass, intent on getting every last bit. "Can I see your tattoos?" he asked.

Jav pushed his sleeves up further and showed the inked designs.

"Nice," Ari said. "They have a story?"

"Everything has a story," Jav said. "These don't have a particularly happy one."

"I'm guessing you save it for date five or six?"

Jav was about to jokingly agree, when he felt a ghostly hand touch the nape of his neck and a remembered voice say, *Tell him. Simple story. You have until the light changes.*

"I lost a good friend on Nine-Eleven," he said.

"I'm sorry," Ari said.

Jav touched the dragonfly. "This one was his. I mean he had it on his arm and I copied it. The wheel is… Kind of hard to explain, but to me, he was one of those *Captain, My Captain* kind of guys. Know what I mean?"

Ari nodded. "Like he's on the other side helping to steer you now."

"Exactly."

"That sucks. I'm really sorry."

"Thanks." Jav pulled his sleeves down. "So. You have any savings for college?"

Ari rolled his lips into a tight line. "Some," he said. "Tom Kingston… Let's say he didn't only screw my mother."

Jav felt his eyes widen. "He cleaned you out, too?"

"Yeah."

"Jesus…"

"We got some of it back after he was convicted. But… Heroin, man. It's like a jealous God. Demands everything, takes everything." Ari's eyes focused intently on his fingers, which were shredding a napkin.

"Do you have any after school jobs?"

"I work three days a week at the library and Starbucks on the weekend."

"Mm." Jav laced his fingers together and set his chin on top. He tapped his thumbs, thinking about all he had to do.

"How long do I have to stay at Lark House?" Ari asked.

"Well. I can take you back to my place in Manhattan. But one, it's a small place. Two, it interrupts your school year and takes you away from your jobs and the precious few things familiar to you. Including your dog. Who wouldn't be allowed in my building."

Ari's eyes stabbed Jav's with bald alarm. "So I have to stay in Guelisten then?"

"Residential details aside, is Guelisten an acceptable place? Is it close enough to Morgantown High, close enough to your work? Close to your endocrinologist who, by the way, needs to see you in a week. Right now I'm most concerned about your safety, your health and your education, in that order. What's the most pressing concern you have right now?"

"I want to be near Roman."

"Staying at Lark House solves that problem."

"I want to keep working. I have to keep working. I want to be near Roman. I want to graduate and go to college."

"And be safe."

"I guess. Yeah." All the poised maturity dropped from his face like flakes of dead skin and now he looked young and frail.

"I'm sorry. You're wiped out," Jav said. He caught the waitress's eye and signaled for the check. "I'll stop asking you questions and take you back."

"Thanks," Ari said. "And thanks for dinner."

LITTLE THINGY

"¿Qué onda, cosita?" Deane's father said as they were driving home from the shelter. He always spoke Spanish to her when they were alone. Deane's fluency was excellent, but reluctant. She knew it made Alex happy when she used his native tongue. Deane wanted to make him happy, but being able to speak a language exclusively with Alex wasn't fair to her mother.

As an athlete, Deane held fairness in high regard.

"It was so sad about that boy," she said.

"I know."

"His mother just…fell down the stairs."

"Unbelievable, right?" He had one hand on the wheel. The other elbow rested on the window ledge and his fingers tapped his mouth. In the last, slanting rays of the sun's light, the lines in his face looked deeper.

Stella always said Alex was killer handsome. Personally, Deane thought he was kind of dorky-looking. Especially with his glasses. Clark Kent on the other side of forty. His ears stuck out a little and he had deep dimples. As he'd gotten older, those dimples lengthened, framing his wide smile like parentheses. He still had all his hair, but lately it showed more grey than brown. If he didn't shave a few days, his beard came in full of silver.

On the other hand, he had beautiful, intense green eyes. He went to the gym before work every morning and ran with Deane on the weekends. His stomach was flat, his shoulders broad, his arms strong, defined and tattooed. When he walked away, Val always stared after and murmured, "Look at that butt."

Sometimes, he took off his glasses and glanced up at whoever was speaking, the lines around his mouth blurred by beard growth, his hair tousled just the right way. And Deane would be filled with a possessive pride, thinking yes, her father could, objectively, be considered an extremely handsome man. Even killer.

Ari Seaver, the boy whose mother died and whose dog was poisoned, wasn't exactly killer, but... *Damn*, Deane thought. She'd barely been able to take her eyes off him. Ari was the polar opposite of Casey Bradshaw's golden good looks. Dark hair tumbling over his forehead and eyes the color of milk chocolate. Long lashes and eyebrows so smooth, Deane kept wanting to run her finger along them. But God, he was thin. Uncomfortably thin. With such a maelstrom of sadness and fear and shock in his face, it tore Deane in two. Half of her wanted only to look at him while the other half couldn't bear what she saw. For a brief moment, when their fingers touched within the dog's fur, she felt his pain crackle up her arm. Then she wanted to run away while only wanting to stay and guard him.

That hurt like hell.

Let me feel it again.

Empathy, she thought, wondering how she could collage it. A hand on someone's shoulder. But not on it. *In* it. She shuffled imaginary pieces of paper, layering them. Human touch sinking beneath the skin to become one with someone's experience. In her mind she touched Ari's shoulder, felt bone and muscle and sinew and pain. All sharp-edged and skeletal.

"He was so thin," she said.

"I saw that. I don't know if that's his build or if something else is going on. Poor kid."

He hurts to his bones, Deane thought. She imagined walking through her front door and finding her mother dead. Val drove her batshit, but it didn't mean Deane wanted to discover her flung on the floor like a rag doll. Her blonde hair spilling across a grey, frozen face, catching in a half-open mouth. Blank eyes staring up at the ceiling. Victim of a stumble.

One misstep, one stupid trip and everything could change.

"You all right, cosita?" Alex said.

I'm upset, she thought, trying to distill her emotion down to a single word. The world was tenuous and uncertain tonight. Ari's plight now all tangled up with her confusion about Casey and sticking in her throat.

She reached across the console to Alex's arm, tracing the two bands tattooed around his right bicep. Her name and her mother's name inked into her father's skin.

"Dad?"

"Yeah, babe."

"When did you first fall in love?" she asked in Spanish.

Alex's head turned toward her, then back to the road. "With your mother?"

"With anyone."

He drew in a long thoughtful breath, then exhaled it. "I guess it was Amanda. I was with her most of college."

"You loved her." Her fingertips traced the long scar across his elbow, then she took her hand away.

"Well, she wasn't the love of my life, obviously. But your first love is important. It goes in your Hall of Fame. Looking back now, it's easy to dismiss it and say I didn't know what I was doing or didn't have a clue what love was. My opinion now doesn't change what I felt then. Back then, I believed it was love. It felt like love."

Deane hummed.

"That's all that matters, cosita. What you believe and what you feel now. Later on, you might feel differently. Later you might be able to explain it better. But it doesn't ever change how you felt at the time. Cachai?"

She didn't get it. What she felt now was ten kinds of shitty and she couldn't explain any of them, in any language. Her throat squeezed the tears out of her eyes.

Alex leaned back long in his seat, reaching in his pocket for his handkerchief. It was another of his dorky ways, one Deane found slightly gross, especially during cold season. But this handkerchief was clean, pressed neatly into a folded square. It smelled a little like spearmint from hanging around the gum Alex always carried on him.

This was her father. He had her name on his arm. He carried a handkerchief and gum. He called her cosita, "little thingy." He answered her questions about love. And when she cried for no reason, he didn't ask what was wrong. He only reached to wrap her ponytail around his hand and said, "Hoy ha sido duro."

Today was hard.

AFTER-DINNER MINT

*J*AV HELPED ARI unpack, putting clothes in drawers and lining books on top of the dresser. All ten volumes of Neil Gaiman's *Sandman*. A compilation of Marvel comics. An illustrated atlas of Tolkien's Middle Earth. A *Peanuts* treasury and a thick tome on the art of Maurice Sendak. He sensed Ari had more books at home, but these were the essential favorites he needed close by.

Ari put pencils and markers into jars, stacked pads of paper and sketchbooks on the desk. Jav wanted to see his nephew's artwork, but decided to wait. The kid needed sleep.

"I'll be back in the morning," he said. "You, me and Lauren will have a meeting to figure out how you're going to get to school. You'll probably have to bus it a while until we can get the deed of your mother's car transferred. Take care of the registration."

"What about insurance?"

Jav paused. "Good question. I don't have any."

"Whose car are you driving?"

"A friend's," Jav said, adding yet another post-it note to the thousand stuck around his brain. "I don't own one. I'll have to call the agent, talk about getting the policy transferred into my name. Or opening a new one. Or buying a car. Maybe leasing one. Never mind, I'll figure it out."

Slowly Ari nodded, as if finally realizing how dozens of logistical details of his life were now being transferred, his personal deed changing hands. "Thanks," he said.

"You don't have to thank me," Jav said. "None of this comes at a price."

The air in the room swelled, looking from one man to the other, not sure what to do.

"You have my cell number?" Jav said.

"Yeah."

"Call if you need anything. I'm here."

Ari took two stumbling steps toward his uncle. He didn't put arms around Jav, only lurched against him and put his head down, hands by his sides. Jav caught him tight, spread his palm wide on the back of Ari's head and held him.

This is my sister's son.

"It's all right," he said. "We'll get it figured out."

Ari exhaled ferociously. His body trembled once, then went still. "I'm so fucking tired."

"Come on," Jav said, rubbing the boy's back. "Brush your teeth and put your head down. Today's finished."

Ari stepped back, dragging the heel of his hand across an eye. "Going to bed at seven," he said. "I haven't done this since I was five."

Jav's own feet stumbled as he walked to his car. Bed didn't sound like a bad idea but he had to get some writing done. Maybe the bookstore, Celeste's, would still be open and he could sit with his laptop and bang out a thousand words.

The intoxicating smell of paper and coffee wrapped around Jav as he collapsed on a stool, face buried in his hands.

"That bad?" the androgynous blonde woman asked.

"Today kicked my *ass*."

"Looks like it."

She poured coffee into a big mug. Generous and round, like a D-cup breast, and just as lovely between Jav's palms.

"Are you Celeste?" Jav asked.

"No, Celeste was my aunt. This was her shop."

"What's your name?"

"Trelawney Lark. No Harry Potter references, please. I was twenty-five when they were written."

Jav laughed.

"You wouldn't believe the number of people who ask if my parents named me after Sybill."

"Is there any significance to the name?"

"Yes," she said. "It's the name of a village in Zimbabwe. My father was doing missionary work there and found me under a tree."

Jav gazed at her over the rim of his cup. "I detect some sass here."

"Enough about me." She leaned on her elbows. "Tell me about your day."

Before Jav could think twice, he pulled the release lever on the dump truck and out spilled the estrangement from his sister, the plight of her death and his sudden guardianship of Ari. Trelawney listened with few interruptions. Then took his cup away and had a short conversation with the other barista before coming back to Jav.

"Hungry?" she asked.

The fries he'd nibbled at the diner seemed a year ago. "Kind of."

"Let's go next door."

He followed her like a duckling, happy for someone else to make decisions. The restaurant next to Celeste's was a tapas winebar. And packed. Trelawney squashed her way through the crowd, a fold of Jav's jacket in her fingers. Turning her head this way and that, smiling, waving, calling hello at everyone. They reached the far end of the bar and two empty stools with "reserved" signs on the seats. Trelawney plucked the signs away and beckoned Jav to sit.

"Nice," he said. "You know the owner?"

"I am the owner," she said.

"Of the restaurant?"

"Of the building." She leaned forward on her elbows to be kissed by the bartender. "Can we get a bottle of the Cono Sur? And two orders of the Brussels sprouts to start."

"Not a big lover of sprouts," Jav said.

"You'll love these. They're deep-fried in peanut oil. You need one order to eat and the other to make out with."

She was right. They chatted with ease, licking their fingers as the bartender set plate after plate in front of them.

"Is your nephew comfortable at Lark House?" she asked.

"For the moment. The tree fort there is unbelievable."

"My brother helped build it."

"Really? Your brother is The Treehouse Guy?"

She nodded as she wiped her mouth. "That he is."

The excellent fare filled up the emptiness inside Jav as the wine smoothed out some of the worry in his head.

"Feel like a walk?" she said afterward.

"Sure," Jav said, wondering if he'd stumbled into a date. Trelawney hadn't touched him, hadn't leaned a millimeter into his personal space or given off a trace of sexual chemistry. He nibbled on the curiosity like an after-dinner mint as he stepped into the cold night and Trelawney made a last round of goodbyes behind him.

"Lark's," he said, pointing to the sign above the restaurant. "I keep seeing that name today."

"This is the Lark Building," she said. "My family's been in Guelisten forever."

"Forever?"

"Well, at least as long as the railroad has."

"And now you own it." Jav stepped back from the sidewalk, taking in the brick facade. "What about Lark House?"

"My great-aunt Billie founded it in the thirties. It's privately owned now, the Larks have nothing to do with the running, although my brother sits on the board."

"And, full circle, he built the treehouse there."

"Well, that's stretching the truth a bit. He worked on it during the construction but he didn't design it. Still, it helped him find his calling. You could say the treehouse built Roger."

"I'm having déjà vu again," Jav said, looking up, then down the street.

"Have you ever been here?"

"No," he said. "But for the second time today, I feel like I know this place." The vague recollection buzzed at the edge of his mind, like a persistent gnat. He couldn't swat it. Was he remembering a sliver of a dream? Something from a movie?

They crossed the tracks and went down to the water, but the wind off the river was brutal and they retreated back to Main Street.

Back in front of Celeste's, Trelawney took out her keys and unlocked the narrow door next to the shop.

"You live here?" Jav asked.

"No," she said. "I'm showing you something."

Jav followed her upstairs, eyeing her slender hips. Come to think of it, getting unexpectedly and spontaneously laid wouldn't suck. One load blown after the awesome dinner and he'd practically go into hibernation. He had a vision of Trelawney's white skin against his dark skin and felt things stirring in his jeans.

Trelawney unlocked another door at the top of the stairs and led him inside an apartment. It was furnished but undecorated.

"This is my brother Roger's place," she said. "Meaning he owns it, but I rent it for him. It happens to be between tenants at the moment."

Jav smiled. "You're not thinking of renting it to a high school student?"

"No, I'm thinking of renting it to you."

"You hardly know me."

One of her shoulders rolled. "I'd ask for references and run a credit check, of course."

Jav moved around the space, looked in the bedrooms and realized he liked it here. Not only here in the apartment but in this picturesque-as-fuck, weirdly familiar town. He leaned on the windowsill, looking over the train station and the bluff to the dark shadow of the river. The Mid-Hudson Bridge lights were like diamond necklaces. A sullen cluster of bulbs on the opposite shore, where Ari's house stood alone and empty.

Theoretically, he could work from anywhere. He'd need to take a few months off, for sure—get Ari settled and see what it was like guarding a teenage boy. To write, Jav only needed a laptop and WiFi access. Escorting might be difficult. Not so much to do as to hide what he was doing. It was either keep it under the radar or stop.

Jav didn't want to stop.

He sighed. It would be a disruption for him, but the least disruptive solution for Ari was right here, beautifully laid out for the benefit of all. Even himself.

"Think about it," Trelawney said. "Take my number and let me know."

"I'm having the weirdest day."

"I'll bet."

He turned from the window to face her. "It almost seems too easy," he said. "All these pieces falling into place."

Her chin tilted and the smile playing around her full lips was a beautiful thing. "Do you believe in coincidences?"

"Today? No." Hands in pockets, he walked over to her. Stood still and let her look at him. "Where to now?"

Her eyes gave him the up-down. "I know what you're thinking."

"Do you?"

"Not really, but it's fun guessing."

He remained still, used to letting women get used to him.

"I like your company and your chemistry," Trelawney said. She looked at her watch. "And on that note, I have to get home." She smiled at him. "Alone. But thanks for wondering."

He was disappointed but not devastated. He'd be content to rub one out and then crash sideways across the king-sized bed in his hotel room. His jaw split in a humongous yawn as they went back down the stairs and out on the street.

A couple came down the sidewalk, walking a dog. The man had his hands in the pockets of a leather jacket. His breath made little clouds in the night. The woman had blonde hair peeking out from a wool cap. Her hand was tucked in the man's elbow. They were laughing.

The tickle at the edge of Jav's mind became a caress.

I know this place.

The couple came closer. Close enough for Jav to see the dimples creasing the man's smile and remember all the nights Jav went out of his way to see that smile. Close enough to hear the staccato peal of the woman's laugh and remember how beautiful it sounded in the dark.

"Hey, guys," Trelawney called. "That's my sister and her husband," she said to Jav.

"The dollhouses," Jav whispered.

"What?"

"Hey," the man said. "What's going on?" His eyes flicked from Trelawney to Jav, blinked twice and then stared. His chin tilted. "Do I…"

"Oh my God." The woman Jav only knew as Valentine stepped back and put her hands over her mouth.

"Alex." Jav bit the name out of the air and let the X hiss against the roof of his mouth. His mind blew dust off an old notebook, opened it to the page where he'd left off and picked up a pen.

Where were we?

"Holy *shit*," Alex said, his mouth hanging open.

Trelawney looked around the gaping trio, confused. "You guys know each other?"

Jav backed away. His shoulder blades thumped the wall of the Lark Building and he slowly sank to sit on the steps. The dog sniffed at his legs. Valentine's eyes were wide above her gloved fingers. Alex's laughing breath made clouds in the night.

"Holy shit, it's Javier Soto," he said. "Walker, nephew and occasional assassin."

Jav put his head in his hands. "Jesus Christ." He looked up and cried out to Main Street, "I am having the *weirdest* day…"

HE MISSES US

"**I**'M GOING TO bed," Alex said. "I'm beat."

Val glanced at her watch—it was ten of midnight. She took off her reading glasses and looked back at Alex. "I'm kind of in a thing here," she said. "I'll wait up for Deane. She should be home soon."

He came in and kissed her forehead. "'Night." He kissed her nose. Then her mouth. Then her mouth again. "Don't stay up too long."

"I thought you were beat."

"I am." He bent and kissed her neck, inhaling long.

Val's eyes jumped around the computer screen as Alex's footsteps went up the stairs and over her head. The scrape of their bedroom door closing. Then water running through the pipes.

She got up and closed the door to her workroom, putting her back to it and letting out the breath she'd been holding for an hour.

Javier Soto.

Or rather, Javier Landes.

He'd howled laughing when Alex dug a business card out of his wallet. Worn and creased after being carried around for twenty years.

"The hell are you doing with that?" Jav said. "Are you kidding me?"

"In case I need someone bumped off," Alex said.

"Man, that's not even my name." Jav plucked the card out of Alex's fingers and tried to tear it up. Alex snatched it back to more hoots of laughter. Meanwhile, Val stood staring like an idiot with a frozen smile stretching her face to the breaking point.

Javier...Whatever his last name was.

Right here on Main Street.

And gorgeous. Still. Maybe even more so. Absurdly, unfairly gorgeous.

"I know him from my nights waiting tables in the city," Alex was saying to Trelawney. "He used to come in after hours to eat dry toast and make the waitresses faint."

"I can see why." Trelawney turned expectant eyes to Val. *And where do you fit into this little triangle?*

Val moved a casual finger between the two men and herself. "Alex met him first. I met by association."

Jav gave her a quick glance, then looked away. "This is crazy."

It took a few minutes standing in the cold to tell the story and sort out what the hell all of them were now doing in Guelisten. Of course Alex already met Jav's nephew that afternoon at the shelter. And of *course*, Alex, being the clueless sweetheart he was, invited Jav and the nephew for brunch tomorrow. Val could only nod and shrug assent. Sure, come over. Why not? Life was too short not to have your old lover come for brunch.

Lover. That was generous.

Jav gave Alex a new card, insisting yes, Javier Landes was his real name. Walking away with Alex, Val turned back, caught her sister's eye and said, "I'll call you."

The Lark sisters did not call each other. Their homes were mere blocks apart and less than fifty feet separated their places of business. They didn't call, they barged in or dropped by or showed up.

In Lark sister-speak, "I'll call you" meant, *I've got a really big, really bad problem and I need to talk to you. Pronto.*

Trelawney picked up her phone within half a ring. "Pronto."

"Fuck me."

"I made popcorn," Trelawney said. "I cannot *wait*. Talk really slow."

Val told, speaking both slow and soft.

"In conclusion, this isn't your typical ex-boyfriend situation," she said.

"Uh. No," Trelawney said.

"Are you disgusted with me?"

"For what? Hiring an escort? Men do it all the time. Why not women?"

Val exhaled.

"You did nothing wrong," Trelawney said. "You weren't even with Alex at the time."

"It was twenty years ago."

"You were young and single. Immersed in your career. You paid him to be the perfect boyfriend when you didn't have time for relationships. You needed a job done and he did the job. It's nobody's business but yours. And his."

"And maybe Alex's now?"

"Oh… He doesn't know?"

Val chewed her thumbnail. "No."

"Are you going to tell him?"

"Christ, I don't know."

Trelawney crunched popcorn. "Yeah, I don't envy you that conversation."

The front door opened and slammed. The strange girl who squatted in this house, whom Val sometimes referred to as her daughter, was home.

"I'm home," Deane yelled.

Val covered the phone with a hand. "I'm in my workroom," she called. They lived in Muriel's old house on Tulip Street. Muriel's sewing room was now Val's. It had a little worktable for Deane as well. The two of them used to spend hours being crafty, but now Deane preferred to produce her tortured creations in her hidden lair. Or bedroom. Whatever the kids were calling it these days.

"How the hell am I going to tell him?" Val said, running a hand through her hair and tugging on it.

Her door bashed open and Deane put her head in. "I'm home."

"I heard. Have a good time?"

"Where's Dad?"

"Upstairs, he was tired."

Esmeralda, their new kitten, squeezed past Deane's feet and came pattering up to Val, squalling her pathetic little mew.

"What are you doing?" Deane came in and sidled along the counter where Val kept notions. "Are you making something?" Her fingers trailed across ribbon spools and dug into boxes of buttons. Of course. Deane typically couldn't stand Val breathing in her presence, but tonight of all nights, she was feeling lovey and looking for company.

"Hon," Val said. "I'm talking to my sister. Would you…mind?" She cocked her head toward the door with a pleading smile. Deane sucked her teeth, flipped her ponytail over her shoulder and banged out.

"Shoot me," Val said to Trelawney. "To death."

"I can't. I need you."

"Do I have to tell?" Val said. "It was a long time ago. Can't I file it under Secrets of the Broadway Dresser? Let it be like an ex-boyfriend situation?"

"That's all well and good if he's passing through town on his way to Denver or something. He could be sticking around. In Roger's apartment. Indefinitely."

"Ugh."

"And if it gets out later, it has *major* potential to bite you in the ass. Like, you could lose an entire ass cheek. None of your clothes would fit anymore."

"We can't have that," Val said. She flopped onto her little couch, putting her feet up on one arm. Esmeralda clawed her way up and curled into a ball on Val's stomach. Her purr was louder than her mew.

"I must say he's quite easy on the eyes," Trelawney said. "How is he in bed? Worth the money?"

"Oh. God. You have no idea."

Trelawney laughed. "Well, good for you. I can't believe you kept it from *me* all these years. Clearly I was too young to appreciate your escapades."

"I liked it being my little secret," Val said. "It goes into my files as the craziest thing I've ever done."

"Seriously. I can't top that shit."

"And I did it for me. It was fun. I don't feel guilty."

"You shouldn't. But you should think about telling Alex."

"I will."

"Think hard."

"I will. You're coming tomorrow, right?"

"I wouldn't *miss* it. I'll bring the coffee."

"I love you."

"I love you more. Goodnight."

Val let the phone slide onto the floor and let her arm flop over her face. *Seriously, is this a joke?*

If so, fate had one bullshit sense of humor.

Once Jav got up off the ground and they all stopped staring and holy shitting, he hugged her. A quick, laughing embrace. But long enough for her to remember his strength. Tucked in a fold of her mind all this time like a jewel. Her brain picked it up and held it out smugly: *Silly girl. You don't forget a guy who could pick you up like a pillow, pin you against a wall and fuck you nine ways to Sunday without losing a breath or getting tired.*

Those were fabulous dates. Easy. Uninhibited. Whether it was because she was paying or simply because their bodies had a good rapport, Val didn't know or care. Not caring was the *point*. She didn't have to do anything she didn't want to. She didn't have to worry about his satisfaction. She didn't have to do or say a damn thing to him.

Jav did and said it all. As their bodies twined and wound and writhed and combined, the dark of her bedroom filled with amazing words:

"Turn over now."

"I want you so bad."

"You're so beautiful when I'm inside you."

"I was so hard for you all night."

"Your body feels amazing."

"Come."

"Let me see you come."

"I love when you come."

He fucked her senseless, until, drunk on pleasure, high on her own ego and stupid with orgasms, Val could only shape one word in her mouth.

"Yes," she said to Javier Soto. Over and over, "Yes." A thousand times, "Yes." A hundred dollars an hour worth of "Yes."

How in the hell did she sanitize and condense all that into a story she could tell Alex?

I can't. It's pointless. What purpose would it serve? It was a long time ago. Another life. Jav's probably out of the business now and just as happy to let it lie.

Did he even remember their nights? Had she been lost in the shuffle of all the favorites that came after her?

She sighed. Esmeralda gave a throaty little mew.

Come on, Val. Don't make this more than what it is. He was a business partner, not a boyfriend. You can't be lying here wondering what life would be like married to Jav.

She was quick to notice tonight that Jav's left fingers were bare.

He's not the marrying kind anyway.

Hiring an escort was a static, one-sided event, but marriage—or any kind of long-term relationship, was dynamic. A constant give and take. And take didn't always follow give. No orderly turn-taking: *you go, I go. You go, I go. I get a breakdown. You get a breakdown.*

Making bridal gowns for a living made Val philosophical about matrimony: a wedding was an event and had nothing to do with marriage. A wedding was exciting perfection. Marriage was in the boring, unglamorous details. It was sitting on the potty discussing finances while your husband trimmed his nose hairs at the sink. In fact, Val believed marriage was what took place in the bathroom, not the bedroom.

"Don't marry the guy who's your drinking buddy," she told Deane. "Marry the guy who holds your head while you're throwing up, then wipes down the toilet afterward."

Jav was a drinking buddy.

Alex is my life.

And Alex could be difficult to live with.

His childhood flight from Chile had left deep scars on his psyche. His heart swam in blood. He had too many nerves and not enough skin to cover their tender ends. He went into a severe depression after 9/11 that put the sword of their marriage into the forge. It was a tense, anxious year when she feared no amount of sobrepasarlo would be enough to get Alex through or over or around the reverberating trauma in his soul.

Val turned down a design offer with the Atlanta Ballet because he needed her. It was a no-brainer decision. He bought a ticket to Crazytown and she got on the train with him to make sure he used the return.

"I know it's dark," she kept saying. "I know you hate the dark. Believe the light is there. Believe it's going to come back on. As long as you believe, I'm not afraid of this."

She saw him through the tunnel and out the other side. Not pulling from the front, not pushing from behind, but hanging out right by his side. Because he was her man. Because their combined bullshit was bigger, better and more important than all their individual crap. He was a nervous wreck but he was *her* nervous wreck.

She understood perfectly what made Alex tick, but it didn't make him any easier to live with. Still, he was the man she could pee in front of. And it was his disgusting little hairs she wanted in her sink.

Val closed her eyes, looking at the deconstructed pieces of her head and heart.

I only feel guilty about Jav because I don't feel guilty about Jav.

Her phone pinged an incoming text. It was Alex.

I miss you. Please come upstairs.

Val smiled, warmth filling her chest and soothing her worries like a balm. She scooped Esmeralda off her stomach and kissed the sleeping feline face. "He misses us," she whispered. She carefully sat up and put the cat in the nest her body left behind. Turned off lights, locked doors and went upstairs.

Sheba was curled up outside the master bedroom door. A mix of Black Lab and Rottweiler, she was a trained therapy dog and Alex's second wife since 9/11. She and Val had a clear understanding about evening hours: Sheba knew when to show up because nightmares were manifesting, and she knew when to get lost because it was business time.

"Cover your ears, bitch," Val whispered, closing the door.

"Come here," Alex said behind her.

She looked back over her shoulder. He flipped the covers open and sat up in one fluid movement. Naked and beautiful on the edge of the bed.

"Come here," he said, hands reaching.

Mouth watering, she went.

"Look at you," she said, kissing each corner of his mouth. "Who's the most gorgeous fucking husband in the world?"

His hands slid around her hips, curved over her ass and then dug under the hem of her shirt and glided up her back. "Me?"

"Damn right. All six feet..." Her hand closed around his erection. "Eight inches of him."

His smile nudged hers. "Seven and a quarter."

"I round up."

His mouth closed soft around her bottom lip, then her top. "Is the door locked?"

"Mm-hm." Her hands ran along his hard arms. Each bicep banded with inked names. His parents, The Disappeared Ones on his left arm. Valerie and Deane on his right.

He drew her shirt over her head, unclipped her bra and spread it open. One warm, wide hand curved around her breast and his mouth opened for it, drawing it in and sucking gently. His other hand eased down the back of her pants, caressing her.

They kissed, holding each other's heads. He fed her fingers to suck on, gave her his tongue, pulled her deeper into his mouth. She licked her fingers and ran them over his penis, which was up hard and high in his lap, a faint pulse under her palm. She undid the drawstring of her sweats and pushed them down.

"Come here," he said, lying back. "Come on me."

She tossed and kicked her pants away and crawled up on him, kissing, a hand tight in his hair.

"Slow," he said against her mouth. "Let me feel it slow."

"Good?" she whispered, drawing him inside her.

"Yes."

"Like that?"

"So good."

He was warm as bread. Simple ingredients, finely crafted. She held his head, hand wide on his face, drawing his voice into her mouth. "I love you," she said.

"Am I yours?" he whispered.

"Mine. Mine and only mine. Only you for me, Alejandro."

SUNDAY

ONE MORE BEAUTIFUL WOMAN

"**D**R. PENDA INVITED us for brunch," Jav said when he picked Ari up the next morning.

Ari had spent another sleepless night, waking up hungry, depressed and grouchy. "The vet invited us for brunch?" He didn't feel like being social but this was an interesting invitation.

"Want to hear something crazy?" Jav said. "I know him. I met him and his wife once, like twenty years ago."

"Seriously?"

"Yeah. Ran into them after I dropped you off last night. Three of us nearly passed out."

"That's nuts. Can I still see Roman?"

"Roman's invited for brunch, too."

Ari got into the car, biting the inside of his cheek to keep from asking if Deane would be at this gathering. He hoped she would. Of course, Casey at the Bat could be there as well, in which case Ari would figure out a way to take Roman on a nice long walk.

To Poughkeepsie.

Roman, free of his IV, came barreling out of his cage and into Ari's arms, turning in circles, leaping, panting and whining. He bounded into the back seat of the Range Rover and sat with his paws on the center console, licking Ari's ear.

The Pendas' house was a beautiful, pale gold Victorian with red trim and white woodwork. The mailbox read *The Lark-Pendas, 14 Tulip Street*. Jav rang the bell and barking ensued from within. Ari wound up some of the slack on

Roman's leash, shortening it. Roman was usually all right with strange dogs, but strange dogs weren't always all right with him.

Dr. Penda opened one of the double front doors. He was unshaven in jeans and a thermal shirt and not wearing his glasses. He looked like a younger brother of the man Ari met yesterday. Heeled tight to his side was the blackest dog Ari had ever seen. Its fur so ebony, it was almost blue, lying like fine velvet along the high-domed head. It moved slightly in front of Alex and sat on its haunches, blinking at the guests.

"This is Sheba," Dr. Penda said. "Come here, Roman. Say hello to the lady."

Sheba sat perfectly still as Roman sniffed her all over, moving only when he tried to get his nose near the base of her tail.

"As if," Dr. Penda said, laughing.

"Dude, not on the first date," Ari said, drawing him back. "Sit."

Jav had crouched down to let Sheba check him out. "She's beautiful. Black lab?"

"Mix of lab and Rottweiler," Dr. Penda said.

"Alex," a woman's voice called from inside. "Are you going to serve them on the porch? It's freezing out, come in."

Mrs. Penda wore skinny jeans, black converse sneakers and an oversize cashmere sweater that might have belonged to her husband. She shook Ari's hand, kissed Jav and ushered them into the large kitchen. The barista from Celeste's was standing at the island, rinsing strawberries in a colander.

"This is my sister, Trelawney," Mrs. Penda said.

"We've met," Trelawney said, shaking Ari's hand. "In my shop yesterday."

"I remember." Ari swallowed, tongue-tied, actually hoping Deane wasn't around because one more beautiful woman at this party and he would be sporting wood. He retreated a nonchalant distance and crouched down by Roman, petting him.

"Orange juice, Ari?" Mrs. Penda said from behind the refrigerator door. "Or I have cranberry juice. Or water. And coffee, of course. Which Trelawney made."

"Of course," Trelawney said.

"I'll have coffee," Ari said. "Thanks."

Mrs. Penda shut the door. "You met my daughter yesterday, right? At the shelter?"

"Deane."

"Yes. She had plans with her friend, Stella, today. Maybe they'll be back before you leave."

"No biggie," Ari said, happy she wasn't with Casey.

"Here you go, my man," Trelawney said, setting a big mug down on the counter. "You can doctor it up yourself."

Ari slid onto a stool at the kitchen island. Down at one end, Jav and Dr. Penda were drinking bloody marys, laughing and speaking Spanish: Jav like a machine gun, Penda slower and sing-song. Trelawney cut up fruit for a salad and her sister rummaged in a low cabinet. Ari peered closer. Perched on Mrs. Penda's shoulder was a grey tabby kitten, clinging with all claws and mewing as her owner stood up and put a heavy skillet on the stove.

Trelawney's cell phone rang, she put down her knife to take the call in the other room.

"Can I do anything, Mrs. Penda?" Ari said. "Or is it Lark-Penda?"

She threw him a dazzling smile over her shoulder. "It's Val. Short for Valerie. My husband is Alex and the cat is Esmeralda. You can take her away before she falls into the hot grease."

Ari disengaged the tiny claws from Val's sweater, taking the opportunity to inhale some heady perfume. Then he sat down with his coffee again, letting the kitten crawl over him.

Trelawney came back in, two spots of color up high in her cheeks. "That was the historical society," she said. "They're going to take the houses."

"Oh thank *God*," Val said, half turning from the stove. "All of them?"

"All that aren't promised elsewhere. We've officially liquidated." Trelawney caught Ari's puzzled eye. "We've been trying to find homes for my mother's dollhouses so we can renovate the gallery space. This is a huge relief."

"Renovate it into what?" Ari asked.

"Not sure yet," Trelawney said. "But it hasn't turned a profit in years and it's such a prime piece of real estate. It's time to transform."

"Trey loses sleep if she's not turning a profit," Val said.

"It's time," Trelawney said. "Keep the memory, let go of the thing."

"What else is upstairs in that building?" Ari said.

"My brother's apartment," Trelawney said. "Which I rent for him. In fact, I was showing it to your uncle last night."

Ari glanced at Jav, then back at the blonde woman. "What for?"

"To see if he wants to rent it."

Ari stared, sure she was saying something significant but he was missing it. "Rent it for...?"

Trelawney's mouth twitched. "For the two of you," she said. "Until you're done with school. Come work for me and I might lower the lease a little."

"Work for you at Celeste's?" Ari said. "Are you kidding?"

"About coffee and books, I never kid, kid. I'll need manual labor next weekend if you're interested. Big estate sale with ten miles of bookshelves I want to pillage. Think it over."

She picked up the carafe and refilled Ari's cup. Esmeralda crept down from his shoulder and into the pouch of his partly-zipped hoodie. He zipped it a little more to keep her safe and she curled up against his stomach, purring. Beneath his stool, Roman sprawled out, nose on paws. The smell of bacon frying curled around the kitchen.

Ari sighed.

My mother's dead.

He drew a deep breath and let it out. Yes, she was. And she'd want him to be somewhere safe. With people making him feel welcome. He was sure of it.

Eat, he could hear her say. *God, you got so thin. Please, honey, try to eat something.*

Trelawney put some cantaloupe in front of him. He ate it. Val squeezed past to get something out of a cabinet and her hand brushed his back. A mother's hand. Strong and loving. He let it feel nice.

Sheba barked, Roman got up, the kitchen door swung open and Deane came in. She was followed by a pretty Asian girl, who was followed by a golden retriever wearing a blue vest.

"Bacon," Deane said in a moan, lurching like Frankenstein to the stove.

"You're back?" Val said, looking back. "What happened to the movie?"

Stella slid onto the stool next to Ari. "I had an aura," she said. "I had one last night, too, but Henry hasn't given me any alerts. I don't know, I got wigged out being in a dark theater so we came here." She looked at Ari. "Hi, I'm Stella."

"Ari. Hi."

"This beast is Henry. He's a service dog so don't be offended if he ignores you. When the vest is on, he's strictly business."

Deane turned from the stove, juggling hot pieces of bacon in her hands and holding another strip in her teeth. "Hi, Ari," she said around it. "You always catch me with food in my mouth."

He couldn't think of anything to say. Her hair was down, tucked behind her ears and sweeping across her back in all its Crayola colors.

"Oh my God, bacon is life," Stella said. "Mrs. Penda, you're the life-giver."

"Call me Val or I'll kill you."

"I can't. If I start, I'll do it in front of my mother and she'll wring my neck."

"She's so formal," Deane said, putting strawberries and melon on a plate.

"I know, she was born with her ankles crossed," Stella said. Her hand moved in slow strokes over Henry's head. Ari was about to reach to pet him when he noticed the two circle patches on the dog's vest. One was a caduceus surrounded by the words SEIZURE ALERT DOG/MEDICAL ALERT DOG/ON DUTY. The other had a black handprint within a red circle and a bisecting line. PLEASE ASK TO PET ME.

Ari kept his hands to himself and guessed Stella had epilepsy.

Val plated up bacon and took a tray of hash browns out of the oven. Trelawney pushed the bowl of fruit salad toward the center of the island. Nobody suggested or gravitated toward a table. Val tossed a stack of paper plates into the fray and everyone dug in, either sitting or standing.

"Scoot over," Deane said, bumping her hip against Ari's side.

"I'll get up."

"No, no. One cheek sneak."

So they perched, each with half an ass on the stool and their sides touching while they ate. Friendly chatter in two languages around and over the counter. Bacon and potatoes and strong coffee. Three dogs at Ari's feet. Sandwiched between two pretty girls with a kitten inside his sweatshirt.

This was a fucking great party.

TICKET TO CRAZYTOWN

AFTER STELLA WENT home, Deane and Ari sat in the den watching TV. Or rather, Deane sat, holding Esmeralda while Ari prowled the perimeter of the room, looking at her artwork. A gallery of her life's creations, starting on one wall with her kindergarten finger paintings and working around to her watercolors and paper collages.

"This is cool," Ari said, running his finger along a narrow, vertical frame. Deane had outlined three portraits—herself and her parents—as if for stained glass or appliqué, then filled in each section using scrapbook paper. "It's so... *fine,*" he said. "You have to work really close-up."

"I like to," she said. "I kind of fall into the paper. Leave everything else behind."

He kept walking around, his arms crossed, peering up close then standing back. The light from the table lamps caught the shadows in his face as he moved, making him appear healthy and beautiful one moment, then gaunt and troubled the next.

Deane tried to remember if she ever saw Casey walk around the den's walls as if he were at a museum. Come to think of it, she could barely imagine Casey at a museum.

Ari touched a black-and-white photo hanging in the middle of all the color. "Is this your dad?"

"Yeah."

In the picture, Alex hugged Sheba's head on his shoulder, his face turned slightly into her neck. His hair was longer, combed back from his forehead and spilling over his ears.

"That's the day he got Sheba," Deane said. "Love at first sight. My mother calls her The Bitch."

Ari laughed, touching the photo. "He looks older here. Older and sadder."

"He was going through a tough time."

"Oh. Is he all right?" Ari's finger traced the tattoos on Alex's arms, and the long scar cutting across the crook of his elbow. Deane bit her lip.

"He's fine," she said.

But he wasn't, she thought. *He made that scar. With a knife. It was bad.*

Ari came over and ran his hand over Esmeralda's head. His fingers bumped Deane's and moved away. "I had a good time today," he said.

"I'm glad."

"But it's weird. Having a good time. You know? Like how can I possibly be enjoying myself when my mother's dead?"

"She'd want you to," Deane said.

"That's what I told myself. Your mom's real sweet. And I thought, *Well she's not my mother. But she's a mother...*"

He was so close to her. Their fingertips kept touching.

"I'm really sorry about what's happened to you," she said.

"Thanks." He cleared his throat and stepped away. "I'm going to get some water. You want?"

"Thanks."

She stretched full-out on the couch and closed her eyes a moment, filled with a guilty confusion and Sunday afternoon lethargy. Esmeralda curled in a ball on her chest, running like an engine.

Ari came back in, holding two glasses. "Sheba never leaves your dad's side, does she?"

"Rarely," she said. "He had to get her after Nine-Eleven."

Ari heeled off his sneakers and sat in the recliner. Roman jumped up and lay across his legs. "Was he in the city that day?"

"No, my mom was," she said. "She went downtown to meet a friend. For breakfast or something. She was on the subway when they began to hear about the first plane hitting. She was talking to my dad on her cell phone about it. Then she came up out of the subway and right over her head—*whoosh*—the second plane. She saw it hit."

"Holy shit. How did she get off the island?"

"She ran south, along with everyone else. Looked back to see the first tower fall and ran faster. Caught up in that big cloud of dust and debris, you know? She jumped on one of the ferries to New Jersey. It took her the rest of the day to get home. And for a long time, cell service was down and my dad didn't know where she was. That's what messed him up. It triggered something that happened to him when he was a kid. He went into a bad depression afterward."

"Wow."

"He's better now, he's fine. But he still has nightmares. Sheba's trained to help him wake up. She can sniff out anxiety like other dogs sniff out drugs."

"What about your mom?"

Deane half-smiled. "Mom's the strong one. Don't get me wrong, she was shook the hell up. I mean she saw people jumping out of the towers. It was horrible. But it didn't…stick to her. I mean, stick in the folds of her brain and just echo over and over. My dad couldn't get away from it."

Ari nodded. "I see."

Do you? Deane thought. She'd never told Casey about the dark year after 9/11 when Alex went away from them.

"Bought a ticket to Crazytown," was the way Alex referred to it now.

"All tickets to Crazytown are round trip," Val always added.

Deane would pick up her cue: "And all rentals are short-term."

They could make jokes about it. Val said as long as you could laugh at something, it couldn't kill you. But Deane didn't do much laughing while her father was renting a condo in Crazytown. She was twelve. And scared to death Alex had lost his return ticket.

During the day, she was armed with a handful of soft, factual sentences she could say out loud:

My dad's having a hard time.

Dad's a little depressed, but it's going to be all right.

It's just a tough time for him right now. It will get better.

Alone, out of the public eye, or in the dark of a sleepless night, Deane whispered things she couldn't tell anyone.

I hear my father crying sometimes.

Dad's going into the closet to hide.

My father had to go to the hospital.

My dad cut his arm with a knife.

I think my father tried to kill himself…

"Nodding off?" Ari said.

"Yeah." Deane faked a laughing yawn. "Don't take it personally. File it away under Sunday Afternoon."

She did fall asleep. When she opened her eyes briefly, Ari had clicked off the TV and was lying back in the recliner, his hand on Roman's head, his chest rising and falling with long, easy breaths. His face was turned toward her, peaceful and composed. His eyelashes made thick crescents against his cheekbones and his neck looked smooth and strong.

With a jingle of his collar tags, Roman yawned, turned his head and looked at Deane. He appeared to smile at her.

"Hi," she whispered. "Isn't this nice?"

She turned on her side, carefully putting the kitten into the crook made by her knees. Pillowing her hand on her cheek, she dozed off again.

When she woke, the recliner was empty and the house had sunk into a deeper level of quiet. Her parents must be napping too.

Or Doing It.

She sat up to drink some water and saw a piece of paper tucked under her phone on the coffee table. On it was a small, penciled sketch of her asleep with the kitten. Her mouth dropped open at its simple beauty. With its illustrative style, it was almost like a comic.

Underneath the sketch, Ari wrote, *Filed under Sunday afternoon,* and signed his name.

Her phone pinged. It was Stella.

OK, Pooky, I don't fake a seizure onset for just anyone, and I don't fake a seizure onset without payback. I gave you the excuse to go home so DEETS, girl. Spill the tea. He's killer gorgeous and a total sweetie. Did you kiss him?

Deane smiled, her eyes rolling. **No,** she typed. **We just slept together.**

PON FARR

*V*AL'S FAVORITE ASPECT of dressmaking had always been the fine work. The intricate hand-crafting of lace and trim. Attaching a thousand bugle beads or sequins. The tiny, often invisible touches that took a dress from beautiful to stunning.

After napping off the huge brunch, Val went down to her shop to finish up a wedding gown. She took the veil and boxes of tiny pearls and glass beads to the easy chair by the storefront window, where she could both watch and be watched.

Trelawney came in through the back room, bearing a pick-me-up.

"Chocolate hazelnut latte," she said. "Whole milk, no sugar."

"Thanks, baby."

Trelawney poked through the box of beads, letting them sift through her fingers. She picked up the hem of the veil and held it at arms' length, studying the design. Then brought it up close, her perfectly-plucked eyebrows knitting. She let the hem fall with a sigh.

Sighing was unlike Trelawney. So were restless, fidgety gestures. As she stared out the window, her expression was hard and frustrated. Her fingers ran through her cropped bangs, drawing them into a straight line across her forehead. If her hair were black and her ears elongated, she'd look exactly like Mr. Spock. And just as the emotionless Vulcans felt an overwhelming, instinctive urge to mate every seven years—the Pon Farr—Trelawney Lark occasionally experienced a similar phenomenon. Every few years, her solitary, independent asexuality came unraveled into a basket of snakes, all writhing in a crazed desire for...something.

More.

Something more.

Something else.

"Needing?" Val said softly, taking a small scalding sip of her coffee.

Trelawney sank into the other chair, drawing her heels up on the edge of the cushion and wrapping arms around her knees. "Bad."

Val hummed, looking out the window. She had her own Pon Farrs, usually around the turn of the season when it felt like her skin was peeling off, exposing the rawest parts of herself. Parts that wanted to indiscriminately fuck everyone and everything.

It was a hard, roving horniness, almost embarrassing in its frank need. Framed in guilt that Alex, besides being an amazing husband and father, was a sensational and ardent lover. Her life was blessed and superb in so many ways. Yet she had those strange phases of wanting more.

More what?

She had no idea, but it made her imagination tempt young men into her car with candy and puppies.

She had her coping mechanisms. The most effective one was simply to accept what was going on. She found feeding the beast made it tire out. So she read a lot of erotica, surfed a lot of porn, fantasized and jilled off at odd hours of the day. Attacked Alex in the middle of the night. Eventually her skin closed around her bones again and her libido came to its senses. Until the next turn of the season.

She had no idea if Trelawney's Pon Farr was anything like it. Trelawney lived a clean, precise life where sex wasn't a driving force. Still, Val knew her sister got lonely every few years. Bone-achingly lonely. Lonely to a fidgety distraction. No doubt it was the reason the dollhouse gallery would be empty soon. Trelawney needed a new project.

"I'm thinking about having a baby," she said now.

"You're forty-two years old," Val said, setting her coffee cup down, far away from the heap of white voile in her lap.

"Apparently my brain is thirty-six."

"Who's the lucky, imaginary father?"

"I haven't gotten that far in the thinking. Although Javier Landes gives me a big shove from behind."

Val held up a protesting finger but the protest died in her mouth. "I could actually support this," she said, "because it would be an *insanely* beautiful baby."

Trelawney lifted her chin with a closed-mouth grin. "Thank you. I could also ask Francis."

Val laughed. Francis was Trelawney's massage therapist. Fabulously gay, built like a bull and, the sisters joked, the only man who got to see Trelawney naked.

"I could also support that," Val said.

"Well, anyway." Trelawney stood up and kissed Val. "Thanks."

"For what?"

"For playing along and not trying to fix."

"It's not fixable," Val said.

She took another careful sip of coffee and settled back into her chair, picking up her work. She was content. It was still winter and her instincts wanted to nest. Hang around home, making soup and stew and bread. Build fires and take naps. Make love and be nothing but married.

She became aware of a presence on the other side of the window and looked up to see Jav watching her, the tilt of his chin showing interest in her work. Against the grey, chilly skies and the backdrop of the train station, he was beautiful. Jeans and a pea coat, a cup of coffee and his car keys in one deft, casual hand. Obviously on his way back to the city, but lingering, watching her. Just like he used to linger at her bedside before leaving.

Their eyes met and he smiled.

Feeling slightly Pon Farrish, she smiled back.

Hey, little boy. Want some candy?

Part
Three

THE SOUTHERN
HEMISPHERE

CALL WEIGHT WATCHERS

1 *FOUND A FRIEND.*

The sentiment was identical, eerily and fabulously identical to when eleven-year-old Alex rode home from his first trip to Stowe with the Larks. Dozing off with Roger in the back of the station wagon, Alex knew, in a warm haze of certainty, everything was different now. Monday at school would be different. After school would be different. The weekends would be different.

I found a friend.

The moment Alex recognized Jav on Main Street, he felt the same crackle of serendipitous relief.

Finally. I found you. You're here. You're back. Are you staying? You want to hang out? Will I see you at school tomorrow?

Within six weeks, Jav had rented Roger's apartment over the bookstore and moved himself and Ari in. Roman presented a problem: the shelter needed the space he was occupying, and Trelawney was protective of her investments and wouldn't budge on the no pets policy. Ultimately, it was decided Roman would stay with the Lark-Pendas, and Ari had carte blanche to come see his dog whenever he wanted.

At first, Jav, running around like the proverbial chicken, had no time for anything. The legal, financial and spiritual details of getting Ari settled and safe took up all his hours.

The emptying and selling of the home in Morgantown was the most draining ordeal. The house was broken down in coordinated waves. First Ari went through, collecting what he wanted to have and keep and cherish. Some things he took to the apartment, some went into storage. Then an auction company came through. Then the Salvation Army. Last, a volunteer group made up of Guelisten residents and Lark House teens—organized by Alex—cleaned out the rest and threw a coat of paint on the entire downstairs.

One hard-working day, Alex saw Jav wrestle a handful of photographs from where they'd fallen behind a bookcase. Long minutes passed as Jav went through them and something in the tense line of his jaw made Alex curious.

"Find treasure?" he asked, looking over Jav's shoulder. Funny how his memory recalled Jav being much taller twenty years ago when they were actually the same height.

The photos were faded Kodak prints, all of the same three kids against an urban backdrop. Two boys and a girl. Playing in the spray of a fire hydrant. Mugging over ice cream cones. Big toothy grins as they sat cross-legged in front of a Christmas tree.

"Is that you?" Alex said, pointing to one of the boys. Gangly and awkward, but already showing signs of being dangerously good-looking.

"That's me," Jav said quietly. "This is my sister."

"Who's the other guy."

"My cousin. Ernesto." Jav flipped over the last picture. This one of just him and his cousin, later in their teen years. Shirtless and laughing, arms around each other's shoulders.

"Do you talk to him?"

"He died," Jav said. "Long time ago."

"Shit, I'm sorry."

Jav shook his head a little, then gave Alex a closed-mouth grin before lobbing the stack of pictures into one of the ubiquitous industrial garbage bags. His stride walking off was so full of hurt bravado, so don't-give-a-fuck, Alex was moved to retrieve the pictures and tuck them in his pocket. Later he put them in his desk drawer, clipped together with Jav's old business card. He wasn't sure why any more than he knew why he'd kept the card all these years, or lunged so quickly to keep Jav from tearing it up.

Maybe he'll want them back someday, he thought, lingering at his desk and turning the old dagger, Albacete, over and over in his hands.

I'll hold them, he thought. *Like I hold this for my dad. Just in case.*

"OUT OF MY way, fucky," Alex said, bringing the pot of boiling pasta to the sink. Val stepped aside, chopping garlic.

"Did you just call her fucky?" Jav said.

"Don't ask," Val said.

His glasses fogged up with steam, Alex put the empty pot on the stove, then put his arms around Val. "She's my wittle fucky," he said into her neck.

Val's knife never broke rhythm. "This is the crowning achievement of my life, Jav."

"It's the point of getting married," Alex said. "To have a fucky."

"And all this time I thought it was a tax deduction," Jav said, reaching up to get the salad bowl off the shelf. Alex smiled at the ease with which Jav now moved around his house. Knowing where to find dishes and the bottle opener and extra paper towel. Answering the phone or taking out the recycling.

I found a friend.

Jav and Alex hung out, or at minimum touched base every day.

¿Qué lo qué? Can you hang? What you got going on? ¿Qué onda? What's up? Want to grab a beer?

The availability made Alex wonder if Jav was still escorting, until one afternoon when Jav called him with a strange request.

"I know this is weird," he said. "But I'm meeting a new client tonight. She lives at 474 First Avenue, apartment C."

"Oh. You're still…in the business?"

"Yeah. We're going to a charity event at the Cloisters, then back to her place. Probably."

"Why are you telling me this?"

"In case things go south and I end up floating in the East River. You have a trail back to her."

"Jesus, man."

"I know, I know," Jav said. "Usually I write it down and tape it to my mirror. I can't really *do* that anymore with Ari around."

"What did you tell him about tonight?"

"That I have a date. Which, technically, I do."

"Of course," Alex said, wondering if he should find this outrageous. Because he didn't.

"Anyway, someone needs to know where I am. It's the rule. You're the someone."

"I'm honored," Alex said, laughing. "Do I get a cut of the income?"

"No."

Alex had less sexier commitments: rescues, adoption events, school meetings or work meetings. He and Val were taking Deane to visit colleges on weekends. Or they had date nights. The proverbial shit happened. But whenever Alex and Jav got together, planned or spontaneous, it was easy as hell and always a good time.

I'm happy, Alex thought. Which was like reuniting with another sort of long-lost friend. He felt good. More relaxed and content than he'd been in years. And holy crap, he hadn't spoken this much Spanish since his childhood.

"Move, fucky," Jav said, pushing Alex aside so he could get into the fridge.

Val laughed from the stove. "Has a nice ring to it, right?"

From her bed in the kitchen corner, Sheba barked. Roman replied and the two dogs headed out. The front door opened and slammed closed. Footsteps pounded up the stairs and across the kitchen ceiling, followed by the louder slam of a bedroom door.

"That ain't good," Jav said.

A big sigh from Val. "Cause of death: adolescence."

Glances slowly lowered and exchanged around the room. Alex and Val shook fists and did a quick rock-paper-scissors. Alex lost.

"Fuck," he muttered. He wiped his hands on a dishtowel and tossed it at Jav. "Cover me."

"Eres el más valiente," Jav called after him.

Alex picked up a stack of mail that had tumbled off the foyer table from the force of the door slam. Sheba followed him up the stairs, where he arranged his face into neutral lines and turned off the power switch on his Y chromosome, shifting from fix-it mode to listen mode.

"Deane," he said, tapping on her door. "You all right, babe?"

From within he heard sniffling and the distinct sound of tears being muffled.

"Cosita." He turned the knob and cracked the door. Deane lay on her stomach with her face buried beneath pillows and stuffed animals. Alex crouched down and put his hand on her hot, damp head. "¿Qué onda, querida?"

"Nothing."

Alex pulled his cheek in tight to keep from laughing. Teenage girls. They'd be holding a knife to their throat or dangling off the side of a bridge and they'd still say, "Nothing" when you asked what was wrong.

"I see," he said. He pulled his handkerchief out of his pocket and reached around to tuck it in her fingers. "Everything nothing? Or a specific nothing?"

"I got dumped a week before prom nothing," she said, her voice falling apart on the nothing.

"¿Qué mierdas pasó?"

"Casey broke up with me."

"Why?" Which was exactly the wrong thing to say. "I'm sorry—"

"Dad, *please?*" She was crying again.

"I'm sorry, honey. That sucks." He'd woken up the bear and was now frantically pelting it with berries.

"Dad, please just leave me alone."

"All right." He kissed her head and got up. "Stay," he told Sheba, who threw him a look of *I got this,* and lay down on the rug.

He went downstairs rolling his eyes and mumbling. Jav looked up as he came into the kitchen. "Everything all right?"

"You may want to go up for this one, honey," Alex said.

Val turned from the stove. "What?"

"Apparently we've been dumped and we're not going to prom."

"Not going to… Oh, good lord." She downed the rest of the wine in her glass, handed the wooden spoon to Jav and walked out.

Alex popped another beer. "I never liked him."

"Casey?"

"Yeah. I don't even know why. I got no concrete reason not to like him. I just don't."

"It's chemistry. Some people rub you the wrong way on sight."

Alex picked a clump of spaghetti out of the colander and ate it, staring out the back window. Concentrating on keeping his Y turned off, otherwise he'd use it to flatten Bradshaw until the kid had to roll down his socks to shit.

Val stormed back into the kitchen. "Life has *rules,*" she said, pointing first at Alex, then at Jav.

"Here we go," Alex said.

"You do not dump your girlfriend a week before prom. *Especially* if she's bought the dress."

"That's a rule," Jav said. "Why'd he break up with her?"

"I guess he found himself a better date."

"Oh for fuck's sake," Alex said, his face in a hand. "Jav, get the shovel. Forty acres behind Lark House, they'll never find him."

"On it." Jav made a show of going to the back door and then jumped back. "Oh look," he said. "It's Stella."

"Hello," she said from the porch. "Cleanup on aisle eleven?"

"God, Stella, you are my favorite," Val said. "Come in. Please. Save us."

Stella came in, followed by Henry. "Hi, Doc. Hi, Mr. Landes."

"Would you call me Jav already?"

She smiled, showing her lovely teeth. "I'm not allowed."

Deane came into the kitchen, her eyes swollen, her face blotchy.

"Oh, Pooky..." Stella walked over, arms outstretched and gathered Deane in an enormous hug.

"Well this *sucks*," Deane said, sniffing and running Alex's handkerchief under her eyes. "He's taking Brenna Scarsgaard. Can you believe that shit?"

"Who's Brenna Scarsgaard?" Jav asked.

"Queen of the drama club," Val said. "Cagey little bitch."

"Reeow," Stella said, curling imaginary claws at Val.

"When did they become a thing?" Alex asked.

"A week before prom he springs this on you?" Jav said.

"It's fucking humiliating," Deane said.

Stella put arms around her again. "Men are assholes," she said, rocking her friend. "No offense, Doc."

"What am I, chopped liver?" Jav said. "I'm offended."

"And the *dress*, Mom," Deane said, her voice rising up. "What am I supposed to do now?"

"I'll take you," Jav said. "I have an Armani tux and a friend who owns a private helicopter. You and I will land on the roof of the venue and dump pig blood on all of them."

"Then set the place on fire," Val said. "I believe in you."

"Oh my God, *do it*," Stella said, staring open-mouthed at Jav. She turned to Deane. "Dude. It would be epic."

"Jav, you're so sweet," Deane said.

"Excuse me," Alex said. "I don't give permission for this. Maybe the tux and pig blood, but not the helicopter."

Val whacked his shoulder. "Be quiet, fucky."

"He's soothing my ego, Dad, do you mind?" Deane give Jav a hug, then slid open the freezer drawer and retrieved a pint of ice cream. "C'mon, Stel. Let's go get fat." She took Stella by the hand and headed out, all three dogs following.

Stella waved over her shoulder at the adults. "If you don't hear from me in an hour, call Weight Watchers."

"Man, I love that kid," Jav said. "Everyone should have a Stella."

ME AND BERNIE

*D*EANE AND ARI were at one of the stainless steel sinks, gently scrubbing down a rescued Bichon. The miserable dog looked like a rat, its wet fur stuck to its little body, pink shivering skin stretched over bones. The triangle of black eyes and nose stared up at Deane and Ari, both grateful and pathetic.

"Poor thing," Ari said, washing a back paw. "He's skinnier than I am."

He felt Deane's sideways glance. He'd already told her a little about his experience with Waterhouse-Friderichsen Syndrome. How it came from the same bacteria that caused meningitis. The doctors thought it *was* meningitis, until Ari started bleeding into his adrenal glands. He was in the hospital a month, fighting both the infection and septic shock in his extremities. He lost two toes off his left foot, and the nails on his ring and pinky fingers still hadn't grown back. The whole ordeal made a wreck of his stomach and reduced him to bones. His mother fought back tears at the kitchen table, watching her once-ravenous son nibble and pick at food, choke it down and fight like hell to keep it down.

When he got back to school, classmates either did double and triple takes before realizing it was Ari, or they walked straight past him with no recognition at all.

"Bunch of the alpha males started calling me Auschwitz," Ari said.

Deane sucked her teeth. "Jesus."

"I know. That's the best you got, dude? Really?"

Their hands worked in tandem, soaping up the little dog. "Will you ever gain the weight back?" Deane asked.

"I'm trying." Ari flicked on the shower hose and began rinsing the suds out. "I think Jav is a little horrified about how much I can eat now." He sighed. "I wish my mom could see it."

Her hands were full, but Deane reached her elbow and pressed it to his arm. "I wish, too."

When he shut off the water, Ari heard soft singing in the hall outside. Alex walked by the door in his scrubs and cap, a blanket-wrapped dog in his arms. He was rocking it and singing over the little whimpers and anxious yips. His voice traveled down the corridor and back again.

"*Caballito blanco, llévame de aquí. Llévame a mi pueblo, donde yo nací…*"

He stopped in the doorway and leaned on the frame, cradling the dog to his chest. "She's having a hard time coming off the anesthesia," he said to Ari's questioning look. He kissed the dog's head. "It's all right, don't cry. You want to walk? Let's walk."

He set off down the hall again. When he began another verse, Deane joined in under her breath.

"*Son los angelitos que andan de carrera. Buscando la leche pa' la mamadera…*"

She glanced up at Ari and rolled her eyes. "It's a Chilean song. 'Caballito Blanco.' He sang it to me when I was little."

Ari smiled. He wanted her so much, he felt like he was dying.

Deane, he discovered, came in two flavors. Her competitive, athletic side was a solid scoop of chocolate. Always dependable, always consistent. As long as Deane showed up to play, everyone showed up.

Skiing was in her DNA and the sport she loved best. In the spring she played varsity lacrosse. Played to win. Suited up and on her game, Deane was *lethal*. Eyes filled with fire. A field general with a foul mouth and a voice that carried authority two hundred yards.

But when she came off the field and kicked off her cleats, Deane softened into something like butterscotch. Her expression went dreamy. It turned into a book, or went looking for a pencil to sketch, a brush to paint, scissors to cut paper. Her strong arms reached to hold and soothe frightened cats. Her voice dropped into a gentle hush as she bathed abandoned dogs, trimming matted fur and picking off ticks. When she thought nobody was around, she sang Spanish nursery songs to the animals, just like Alex.

Ari couldn't figure out if the athlete was the real Deane and the artist a secret alter-ego. Or the other way around. He liked both manifestations.

Sometimes he thought he loved both.

THE DRAMA OF prom was behind them. Deane and Stella gave the collective male race the finger and went stag, accompanied by Henry. The service dog was resplendent in a black satin vest Val made for the occasion and at the end of the evening, he was unanimously voted Prom King.

With the grind of final exams and Regents finally over, Deane was relieved to be getting away from Guelisten's social politics. She was going to Chile with the ski team on a three-week exchange trip.

"In June?" Ari said.

"June's the start of the season in the southern hemisphere."

"Oh duh," he said. "That's cool."

Actually, that *sucked*. Ari was looking forward to school being out and longer hours to hang with Deane at Celeste's or the shelter.

As her trip date approached, he worried through an anxious fear she would forget him.

Don't meet a hot guy over there, he thought. *Don't not come back. Don't forget me.*

He'd give anything to be going along. But he didn't ski.

Then he got an idea.

He drove over the bridge and back to Morgantown, where he remembered a Catholic Book and Gift shop. "Who's the patron saint of skiing?" he asked the shop worker.

She looked it up and while the canon showed no saint specifically for skiing, St. Bernard was the patron of mountaineers and alpinists. The woman checked her inventory and held up a handsome silver medal with the saint surrounded by snowflakes and the entreaty engraved on the back. It hung off a thin black leather cord. It reminded Ari of Deane's silvery grey eyes, fringed with black lashes.

"It's perfect," he said.

The day before she left, he took it over to Tulip Street. Deane was upstairs in the guest room, packing. A heat wave had come through Guelisten and Deane's skin was flushed and her hairline damp as she folded and packed her layers of ski gear.

"I can't imagine wearing all this in a few days," she said, drawing a forearm across her sweaty brow.

"Are you excited?"

"Kind of freaked. I've never been this far from home alone before. I mean, I won't be alone. But I'm used to traveling far with my parents."

Ari leaned against the dresser. "Why isn't your Dad chaperoning? You'd think he'd jump at the chance to go back to Chile to ski."

Deane's mouth twisted as her shoulder shrugged. "Everyone thought that except him. I guess it's too upsetting. Even after all this time."

"Jav told me a little about what happened in Chile in the seventies. And how your dad hasn't seen his parents since he was eleven."

Deane nodded. "All the emotional stuff from the past, plus he hates to fly."

"Really?"

"He needs like three Valium to get through security."

"Huh." Ari always had trouble reconciling this dark, troubled side of Alex. At the shelter or in passing, Ari never saw Alex depressed, agitated or fearful. He was always smiling and gentle and even-keeled. His touch with animals was magic. He could charm the nastiest, spitting cats and soothe the most high-strung, mistrustful dogs. Rabbits, ferrets, guinea pigs and rats: they looked daggers at their owners, then turned and ate out of Alex's hand.

Everyone nibbled on Alex's chill demeanor. "Not a problem," he said when things got stressful. "No worries. We'll work it out."

He projected such a Zen façade, you'd never guess he carried around a strange, ghostly pain from the past. That he'd nearly had a nervous breakdown once. That Sheba often woke him up from nightmares and he had odd little phobias tucked in his pockets.

Esmeralda jumped up on the dresser and started rubbing against Ari, breaking him out of his thoughts. "I brought you something for the trip," he said.

"You did?" Deane said, putting down a fleece.

"It's nothing." He held out the tiny pouch. "I mean, it's just a thing. For good luck."

"Dude, you shouldn't have."

She unwrapped the medal and held it up to the light, squinting. "Saint Bernard?"

"Patron saint of mountaineers. And skiers, if you take a little poetic license."

She laughed. "Oh my God, it's perfect." She put it on right away. "I love it. I'll wear it the whole time. Me and Bernie."

Ari smiled as his stomach collapsed in relief. She liked it. She wouldn't forget about him.

"All right," he said. "I gotta go. Have a great time." They hugged quick and with a last wave, he turned to leave.

"Ari, wait."

He turned back, his chest immediately tight. Deane walked toward him, one hand touching the St. Bernard medal. The other slid around the back of Ari's neck. Her face came close, then stopped with her mouth an eighth of an inch from his. Ari closed his eyes, feeling the floor sway under his feet.

A long breathing moment. Then he felt her smile.

"Thanks," she said softly.

"You're welcome," he whispered, opening his eyes. His smile curled up, matching hers. They didn't kiss. Not yet. Only smiled close together, breathing each other.

Ari could smell chocolate and taste butterscotch. His hand touched Deane's hip. Inched into the curve of her waist. And finally settled in the small of her back. Her lips touched his gently and her fingers tightened in the hair at the back of his head.

"How about we talk more about this when I get back?" she said.

"Okay."

Their mouths brushed again. A long shared inhale and exhale.

"Bye," he said. "Be careful."

"I will."

T FOR TÍO

*D*EANE'S SKI TRIP overlapped with Jav's own jaunt to South America. One of his longtime clients was on the board of Banco Santander and hired him for a long weekend down to Buenos Aires.

Jav had left Ari alone overnight a few times, but now he'd be gone four nights and five days. He felt confident about it. Ari was a good kid. Being raised by a single mother had given him both heightened independence and heightened responsibility. He was making friends in town, but Jav sensed Ari respected Trelawney far too much to host a keg party in her apartment. Plus, working two jobs kept him busy. And monitored. Between the shelter and Celeste's and Roman living at Tulip Street, one of the Larks would always have an eye on him.

While Jav packed, Ari lay around and ate. Used to eating out or shopping for one, Jav was still getting the hang of feeding his nephew. He was pleased Ari was finally putting on some weight, but good lord, the kid was a bottomless pit at one end and a mass consumer of toilet paper at the other.

"Remember Val said to go over for dinner," he called out to the living room. "Anytime you want."

Ari grunted. He was flopped on the couch with a book, his card with the cut-out window pressed to the pages, keeping the visible text to a minimum. Jav passed back and forth three times before noticing Ari was reading *Client Privilege,* his short story collection.

He had a panicked, parental moment of *Oh my God, you can't read my book.* Then a flattered curiosity took its place: *You chose to read my book? Unbidden? Really?*

He kept quiet and continued packing. Feedback wasn't any fun when you had to fish for it.

"Know something, T?" Ari called.

"T?" Jav said.

"T for Tío. That all right?"

Jav smiled at the sliver of Ari's head against the arm of the couch. "Works for me."

"You write short," Ari said.

"What do you mean?"

Ari came in with the book and wormed between piles of clothes to lay on the bed. "You write short chapters. And inside the chapters, you write short paragraphs. Like each one fits exactly inside my little card window here."

"I write the way I like to read," Jav said.

"But it reads like a comic strip. These blocks of action would totally work as a graphic novel."

"You think?"

"I'm surprised no one's approached you about it."

"Huh. I'll mention it to my agent."

"You should." Ari fanned through the pages with his thumb. "What's your next book about?"

"I don't have the elevator pitch yet, but shortest summary is a woman who's in an abusive relationship finds a way out after Nine-Eleven."

"How?"

"She works in the World Trade Center and everyone who knew her before Nine-Eleven now believes she's dead."

"Wow," Ari said. "You think that could've actually happened?"

Jav got the Post Secret card and showed him. "I don't know if it's real or not, but it made me think a story was in it. If the muse pitches me an idea, I swing."

"What's the title?"

Jav hesitated. Typically the title was the last thing to reveal itself to him and the last thing he revealed to others. Once something became typical, it became superstition. But this book was different. And this was a good conversation.

"I think," he said, "it's going to be called *The Trade*."

"*The Trade*," Ari said slowly. "Trade like the World Trade. And trade like trading one life for another. I get it. T, that's fucking genius."

Jav felt his face get warm. "You think?"

"Totally. The muse will aim a knuckleball at your head if you don't use it."

"She's such a bitch."

Ari turned on his side, his expression thoughtful. "Is this woman in Argentina your girlfriend?"

"A girlfriend."

"You have a lot of girlfriends."

"In other news, water is wet."

"But you don't have anyone special."

"Well, what about you," Jav said. "Who's your main squeeze?"

Ari snorted. "Girls only hang with me so they can get to you."

Jav laughed. "Please."

"Think you could see Deane while you're down there?"

"Down there? Dude, look at a map. South America is a big ass continent."

"Yeah, I don't know why I said that." Ari pulled the pillow partway over his red face and slung one knee over the other, his foot jiggling. "I kind of kissed her."

"Kind of? What, with one lip?"

"Shut up."

"You tripped and fell and your mouth landed on hers."

"Whenever you're done," Ari said.

"I'm sorry. Tell me about the *kind of* kiss."

Ari stayed hidden under the pillow. "It was more than a peck. Less than a full-blown makeout session."

"Well," Jav said, rolling socks. "That's something."

"Yeah."

"Where'd you leave it?"

Now the pillow was moved a little. "We're going to talk about it when she gets back."

The temperature in the room dropped five degrees. The hairs stood up on Jav's forearms and a faint roaring filled his ears.

When I come back, we should have a conversation.

Jav swallowed, waving mental arms to clear the fog. "Sounds like a good plan," he said, trying not to think of Deane's ten-hour return flight.

We'll talk about it later.

Ari rolled over, shoving the pillow under his chest and wrapping his arms around it. "I like her a lot."

"She's a great girl. And you already know her parents like you."

"Mm."

Jav went on packing. He tried to whistle and project casualness, but his mouth was dry. Echoes of the past ricocheted off the insides of his skull. It had been a long time since he planted Flip in his everyday activities. A while since he imagined something ordinary like packing a suitcase, while Flip lolled around on the bed, watching him. Asking questions.

"¿Qué lo qué?" Ari said. "You look morose, T."

"I'm remembering someone I loved," Jav said in Spanish.

"You talk too fast." Ari put his forehead down. "Think you'll ever get married?"

"Nah. It's not my style. Dude, you're wrinkling my sport coat, get off."

Ari got up, swatted Jav playfully with the book and headed for the couch again.

JAV HAD BEEN meeting Marianna Sastre-Vaca in various places in South America for years. She practiced international law in Rio before becoming Vice President of Legal-Latin American Affairs at FedEx. She served on the board of Santander and if things went her way, she'd be named its next chair. Things typically went Marianna's way, either by skill, reason or force. But in the bedroom, she liked to beg for things.

"It keeps me humble," she said.

Whatever, sweetheart, Jav thought. Every client had a right to their little quirks. If she was paying, he was playing. He made her ask for everything, and benignly ignored her treaties until she was on her knees. He could hold her on the razor's edge of an orgasm until her whimpered pleas became screams. She begged to come, but wouldn't until he let her.

"What do you say, querida?" he then asked over the limp heap of her body in the sheets.

"Thank you," she whispered.

Properly humbled, Marianna threw on suit, heels and her face. Then she was off to meetings and Jav was free to wander until she called for him.

He sat in Plaza Dorrego, enjoying the crisp fall day, a beer and the street tango dancers. His pen hovered over his notebook, trying to pin something down. Something more than the obvious. The wedding cake building at the corner of Defensa and Humberto Primo had to have been described a million times already. What could he write about tango that hadn't been written before?

He ordered another beer. He jotted words and crossed them out. His phone pinged an incoming text. It was Alex, and the text simply said: **Help me.**

Jav smiled, knowing what was coming next. Alex was always texting him photos of the veterinary crisis du jour. A cat who nonchalantly destroyed the exam room. An X-ray of a dog with a TV remote in its stomach. A vomiting snake. Two mating lizards who couldn't uncouple.

Minutes went by, but no hilarious picture came in. Only another text: *¿Está ahí? PF ayúdame.*

Are you there? Please help me.

Jav squinted at the phone as if the text were in Chinese. Something was wrong. With cold fingers, he typed *I'm here. What's going on?*

Another ten minutes went by before Alex replied: *Deane crashed in Portillo. Severe concussion, brain bleed. Bunch of broken bones, maybe a vertebra. They air-lifted her to Santiago.*

Jav's mouth dropped open. *Holy shit. Call me.*

Can't, on hold with 3 different airlines. Scrambling to find a nonstop flight.

Who's with Deane right now? Jav texted.

No reply.

Once again, cold swept Jav's limbs and the air roared up in his ears. He stared at his phone, his beer ignored, the breeze rifling the pages of his notebook.

This isn't happening, he thought. *She and Ari have to talk about it later. Ari is waiting and she will come home and they will talk. Ari will get that conversation if I have to bring Deane back myself...*

His finger scrolled up and down the screen, reading Alex's texts.

"Brain bleed," he said under his breath.

We'll talk about it when I get back.

The beer soured in his stomach. Flip's words sat down so hard in his lap, his chair rocked back.

You're all I have. You have to get me down.

He texted Marianna: *PF llámame, tengo una emergencia.*

Five minutes later his phone rang. "Querido, what's wrong?"

He explained the situation, saying his niece had been badly injured in a ski accident in Chile.

"Oh no," Marianna said.

"She was air-lifted to Santiago. If her parents can't find a nonstop flight from New York, it could take them—"

"Oh my God, you have to go," she said. "Right away."

"I'm sorry to—"

"Don't be ridiculous, Javier. Get a cab back to the hotel and pack. I'll call my pilot and he'll take you."

Jav dropped some pesos on the table and ran to find a taxi. He was starting to text Alex when Alex pinged him first:

Booked our flight, leaving 9PM tonight JFK. Nonstop to SCL. 11 hours. Javi, please help me. I know you're working but can you go to Santiago?

In a cab already, Jav texted. *Heading back to my hotel, they're gassing up the jet for me and I'll be in Santiago in 2 hours. 3 at most. I'm on the way.*

God, thank you... I can't thank you enough.

Tell me what hospital.

Clínica las Condes. I'll get you the address.

I'll get it myself. You just get yourself on that plane.

Val's crying. She says she loves you. I fucking love you too. Thank you.

Love and thank me later. Go pack. Tell hospital I'm coming. I'll tell Ari to take care of the dogs. We got this. Vamos a superarlo, cachai?

ANYTHING YOU
WOULD TELL ME

*D*EANE WAS HALF a world away.

The sheer helplessness to do anything about the distance made Val want to scream. The limits of twenty-first century technology and the natural laws of the universe didn't mean *shit* when it was your child. Fuck how fast a jet could fly and fuck the curvature of the Earth. North and South America were three inches apart on a map, why the hell would it take them until tomorrow to get to their daughter? They needed to be there *now*.

"Jav's going," Alex said, turning his phone to show her the text. "He's on his way, he'll be there in two hours."

Val burst into tears, the relief buckling her knees. Jav was in Argentina. He was dropping everything and going to Santiago. Jav would be with Deane. And Jav being there was the only reason Val then went calm and stayed calm as she and Alex packed up. Her stomach was in a knot, her chest was a clenched fist, but her hands swiftly grabbed clothes and made lists and arrangements. She could function because Jav was on his way to Chile.

While Alex dealt with the flight, Val called Ari. "Can you dog sit?"

"Jav already called me," he said. "Don't worry about a thing."

"We're low on their food, you'll have to—"

"I'll take *care* of it, you just go."

They were going. So was Jav.

As Val emptied food containers out of the fridge and poured perishables down the sink, Alex paced the kitchen, on the phone with the hospital. A flood of Spanish. A pause. Another flood. "Si" repeated over and over. Val gritted her teeth against resentment she couldn't understand the conversation, only pick out a couple words here and there. It heaped kindling on the bonfire of helplessness. Her eyes stung as if exposed to smoke.

"Parenting," she said under her breath. "It ain't for sissies."

When the call came late this morning, she and Alex were naked in bed and slightly hungover. They tied a huge one on at Lark's Winebar last night, celebrating their seventeenth anniversary. They demolished six tapas courses and two bottles of Cono Sur, then wrote out their annual pledge to desire: *I'd like to be faithful to you another year.*

After a marathon of raucous, home-alone sex, they slept in late. They took coffee back to bed and lay around, reading and talking and dozing.

Life *lived* for such moments. It fucking loved to find you relaxed and blissful and hit you like a car bomb disguised as a phone call.

Hit me, Val thought, throwing cups and containers into the dishwasher. *I can handle your bullshit. Don't you dare do anything to my baby. She is my only child. She is the sole bud on our tiny family tree. Don't you even think about...*

She turned from the sink and Alex caught her gaze. His hand slid around the back of her neck and his next sentences were slow and deliberate, for her as well as his audience:

"Mi hermano Javier está en camino desde Argentina esta tarde. Sí, mi hermano."

Val nodded, taking a long, deep breath and understanding.

My brother Javier is coming. Yes, my brother.

Alex touched his chest. "Hasta que llegue,"—now his finger pointed to an invisible presence—"mi hermano actuará en mi lugar como mi apoderado. Sí. Puedes decirle cualquier cosa"—the finger jabbed his chest again—"que me dirías a mí. ¿Cachai?"

"Cachai," Val whispered. She got it: until Alex arrived, Uncle Javier was in charge. *You can tell him anything you would tell me.*

On the way to JFK, Alex's phone started lighting up with texts from Jav.

Just landed, grabbing a cab.

Twenty minutes later: ***I'm here. I'm right next to her.***

The Lark-Pendas exhaled.

Everything focused on head injury right now. Brain bleed is minimal but the first 24 hours are critical. She stays in the ICU.

Another half-hour: ***X-rays say no broken vertebrae. Only tiny hairline fracture in the L2. She can move all limbs, turn head, wiggle fingers and toes.***

Broken collarbone and 4 broken ribs right side, 1 punctured her lung. 2nd hairline fracture right femur. Minor, should heal on its own. No other broken bones.

It wasn't anything they hadn't already been told by the doctors. But somehow, texted from Jav, it made more sense.

She's sedated and intubated right now. SHE CAN BREATHE ON HER OWN. Doc wants to make it as easy for 6-8 hours. Give her brain and body as little to do as possible.

"She can breathe," Val said. "It's like when she was born. Fingers. Toes. Breathing. We're good."

Alex nodded, drawing a deep breath of his own but not talking. He'd pulled all his loose ends tight, reducing himself to a brick.

As they were boarding, Jav sent one more text: **Hey, just found out Doc's name is Eduardo. Your father's name, no? THIS IS A SIGN. We got people on the other side helping.**

Alex pushed the heel of his hand hard into his eyes after reading that one.

Thankfully no one showed up to claim the third seat in their row so they were able to spread out a little more. Val thought she might even be able to sleep on the flight. At the very least, she could open a book and attempt to get lost in someone else's story, something she wouldn't allow if Deane were alone and injured on the other side of the world. Without Jav, Val would sit upright and motionless, staring at nothing in a communion of misery.

Alex knocked back a Xanax during the flight safety talk. "I'm not fucking around," he said. "The only way I'm getting through this is unconscious."

"Take two," Val said. "No points for style."

Alex detested flying. It was best he slept, or put himself to sleep. Deane would need him. Alex was always her go-to guy in a crisis. He was a pro at soothing both frightened animals and little girls.

Val sighed.

Little girl.

A big little girl now, who didn't seem to need her mother much.

Val had been fully prepared for the teenage years being a nightmare. *She* was a nightmare in those years, just ask Alex. But what threw her off guard (and what she'd conveniently forgotten) was how sudden the years were upon you. Your daughter went to bed on the eve of her thirteenth birthday as a sweetheart, and woke up the next morning a bitch. You never stopped loving her, but goddamn, you had a lot of days when you didn't like her.

At all.

Eighth grade to sophomore year, Alex often referred to Deane as "the exchange student." For a time, they literally didn't speak her name. She. Her. It.

The spawn. Val's head ached from perpetually butting against the alien living in her house. Riding out the unpredictable mood swings. Running interference on the senseless drama. Val couldn't say good morning without rolling eyes or an exasperated sigh in return. A simple request for household chores was treated as an order to cut one's arm off and eat it. Nothing was simple. Everything turned into a negotiation with life-or-death terms.

Val read once that teen years were harder on a marriage than the newborn months.

She believed it.

Still…

She raised up the window shade, looking out at darkness and her own reflection.

Oh Deane, I'm sorry.

She didn't know for what, but the thought released something in her heart. She rubbed her temples, her eyes welling up.

Did I do enough? Did I try hard enough? Was I too hard on her?

She sniffed, drawing ragged breaths as her hands clenched in fists.

Little girl. Our one little bud on a tree.

Did I tell her I loved her before she left?

Of course she did. After losing her parents and grandmother in that accident, Val never didn't hug and kiss goodbye. Never didn't say I love you.

"I love you," she whispered. "It's all right, Deane. We're coming. Daddy's coming. Just hold on."

She jumped in her seat when Alex took her hand and squeezed it. His other hand held out his handkerchief.

"Jav's there," he said.

Val nodded, wiping her eyes. "And the doctor's name is Eduardo."

"You wouldn't believe how much better it makes me feel. It's a sign." He pushed up the armrest. "Come here. Put your head on me."

Val stretched across two seats and laid her cheek on Alex's chest. His expression was serene and his hand moved slowly along her hair, but beneath her ear his heart thudded hard.

"You're going home," she said.

"After thirty-three years."

"Are you nervous?"

"I'm scared for Deane, not me." A corner of his mouth twisted and a shoulder shrugged. "Yeah, maybe a little nervous."

She ran the backs of her fingers along his cheek. "You never wanted to go back, did you?"

"Someday maybe," he said. "But not like this."

"Jav's there."

"Thank God," he said. "It's crazy. I mean, how we met…and then met again. What he's come to be for us." He yawned. "It helps so much." He yawned again. "So does the Xanax."

"Close your eyes," Val said. "It's not the place you fled from. The soldiers are gone and nobody's getting left behind this time." She touched her fingertip to his nose. "Cachai?"

He nodded. "Cachai."

"Jav's there now. He won't let her disappear."

⌒

WHEN THEY LANDED in Santiago, Alex's phone exploded with backlogged texts from Jav.

She's sleeping. Tube's out. Breathing fine, just lot of pain.

You must be on the plane now. I'll just keep sending updates as I get them.

Not doing so well with morphine, it's making her sick. They switched drugs and now she's sleeping.

Still sleeping. Her coach had to get back to Portillo, he'll call you tonight.

She opened her eyes. Looked right at me, knew who I was and where she was. She's awake and with us. I told her you're coming.

Lot of pain. She's sleeping again.

Io lovr yoiu don wory.

^That was Deane typing. Her vision's doubled but she did it herself.

She's running a fever, pain is pretty bad.

OK, she's on antibiotics and a stronger sedative. She's out like a light. I need to grab something to eat. See you soon.

Traffic was slow. Their nerves were shot. When they staggered into Deane's room in the ICU of Clínica Las Condes, Val was so tired and shredded, she felt she was having an out-of-body experience.

Their daughter was sound asleep, her bruised face flushed and hot. Alex and Val pulled chairs to either side of her bed, kissing and touching her. She turned her head from one side to the other, hummed in her throat when Alex laid his hand on her brow. Then went still again, breathing slow and deep.

Val kissed her daughter's limp fingers and held them to her cheek. Alex held Deane's other hand, softly humming "Caballito blanco."

"You're here," Jav said. He stood in the doorway, unshaven and rumpled, dark circles under his eyes.

All three of them stared a moment. Val's vision bubbled up hot and wet. Her heart surged with an intense memory of her bedroom in New York and her last date with Jav. All those fragile words in the dark.

The people who should've known and loved you best threw you away. I don't understand how, because you're so good.

"Jav," she whispered. A sob ripped out of her throat and all the tears she'd held in check spilled down. Jav opened his arms and she ran to him.

"It's all right," he said, picking her up off her feet, his arms strong around her shaking body. "Everything's all right."

"Thank you," she cried.

You good, dear, fine man, I will never throw you away.

"Shh… Don't cry."

"I love you," she said against his neck. "I will always love you for this."

"I love you too. It's all right."

He shifted her into one arm and then he had Alex gathered up against his other shoulder.

"Te lo agradezco mucho," Alex said.

"You don't have to thank me."

"No sé cómo agradecértelo."

"Stop." Jav kissed his head. "You guys are my family. I'd do anything."

He kissed Val's head. Then six arms wove and wrapped and they held each other tight.

PINWHEEL

*1*T WASN'T HER fault.

She'd been making a clean run down one of the intermediate slopes. Not showing off or hot-dogging. She was at her top speed, but a half-dozen other skiers were passing her.

The trail merge was up ahead. One universal rule of the mountain was you always yielded to anyone below you. Another was you didn't assume the uphill skiers could always anticipate you crossing their path.

Clearly no one ever thought to make a rule against treating the merge like a U-turn and trying to ski *up* the trail. But that was exactly what some guy did. Straight into Deane's path. She veered to her right as he dodged to his left and she flew into him at forty miles an hour.

The chest-to-chest collision blew her out of her gear, cracking the bindings on both her skis.

Mommy, she thought.

A pinwheel of sky and snow.

Mommy, I'm not supposed to die this way.

Another pinwheel, tinted pink and orange by her goggles.

But I might.

Someone screamed. Was it her? Then another big crash and a stream of cursed Spanish. Something hit her head. Or her head hit something.

Mommymommymommymommy...

Then her thoughts stopped.

She woke up in the hospital and was told she was lucky. Insanely lucky. The X-rays and scans showed only a tiny, hairline fracture in one of her lumbar vertebrae. Her helmet couldn't prevent a serious concussion, but it had kept the brain bleed to a miraculous minimum. Without the helmet she'd be dead, the nurses said.

Deane wished she were dead. From shoulder to kneecap on her right side, she was one giant, tender bruise. Every breath like a spike through her chest. Every cell in her stunned, battered body crying *Mommy.*

The pain crawled through her head like a sick slug, oozing across her chest and down her back. She never knew pain could have a texture. Hers was cold and slimy and sickening.

I want my mother.

Her brain clanging in her skull. The horrible nausea and disorientation after they started her on morphine and her body revolted. Her team of nurses rolling her on her uninjured side and keeping her immobile while she threw up.

I want my mother.

Heaving was agony. Moving or being moved was agony. Even thinking was agony as she thought, *I will never say I'm miserable again. Ever. I will never be more miserable than this. This is ground zero.*

The frazzled thought bumped into a memory and flipped up an image of Alex pacing the house like a caged panther while the TV carouseled images of smoke, fire, falling buildings and airplanes. Val lost somewhere in the middle of it. Down at ground zero.

Mommymommymommymommy...

"Shh," Jav said, a cool hand on her burning forehead. "Eres la más valiente."

You're the bravest.

She couldn't believe he had come. She knew it would take her parents a whole day, maybe even two, to fly from the other side of the globe and get to the hospital. When she opened her eyes and saw a strange man dressed in street clothes sitting by her bed, she thought she was dreaming. When her scrambled brain identified him, she thought she'd gone insane.

"Jav?" she whispered around a throat still raw and sore from the breathing tube.

He smiled. "At your service."

"What are you doing here?"

"Oh..." He hitched a little closer to the bed and stroked her cheek. "I was just in the neighborhood."

She burst into tears, which hurt like hell, but she couldn't stop them. He carefully gathered her head in the crook of his arm, gently patted under her eyes with a corner of the sheet. He smelled musky and strong and she cried all over him.

"It's all right," he whispered over and over. "I'm here now. Everything's all right."

"I want my mother," she cried, surrendering. "I want my mother, please, get my mother. Please get her. Get my mother."

"I did, honey. She's coming. She's on a plane right now with your dad. They're coming, honey. You hold onto me. I'll stay right here the whole time."

He never left her bedside. Once when she woke from a doze, he showed her his phone and an email from Ari:

Tell her I'm so sorry about Bernie. He turned out to be a jinx.

"Who's Bernie?" Jav asked.

"I don't know." Inside Deane's aching head was a frantic huddle-up: *Bernie? Who's Bernie? I don't know anyone named Bernie.*

"Don't cry," Jav said, stroking her forehead. "You've had a shock. Everything's all jumbled in your head still. It's all right." His hand slid and he gently pulled on one of her earlobes. Deane reached to touch the other—it was bare.

"My earrings," she said. She had a vague memory of the nurses cutting her out of her clothes. They must've taken off her jewelry, too.

"Oh," Jav said, patting his pockets. "Wait, they gave your stuff to me."

He drew out a small buff envelope and tipped the contents into his hand. Her earrings, bracelets and a thin leather cord with…

"Oh, *Bernie*," Deane said.

Jav looked ridiculously pleased with her. "See? You remember. It just takes a minute."

Relief made Deane sink deeper into the pillows as the huddle in her head exchanged high-fives and trotted back into the game. Jav carefully fastened the cord around her neck and the St. Bernard's medal fell cool on her chest. "Ari gave me this," she said. "For luck."

"Well, in my opinion, it did its job," Jav said. "This could've been a lot worse."

Deane closed her eyes. One player from the huddle lingered on the sidelines of her mind, worried. Trying to connect circuits that couldn't quite reach. Buzzing sparks of disjointed recall. Something about Ari. And the saint's medal. Casey. Stella. The kitchen. Her house.

Home. So far away. Buildings burning at ground zero. Alex pacing through a cloud of foggy dust because Val was lost somewhere inside.

"Where's Mom?" she said. "I need my mother."

"She's coming, honey," Jav said. "She'll be here soon."

LAST SEEN HERE

*T*HREE DAYS POST-CRASH and Deane was out of the ICU and over being a coddled invalid.

"Dad, you can't fly five thousand miles to the city where you were born and not go looking for your house," she said. "Now all of you get *out* of my room so I can have a sponge bath in peace. Don't come back without pictures."

"I guess she told us," Jav said after their dismissal. He turned to Alex. "Lead the way."

The little Alex had seen so far of Santiago was unrecognizable, but certain locales had stayed firmly in his memory all these years. He lived at Calle Isabella, 42 and his father's bookstore was on Calle Trinidad, off the Plaza San Margarita. Eduardo walked to work so it couldn't have been too great a distance from the house. Of course it felt like forever to him when he was eleven. Because he was eleven.

The hotel concierge got them a map and showed them bus routes. They hit the Plaza first. Alex stood at its center by the fountain and turned in all directions.

"No?" Val said.

He shook his head and shrugged at the same time. "I can't..."

"Take your time."

He turned again, laced hands at the back of his neck. "I remember the fountain," he said. "The fountain is the same, but I don't recognize anything else. I can't orient the fountain to where the shop was."

He looked around, sighing heavily. "I have an old photo at home of my dad outside the shop, maybe if I had it..."

"Where is it?" Jav said. "Ari can take a picture of it and send it to us."

They put the Plaza on hold and followed the map to Calle Isabella. Along the block of the fifties, Alex's steps grew slower. He kept looking around, chewing on his lower lip. They crossed a wide avenue. Passed number 48.

"Forty-six," Val said. "Forty-four."

"Holy shit," Alex said under his breath. They all stopped and stared up at number 42, a pale yellow stuccoed building with white trim and red railings.

"It's the same colors as our house," Alex said. "Look at that."

"I know," Val said.

Jav went a few paces away, taking pictures.

"Do you remember?" he heard Val say.

Alex nodded. He went up on the stoop, turned and faced the street. Came down the steps again. Closed his eyes and opened them. He looked up at the building facade and pointed, lips moving as if counting. "Third floor, second window in," he said. "That was my parents' bedroom."

He walked a few paces down the sidewalk, looked up at the window again. He moved closer to the front of the building. His foot scraped over the sidewalk, then he crouched down, a hand against the bricks. The other hand at his brow.

Val hunkered down next to him. "Here?" she said. "It was here?"

Alex nodded.

Jav watched, his eyes growing wet. He couldn't imagine what happened *here* and didn't want to. Whatever it was, it could still bring Alex to his knees thirty years later.

Jav couldn't look away. His heart rumbled in his chest, like an earthquake stirring in his soul. Waking up. Lurching to life. Grabbing him by the shoulders and shaking him, *Don't you see? Don't you see?*

Alex got up, wiping his eyes. But he was smiling, even laughing a little. "Jesus."

He and Val posed on the steps and Jav took a picture. His phone pinged an email then, with the picture Ari took in Alex's study. They headed back to the Plaza San Margarita. Alex held up the phone with the photograph of his father. Enough of the fountain was in the shot that he could line himself up. He lowered the phone and stared straight ahead. Jav followed his gaze to a cafe with bright blue stucco walls.

"Is that it?" he asked.

"No. I mean, clearly it was right there," Alex said, looking down to the phone and up again. "But it's not the same building."

They walked closer to be sure. Jav stopped a policeman to ask if he remembered a book shop on this corner. The officer apologized, saying he wasn't from Santiago. Undeterred, Jav asked an elderly gentleman sitting on a bench in the plaza, throwing bits of bread to the pigeons and dogs.

"Librería?" the old man said. "Se quemó. Setenta y tres."

It burned down in seventy-three.

"The whole building?" Jav asked. "¿Se quemó todo el edificio?"

"No, no," the man said. "Just the shop. During the coup. They tore the building down in eighty-four, eighty-five."

"I see. My friend. Over there. His father owned the shop."

The old man eyed him a long moment. "¿Desaparecido?"

"Yes," Jav said. "Both my friend's parents. He was only eleven. He got out of the country but never saw his family again."

The man threw a handful of breadcrumbs. "My son was disappeared," he said. "And my brother. I was a guest of Pinochet for two months."

He held up his other hand. Or what was left of it. Just a flat palm and a web of scar tissue. Every finger gone. Severed. Disappeared.

"Lo siento, señor," Jav barely managed to say.

"Bring your friend over here."

The old man introduced himself as Espinoza, without a first name. He shook all their hands but then shooed Val and Jav off. They got an outdoor table at the cafe, ordered coffee and watched the two Chilean men communing.

"What happened outside his building?" Jav asked. "What was that about?"

Val opened her mouth as if to answer, then closed it and shook her head. "It's his story to tell, Jav."

"I understand."

She put her hand on top of his. "I have a feeling he'll tell you someday."

Her gaze went back across the plaza but their hands stayed linked, and Jav kept looking at her. The sun in her hair. The firm clear line of her jaw and the fine lines etched by her eyes.

"She wanted you," Jav said.

Val blinked at him. "Who?"

"Deane. She cried for you."

Val's fingers went tight in his. "What?" she whispered.

"The whole time I was with her," Jav said. "She was crying, *I want my mother. Please get my mother, I need her.* Even when she slept, she mumbled *Mommy* under her breath."

"She did?" Val said, her eyes brimming. Her fingertips touched her collar-bones, as if this was a gift when it wasn't her birthday.

"Why wouldn't she?"

"I... She usually goes to Alex. She and I haven't... I mean, it's been..." Val was crying now. "She wanted me?"

Jav yanked some napkins from the table dispenser. "Jesus, Val," he said, wiping her face. "Of course she wanted you. You're the strongest person she knows. You're the strongest person I know."

She cried and laughed, mopping her face.

"I really need to start carrying a handkerchief," he said. "It's so much more classy."

Her damp eyes rolled but her smile turned up wide. "I'll never be able to thank you enough."

"This is a good story," he said. He was so suffused with love and affection, his well-being feeling so well-done, he'd never be able to tell it properly.

He brought her fingers up and rested his mouth against them.

It's so good right now. It's excellent.

Finally Alex stood up from the bench and extended a handshake, but Espinoza heaved himself to his feet and embraced Alex instead. Dogs and pigeons circled their feet.

Alex crossed the street and came over to the table.

"What did he tell you?" Val asked.

"Everything. I mean, we just shared our stories."

"Did he know your father?" Jav asked.

"He knew *of* him. Knew the bookshop and how it was a place where... They weren't acquainted but Espinoza knew who my father *was*." Alex broke off and rubbed his face. "Give me a minute. This is a lot to take in."

"You want a drink?" Jav said.

"No. If you're done, I want to go one more place."

They found the old U.S. embassy, which was now part of the chamber of commerce.

"Wow," Alex said. "Now this is vivid."

"You remember?" Jav said.

"Oh yeah. This was the entrance. A little hut was here for the guards. The gates were shut. Different gates but right here." He stood, centered in the gateway, pointing to the ground. "Right here I saw my father for the last time. The guards pulled me in. The gates shut. Like prison, you know? *Clang.* And I held onto the bars and turned my head sideways to watch him." He pointed down the sidewalk. "No trees back then. Or they were smaller. It was much more open. I could see all the way down to the end. He waved. Right there. Right on that corner…"

Jav watched Alex walk down the sidewalk, following his memory's trail of breadcrumbs to the corner. He stopped and stood still, hands on hips. His feet turned in a slow circle, his gaze swept the sidewalk all around. Then slowly he came back to the gate.

He looks good to me, Jav thought. A smooth feeling in his mind, like something from a remembered dream.

"Weird," Alex said. "It's so ordinary. You know? Like I'm looking for a plaque in the wall or a marker on the sidewalk. Something that memorializes it. *Eduardo Penda, last seen here.*"

"Espinoza knew who your father was," Val said. "Your father *was* seen here. He can't be disappeared."

Jav reached and put an arm around Alex. Alex moved closer under its drape. His leather jacket was warm from the sun. The wind picked up the edges of his hair. His hand rested on Jav's back, his other arm curved around Val.

Alex began to speak. "Espinoza said…" Then he trailed off.

"Tell us," Val said softly.

"He said it's a life," Alex said. "And not everyone gets one."

"Second chances are given or made," Jav said.

"This was good," Alex said, his smile an open beautiful thing. "I like today. I'm glad we did this." His voice dissolved. Then his head slumped and his shoulders trembled. His eyes squeezed as he rolled his smile in and bit down. Jav and Val folded in like a closing book, taking him in between their four arms. Alex laid his head on Val's shoulder. Jav laid his cheek on Alex's head.

"He's glad you did, too," Jav said. "He sees you. He's on the corner and he sees you…"

A COUCH IN THE SKY

*D*EANE SPENT TEN days in the Santiago hospital and came home the first week in July. On a private jet, which Jav's mysterious friend arranged.

It was *ridiculous.* Deane had visions of suffering in a coach seat for ten hours, trussed in her support brace and going out of her mind. Instead, she lay on a couch, reading and watching movies while her parents reclined in cushy leather seats.

"I'm on a couch in the *sky,*" she kept saying.

"I'm ruined," Val said.

"And look at you, Dad. I believe you're actually enjoying the flight."

Alex smiled behind closed eyes. "Private jet and Xanax. This is the only way to do it."

"Who is this friend of Jav's?" Deane asked. "Can she be my friend too?"

"You can't afford her," Alex said and Val kicked his leg, laughing.

Deane was still suffering headaches and nausea. Her vision split when she was tired, doubling the world. And tiny bits of her long-term memory had gone numb.

She knew her house, but stared at one or two possessions, their provenance vanished. *This is mine?* She admired a picture on the wall and was puzzled when Val said Deane herself had drawn it. *I did?* She looked at the gorgeous formal dress hanging in her closet and had zero recollection of wearing it. *When?*

"To prom," Stella said. "I was your date, remember? We went stag because men are assholes?"

"Of course," Deane said, not remembering.

Casey came to see her. Stella said he flipped out when he first heard about her crash. A dozen other students concurred he *really* flipped out. It all made for a rather pleasant eyewitness account.

"Oh man, it was bad."

"I've never seen him like that."

"He was in tears. Dude, it was crazy."

"He made me come to church with him and light a candle."

What wasn't pleasant was the small void in her memory regarding Casey. They'd broken up, but the reason seemed to have escaped her.

She remembered Casey, she knew who he *was*. She remembered their relationship, remembered dates, remembered sex and she could put him in context. When he came to the house with roses and seven bars of her favorite chocolate, she recognized his concern was laced with something else. Regret or remorse. Or both. She vaguely recalled being mad at him. Did they have a fight? About what? She felt stupid asking Stella. She couldn't construct the question in a way that didn't make her sound like a soap opera heroine emerging from a coma.

Do I know you? Where am I?

She didn't want to ask her mother either: bad enough Val got all teary when Deane didn't recognize shit around the house. Why upset her more? And how important could it be anyway? Casey was here now. He sat on the floor by the side of the couch and laid his head by Deane's hip. One hand held hers, the other ran in long strokes down her legs.

"You got so thin," he said.

She pushed her fingers through his hair and let them trace over the lines of his face. He held still, his eyes closed.

"I missed you so much," he said. "And I'm so sorry. I was an idiot."

She went on caressing him. If he was sorry, she'd let him be sorry.

"This time we've been apart," he said. "It's made me see a lot of things."

"Like?"

His mouth opened and closed a few times. "It's hard to explain."

"Try," she said. "I won't laugh at you."

"I don't know, I just...I just love you."

"Why?"

"I don't have a reason. Isn't that what love is?"

He rolled up on his knees and put his head on her good shoulder.

"I love you," he said. "And I want you back."

She was young. Holes dotted her memory. She was vulnerable in her injuries and a sucker for a cute boy's earnest penitence and attention. It soothed her.

She ate it up like cake.

"I want you back, Deane."

She let his hair sift through her fingers. "I know."

LITTLE
WOMAN-GIRL

ONE GIANT TOOTHACHE

AUGUST 2006

1 T MADE ARI crazy.

Crazy.

"T, if you love me, kill me," he said, half-slumped on the coffee bar at Celeste's.

"Don't kill him in the apartment," Trelawney said to Jav. "I have to disclose it if I ever try to sell the place."

"I'll kill him in the parking lot," Jav said, not looking up from his laptop.

"Hurry," Ari said, groaning in misery. He couldn't escape it. Every time he stepped outside, he saw Casey driving Deane to physical therapy appointments. Casey loping up the porch steps at Tulip Street. Casey picking Deane up at the animal shelter. Casey and Deane having coffee at the bookstore.

Wanting Deane felt like dying. This crushing disappointment felt like not dying when you were terminally ill.

What the fucking fuck?

How about we talk more about this when I get back?

Her exact words. Now she was back and acting like *this* never happened.

"No rush," Ari mumbled. "Whenever you want to disengage your face from Casey's, I'll be glad to have a chat."

He was wounded to the core. A victim of emotional assault who couldn't press charges. He had absolutely no leg to stand on. Deane had a horrendous crash in Chile. She could've been permanently injured. Hell, she could've died. She was expected to make a full recovery but she wouldn't be playing sports for a while. That had to suck. Obviously the whole ordeal had made her think twice about Casey. She had a thing with him for nearly two years. What was Ari going to do—lodge a complaint based on a kind-of kiss and a rain check? He'd look like a whiny bitch. He had some pride.

And he had a permanent scar across his tongue from biting it in Deane's presence. His entire body felt like one giant toothache. The only thing that gave him a shred of comfort was she was still wearing the St. Bernard's medal. That had to mean something.

Didn't it?

Only Jav and Trelawney knew of the almost-kiss up in Deane's bedroom. Ari told a lot of things to Trelawney. She was one of those people whose ear was a funnel for shit. A good listener and pretty much un-shockable.

After a few weeks of enduring Ari's pissy moods, Trelawney laid a cool hand on his forearm. "You know, I've been thinking," she said.

"What?"

"I talk to Deane and I notice she's forgotten things. Little things she's told me or done with me. She's lost memories."

Ari stared at the luminous face. Trelawney looked so much like an elf out of *Lord of the Rings*. Full of some centuries-old, enlightened wisdom he'd never attain.

"She had a bad head injury," she said. "She bled into her brain. So maybe tuck it in the back of your mind that she doesn't *remember* she kissed you." She squeezed his arm. "All right?"

He nodded, feeling chastised and stupid. The theory didn't ring one hundred percent true. After all, Deane remembered he'd given her the St. Bernard medal, which was right before the kiss. Still, if the snub was beyond everyone's control, it helped take some of the sting out of his sunburned feelings.

He threw all his energy and focus into working out. All summer, he ate six meals a day and went with Jav to the gym every morning. At first, he just gained weight and got chunky. Then, around the middle of August, the chunk started to streamline into muscle. He'd always be slim, but the leanness was defined in a way that made him loiter in front of the bathroom mirror, pleased. He had shoulders now, and something to put in the seat of his pants besides air.

One day he picked up Jav's hat, a short-brimmed, dark grey cap with a little feather in its black band. Jav often wore it when he was writing and, interestingly, he didn't look good in it. Something about the hat's size and shape made Ari's drop-dead gorgeous uncle look dorky.

Ari put it on and glanced at the mirror. He looked good.

"This a fedora?" he asked Jav.

"Pork pie," Jav said, giving it a tilt. "Also known as a stingy brim."

"Can I wear it?"

Jav gave him a skeptical look. "It's my lucky hat."

"Where'd you get it?"

"It belonged to someone I knew."

For a moment, all the skin of Jav's face seemed to yank sideways and a flicker of pain shot across his eyes.

"Who?" Ari asked.

Jav's eyes softened and his face pulled itself together again. "You can wear it. But take good care of it. Lose it and I'll kill you."

"Don't kill me in the apartment," Ari said. "Trelawney won't be able to sell it."

He started wearing the hat to work. Then to school. He took care of it the way he was taking care of his body. When the senior class made a trip to Bard Rock for Homecoming, Ari could feel appreciative female eyes on his new physique. Girls were flirting with him. Play-fighting for a turn to wear his hat. Hyper-aware of his uncle's trust, he kept it out of their hands and on his head.

"Wow, look at you," Deane said, touching his sculpted arm as she passed by.

"Look at me," he said.

She gave the brim of his hat a little flick with her finger. "Nice lid."

The sun went down and the kids built a bonfire. The air was full of guitar and songs and pot smoke, overlaid with the sweet sadness of summer's true end. Deane was with her girlfriends, singing and roasting marshmallows. The flames turned her hair to amber and glinted off Bernie at her neck. Ari was drunk and horny and he wanted her.

He went for a walk down the beach instead. Kicking at the sand, chucking rocks into the river and mumbling to himself.

He came upon a lifeguard chair turned on its side, bedded down for the night.

It was rocking back and forth slightly.

A girl was on her knees with her forearms on one of the trusses, her skirt up around her waist. A boy knelt behind her, holding her hips and fucking the living shit out of her. Little cries and yelps rose up over the night. *Harder. Oh yeah. Do it. Yeah. Give it to me.*

Ari's eyes widened, then squinted. A corner of his mouth smiled. His chest released a chuckled grunt of judgment. He turned around and loped back to the party.

Deane was coming toward him, looking around. "You seen Casey?" she asked.

Ari flipped his thumb over his shoulder. "I think I saw him down that way."

OBESE EMOTIONS

"**W**ERE YOU SLEEPING?" Deane said. "Did I wake you up? I'm sorry."

"No, I was awake," Alex said, "I was reading. What's wrong?"

"I need to get out of here. Can you come get me?" She'd never played this card but it had always been in the deck since she started going to parties. *If you're in trouble, call. Anywhere you are, any hour, you call and I will come get you. No questions.*

"What's the matter?" Alex said.

"I'm not hurt, I just need to go home. Please come get me?"

He gave a huge sigh of inconvenience, but he didn't renege on the bargain. "Can you get somewhere safe to wait for me?"

"I'm at the front gates. By the stone wall."

"I don't want you waiting out by the road alone at this hour."

"Ari's here. He wants to leave, too."

"All right, cosita. I'll leave in five minutes."

"Thanks, Dad."

She hung up and looked at Ari. "I don't want to talk about it."

He put his palms up and shook his head. "I got nothing anyway."

He lay down along the top of the stone wall, hands behind his head and his hat on top of his face. Deane sat on the ground, back against the wall, tearing up handfuls of grass.

"Son of a bitch," she said.

Ari grunted.

"I can't believe I was so stupid."

Ari said nothing.

She closed her eyes. The image of Casey and Brenna was burned there with a sickening fascination. The way he was fucking her. You couldn't call it anything else. She'd stared at Casey in a sort of weird amazement, never having seen him like this. They'd only had sex with him on top. And the couple times they'd done it since her accident had been slow and careful and sedate. Deane hyper-aware of her healing body and trying to ease the pleasure around her little aches and bigger pains. Casey quiet and conscientious above her.

Tonight, Casey astonished both Deane's eyes and her ears. On his knees, taking Brenna from behind. His head thrown back and moaning, grunted words coming out of his chest and throat: *I love fucking you*, he said. *God, I love this pussy.*

He groaned and babbled, holding Brenna's hips and *banging* her with a reckless, animal abandon.

Dude, Deane thought for a surreal instant. *Where'd you learn to do that?*

"What an asshole," she said, slumping against the stone wall.

"I'm sorry," Ari said.

She glanced up. "You drunk?"

"Mm."

"Try to get it together when my dad gets here? Don't puke out the car window or anything."

He laughed slowly in his chest. "Don't worry, I have it all under control." He took the hat off his face and set it on her head. The warmth inside settled on Deane's crown like a soothing palm. "Your dad's cool, anyway," he said. "I love him."

"Do you?"

"He's good people. You're so lucky. Holy crap, look at all the stars."

Deane shifted her gaze and stared up at the twinkling sky. The vast, incomprehensible dome of distance and time and infinite multitudes. Deane and her problems a measly speck of dust below it. She drew her knees up, set her forehead on them and imagined Alex pulling on shoes, finding his keys. A hand on the doorknob ready to go, then he'd look back at Sheba. He'd smile and jerk his head. *Come on, let's take a ride. Deane needs to be rescued.*

"Can I ask you something?" she said.

"Mm."

"What happened to your dad?"

"My real dad?"

"Yeah."

He didn't answer. The silence behind her grew heavy and she bit her lip. "If it's not too personal, I mean," she said.

"I don't know what happened to him exactly," Ari finally said. "He and my mom were never married."

"But who was he?"

"Just some guy she met," Ari said. "Mom never talked about it much, said it wasn't much to tell anyway. She met a guy and they had a summer romance, but then he left. Not left in a cruel way, not like he abandoned her. They parted as friends and moved on, and when she found out she was pregnant, she decided to have me on her own. And give me her name."

She chewed on the ends of her hair. "What's the name you were born with?"

"Aaron Gil deSoto. When Nick adopted me, I became Aaron Seaver."

"Do you know what your father's name was?"

"Rogelio Alondra," Ari said, in such an exaggerated sing-song, she wasn't sure he was serious.

"Really?"

"Rogelio Alondra," he said again. "It's on my birth certificate."

"Did she ever tell him he had a son?"

"She said she couldn't find him. Or maybe she didn't want to."

"Did you ever want to?"

He was quiet a long moment. When he next spoke, he sounded much more sober. "When I think about dads, I only see Nick. He was a great guy and I think about him all the time. Think how my life would be different if he hadn't died. And I guess... Maybe I don't want to go through that again. Know what I mean? Go looking for my real father and have it end up being disappointing? Or tragic?"

"I get it," she said.

"I Google the name every now and then. I only get a bunch of Spanish results. Genealogy sites. Usually with Rogelio as one person, and Alondra as another person. Once I found a Rogelio Alondra but he was some Spanish lord in the seventeenth century."

They were quiet a while. The crickets chirped and chattered. The hair on Deane's neck rose up, a prickling awareness at her nape. Then Ari's finger touched her. She shivered in her skin as he drew along the thin leather cord.

"You still wear this," he said softly.

"It's good luck."

His finger caressed her neck and slowly moved into the soft, secret spot behind her ear. She bowed her head, let the hat fall to the ground and her hair tumble toward her face. His fingers started to play with it. Her stomach tightened, then relaxed. A thickness in her chest, tumbling down a chute toward her lap.

"Can I ask you something?" he said.

"Mm."

"Do you remember kissing me?"

She picked up her head, looked back at him, blinking. "When?"

"At your house. Right after I gave you this."

For a moment she thought she would cry. She hated these potholes in her memory. Hated the vulnerability of the narrative being taken away from her. Anyone could mess with her head and tell her she kissed someone. Fucked someone. They could tell her she blew the track team and she'd have no way of knowing if it were true.

Ari's face was soft in the moonlight though. His hand still stroking her hair.

"It's okay if you don't remember," he said.

She tried to. He gave her the St. Bernard medal. She remembered a little black bag. She remembered being touched. Delighted. Putting it on right away. But then…

"I don't," she whispered. "I'm so sorry."

"It's all right," he said. "I wondered if it got lost on the mountain. It's not your fault."

She turned her head away again. Ari pushed her hair to the side and his palm settled warm on the back of her neck.

I kissed him.

"Now I really wish I hadn't gotten back together with Case," she said.

"Tell me about it," he said.

She closed her eyes. "Ugh, and I slept with him again."

"Don't tell me about it."

She laughed. "You sleep with anyone?"

"Right now?"

"Ever."

"Yeah." His thumb moved along the bumps of her spine. "Few times."

"Only a few?"

She could feel him smile behind her. "I had a girlfriend. We started to mess around and… It was only twice, then I got sick. I missed a ton of school. When I came back, I was so run down and looked like shit."

"Mm." His hand felt so good in her hair. Her head lolled, her chin tracing pendulum arcs.

"She kind of moved on," Ari said. "But even if we stayed together, it was like… I was skin and bones and I didn't want her to see me. I was embarrassed. I could hide it with a lot of layers of clothes. But the thought of being naked with someone wasn't a pleasant thought anymore."

Deane had a sudden, intense vision of Ari lying naked on a bed. A girl folded in his arms, her head on his chest. His eyes closed and a tiny smile curling up his mouth as he ran fingers through her hair.

"I've always been self-conscious since," he said. "Something in me still feels so skinny and fragile."

"You're not fragile," Deane said. "You're sparse."

"Sparse?"

"You're rake thin with obese emotions."

His wandering hand held still and squeezed gently. "I like that."

"You don't have anything you don't need."

"Still," he said. "I need to gain the weight I want. The weight of things I want."

"What's a thing you want?"

"I want to be inside you."

His tone was conversational, his hand played in her hair again, easy and undemanding. But the night pulled in close and Deane felt herself expand to meet it.

"That's not a thing," she said.

"Yes, it is."

She touched the edges of the night and suspended there, swinging in the hammock of the moment, purely alive. Then a sweep of headlights, a crunch of tires on gravel and Alex's car turned into the park entrance. The night slipped back into place as Ari sat up and Deane handed him his hat.

STATE OF EMERGENCY

*A*LEX AND VAL were lying around in bed with Jav. Figuratively speaking.

"Jesus Christ," Val said. She closed her copy of *Gloria in the Highest* and tossed it aside, pulling the sheet up to her face to wipe her eyes.

Alex didn't look up from *Client Privilege*. "That bad?"

"Oh my God. I'm a wreck." She got up and went into the bathroom, splashed cold water on her face. "Son of a bitch."

As she lay back down, exhausted, the dogs started barking downstairs. After a minute, Deane tapped her fingers on the half-open door.

"¿Qué onda, cosita?" Alex said.

"Hey," she said, coming in. "Look at you two reading so cozy." She flopped down at the end of the bed, curving her body around their feet and snuggling against Val's legs.

Val and Alex exchanged a quick glance. Since she'd started dating Ari, Deane was hanging out with them more. *Talking* to them. Not only about the new relationship but about everything going on.

Even after a summer of intensive physical therapy, Deane's doctor wouldn't sign off on her playing soccer or racing with the ski team. With their active daughter benched for first semester, possibly for all of senior year, Val and Alex braced themselves for an adolescent state of emergency.

It never came. The exchange student departed and the spawn matured overnight. Deane went to bed a pill and woke up the next morning a pleasant adult.

"It's actually nice to have all this free time," she said. No doubt because she was spending so much of it with Ari. They'd joined the school newspaper together. Ari was putting out a weekly comic strip—he did the conception and the drawing, Deane did the ink and color. They were taking a digital media class at Dutchess Community College. They worked at Celeste's and volunteered at the shelter.

"She never did all this kind of stuff with Casey," Alex said.

"I know," Val said. "In two months I've seen Ari in my kitchen more than I saw Casey in two years."

Deane's eyes were filled with happiness, her mind full of plans. She wanted Ari and Jav to come for Thanksgiving dinner and to Stowe when ski season started.

She's falling in love, Val thought, gazing down at her daughter, who was flipping through the pages of *Gloria in the Highest.*

"Was this good?" she asked.

"Insanely good," Val said. "Jav writes so seamlessly, you forget you're reading."

"That makes no sense," Deane said, but Alex popped up from his pages and pointed a finger at Val.

"Get out of my head, I was *just* thinking that."

Deane hummed, now reading at the beginning of *Gloria.*

"It has a lot of sex in it," Val said. "FYI."

"I've read books with sex. FYI." Without looking up, Deane scooted off the bed and headed toward the door. "'Night," she said. "Love you."

"'Night, honey, I love you."

"Te quiero, cosita."

Still reading, Deane stepped around Sheba and pulled the door softly closed behind her.

"Who are you and what have you done with Deane?" Alex said.

"Right?" Val said. "I love it. I hope it lasts." She curled up by his hip.

"I think it will," Alex said, a hand on her head. "He's a good kid. If anyone's her first foray into sex, I'm glad it's Ari."

"What?"

He glanced down, eyebrows raised and face smug. "Aren't I hip?"

"Tragically hip. It's not her first foray."

He looked at her a long time. "You've ruined my life."

"Sorry."

He scooched further down in his stack of pillows and put the book in front of his face again.

Val moved her leg over his. He gave a soft grunt of acknowledgment. She smiled. It was difficult to distract Alex when he was sucked into a book. Difficult, but not impossible. She ran her palm up his thigh.

"May I help you," he murmured.

She pulled the drawstring on his scrubs and slid her hand inside.

"I'm reading," he said.

"Where is it?" she said, searching around. It always amazed her how a massively erect cock could shrink into such a shy toadstool.

"Hey," Alex said. "'Where is it' are not words to be using when your hand is in a guy's pants. We've discussed this many times."

"He's hiding. Is he cold?"

"He's *reading*, fucky. You ruined my life and now you insulted him. Get out."

Val withdrew her hand and rolled away. "If you find him later, wake me up."

She turned off her night table lamp and pounded her pillows into place. A few moments of page-turning quiet passed.

"How do you know she was having sex with Casey?" Alex said.

"She told me."

"When?"

"Only recently," Val said. "The other day when we were baking."

"Oh."

She looked back over her shoulder. "It was a good talk."

It was a golden day. A keeper. Deane and Val baked all afternoon, talking about creativity, art, love, college and relationships.

Unprompted, entirely of her own accord, Deane started talking about Casey. Val, having finally learned a thing or two, kept her mouth shut, offering only the occasional, precipitating comment.

"You know what I wish?" Deane said, licking the batter off the beaters.

"What?"

"I wish I could take back the sex. Know what I mean?"

"Mm," Val said. The last breath she'd taken didn't want to exhale.

"It's not that I felt pressured," Deane said. "It was a mutual decision. It was consensual. It just never felt like anything…special."

"I see."

Deane dumped the beaters in the sink and leaned forearms on the counter. "He was the wrong guy," she said, sighing. "He was a good guy. At the time, I mean. He turned out to be a shit later on. But in the moment, he was the one I chose."

"Of course."

"He was the first guy, but the wrong guy. And that kind of sucks. He got my virginity. I wish I could get it back. You know?"

A moment of silence swelled like a blister. Val was washing the mixing bowl and in the soapsuds she could only see her little girl, naked and uncertain in the dark, lying under a boy. And in Deane she saw herself at eighteen, with a boy who wasn't cruel, a boy who didn't force her... But a boy who wasn't the *right* boy.

Then all the not-right boys after.

And the bone-deep, introspective sadness after she stopped hiring Jav for sex. *I never made love.*

"You got a weird look going, Mom," Deane said. "Is this too much information?"

It wasn't the amount of information being offered, it was the information Deane wanted in return. It was those two words: *You know?*

Watching sudsy water swirl away down the drain, Val was keenly, profoundly aware of Deane's trust in her right now. This vulnerable, insecure moment and its need for a litmus test. *What's normal here, Mom? Tell me what you did. Tell me how you felt. Give me something to measure against.*

It's no wonder she wanted you, Val thought in Jav's voice. *You're the strongest person she knows.*

She turned off the faucet and reached for a dish towel. "Yes," she said. "I mean, yes, I know what you mean." She turned around, running the back of her hand over her forehead, as if trying to press an idea into place. "You trusted him on a lot of levels, especially after you came home from Chile. If the first time he let you down sucked, the second must've been ten times as shitty."

Deane stared back at Val, eyes bright and lips pressed, nodding the tiniest bit.

"So I can totally understand wanting to take it all back," Val said. She crossed her arms, leaning against the counter. "Unfortunately, honey, it's part of becoming sexually active. It's like a whole new arena of judgment you have to learn to negotiate. It's hard. You misjudge, you make poor decisions and pick the wrong partners. Everyone does. I did. It hurts sometimes. Leaves you feeling like an idiot. Or even ashamed." She spread her hands out, one corner of her mouth twisting. "But then next time..."

"You're smarter about it."

"I always thought physical virginity and emotional virginity are two different things anyway." Val tried to keep her hand steady as she smoothed a piece of hair behind Deane's ear. "First time I went to bed with your father I was a complete emotional virgin. Going to bed with all our history and affinity and years of knowing each other. Sex in that context... It was like nothing I'd experienced before. I know this sounds corny, but it humbled me."

"Really?"

Val nodded. "I don't know everything, honey, but I guarantee you this: you're going to feel a whole lot better about making love when you're making it with someone you love."

Deane drew a long breath in through her nose. "I like Ari," she said softly. "I think I like him a whole lot."

"He's different."

"Way different." She didn't say anything more, and Val chose to let it be. She tapped the tube pan on the countertop to get the air bubbles out, then slid it into the oven and set the timer.

"This'll be an hour." She put arms around Deane and put on her affected Slavic accent. "I for to go to take leetle nap now."

"You for to have nice nap. I for to take cake out of oven." Lingering inside Val's hug another moment, Deane exhaled a sigh. "Thanks, Mumsy."

Val touched a fingertip into her daughter's dimple. "Anytime, girl of mine."

Little woman-girl.

Val sighed into the dark of her bedroom. *Be safe, little woman-girl,* she thought. *Be safe. Be smart. Be happy. And if you can't, come home. Just come home to us...*

Alex clicked off his lamp and scooted up close to Val's back.

"May I help you?" she said, smiling as his erection pressed cheerfully up against her butt.

"I found him," he said.

ADULT PRIVILEGE

1 T SUCKED THEY had to make out in the car. But on cold fall nights, Ari and Deane didn't have much choice. If they hung out at Ari's apartment, Jav was always there. He politely took his laptop into his room to write, and closed the door. But he was there. If he went into the city, he finked to Val and Alex, who then insisted the two teens hang at their house.

The rule at the Lark-Pendas was when Alex and Val went to bed, Ari went home.

"Are you serious?" Deane said. "Why?"

"Because we rule the roost," Alex said.

"We're just watching TV."

"Bullshit you are," Alex said, laughing. "It's non-negotiable, cosita. I love Ari to bits. You picked a winner and he can stay as long as one adult is awake and upright in the house."

"Mom, come on."

Val shook her head. "Sorry, hon. United front on this one."

"So you'd have no problem with me fooling around with him in a car?"

"As long as it's parked," Val said.

"Ha ha. You're hilarious, mother."

"Cars are where you're *supposed* to fool around," Alex said. "I had to clock my time in cars, your mother had to clock her time in cars."

"Soft, horizontal surfaces are an adult privilege," Val said. "So is privacy."

"You know," Alex said to Val, "we haven't done it in the car in a long time. You want to go for a ride?"

"I think I'll go throw up," Deane said.

Alex pulled her ponytail. "As parents, we're obligated to keep our teenager slightly frustrated at all times," he said. "Don't test me on this one, Deane. I find him here in the middle of the night and it's going to be unpleasant."

Sometimes Ari could beg Jav's SUV, and then at least they could lower all the back seats and stretch out. But more often than not, they were squashed in Ari's Honda.

Which wasn't *entirely* bad.

"It's so good," Ari whispered.

Deane straddled him in the pushed-back driver's seat, tilting his head back and pulling his mouth up into her kiss. Pulling the breath out of him. Making him make that adorable, hot noise in his chest. He kissed like a fucking dream. Like Deane filled out an application, requested, "Send me a boy who kisses like *this*," and the universe followed instructions to the letter.

Ari's kiss went from soft to hard, from teasing to hungry, from shy to aggressive. The perfect amount of give and take. The perfect amount of tongue at the perfect time. And that *sound* he made in his chest. It made her crazy.

"God, you drive me crazy," Ari said, breathing hard. His lips were swollen and she'd pulled his hair into a tousled, sexy mess.

She hummed, grinding her hips back and down on his erection. His hands curved over her butt, pulling her in tighter, pushing her where he wanted. It felt so fucking good. Happiness and desire tugged her in seven different directions until she felt spread out over the night, like sticky sweet jam on warm toast. She wanted to bite and crunch, chew and savor all of it.

"I want you so bad," he whispered, his fingertips drawing down from her collarbones. He unclasped her bra and gently pushed it open. Then his hands curved around her breasts, his palms warm and dry. He gathered one into his mouth, his thumb moving in slow circles on the other. Deane kept grinding down on him, hitting her sweet spot.

"This might make me come," she said.

"I've never made a girl come," he said. His eyes shone in the dim light as he gazed up at her. "I've never *seen* a girl come."

"Want to now?"

"God, are you kidding? Show me…"

So the cold crisp nights of autumn melted away within the fogged-up windows. They took it far, but took it slow.

"I'd like to wait," Deane said. "Having actual sex, I mean."

"I know what you meant."

"It's only… After everything with Casey, I'm more inclined to go slow this time. Wipe the slate clean and start over."

He laughed. "Dude, I had awkward sex twice. My slate is shrink-wrapped." He kissed her, threading his fingers through her hair. "And it's all yours."

SCHNOZZ

"**S**o all summer long," Roger Lark said, "Val was playing her goddamn Abba album."

"It was my goddamn Linda Ronstadt album," Val said. "If you're going to tell the legend get it right."

"Sorry," Rog said. "Linda Ronstadt. And Alex was going out of his gourd."

Val belted out the opening lyrics of "When Will I Be Loved?"

"Oh my God, all summer long," Alex said, going around the table to pour wine. "That one and 'You're No Good.' Until I wanted to kill myself."

"What happened?" Ari asked.

"He busts into Val's room," Rog said. "Takes the record off the turntable, then makes a run for it."

"Locked himself in the bathroom," Trelawney said. "Held it for ransom."

"Except Val here," Rog said, "doesn't negotiate with terrorists. She backs up down the hall and charges."

"No way," Jav said.

"*BOOM*—she kicks the door down."

"Holy shit," Ari said.

"This is my favorite story," Deane said.

"I honestly didn't think it was going to work," Val said, going a little pink in the face.

"Oh, it worked," Alex said.

"The door went right off the hinges and toppled half into the bathtub. I couldn't believe it."

"*You* couldn't believe it?"

Val laughed. "You screamed like a little girl."

"I did. I actually screamed."

"And then what?" Jav said. "Did you beat the shit out of him?"

"No," Val said, as Alex said, "Yes."

"Oh stop, I didn't beat you," she said. "Just...touched you rather vigorously."

"I came out of that one bruised and broke," Alex said. "We got in so much trouble."

Val closed her eyes as her shoulders gave a little twitch. "That was a long month."

"It was fantastic," Trelawney said. "Rog and I had complete control of the TV. We came and went at leisure, leaving the two sulking waifs behind. I don't think they spoke to each other until Halloween."

"Guys, don't stand on ceremony," Val said, shaking out her napkin. "Start serving yourselves. Eat. Happy Thanksgiving."

"Val, did you save me the tail?" Trelawney asked, passing a platter.

"Don't I always?"

"Look at the nose on this guy," Alex said, stopping by Roger's chair to top off his wine glass.

Roger tipped his profile up to the ceiling, showing off both sides of his prominent nose.

"I swear it's getting bigger in your old age," Alex said.

"It's not the size of the honker, it's what's *in* it that counts." Roger grinned at Ari then. "You're no slouch in the schnozz department, either, kid. Let me see."

Ari turned his head good-naturedly.

"You got the chin to pull it off," Rog said. "When you got a big nose and a weak chin, you're fucked."

"Does everyone have a drink?" Val said, picking up her glass. "Alex, give us a toast."

Alex put a hand on Jav's shoulder. "Help me out, man."

"Arriba," they said, and glasses were held high.

"Abajo." Glasses lowered.

"Al centro." Glasses into the middle of the table to make a bouquet.

"Y adentro." Everyone drank.

Roger put his glass up again. "And in the words of Roland Lark: here's to those who wish us well, all the rest can go to hell."

"To hell." They clinked and drank once more, then attacked the feast.

Jav hadn't known anything like it since his childhood. A hundred years since he'd sat at a pulled-out, multi-leaved table with loved ones. Hardly able to eat for laughing as dishes, jokes and cracks passed up and down and across. The tableaux of four golden-blond larks and three dark tigers filled his eyes and squeezed his heart. Roger and Trelawney were laughing. Ari had his hand casually on the back of Deane's chair. Val rested her chin on a fist, beautiful and happy as she gazed at her empire.

"It's a life," Alex said under the hum of chuckles and chatter.

Jav looked at him. "And not everyone gets one."

Alex winked and looked away but Jav's gaze got stuck, lingering on strange details. Like how Alex's light blue sweater leached the grey out of his eyes, leaving them mint green. One sleeve was pushed up, showing the tattoo of the Unisphere. A little above it, a scar cut a long, pink line across his elbow. Jav wanted to touch it. Wanted its story.

Stop it, he told himself. *You're not doing this again.*

Now ideas of warm skin were in his head, tugging at his shirt and feeling dangerously familiar.

We should talk about this later, they said.

No, we shouldn't, Jav thought.

Val was circling the table, topping up wine glasses. Her hand caressed the back of Jav's head. "Happy?" she said as she leaned to pour for him.

"I've never felt so at home," he said, his nose full of her perfume.

She kissed his temple. "That's huge coming from you."

On his other side, Alex laughed, dodging a backhanded swat from Roger by leaning into Jav's space. Jav took another bite of turkey and stuffing. It took an hour to chew and swallow it, as his mouth suddenly wanted to be full of something else.

Good Christ, if you're going to do this, do it with Roger. At least your chances would go from impossible to infinitesimal.

He did like Roger. He was good-looking, but in a shaggy, relaxed way. Not a hunk but a lunk. A Golden Retriever of a man, he occupied space like it was a hammock. He could probably lounge on a cactus and convince others it was more comfortable than a couch.

As Rog raised arms to the ceiling in a luxurious stretch, Jav noticed he had his own tattoo: a compass rose along his left forearm, the central axis stretched out long, a single letter N at its point beneath the heel of Roger's hand.

Jav's eyes narrowed, finding a story. *His tastes and emotions were simple,* he thought. *The Compass never worried. He patted problems on the head and told them to run along. If he was cold, he put on a sweater. If he broke something, he swept it up. If fear struck, it was a sign he was doing something wrong and he changed direction.*

"Uh-oh, Jav's in the zone," Ari said.

Jav blinked. Everyone was looking at him. "Sorry," he said. "I can't control when the muse shows up. Anyone got a pencil?"

———

THE MEN TOOK an after-dinner walk with the dogs, climbing Bemelman Street up to Lark House.

"Dude, Ari's a great kid," Roger kept saying to Jav.

"Thanks," Jav said each time, feeling odd. It was praise for a parent, not for him. Ari's greatness was none of his doing.

"I mean it," Rog said. "He's going places."

Ari had a thousand questions about the tree fort, the HGTV show and the countries Roger had been to. Roger gave a guided tour as he answered them all.

"¿Qué onda?" Alex said, coming to join Jav on the highest platform of the fort. They leaned on the railing and gazed out at the lights along the Hudson.

"Best Thanksgiving I've had in a while," Jav said. "Possibly ever."

"Good," Alex said, putting an arm around him. "You belong with us."

"Rog is hilarious."

"Isn't he? I don't know anyone with a bigger heart."

"Must be tough when he leaves."

"Yeah," Alex said, and slapped Jav between the shoulder blades. "I'll have to buddy up with you instead."

"Oh, I'm the consolation prize. Great."

"You're a lot more interesting than Rog. Don't tell him I said so."

"My silence is expensive."

"What's the going rate these days?"

"Forget it. I'll write you off as a charitable donation."

"Thanks, fucky." Alex unzipped his jacket a little and reached inside. "I've been meaning to give these to you. Or rather, let you know I have them."

He handed over a stack of photos. Jav took them and his eyes bulged. They were snapshots of him in his youth. Him and Naroba. Him and Nesto. The three of them as kids in Queens.

"Where the fuck did you—" Then he remembered. He'd found them when they were cleaning out Naroba's house. "I thought I threw these away."

Alex shrugged. "I'm a sucker for lost families. I don't know, I felt bad for you. I felt bad for all of it, so I took them home. The one of just you and Naroba together is nice. Maybe Ari will want it."

Holding the pictures tight, Jav stared at him, touched to his bones. "Thanks," he said softly.

"Hey, Schnozz," Roger called from below. "Come down here, I want to show you something…"

AN AXE IN HIS HAND

DECEMBER 2006

AUGUSTO PINOCHET, DICTATOR WHO
RULED BY TERROR IN CHILE, DIES AT 91...

COFFEE CUP FROZEN in mid-sip, Jav blinked at the *New York Times* headline. "Shit," he said slowly.

He clicked on the article, read it. Then texted Alex.

Dude, I just read in the newspaper Pinochet's dead.

No reply. After ten minutes, Jav texted again:

Are you OK? A lot of mixed feelings, I guess. I'm around if you want to talk.

Nothing.

The day had a weirdly ominous feel to it, made worse by Jav typing "Pinochet atrocities" into Google and falling into a horror show of documented human rights violations. The Caravan of Death. The detentions and torture centers. "La Parrilla"—the grill of metal bedsprings where prisoners would be strapped and electrocuted. Prisoners with their legs run over by cars, their ears beaten into deafness. A detention center known as Discothèque devoted to sexual abuse. Women raped to death. Forced to commit incest. Even testimonials from women raped by trained dogs. And rats.

Pinochet returned to Chile under house arrest in 2000. Now he was dead, before he could be convicted of any crimes.

Jav shut the computer off and stared at the blank screen. He saw Alex kneeling down on Calle Isabella, a hand to the yellow-gold facade of his old home as Val asked, "Here?"

I have a feeling he'll tell you someday.

In the afternoon, Jav took a walk up to Tulip Street and rang the doorbell.

"You know you've earned walk-in privileges by now," Val said, kissing him. "You don't have to ring."

"I know, but…" He wiped his feet and went inside. "In case you and Alex are fucking on the kitchen floor, I like to give warning."

Her smile was sad as she shut the door and he knew he didn't have to explain why he was here.

"How is he?"

"Not good," she said, crossing her arms. "Fine when he first heard, but over the course of the day it's sinking in and bringing up all kinds of… Well, anyway, he's out in the back yard, splitting wood."

"I'll go say hi."

"I need to go down to the shop and finish some things."

"All right," Jav said, feeling like she was telling him something else. "Are you okay?"

"Be careful," she said. "He's moody as fuck and he has an axe in his hand."

"I will."

She caught his sleeve as he made to pass. "Has he told you anything yet?"

"About Chile? No, not really."

She nodded, looking past him. She wore a black turtleneck and in the watery sunlight coming through the front doors' glass panes, she was beautiful, yet fragile.

"Hey," Jav said softly, putting a hand on her shoulder.

"He likes you so much," she said. "I mean, he really relies on you."

"I know."

"He had a terrible experience, and a lot of the time he feels the way it impacted his life isn't justified. That it wasn't as bad as it really was. He has a sadness in him, Jav. A survivor's guilt that just doesn't ever…"

The sunlight through the glass intensified and Jav remembered this was a woman who kicked in the bathroom door to get back what was hers. He imagined Alex came to America with a half-dozen barricaded doors in his heart, and Val either bashed them down, took them off the hinges or picked the locks open. She'd let nothing come between her and her man.

"It can't be easy," Jav said.

"He's—"

Jav put a fingertip on her lips and didn't let her finish. "I meant it can't be easy for you," he said.

She shook her head, lips pressed in a tight, wobbling line. He pulled her close and held her, remembering now the street outside the embassy in Santiago, where he and Val held Alex between them. The clear, pure love for his friends coursing through Jav's veins. The joy of the moment. And the solemn responsibility that came with it.

I want this job, he thought. *I will be excellent at it.*

His coming over today could be a symbolic passing of a baton. Val could leave the house, leave Alex moody as fuck with an axe in his hand, and go down to the shop because Jav was here. He could be relied upon.

I will do this and you will give me... Nothing. This does not come at a price.

"Thank you," Val whispered against his coat. "You're so good."

He took her head and kissed her above the eyebrows. "You guys are my family," he said. "I'd do anything."

Val patted him, stepped back and reached for a jacket on the row of pegs. "I'm going. Don't burn the house down."

"You never told him about us, did you?"

Val glanced at him as she drew her hair out from under her collar. "No. What purpose would it serve?"

He nodded and drew pinched fingers across his lips.

JAV WENT DOWN the back steps into the yard. Sheba lay on the ground by Alex and didn't get up. Roman came running though, with a tennis ball in his mouth.

"Hey," Alex said, without breaking the rhythm of his work.

"Hey."

"Sorry I didn't text you back. I'm in a foul mood."

"Yeah, I figured."

Jav tossed the ball to Roman a while. Alex went on splitting logs and Jav started picking up the wood.

"Where do you want this stacked?"

"Back porch. You'll see where I started."

They worked for nearly an hour. Alex said barely a word but somehow, Jav sensed his company was appreciated. He kept quiet and let his presence do the work.

"Want a beer?" Alex finally asked.

"Sure."

He brought out two bottles and they sat on the steps. Sheba came to sit between Alex's feet, her muzzle on his knee.

"I'm so fucking angry," Alex said. "All day it's been building up."

"I don't know what to say, man. I'm sorry."

"There's nothing you could say. Nothing you could do. There's no fucking thing for it, I just have to take it out on the woodpile until I don't feel pissy about it anymore. Son of a *bitch...*"

He stood up and fired the beer bottle across the yard. It hit the side of the shed and shattered in an explosion of foam and green glass. Sheba stared up at Alex. Roman trotted toward the shed, barking

"Feel better?" Jav asked.

"Yeah." Alex sat down again. "No. I wasted a beer and now I have to clean that shit up. Roman, get out of there," he called, then gave a sharp whistle through his teeth.

"Throw another one." Jav drained his beer and handed it to Alex.

"Nah."

"Throw it."

"I don't need to—"

"Throw it, bugarrón," Jav barked.

He reared back a little at the speed with which Alex seized the bottle in his right hand. He flipped it to his left as he rose to his feet and lobbed it like a grenade at the shed. It hit dead center in the splash of beer from the previous bottle and disintegrated. Sheba put her front paws on Alex's hip and stretched up to sniff at him.

"Yeah, that was pointless," Alex said, petting her. "It's all right, honey. I'm okay."

"I didn't know you were a southpaw," Jav said. Which seemed to strike Alex as hilarious because he started laughing. Kept laughing as he and Jav shooed the dogs inside and started sweeping and collecting the glass from the concrete slab under the shed.

"You got a picture of your parents?" Jav asked. "I only saw the one of your dad when we were in Chile."

"Sure." Alex ran his foot across the gravel path, picked up another piece of glass and chucked it in the garbage. Then he looked at Jav. The sun glinted in his eyes and sparkled off the silver in his beard growth. He smelled like dust and metal, like sweat and sadness. He smelled like war. He smelled like a brother.

The brothers served under Captain Trueblood until his demise, Jav thought. *The ship was theirs then, and they swore a blood oath to sail together until their death.*

Jav's mouth was dry and he could feel his eyes growing wet. He looked away.

The love was strong between the brothers. Although for one, it was too strong.

"Be right back," Alex said, and went inside.

Jav stood alone in the yard, staring at the back door, his feelings hurt.

Where the lark went, the tiger longed to follow.

Then he thought about being inside. Alone with Alex in the empty house.

They would burn the ship before they let it be taken from them.

A flame ignited in the center of his mind, curls of orange around a blue-black heart.

The heat spread through him, setting the grass alight. A line of flame straight to the porch steps, rearing up high and hot at the door. He burned with images of walls to lean against, couches to sink into, stairs to go up. Beds to lay in.

Two desire-filled voices in the ship's cabin now, still calling softly to the velvet dark, "Trueblood." *A secret code word. A signal their blood was high.*

His blood running molten in his veins, Jav thought of Flip at the door of his apartment, smiling back at him for the last time. The skies of Manhattan filled with ash. A smoking crater in the earth of Pennsylvania. Second chances carelessly wasted. He took a step toward the house, his unblinking eyes fixed on the door.

Don't let him go. Don't let him slide through your hands again.

He put a foot on the bottom step, about to follow, but then the door opened. Alex came out with two more beers, some pictures and an antique-looking knife.

"This was my dad's," he said. "Bequeathed to me for safekeeping." He reversed the hilt over his wrist and let Jav take it. "Went right through customs with that in nineteen seventy-three. Can you imagine me getting on a plane with it today?"

His heart pounding hard, Jav managed to laugh, drawing the dagger out of its sheath. "You'd be calling your lawyer. Wow, look at that."

He looked at the faded Kodak snaps of a young Alex and his parents, posing at home, on the street, at the ski slopes. He listened to Alex tell of a mass grave found at a site called Patio 29, and how Alex had registered with the database maintained by the Medical-Legal Institute in Santiago. All he could do was wait while the DNA analysis was done. And wonder.

"I'm sorry," Jav said, feeling useless and impotent, even as his blood boiled and an erection kicked from within his jeans, wanting out. Wanting in.

I want him.

His breath burned in his chest.

This is happening again. It's all happening again. I have it in my hands and now I have no choice but to let it slip away, because he relies on me. Because Val relies on me. She told me not to burn the house down.

He passed the photos back and their fingertips grazed. Jav bit the inside of his lip. He wanted to put his hands not only *on* Alex, but *into* him. Touch the pain he kept buried inside. Cup it in his palms and taste it.

I want to come into your house and touch things.

He gripped his beer bottle tight between his hands and kept his gaze forward. *Don't fucking do this. Don't want. I lose this and I'm done. I can't do it again.*

"Thanks for coming over," Alex said, getting up. He collected his mementos and beer bottles and went inside. Jav stayed where he was.

Don't go in there. This is not your second chance. This isn't for you.

"I wore myself out," Alex said. "Think I'm going to crash for a while. I don't know what's going on tonight but I'll ping you later, maybe we can hang?"

"Sure," Jav said. He faked a non-committed yawn as he stood up and turned around.

Alex lounged against the door frame, arms and work-booted ankles crossed. His eyes surveyed the yard, then he looked down and smiled at Jav.

The smile of a mariner.

It caught Jav under the ribs and his teeth trembled together. He felt the ground tilt beneath his feet. His heart flailed, making desperate minute adjustments, frantically trying to find center. Find his way home, even as home insisted it was here. Right here in this house. With Alex.

Let me come in. Let me stay. Let me touch you.

I want to come home and talk about it.

COORDINATES

TIGUERISMO

MARCH 2007

WINTER BREAK AND Alex was pure joy on the drive up to Stowe, Jav riding shotgun and Ari in the backseat. Deane and Val had gone up yesterday and Trelawney might come later in the week. All of them together at the Lark's ski house, which Roger now owned.

"He doesn't live there full-time, does he?" Jav asked.

"Only from January to March, when he's not working. Then Trelawney rents it for him."

"Will he be there now?"

"Yeah, we'll overlap a few days."

Sunset colored the western skies pink and orange behind hills and through trees. Excitement colored Alex's heart bright red. He was on his way to his happy place. Rog was waiting for him and Jav was coming.

"You ski?" Alex had asked Jav when he extended the invitation.

"Sure."

"Where'd you learn?"

"I had one client with a place in Aspen and another who took me to Switzerland."

Alex glanced in the rearview mirror. He kept forgetting Ari was in the car with them. The kid had been silent the whole drive, either plugged into music or sleeping while Alex and Jav talked the miles down.

"Is it mostly regulars these days?" Alex asked quietly. "Or do you still get new clients?"

"I don't actively look for new clients anymore. They typically find me through word of mouth. I'm more picky about who I take on."

"But you don't...*have* to take on anyone. I mean, it's not your sole income and if you stopped, you wouldn't be financially screwed."

"Nah."

"But you still do it."

"I like it."

Something in Jav's tone made the three words into a closing statement. Alex let it go and reached for the radio dial to turn up the volume a bit. They drove to the music, not speaking. A dozen convoluted questions tried to sort themselves out in Alex's head while Jav stared out the window. His lips moved faintly. Paused. Then moved again, shaping silent words.

"Private conversation?" Alex said.

Jav flicked his head and looked over. "Hm?"

"You look like you're talking to someone."

"To myself. I swear it gets worse as I get older."

A few miles of silence rolled by.

"What was your dad like?" Alex asked.

Jav put a foot on the dashboard and an elbow on his knee. "Simple," he said, after a reflective moment. "Simple and spiritual. He didn't like conflict, didn't like messes, didn't like complication. Wanted everyone to get along, be happy, not worry. Work hard and good things would happen."

"When was the last time you saw your mother before she died?" Alex asked.

"The day I left home."

"No contact at all?"

Jav shifted in his seat. "I tried... The last time I called her was on Nine-Eleven."

"And?"

"She called me a few names and hung up."

Alex's cheekbones winced, as though he'd been slapped. "Jesus."

Another few miles went by and the silence in the car swelled. *Ask me,* Alex heard it say.

"What happened that made her...treat you like that?" he said.

Jav started to speak but then paused, as if weighing the risk against their friendship. Alex's mind ran a gamut of dire scenarios—murder, rape, grand larceny, embezzlement, drugs, an illegitimate child—that would make a family cut off one of their own. He felt cold all of a sudden, genuinely anxious this confession would drive him to do the same.

Please don't have killed anyone. No rape or murder. Anything else I can deal with.

"I got caught messing around with a cousin," Jav said.

The crime was so benign, Alex almost laughed. "Messing around. In the biblical sense?"

"Yeah. Not full-blown sex. Just kissing and hands where they shouldn't be."

The anti-climax kept building up as laughter in Alex's throat. He had to swallow hard and tell it to cut the shit, this was serious. "And that was the big scandal that got you disowned?"

"Well," Jav said slowly. "It was a male cousin."

The laughter beat a hasty retreat, leaving Alex's mouth open in a silent "oh." He studied the road, rearranging his thoughts. "I guess that's different."

Jav's laugh had no humor in it. "To a Dominican family, it's unforgivable."

"Why?"

"Short answer is Tiguerismo."

"Tigers?"

"Long answer is homosexuality goes against everything my people see as the ideal male. The tiger. Being gay isn't only against the laws of God and man, it's against what it means to be Dominican. The tribe doesn't like foreigners."

"But you weren't... I mean, you aren't...?"

"Gay? No. But..." Jav shrugged. "They saw what they saw. I won't lie, we were kissing with a hand down each other's pants and I'm not sure where it would've gone if my uncle hadn't shown up. He went ballistic. I couldn't escape because we lived with him. My dad sheltered me from the abuse as long as he could. Then he died and it was open season. My cousin threw me under the bus and sicced his posse on me. My uncle went on a campaign to get rid of me. I tolerated it until my mother joined in. Then I left."

"What about your sister?"

"Naroba was a follower, not a leader."

Alex took a quick glance over his shoulder. Ari was curled against the window, ostensibly asleep, but teenagers had highly selective hearing. Plus, he suspected Ari understood a lot more Spanish than he let on.

"Does he know the story?" Alex asked.

"To an extent."

"Jesus," Alex said. "That's the shittiest thing I ever heard."

"Yeah. Well. Thanks for not freaking out."

"The hell you mean?"

"You know what I mean."

"What, you think I was going to throw you out of the car?"

"Wouldn't be the first time I got thrown somewhere."

"Keep your seatbelt on, this doesn't scare me."

"Well, I appreciate that." Jav's tone was jovial but his fingers patted his thighs and ran along his arms, as if confirming he was intact.

"Christ," Alex said, thinking it over. "How old were you when this happened?"

"We were both seventeen and shit-faced."

"For fuck's sake, nothing counts when you're drunk at that age. You were fooling around. Big deal. Now I'm pissed off."

One of his hands made a fist on the rim of the steering wheel. His mind was a jumble of outrage and curiosity, the latter subdivided into fascination and revulsion. He imagined a teenaged Jav with a hand down a cousin's pants. Then he noticed the hand that had been in a fist was now consciously wrapping around the steering wheel. Relaxing and sliding, then gripping again, as if...

Dude, what the fuck?

He let go the wheel and ran his palm along his hair. "Was he the cousin in those pictures you found? When we were cleaning out your sister's place?"

"Yeah."

"And he died, you said?"

"Yeah."

Vulnerability wafted like air freshener and the single-word replies were razor swipes through it. Jav's story sat like a stack of poker chips between them. Alex didn't think it was necessary to raise the bet but he wished he could at least see it. Quid pro quo. But what did he have? At seventeen he was safely fostered at the Larks and loved like a son through his successes and screw ups. He and Roger shared a room through their adolescence, talking about girls in the dark, sharing their pathetic conquests and monumental frustrations. He could remember getting drunk and emotionally sloppy with Rog on occasion, but never...

Well. Wait a minute.

Alex started chuckling as a memory winked at him from the past.

"What?" Jav said.

"Well." Alex rubbed the back of his neck. "One time, Rog and I, we must've been fourteen. It was before my uncle Felipe died. Rog found a porn video in his father's closet. We'd exhausted our supply of *Penthouse* magazines so this was *huge*."

"Porn is so easily accessible now," Jav said. "These coddled kids don't know what it was like to hunt down smut."

"Spoiled shits. Anyway, we smuggled it up to his bedroom. His room had two twin beds, opposite sides. He's over there. I'm over here. The tape is on the TV. And we watch."

"I know where this is going."

"After a while, his hand's in his pants. Mine's in mine. Next thing you know, we're both jerking off and not a word. Not a *look* exchanged."

"Business as usual."

"It was so blasé. And so…not a big deal. Afterward he threw the box of tissues at me. 'Here you go.' 'Thanks, Rog.' He rewound the tape, took it back to where it belonged, I went to sleep."

"End of story?"

"Well, it happened like two more times."

"Same tape?"

Alex laughed. "It was all we had. We got bored with it, so I figured if Rog's respectable father had porn hidden away, why not my uncle? So one night when Felipe was out, we snooped. And sure enough, we found a tape."

"Score."

"We set up shop, we started the tape…"

"And?"

"It was gay porn."

"Oh, Christ."

"*Killed* the mood."

"Did you know your uncle was gay?"

Alex ran a hand over the top of his head with a whooshing noise. "No clue. None. Yeah, he was a little light in the loafers but he had women around all the time. Women *loved* him."

"Yeah, women loved Rock Hudson, too. Just saying."

"I had no freakin' idea. So here's Rog and I having engaged in…not mutual masturbation but… What would you call it?"

"I don't know. Adjacent masturbation?"

"Well, whatever you call it, it was no big deal to us. Now we're watching men jerk and blow each other and whoa, is *that* what we were doing? We were both slightly freaked."

"And that was the end of the synchronized spanking, I take it?"

"Yep."

"You ever talk about it after?"

"Every now and then it's hinted at. Like if one of us prefaces something with, 'This is kind of hard to talk about,' the other gives a look like, 'Dude. Please.'"

"Your uncle ever come out?"

"Not to me. I snooped some more and found other tapes. Magazines and books in his bedside table drawers. When he died, I felt really protective about his privacy. That night, I went in his room and gathered all that stuff in a trash bag and I took it to Beatriz. I said, 'I don't want anyone to find this.' She looked inside, nodded and got her car keys. We drove over to Hudson Bluffs, found a dumpster and threw the bag in. That was the end of it."

The silence slumped between them, tired but satisfied, as if it had finished a tough workout.

"Did you ever have male clients?" Alex asked.

"No."

A beat. "Why'd you give me your card?"

"The first time? Because you asked for it."

"What about the second time?"

Out the corner of his eye, he saw Jav's head turn to him. The flash of his white teeth as he smiled. "I don't know, you seemed like a cool guy. I'd have killed someone for you."

"So it wasn't an attempt to get my business?"

Jav laughed. "Not on my resume, man. No pay-to-gay. No couples."

"No couples?"

"No. Did it once and had a bad feeling about it. Did it again to be sure and got a worse feeling. Left the money behind and crossed it off my CV. Three in a bed is too complicated. And paid or not, fucking another man's wife in front of him is just asking for trouble."

"I'm hungry," Ari said. "Can we stop and eat?"

BLACK DIAMOND

"**W**HERE'S MOM?" DEANE asked.

Roger, ensconced in an easy chair by the fire, flipped a thumb toward the window. "Out there being happy."

"Are you happy?"

Roger laced hands behind his head and gave a big grin. He had a beautiful compass rose tattooed along his forearm. It helped cover up a scar from when he'd broken his arm building the tree fort at Lark House. Only the letter N was inked, at the topmost point.

Deane peered through the frosty window panes. Val was building a snowman by the driveway. She always wore her hair in two braids during a ski trip. They hung from beneath her striped stocking hat with its big pom-pom at the end. She looked cute. Young. Pink-cheeked and busy in the snow. Deane started braiding her own hair as she watched, then pulled on her own snow pants and boots.

Val gave a big wave when Deane came out, yelling with her Slavic accent, "You for to come to play with me?"

"Jes, I for to come to help you," Deane called back.

They built a long receiving line of snow people. They were sticking branches into the spheres for arms when headlights turned into the driveway, slicing beams into the falling snow. Alex's SUV slowly rolled up. The front door of the house flung open with another shaft of warm gold light. Roger stepped onto the porch, big and bearded in snow pants and a fisherman's sweater, arms flung wide.

Alex was out the passenger side before the truck was in park, running toward the house and yelling as Rog came down the steps yelling. Then they were down in the snow, rolling and punching and laughing.

"My bromance," Val sang softly. "Doesn't have to have a moon in the sky..."

"They just *saw* each other at Thanksgiving," Deane said.

"Doesn't matter," Val said. "Hey, handsome." She laughed as Jav lifted her up in a big hug. Then Jav scooped up Deane and twirled her. He smelled like his delicious self, with a touch of fast food perfume in his hair.

Ari emerged then from the back of the SUV. Deane's heart rolled over and died. She stood still with sticks in her hands and a wobbly smile on her face, shy about embracing him in front of the adults. They opted for a quick side hug, Ari's hand trailing down her back as their arms dropped.

"Hey, Schnozz," Rog said. "Good to see you." No such shyness for him, he wrapped Ari in a bone-crunching, fist-pounding hug, one hand ruffling his hair. "Grab your stuff and come in."

The ski house had three bedrooms upstairs: one with a king-sized bed and en suite bathroom. The other two had a jack-and-jill bath between. Downstairs was the bedroom with two sets of bunk beds, pushed head-to-head along one long wall. The Lark siblings and Alex had slept here when they were younger. Deane was set up in one of the bunks. With Ari's arrival, the adults concerned themselves with sleeping arrangements.

Roger yielded the king room to Val and Alex and sidled up to Jav, saying, "Leave your side unlocked for me tonight?"

Jav replied by wrestling Rog face-down onto the kitchen counter and pretending to dry hump him.

"Easy, man," Roger cried. "It's my first time."

"You'd never know," Jav said.

"Where's Ari going to sleep," Val said, stirring something at the stove.

"Can we trust two teens alone in the bunk room?" Jav said.

"Yes," Roger said, at the same time Val said, "No."

"Mother," Deane said.

"I know, I'm such a bourgeois twit."

"You are." Deane said.

"I'll sleep on the couch," Ari said.

"Sleep with me," Jav said, grabbing him from behind and pummeling him.

Ari barked a laugh. "No, thanks."

"I'll feel bad if you have to sleep on the couch," Val said.

"No you won't," Deane said.

"For Christ's sake, Val," Rog said, "you and Alex shared the bunk room for years."

"We were *twelve*," Val said.

"Ha, you weren't twelve when you snuck off with him to the master bedroom." Rog glanced at Deane. "You know you were conceived in this house, right? On second thought, Schnozz better sleep upstairs."

Loud laughter. Ari turned bright red and Deane wished she could die.

⌘

VAL HUNG BACK the next morning to food shop and get something going in the crockpot. The rest of them headed to Smugglers' Notch. Ari took a group lesson on the beginner hill while Deane headed up Madonna with Alex, Jav and Roger.

It was her first time on the slopes since her accident and she was more anxious than she wanted to admit. So was Alex. She could tell he was trying not to hover, but every time she stopped to negotiate the trail or enjoy the view, he was on her. *Are you all right? Are you tired? Are you cold? Does your back hurt? Are your legs all right? Do you want to stop? Should we rest?*

Even Roger, usually so chill, clucked over her, until Deane wanted to skewer both of them with a ski pole.

"Do me a favor and wipe out," Jav said to her privately. "Have a yard sale, get it over with and we'll all relax."

"No shit," she said.

She gravitated toward Jav. He was a solid, simple skier. No tricks, no risks, no thrill-seeking. He wanted to enjoy getting down the mountain and live to do it again. Deane followed his tracks, copying his wide, elegant turns, dialing back into fundamentals. She felt good, although the trail merges spooked her and she moved to the far middle of the slope to avoid them.

Alex turned his skis across the mountain and waited for her to catch up. She plowed in beside him with neat, precise spray of snow across his legs.

"You look good," he said, busying himself with his bindings.

"Thank you."

Jav sliced to a stop, followed by Roger on his telemark skis.

"Feel all right, Deanie?" Rog said. "Tired?"

"The only thing tired is my brain," she said. "I'm *thinking* so much."

They met Val at the lodge for lunch. Ari was signed up for a private lesson afterward. Val and Alex wanted to ski together. Rog called it a day, saying he had phone calls to make and packing to do.

"I'll go up with Jav," Deane said.

The first lift ride after lunch was always the worst: all the blood in your stomach and your feet not happy to be buckled back into boots. Jav closed his eyes, snow collecting on his lashes.

"After lunch is such a great time for a nap," he said.

"I know," she said. "Later we'll all crash."

"Did you just say crash?"

"Oh yeah, I said it. Crash," she called out as they rose above the tree tops.

"Rhymes with cash," Jav yelled.

The mountain vista unfolded on either side of them. Deane pointed around, naming the peaks. Over at Stowe Resort, the "Front Four" cut wide, white arteries down the mountain face: Goat, Starr, National and Nosedive.

They passed over trees filled with Mardi Gras beads and assorted brassieres.

"There go your parents," Jav said, pointing.

Coming down the slope below them, Val and Alex skied in sync, their tracks making perfect figure eights. Jav and Deane whistled, applauded and yelled out scores.

"Dad's always so happy up here," Deane said.

They did a couple intermediate runs on Madonna, then took the lift up Sterling to try a black diamond.

"Feel good?" Jav said, looping his pole straps around his wrists.

"Let's do this." Deane pulled her goggles down and pushed off.

She fell only a few turns in. She laughed it off, got up and kept going.

And kept falling.

She couldn't pull a turn to the right, couldn't remember the simple mechanics of holding an edge. The trail was too steep. It narrowed and her spooked perception made it even narrower, hemming her in. She had no room. People were flying past her from behind, cutting close to her sides. All her confidence crumbled and the knowledge in her limbs slid away like an avalanche.

"All right?" Jav said as they paused at a bluff.

Her throat was seized up and within her goggles, her vision was watery. "Yeah, you go first," she said. "I like following you."

He went on ahead. She followed but made only one wobbly turn and her tips crossed. She tripped herself and wiped out onto her hip. She got up, furious and frustrated. Then lost complete control of her next turn and fell again on the same hip, losing a ski this time. It slid down the mountain like a propeller and Deane watched it go. The wincing impact of the double fall howled along her side and she was done. She lay in the snow, broken.

I'll never get down, she thought.

FINAL RESTING PLACE

*J*AV PANICKED WHEN Deane lay limp and still after the last fall. Then she pushed up on an elbow and gave him a weak wave that was half *I'm all right,* and half *Save yourself, just leave me here to die.*

He retrieved the lost ski and sidestepped back up to her.

"Yard sale," he said. "We can relax now."

"I can't do this," she said. "I can't find my stuff. I can't stop thinking."

"It's okay, honey. Take a minute."

"It's like I'm afraid of the mountain," she said, the tears breaking through.

"I know. It's all right." Jav popped out of his skis and speared his poles into the ground. He made Deane pop out, take off her helmet and sit with him along the edge of the trail. She buried her face in his chest and cried, long and hard. He held her tight.

He was a professional holder, after all.

"I don't think I can get down from here," she said.

Jav stared down the steep slope between them and the lodge.

You have to get me down from here.

His mouth shaped remembered words. "I'm with you," he said against her head. "I'll get you down."

The wind whistled along the trail, blowing the snow around them. Jav closed his eyes and imagined Flip crouched down with them, a soothing hand on Deane's back. His smile shining warm on Jav.

"Sorry," Deane said, lifting her head. She sniffed hard and ran the tips of her gloves under her eyes.

Jav dug in his chest pocket and pulled out some tissues. "We're going to get down," he said. "You can ski down, walk down, slide on your butt. However you want to do it, I don't give a shit. I'll be with you the whole time."

"All right," she said, exhaling.

"What's it going to be?"

"I'll ski," she said, blowing her nose.

"Good girl."

They clicked back in, and one wobbly turn at a time, along with some sideways sliding, Deane Lark-Penda conquered the mountain.

"You're the bravest," Jav said, hugging her when they sliced to a stop at the base lodge.

ROG SAID HIS goodbyes. He'd be building and filming in Canada the next six months. He ran the gauntlet, giving squishy hugs to the girls, back-thumping ones for the guys. And a hair ruffle with nose pull for Ari. "Take care, Schnozz. I'll see you again soon."

"Man, I like that kid," he said to Jav as they loaded his things in the trunk. "Even if he is trying to get in my niece's pants."

"More like your niece is seducing my nephew."

Rog laughed, slammed the trunk and gave Jav another hug. "Take care of my brother, all right?"

"Does he need taking care of?"

Rog flipped his keys from hand to hand. "Not so much up here. On the mountain, Alex is at peace. It's the one place his demons can't touch him. The place where he doesn't think about his parents and where he feels he's been a good son."

"We all want to be good sons."

"Ain't that the truth?"

Jav watched until Roger's taillights vanished down the road, then he went back inside.

In the kitchen, Alex was mixing up a round of pisco sours. "South American classic," he said. "Personally I'd rather drink beer but I like pisco every now and again." He handed Jav a glass. "Con muchos abrazos, amor y besos."

"Pero no pesos."

They clinked and drank.

"Not bad," Jav said.

"Peruvians add bitters," Alex said. "And a big froth of egg white on top. It's pretty gross." He hitched up to sit on the countertop.

Jav stared a minute, then chugged the rest of his glass. Crossing his arms tight, he leaned back against the counter, his hip by Alex's knee. Staring anywhere but next to him.

"Deane said you helped her out of a hairy situation," Alex said. "Up on Sterling."

Jav shrugged. "She helped herself. Pulled it out at the end like a champ."

He kept looking away, hearing Alex down the rest of his pisco sour and set the glass on the granite. He jumped a little when Alex touched the back of his neck.

"Easy," Alex said, laughing. "I'm not making a pass at you."

"Bummer."

"I just want to see your ink. What's this?" He drew Jav's collar down and touched Jav's skin, where Trueblood and his coordinates were tattooed.

"Friend of mine who passed away," Jav said. "Final resting place."

"Lo siento."

Jav thought that would be the end of it but Alex's finger stayed hooked in his shirt.

"It's so fucking weird," he said slowly.

Jav glanced back. "What?" He glanced up. He could easily reach, take hold of Alex's head and kiss him.

Alex slid down the counter and turned away, pulling up his shirt.

Christ, Jav thought, stuffing his hands in his pockets as he looked at Alex's back and the coordinates inked dead between his shoulder blades:

9.11.1973
33° 27′ 0″ S, 70° 40′ 0″ W

9.11.2001
40° 42′ 45.72″ N, 74° 0′ 21.24″ W

Jav fisted his hands to keep from touching, as he guessed, "The bottom set must be for New York?"

"Yeah. The top is Santiago. Pinochet's forces took over on September eleventh. It was twenty-eight years to the date. When the first plane hit, it was almost to the hour when the presidential palace was bombed in seventy-three."

"Holy shit," Jav said.

"Why have one Nine-Eleven when you can have two?"

"That's insane."

Tell him, he thought. *Tell him what's really on your neck. Tell him the story.*

"But weird how we both got maps on us," Alex said, pulling his shirt back down.

For the same date, Jav thought. "From the start it was weird. When I saw the Unisphere on you."

Alex held out that forearm. "I remember. A giant's abandoned plaything."

"Don't you love me anymore?"

Alex laughed, collecting their glasses and mixing up another round of drinks. *Tell him about Flip.*

Jav fisted his hands in his pockets and instead asked, "What happened to your elbow?"

Alex gave a quick glance to the scar above the tattooed globe. "Oh, I cut myself."

Deane came into the kitchen, her hair wet from the shower. "Look at you all happy, Dad," she said. "Usually you're crying in the bathroom after your boyfriend leaves."

"I'm his boyfriend now," Jav said.

"Ooh, I'm telling Roger."

"Quiet, you," Alex said. He grabbed Deane and wrestled with her.

"My silence is expensive," she said, laughing through his grip.

"As it should be," Jav said.

"Can I have a pisco sour?" Deane asked.

"No."

"Come on. I'm not driving anywhere."

Alex poured some sour mix in a glass and threw an ice cube in. "There. Go crazy."

"You're no fun," she said, walking out.

"My fun is expensive," Alex called after her. He shook his head and chuckled as he handed a drink to Jav. "Kids."

"You want to string some bells across the bunk room door tonight?"

"Good idea." Alex took a drink, then ran the back of his hand across his mouth. His green gaze squinted at Jav. "Where you been all my life, fucky?"

"You want the exact coordinates?"

Alex's head fell back as he laughed, showing his throat. Then his chin dropped, his dimples deep around his smile.

Jav smiled back, wanting to kiss him.

CREAK AND THUMP

"*I*S THAT YOU?" Deane whispered.

"I hope you weren't expecting someone else." Ari eased the door shut with barely a click, then moved on silent, socked feet to Deane's bed.

"Is everyone asleep?"

"I think everyone's dead. They killed two bottles of that pisco shit, they could barely get up the stairs."

Deane shivered as he slid in next to her. They kissed around stifled giggles, freezing up and analyzing every little creak and thump the house made, then dissolving into laughter again.

"I think it'll be all right," Ari said. "They were freakin' plowed."

"Which makes us the adults in the room."

The kissing slowed down and sank deep, their bodies relaxing and becoming one with the silence.

"It's so nice in a bed," she said. "I can see why people like to do this."

"Mm." His hands slid beneath her shirt and closed gently around her breasts. "You're so soft."

"Your hands are always so warm."

She arched into him, her skin wanting more. "Can we take our clothes off?"

His kiss hesitated against hers. "I can't… I don't want to do it here. Not with everyone upstairs."

"No, no, I didn't mean we'd do it. I just want to feel what it's like to be naked in bed with you."

"I do, too. God, I wish we were alone. This would be such a perfect place for the first time."

"I know. Just for a minute, can we?"

He laughed against her neck. "A minute. Right." But he reached for the buttons on his flannel and started undoing them. Deane wriggled out of her shirt and sweatpants. Clothing was kicked out item by item, then they inched into each other's arms.

"Hi," he said softly.

"Hi."

"This was a really bad great idea."

"I know." She slid her body as close as she could to him, then kissed her way closer. Desire pooled thick like pudding in her chest, sweet along the back of her throat.

"I can't wait to make love someday," he said.

A sudden aching damp swelled between her legs. "Soon," she said. "Someday soon." She sank into his mouth a little more, opening for him. Tasting him. Feeling his penis hot and stiff against her stomach. Wanting to feel it glide inside where she was wet and craving.

"This feels so good," he said.

She ran her fingers along the edges of his shoulder blades. Along the bumps of his backbone and the long spaces between his ribs. Along his hard, slim arms and down his tight stomach. Up again over his chest and throat and threading them through his hair. "I love your body."

His hands pressed into her back. His arms and shoulders rose in goose-bumps. Even the fine down of hairs on his chest looked up. "For real?" he whispered.

"It's beautiful." She pulled tighter toward him, wanting to pass clear through the barrier of his skin and meld with his muscle and bone. Melt together and never separate. Leave a piece of her lodged deep within so she could be in him even when they were apart.

I'm so happy.

"Ari?"

"Mm."

She perched on the edge of herself. Hesitated a split second. Then stepped off. "I love you."

His chest filled up with air as he slid hands along either side of her face. "I love you, too," he said, exhaling and pressing her forehead to his.

"For real?"

"For real." He kissed her. "It's beautiful."

THE DAMAGE WAS great the next morning. None of the adults could get out of bed. Ari and Deane left a note and took the shuttle bus to Smuggler's Notch. They started on the easy trails until Ari felt comfortable, then gradually moved on to the intermediates.

Now at the tail end of winter break, the resort was mellow. Often they had trails entirely to themselves, the wide open boulevards theirs to barrel down at top speed, or meander across with gigantic turns.

I'm in love, Deane thought, throwing her head back to the bowl of the blue sky, the snow-frosted trees and the folds of the mountains.

They kept stopping to grab each other. Coming to a breathless, laughing halt at the side of the trail. Trying to kiss, laughing as they bonked helmets and goggles. Laughing as they yanked their head gear off so they could get close, wrap arms around each other and kiss, their poles sticking out in all directions.

"God, I love you," Ari said, unzipping her jacket a little so he could get at her neck. "I can't believe this is happening."

"It is," she said, leaning back in his arms, toppling off the edge of the world. Love caught her in its palm, kept her cradled in a soft joy all the rest of the day.

On the drive home to Guelisten, she and Ari rode with Val. They sat in the backseat holding hands, falling asleep on each other's shoulders, or contentedly staring out the windows while sharing a pair of earbuds. Playing songs for each other, the lyrics filling Deane with a teary affinity with the world. The memory of being naked in Ari's arms tightening her chest and belly, nearly to the point of tears.

I'm in love.

Val reached around the back of her seat and tapped Deane's leg. Deane caught her hand and they twined fingers. Out the corner of her eye she saw Ari smile before he looked back out the window at the snowy countryside.

Val freed her fingers, then reached to Ari, her hand making circles. Ari caught it up in his and gave a squeeze.

"Everybody for to hold hands," Val said. "For we to get home safe."

Deane unbuckled and hitched toward the driver's seat, sliding her arms around Val.

"Hi, Mumsy," she whispered.

Val turned her face, smiling. "Who for to be the happiest girl in the world?"

"That for to be me."

SAME DESTRUCTION

*A*LEX SEEMED TIRED on the way home from Stowe. No conversation in Spanish, no jokes or stories. He kept turning the radio knob, following the NPR lineup. *Wait, Wait, Don't Tell Me,* followed by *Car Talk.* Then *Moments in Time.*

"Can you keep a secret?" Jav said.

"Sure."

"This journalist talking? Camberley Jones?"

"Yeah?"

"She was one of my clients."

Alex's face didn't change a millimeter. "When?"

"Back in two thousand three. Or two, maybe? She won the Peabody Award for a story she produced on that college shooting down in Philadelphia. I went with her to the ceremony."

"Huh." Alex turned the volume knob up. He shifted a little in the driver's seat, tugging at the legs of his jeans, then settled back. His demeanor closed up like a fan while Jav was wide open, desperate with longing. Wanting Alex's attention.

Are you mad at me?

His shoulders flicked. What was he, in seventh grade and needing an emotional weather report? The guy was tired.

He tried to chill, but the air in the car was electric and dripping. It sank claws into Jav's skin, yanking and pulling him in all directions. His hand curled in a fist to keep from straying toward Alex. The pull in his bones was both sexual and soulful and it infuriated him. He had friendship. He had acceptance. He'd found a family. Why wasn't it enough? Why, in his mouth, on his tongue, resting like

pearls, were these impossible opalescent questions: *Do you want me around?
Do you want me?*

Do you love me?

Every cell in his body cringed. His fist opened and closed in a reflexive response to fight this feeling.

I don't need his love.

I don't want it. I don't want to need it. Not from him. Not from anyone.

I don't want this strangle in my chest, this heat in my belly, this agony in my bones. I don't want it.

He turned his head toward the window, desperate to hide. He'd never felt more exposed in his life. Didn't understand why his gigantic emotions weren't broadcasting through the car speakers, wanting this moment in time to be preserved. Not end up a giant's abandoned plaything.

Don't you love me anymore?

"Do you miss anyone from your family?" Alex asked. "Or did they all hurt you beyond repair?"

"I miss my dad," Jav said after a moment.

"Yeah. Me too." Alex took a hand off the wheel and turned the radio down a bit. "Hey, this is kind of a weird question, but—"

"Whoa, I don't know, man. We haven't jerked off together yet."

Alex laughed and the back of his hand whacked Jav's shoulder. "Shut up."

"Go ahead," Jav said, laughing above his burning stomach.

"Did your clients change after Nine-Eleven?"

"In what way?"

"I don't know. Did you have more work? Less work? Different work? Were more people, women, I mean, looking for companionship? Bad enough to pay for it?"

Jav twisted his mouth, thinking. "I don't really remember," he said. "I do remember this pervasive sadness in the city, though. It was a presence. A layer of dust that never went away. You could always feel the smoke and smell hanging in the air."

Alex grunted, fingers drumming on the wheel. "I tanked," he said. "Big time."

"From it being the second Nine-Eleven?"

Alex glanced over, nodding. "Yeah. Something in me couldn't get past the coincidence. It felt...personal. It dredged up shit I didn't even know I was carrying around."

"Like?"

Alex licked his lips, teeth dragging on the lower one a moment. "The planes."

"What about them?"

"Pinochet's secret police disappeared people by throwing them out of airplanes and helicopters. In the Atacama desert. Or prisoners trussed to railroad ties and flung into the Pacific."

"Jesus Christ." So much anxious adrenaline coursed in Jav's veins now, he wondered if he might pass out. "You think that happened to your parents?"

"I have no way of knowing if it did, but after Nine-Eleven, I was fixated, *obsessed* with planes as instruments of death. Constant nightmares about planes flying into buildings. I'm not exaggerating about *constant*. Every night I dreamed of people being trapped in or pushed out of planes. Sometimes my parents. Sometimes Val and Deane. Sometimes me."

Jav squeezed his fists, all his own nightmares about Flip's last moments on Flight 93 breathing down his neck. He'd never had the nerve or the bad taste to actually ask Talin Trueblood how Flip's remains were identified or returned to the family. What for? The answer would've been simple, grim and obvious: *he came back to us in fucking pieces.*

"No wonder you hate flying," Jav heard himself say.

"It's so pathological it's stupid. My whole depression was fucking embarrassing to me."

"What do you mean, embarrassing?"

"I mean Val was the one in the city that day but I'm the one having a breakdown? It made no sense. I had no war story. I'm safe, my family is safe, thousands of people are far worse off from this tragedy. What the hell is going on that all of a sudden, I can't get out of bed in the mornings?"

"But you did have a war story. Your family wasn't safe. You had it worse."

Alex gave a wry smile. "I know that *now*, thanks to about ten grand of therapy. But back then..."

"Bad?"

"Bad. Lowest I've ever been in my life." He pointed with his elbow across the console. "You asked about the scar. When I said 'I cut myself,' I meant it literally. I did that deliberately. With my father's dagger."

"Jesus."

"Twenty stitches. Nine plus eleven make twenty, you know. Because I like everything to be poetic."

"Did you get help? I mean, obviously you came through, but did you just tough it out?"

"No. Maybe if I'd been single and stupid I would've soldiered on. But when you got a wife and kid…" He trailed off and ran his fingertips over his brow. "It's not just your breakdown, it's theirs, too. Depressed, anxious, suicidal—you're still a parent and your kid is watching to see how you deal with it. Deane was twelve and she wasn't stupid. I didn't have to pretend nothing was wrong, but I couldn't lay down and give up either. I had to walk that walk and let her see me crawl sometimes.

"Anyway, I went on meds and did some counseling. Lot of counseling. The trauma and grief about my parents was on a thirty-year delay but it was all there. All the shit I never processed in the moment. God, it sucked."

"But you got through it."

"I got Sheba, and she gave me my sleep back. I started running again, going back to the gym. Working out and working through it."

"It was such a fucked-up time."

"I kept coming back to the image… It was a picture taken at ground zero. This chunk of the building. This jagged piece of the facade stabbed into the middle of the debris and dust. Smoke rising up from the ground, hovering over everything. No color. Everything black and white and grey. The light is sickly. You know which picture I mean?"

"I know it," Jav said. "It almost looks sci-fi. Like an apocalypse. Nuclear fallout."

"I showed that picture to my therapist and said, 'This is what leaving Santiago felt like. This is how it feels not to know what became of my parents. This is my childhood. This is me when I was eleven. Right here.'"

"And now it's you again at forty."

"All over again. Same date. Same destruction. People just disappeared. Airplanes…" Alex shifted in the seat and cleared his throat. "I don't tell too many people about this."

"Why not?"

Alex shrugged.

Jav's eyes followed the lines bordering the highway. "Why you telling me?"

A beat. "Because someone staged a coup on your life, too. Left you a kid standing in the rubble. And you toughed it out and rebuilt. Even though no kid of your own was watching you. I admire that. At the same time, I wonder how bad it hurt."

It hurt so bad.

Jav licked his lips, dragging his teeth and taking a slow deep breath. "The coordinates on my neck are for Shanksville, Pennsylvania," he said. "My friend Flip Trueblood was on Flight Ninety-Three."

Alex's head flicked to him, stayed a little too long and he had to veer the car back from the shoulder. "¿Qué mierdas... Javito, are you shitting me?"

"I was on the phone with him. Right until the end."

Alex hit the brake and slowed the car onto the shoulder. He put it in park, switched on the hazards and half turned in his seat. "He called you from the plane?"

"Yeah. I was like a secretary. Writing down things to tell his family."

"Holy shit."

"Hardest story I ever wrote in my life."

Alex slowly nodded, eyes brimming, wide and fixed on the dashboard, mouth slightly parted. "He called you from the plane..."

"Fucked me up bad, too," Jav said. "I couldn't sleep and I couldn't get out of bed. Couldn't eat, couldn't stop crying. Couldn't write. I could screw, that was it. I don't know if my clients changed but I know I did. I made a shitload of money after Nine-Eleven because sex was the only way I could get my thoughts to turn off."

"Man, that's..." Alex closed his eyes. "He called from the plane. I can't even fucking imagine."

"Yeah, you can," Jav said. "If anyone can, you can. That's why I'm telling you."

Tears dripped down Alex's face, which kept disappearing in and out of headlight beams. A long moment passed, the only sound the click of the hazard lights and Jav's silent, echoing thought of *I want you so bad I want you so bad I want you so bad...*

Alex brushed one cheek, then the other on his forearm. He sniffed hard, put the car in gear and pulled back onto the highway. "You and I," he said after a minute. "We're so alike. It's no wonder."

"No wonder what?"

"That we kept finding each other. I'm having a hard time thinking it was coincidence. Cachai?"

"Cachai."

The miles fell away in silence. Slowly Jav's hand crossed the console and dropped on Alex's arm. Alex's head made the slightest dip down, regarding it, before returning to the road. His expression unreadable.

Heart pounding, walking the line, Jav slowly moved his palm. Over a scarred elbow. Along a tattooed forearm. Alex was stone still, staring down the highway.

This was a mistake.

Then, on the steering wheel, Alex's fingers unfolded. Raised up. Stretched out.

Jav's hand slid over Alex's wrist. His own fingers stretched, reached, and settled between Alex's, entwining, squeezing and settling back down, piggy-backed on the wheel again.

"Nine-Elevens, planes and coordinates," Alex said softly. "It's no wonder, Javi. Not to me."

"Me neither."

After a moment, Jav took his hand away. He crossed his arms over his soft, limp chest and sighed the last of the worry stored there.

DOWN HIS FOREARM

"**O**H MY GOD," Val said. "I feel sick."

"I know," Alex said.

"He called Jav from the *plane?*"

"Yes."

"Oh my God."

"Had him on the phone right until the end. Literally to the end."

"Jesus." Val inched over on the mattress, reaching for him. "Hold me."

"Hold *me*," Alex said, quivering inside his skin. "What a fucked-up…"

Inside his head, his mind was running around and around in a screaming circle, trying to escape the story. Shaking a foot like it had stepped in dog shit. *Get it off me!*

He clutched at Val, remembering the sharp edge of her scream when the second hijacked plane went right over her head and sliced into the south tower.

Get out, he'd yelled through the phone. *Get out of there now, get off the island.*

She called him once more as she was making her way to the tip of the island. Then the first tower fell. The call dropped. All cell service went to shit and Val went dark, swallowed up in the chaos.

A tiny hairline fissure cracked Alex's mind and each agonizing hour that passed widened it.

If I lose her, I'm done. If she's disappeared, I'm finished. I will not survive. I can't flee this coup. I have no embassy to help me escape.

He had no memory of picking Deane up from school. He all at once found himself holding her in his lap as they stared at the TV. His outward manner calm and reassuring, answering questions as best he could, while inside he was cracking into pieces. The dragons off their chains. An unbearable urge to go running for the closet and close himself inside. He nearly collapsed like another tower when Val finally called, safe in New Jersey, on a bus headed for Rockland County. Shocked to the point of numbness. A fine veneer of hysteria over her exhausted voice. But alive and coming home to him.

What if she'd called him from a plane? *We're going down. It's the end. I love you, Alex. You're the love of my life. I love you.*

"I love you," Val said. "Come back, Alex. I'm right here. Deane's safe in her bed."

He held her tighter, projecting backward, contemplating life as a widower with a twelve-year-old motherless daughter. Which made him think of himself, orphaned at eleven.

Who did you cry for at the end, Mami? Were you all alone, Papi? What did they do to you? How did it end?

The dragons in his heart screamed fire and blood. Constructing grotesque tableaux of torture and death. And the planes. The planes, the fucking planes. Prisoners bound to railroad ties. Unable to call anyone before the final shove. Eduardo broken and battered in the Atacama desert. Clementina screaming above her outstretched arms as she and her giant belly plummeted from the sky to the Pacific Ocean.

Mami. Mami. Did they kill you and the baby? Did you have your baby? Did they take it away? Where is my brother? My sister? What did they do to you? How do I find you? The planes. Papi said to wait. This is my job. What do I do now? The planes. My brother, my sister, do you even know who you are? Are you even alive? The planes, they threw them out of airplanes...

"You're shaking so bad," Val said.

"I woke up the dragons."

Sheba nosed open the bedroom door and came straight up onto Alex's side of the bed. Val got him a Xanax. She took half a tab herself then lay down again. Alex pulled her hard against his chest while Sheba pushed herself tight behind him. He couldn't put his mind down. Every thought upset him, or free associated to another upsetting thought. The dragons opened their jaws and set the world on fire. Everything was burning.

"Hold onto me," Val said. "I love you so much."

"I hate this," he said, powerless against the tremors in his limbs. He hated the helplessness, hated having nothing for it but to shake it out. Most of all, he detested the compulsion to go in the closet and shut the door.

He started hiding after 9/11. Stealing secret minutes from the day to escape into the dark he feared. The shoplifted time grew longer, the need grew greater. Until the day he couldn't come out. Val found him, curled up under their clothes with his mouth on his kneecaps, his father's antique dagger in his hand.

Albacete had made the street go silence once. Alex thought she could make his head go silent. She failed him. Blood poured down his arm but the noise between his ears didn't stop.

He shuddered now, remembering how weak and worthless he'd felt that day. Dizzy from blood loss. Half in shock. Cruising on pure adrenaline. Blinking up in the light of the opened closet door and whispering to his wife, *I think something's wrong with me.*

"What's wrong with me?" he whispered to Val.

"Nothing, Alejandro."

"I wasn't on the island that day and nobody called me to say goodbye."

"You had a Nine-Eleven," she said. "You had a terrible experience. You didn't remember how terrible it was until it happened the second time."

"I know," he said, burying his face in her hair. "I know, but I forget."

"This isn't you," Val said. "This doesn't define you and it's not who you are to me."

His teeth chattered. "I love you."

Her arm arced back to hold his head. "You're strong. You're brave and you're resilient. You're a survivor."

He held her tighter. "God, he called from the plane."

"I know," she said. "It's no wonder you're upset." She ran her hand down his forearm and twined her fingers with his.

The shaking stopped. For a split second all was tranquil—*It's no wonder*—then the quaking started once more.

"Do that again," Alex said.

"What?"

"The way you ran your hand down my arm…"

She did it again, her palm warm and dry along his skin, her wedding band clicking against his as she wove their fingers together.

"Something about that is soothing," he said. "Do it again."

Over and over, she caressed his arm and squeezed his fingers.

"You're all right. You're with me and everything's all right."

Sheba laid her head on Alex's hip. Alex glanced through his eyelashes, and the dog's black silhouette morphed into a man's head.

It fucked me up too, Jav said. *Couldn't get out of bed. Couldn't stop crying. I changed.*

Jav was here. Hiding behind him. Peeking around Alex's side. Afraid to go into the tunnel.

Alex reached behind and closed his hand around Sheba's paw. He found Jav's hand in his mind, twined their fingers and squeezed.

Cálmate, hermano.

His focus shifted. The dragons roared in protest, hating to be ignored. Alex imagined thrusting a torch into their fiery breath, lighting it up bright. Holding it to the tunnel entrance and squeezing Jav's hand behind him.

We both have maps on us. Come this way. Follow me. We have to walk this walk.

Val squeezed his hand. "I'm right here. Stay with me."

Alex moved forward into her solid presence and pressed back against Jav's imaginary one. Safe between. The way they'd hugged him outside the embassy gate in Santiago. Everything made circles. Tattoos and dates and coordinates. A predestined map.

It's no wonder we found each other.

Into the tunnel, one foot in front of the other. A strange desire gripped him from behind. A tongue of flame and a reptilian roar. He squeezed Val's fingers. He held onto Jav, guiding him through. He relaxed into the imagery. The panic released its chokehold, slowly dispersed and let him alone.

"Alejandro," Val whispered. "All right?"

"Sí," he said.

"Just rest."

He could see the light up ahead. They were almost out the other side. They'd made it. It was a wonder.

No. It's no wonder...

⸻

HE DIDN'T USUALLY dream on Xanax, but that night he dreamed of many things.

He was a boy in Chile, behind the gates of the American embassy. Watching his father walk away but this time Alejo fought to follow. Wormed his feet and fingers through the iron bars and began to climb, calling for Eduardo. Calling out group names of animals in an attempt to prove himself, prove he could do this job.

Hands seized him from behind and pulled him down. He kicked and writhed, screamed for his father. A pair of arms closed about him, strong and powerful, drawing Alejo's shoulders against a broad, hard chest.

Cálmate, hermano, Jav whispered. The forearm with the ship's wheel lay across Alejo's collarbones. The other curved about his head, cradling him in the crook of a bleeding elbow. The embrace pulled tight like a knot, gathered Alejo close, rocked him in arms. The solid pressure all along his spine understood how terrible everything was. And it was so sorry.

Disculpa, Jav whispered. *Lo siento, Alejo. Lo siento mucho...*

All at once the gates of the embassy were flung open. A stabbing burst of sunlight off water and it wasn't a gateway to a street, but an open door of an airplane. Over the roar of the engine, the soldiers were pushing the women out. The women were screaming. Alejo was screaming. He tried to get to his mother but he was caught fast in the powerful embrace from behind. This time, a palm slid to cover his eyes.

Don't look, Jav said. *You mustn't look. You mustn't think about this.*

Mami, Alejo screamed into the dark of Jav's hand. He didn't like the dark.

She's gone, Jav said. *She's gone and Trueblood is gone. We are brothers now. Cachai? You and me. We're family. We have each other. We have the map and we have to walk this walk.*

Jav's tall, strong body curved like a comma over Alejo, hiding him. Protecting him. *It'll be over soon,* Jav whispered. *Hold onto me. We found each other and we have to walk together. Come on now. Into the closet.*

Jav flung open the door and they darted inside.

It's like Narnia, Alejo said, flinging aside coats and shirts. He seized two cardigans and pulled them on. Jav wore a hat and a rucksack. Snow crunched underfoot. They were on skis. The wind gusted. The Andes punched out of the ground like fists.

Go now, Jav yelled over the gales. *I'm right behind you. Until the end.*

This way, Alejo said. His voice was changing. Deepening into Alex's voice as they pushed off the mountain, carving turns through the powder and shooting into the tunnel. A screaming rush through a pillowy, inky blackness. A million dogs barking. Gunshots and helicopter rotors. Then out the other side and Val was there. Her belly big and curved, the Unisphere tattooed over that magnificent arc. Her hair soaked with ocean water. Tatters of rope around her wrists. She was a piece of expensive chocolate saved for a rainy day. Delicious in Alex's mouth as he kissed her. Ate and swallowed and consumed her.

Jav came up behind, slid hands along Alex's forearms and twined their fingers. His skin was inked all over with coordinates. He was the map of the world. He used it to find Alex. He'd never leave.

You know, he said against Alex's neck. *That's why I'm telling you.*

The dream fell horizontal, tumbling down on the day bed in the back of Muriel's dress shop. Jav's gorgeous force pressed into Alex's shoulders, back and legs. Pinning him down, both commanding and loving. While at the same time, all along his front side, Alex was buried in the hot velvet of Val's body. Aggressive and passive. Crushing her while being crushed.

I love you, Val said.

You crush me, Jav said.

Alex woke the next morning feeling he'd returned from a long journey as a changed man. He held out his hands, looking for tattoos he didn't have. Twice he glanced back over his shoulder, expecting to see something. Or someone.

Driving to work, he ran his left palm down his right forearm, slid his fingers together and squeezed the wheel.

"We're so alike, you and I," he said to the windshield.

His hand down his forearm, over and over. Linking fingers.

It's no wonder we kept finding each other.

BIG

*E*VERY DAY, DEANE'S love broke down the walls of self-conscious uncertainty and showed Ari what he could be. She freed him from his own body. They were taking the wet clay of their sexuality and throwing into the center of a potter's wheel. Together they shaped it into a beautiful bowl. Coaxed the sides up, curved and strong. Fired it hard with trust. Glazed the outside the dark brown of his hair and colored the inside with the silvers and greens of her eyes. Into this vessel they put their secret selves, until very little was left deemed too private to share.

He figured their first sex would be in the car. But the planets aligned and gifted them a weeknight evening with Jav in the city and the Lark-Pendas at a concert at Marist. So their first time was in Ari's bed.

"Let me put this on?" Deane asked, opening the condom.

"Sure," Ari said, swallowing hard above his thudding heart.

"Can I be on top?"

"You can be wherever you want," he said, barely able to get the words out.

The braid of her hair swung past her shoulder as she kneeled over his thighs, guided him inside a little, then lowered her hips down.

Ari exhaled as she closed like a tight fist around him. She arced over his chest like the sky, taking hold of his head and kissing him. The St. Bernard's medal touched his skin, cool and smooth. Her legs flexed and she pulled up along the length of him, then sank down again.

"Oh my God, Deane," Ari whispered in her mouth.

"Feels so good." Her mouth sweet and deep as she slid him in and out of that swollen, squeezing heat. His fingers peeled the elastic off the end of her braid and combed the tresses out long, letting it fall like a curtain around their heads.

"Sit up," she said. "Come here." She pulled him up and unfolded her legs, wrapping them around him. "Hold me like this."

They wound their limbs around each other tight. "Are you all right?" he whispered, hands fisted in her hair.

"Yes."

"It feels all right?"

"It feels…big?"

"Um…" He gasped a laugh. "Thank you?"

"You're welcome?" She burrowed her giggling face into his shoulder. "I couldn't think of another word."

"No, big is good. This is good. Don't…change a thing."

They laughed, sniffed, clutched at each other. Then Deane fell back on her hands, pressed her toes to the headboard and moved on him. Holding her hips, he watched himself disappear up into her body, then reappear again like a miracle.

"Ari, it's so much."

"I know. I had an idea it… No, never mind, I had no idea. This is the first idea I've ever had."

Her head fell back as she laughed. He didn't know you could make love and laugh at the same time. That sex could put a lump in your throat even as it made your body writhe and scream. That a girl could be beautiful when you looked at her through a thin haze of tears. He didn't know it could be this way. He didn't know *he* could be this way.

It was like tearing off a too-tight garment and flinging it aside. His body, lean and strong and healthy, returned to him. The world could call him a kid but in his heart, he was a lover. Deane's lover. Confident and conscientious. Able to roll her down and rise up over her. Move her legs here, turn her body there. Ask for what he wanted and give her what she needed.

"I'm so in love with you," he said, the words tumbling out fearlessly. He loved their shape in his mouth. Loved when they splashed into the icy sea of her eyes. He loved the diamond her bent legs made when they opened to him, loved the push of her hips against his hand and the hungry pull of her mouth. He loved knowing she liked to be kissed like this and touched like that. He loved her wanting him. He peeled off his skin, unlocked his heart and showed her everything he had.

EXTRA SENSITIVE

*J*AV KNEW RIGHT away.

It wasn't that his nephew looked any different. Or acted any different. It was a new way he occupied space. The way space made way for him as he walked around the apartment. A small but significant rearrangement in his atoms. Jav looked at the confident set of Ari's shoulders and he knew.

Oh yeah, he's banging her.

Jav thumped his chest in contrition. It was a crass way to put it when clearly the kid was in love.

Good for you, sobrino, he thought. *You deserve it.*

He struggled with whether or not to have a talk with his nephew about the perils and responsibilities of being sexually active. Sperm and eggs, STDs, blah de fucking blah. Jav *was* the legal guardian here. Still, he felt caught up in a delicate dance of how much Ari already knew, partnered with how much counseling Jav was obligated to provide. And how it would be received. The kid was eighteen, after all, and hell, nobody counseled Jav at eighteen.

Then again, the kid *was* eighteen.

And nobody counseled Jav…

…after all.

Not long after, a day came when he was in CVS and he pinged his nephew: **Need anything while I'm here?**

Ari texted back: ***Razors, shaving cream, toothpaste. Gum.***

Jav hesitated, seeing an opening. **Need condoms?**

No reply for a minute, then: ***Yeah, actually.***

Preferences?

Durex Extra Sensitive. If they don't have, then LifeStyles THYN. The blue box.

Jav raised his eyebrows at the specifics. The kid knew his rubbers. He replied: You want these with or without the man-to-man chat?

LOL. Without. Thanks.

Well. Not bad for an overture. Jav went around collecting items. Though he'd been a long-time Trojan man, he got an extra box of the Durexes for himself.

While Jav was standing in line, Ari pinged again: *Actually, I do have a man-to-man question... It's kind of embarrassing. Don't laugh.*

Fire away.

OK... The condom goes on ME, right?

Jav burst out laughing so loud, the woman in front of him turned around. He waved her off, kept chuckling as he texted back. *Yes. On you, smartass. Every time.*

Thanks. I was pretty sure, but...

That means a DIFFERENT one every time.

Got it. Wait. Different one with a different girl? Or different one even if the same girl?

We're having that chat. Actually, clear your day, this is going to be a full-blown TALK.

Can't wait. Can I invite some friends? Do we have a cucumber in the fridge?

Jav was still shaking his head and laughing under his breath as he walked to his car. He turned the ignition and put a hand on the gearshift, but then fell into stillness a moment, the smile curled halfway up his face. A distinct sense of done-the-right-thing-ness filled his chest. Along with something that felt a lot like love.

Part Four

SONROJANDO

WITH MUMBLED COMPLIMENT

MAY 2007

*T*HE CHAMPAGNE CORK hit the ceiling and a froth of bubbles erupted from the bottle. Cheers and whistles as Alex poured around the circle of raised flutes, even for Ari and Deane. It was their celebration, after all. Decisions had been made and offers accepted: Deane was going to UVM in the fall, and Ari to New Paltz.

"Arriba," Alex said, raising his glass and leading the toast. "Abajo. Al centro. Y adentro." A final clink over the kitchen island and everyone drank.

"I for to be so proud for you," Val said, hugging Deane tight to her side.

Jav had an arm hooked around Ari as well, his heart so full he was on the verge of bawling. *Your mother would be so proud,* he thought. He wanted to say it but he didn't trust the lump in his throat with anything but some glib humor.

"College makes your ass look fabulous," he said, touching his glass to Ari's.

"My ass is always fabulous." Ari took a generous sip and chewed on it a moment, his nose wrinkling before he swallowed.

"It's an acquired taste, Schnozz," Roger said.

Rog was home for Lark House's annual spring fundraiser. The next day, a huge outdoor festival was staged on the bluff and the community turned out in full force, running vendor booths and games, with local entertainment acts throughout the weekend.

Jav strode around the fair, browsing, visiting and socializing. He arrived at the little pavilion where Celeste's Bookstore and Café had its satellite setup, with Deane, Stella and Trelawney serving coffee and baked goods.

"How's business?" he said.

"Little slow," Trelawney said. "Hard to compete with the wine bar."

"You own the wine bar," Stella said. "You're competing with yourself."

Trelawney smiled. "Celeste's is my baby. I like to see her win."

The day was soft and cool. More like fall than spring, and Jav remembered another autumn day when business was slow.

"I can help you guys out," he said. "I need some cardboard."

He made two signs: FREE HUG WITH ANY PURCHASE and HUG WITH NO PURCHASE, $2.

"Oh my God, Mr. Landes," Stella said over his shoulder. "I think I love you."

"You can't love me unless you call me Jav."

"I can't," she said. "Holy crap, this is going to be *epic.*"

By late afternoon, Roger had joined the campaign, holding up a sign: HALE, HEARTY HANDSHAKE, $3.

Ari, who was running a meet-and-greet with the animal shelter, took a turn. HUG WITH PUPPY $5. FREE HUGS FOR LIFE WITH ADOPTION.

One nerdy teenager hung out a shingle: AWKWARD EYE CONTACT WITH MUMBLED COMPLIMENT, $4.62 (EXACT CHANGE ONLY, PLEASE).

He was outdone by a man with multiple facial tattoos and piercings: AVOID ME ENTIRELY, $20.

Even the priest of St. Augustine's Church did his part. INDULGENCES, 50¢.

At the end of the day, the coffee booth had raised close to $750 in perks.

"Last call," Trelawney cried.

"Last hug." Jav turned in a slow circle with his sign. He caught sight of Alex and yelled, "Alejito, come on, don't leave me hanging."

Alex reached in his pocket and counted off some bills. "What does forty bucks get me?"

"Hug and an ass grab."

"How about sixty?"

"All of the above with fifteen-second makeout."

To wild catcalls and hoots, Alex dropped the cash into the booth's collection jar and advanced on Jav, miming a Binaca spray into his mouth before going in for the clinch.

"Get ready to be ruined," he said in Spanish. His hands reached toward Jav's head and for a moment, the universe ceased. The laughing cheers of the crowd stretched out long, like a record slowed down. Faces blurred into one face. The wicked grey-green of Alex's eyes and the bright, clean outdoor smell coming off his clothes. Muscle and bone, white teeth within the red of his smile.

Holy shit, he's really doing this.

Jav's heart screamed like a boy at his first heavy metal concert, right before Alex slid his hand between their mouths.

"You chickenshit," Jav said.

"What do you want for sixty bucks?"

They played it up big for the crowd—Jav dropping the sign and flailing his arms around as Alex twisted him roughly down to the ground. Alex backed away, making a telephone gesture at his ear and mouthing, "Call me."

Jav, sprawled on his back, lifted a single finger into the air. "Can I get a cup of coffee..."

THEY GRILLED STEAKS at Tulip Street that night. Then Deane and Stella headed to a party and Ari went home to work on his portfolio. His art teacher had recommended him for a summer program in animation design at the Vancouver Film School and Ari had a fire in his belly about it.

Roger had a different fire in his belly.

"Too many hot dogs," Trelawney said, rubbing her brother's swollen gut. "And jet lag. Bad combination."

"I'm getting old," Rog said. He reached in his pocket and flipped a dime bag to Alex. "Here. Hydroponic Yukon Gold. Don't say I never gave you anything."

Trelawney took him home. Alex, Val and Jav got high and lounged around the living room, eating popcorn. Alex lay on the couch, his feet in Val's lap. Jav was sunk into the easy chair, Esmeralda curled up on his stomach.

"What's the weirdest thing a client ever made you do?" Alex asked.

"They don't *make* me do anything," Jav said.

"You're going to argue semantics?"

Jav laced his hands behind his head. "Client privilege."

"Oh, now you're arguing legalities."

Jav glanced at Val. Her head was turned in his direction but she wasn't meeting his eyes. He felt a wicked compulsion to test both their poker faces.

"All right," he said. "I had this one client..."

Now Val was looking at him.

"Let's call her Mary," Jav said. He held Val's gaze for a count of five, then winked. "Mary hired me to spank her."

"Shut up," Alex said. "For real?"

"For real."

"Like over your knee?" Val said.

Jav nodded. "Skirt up, panties down. Whale on her ass until she said she was sorry. She was a stubborn shit, too."

"Talk slower," Alex said, sitting up on his elbow.

"Did I mention the school girl outfit and the ponytails?"

"And *she* paid *you* to do this."

"Quite well," Jav said. "It pretty much covered my rent."

"Jesus Christ," Val said, then pointed a finger at Alex. "Don't get any ideas."

"C'mon, I'll pay you."

"What, out of our joint account? How do I profit from this?"

"Oh my God, I'm wasted." Alex fell back in the cushions. Something in his flopped position, one knee pointing to the ceiling, the other toward the room, was wanton. He looked loose, Jav thought, yet he looked *tight*. He wasn't sure what he meant but his expanded mind nodded agreement.

Yeah, man. Tight.

"Quid pro quo," Jav said. "What's the weirdest thing you two have done?"

Alex picked up his head and exchanged a glance with Val.

"Or individually," Jav said.

Val looked at Jav, her eyes narrowed and a corner of her mouth slightly lifted. *You are a naughty thing,* her expression said.

He flicked his eyebrows as he took a pull of his beer. *I know. I need to be spanked.*

"I don't know, honey," Alex said, running a hand through his hair. "The first time you got your finger on my prostate was kind of weird."

Val buried her head on the arm of the sofa, while Jav sucked beer down the wrong pipe and coughed it up laughing. "First time? Meaning there were subsequent times?"

Alex was laughing too, deep from his chest and belly. "Well, I came for like a minute and a half so I got past the weirdness."

They laughed so hard Esmeralda ran away and the dogs came in to investigate.

Well, I guess we've established Alex isn't averse to ass play, Jav thought. *Good to know.*

Wait, what?

Val got them more beers, then sat on the floor, her back against the couch. Alex's hand caressed her and Jav's eyes followed its path.

I'm so fucked, he thought, stoned and horny. A feast in his lap and no knife and fork. You couldn't pay him to leave now.

You could pay me to stay. Now that's an interesting idea.

The high got higher, erasing filters and inhibitions. Alex started telling the story of the first time Val went down on him. "In the back room of the dress shop."

"During business hours?" Jav asked.

"No, no," Val said. "I'm not that crazy."

"I'm telling you, it's one of the top five moments of my life," Alex said.

"Why's that?" Val said. "It couldn't have been your first blow job."

"No, but it was the first one I didn't have to *ask* for."

Jav laughed and Val turned a little pink, biting a corner of her bottom lip. "I did offer."

"If you call slamming me up against the door and dropping to your knees offering," Alex said. He looked over at Jav. "Dude, it was the first time a girl let me come in her m—"

"*All* right," Val said, punching Alex's shoulder. "He doesn't need the details."

"Oh but I do," Jav said, crossing his ankles. He was getting an erection.

"Greatest moment of my *life*," Alex said. "To date. Well, no, wait, not to date. I mean I've had moments since."

"Or a moment and a half with a finger in your ass," Jav said.

"Exactly. But *that* moment goes in the hall of fame. It was—"

"We get it, dear," Val said, patting him. "Val gives good head."

Erection attained. Val did, indeed, give spectacular head. And she'd once paid to slam Jav up against the door and drop to her knees so he could come in her mouth. No fingers, though. Bummer.

Wait, what?

He blinked, scattering the memory. Alex was propped up on an elbow, gathering up Val's hair and pulling her head back on the cushions. The column of her throat white and soft. The tendons flexing as Alex kissed her.

High and existential, Jav watched the slow, exploring dance of mouths. The meet and part of lips. The flicker of tongue. He put himself first in Alex's body, took a look around Val's kiss as if he was visiting his old high school.

Then he put himself in Val's body.

And stayed there.

For a minute and a half.

Now it was his head tipped back for Alex's kiss. Alex's hand running along his throat. Alex's thumb on his chin, holding his mouth open.

Val's mouth taking turns in their laps.

Holy motherfucking Christ, I want this.

He could barely look at them.

He couldn't bear not looking at them.

I want you so bad.

Which *you* did he mean?

Alex and Val broke out of the embrace and looked at him.

A long, triangular staring moment.

This is it, Jav thought.

He didn't do couples but if it meant he could stay, he'd do them.

Go. Hold their eyes, crawl over there and do it. Tell him to keep kissing her and then unbutton her shirt. Kiss her breasts while he's got her mouth. Slide a hand up the leg of her shorts. She's not wearing underwear. She never did. Kneel across her legs, pin her up against the couch and take a turn kissing her. Run a hand up Alex's thigh. See what he does. Let him lead. Do it.

Take it. Take both of them. You'll never have another chance.

Do it before they get on the plane.

"God, I'm wasted," Alex said, falling back on the cushions.

"Mm," Val said, her eyes closed. Her nipples pressed against her shirt.

Jav swallowed. "I better see myself out," he said, getting up. "Before we get into trouble."

Was he imagining it or did the air taste disappointed?

"'Night, man," Alex said.

"Safe home," Val said.

Yeah, he was imagining it.

He went home. Ari was passed out on the couch, his artwork carefully spread out to dry on the counters and dining room table. He'd opened all the windows to clear the paint fumes and the apartment was chilly. Jav turned off the TV and threw a blanket over his nephew. Then he went into the shower and jerked off with a petulant vengeance. Alternating between making his hand into Val's mouth, then Alex's mouth.

Alternating between wishing they'd just hire him already, and feeling if they did, it would break his heart.

No Points for Style

*A*s soon as the front door closed behind Jav, Alex pulled his shirt over his head.

"Get over here," he said, tackling Val to the floor. His knees hemmed in her writhing body and his hands pinned hers to the rug.

"We better go upstairs," she said around his kiss. "The spawn will be back soon."

"God, I can't wait until she goes to college."

"Right?"

They stampeded up the stairs, shut and locked the bedroom door. It rattled as Alex corralled Val against it, kissing hard, sucking and biting while his hands yanked off her shirt and unclipped her bra. "This isn't going to be romantic," he said.

"Romantic's overrated." She ran her hands along his body and her tongue along his neck. Greedy, hungry strokes, wanting to stuff his skin down her throat and feast. She was so high, turned on and tuned in. Blind with need and swollen with impatience as Alex stripped her shorts off and pushed her toward the bed.

"Bend over for me," he said, his voice husked out. Barely had Val settled on her elbows when Ales pushed into her, hard and huge, making a groan tumble out of her mouth.

He laughed softly at the nape of her neck, collecting her hair in one hand. "So wet," he said. "Who got you all worked up like that?"

"You."

And Jav, she thought.

"Good." Alex's big, strong hands slid down her back. "Now hold still."

He took her by the hip bones and then it was every man for himself. Self-preservation screwing. No points for style or stamina. Whoever came first won.

Val's hands clenched around the sheets. Head lolling, eyes rolling, her gaze wobbled on the armchair in their bay window. She licked her lips, smiling at an invisible presence sitting there.

You like that, Jav? she thought. *You like watching? I saw you downstairs. You were thinking about it.*

She imagined him unbuttoning his pants, taking himself in hand. Beautiful and arrogant, stroking off and never losing her eyes. Arousal gripped her tight, wrung her out.

"So hot," Alex whispered, an edge in his voice and a hitch in his breathing telling Val he was close.

From the armchair, Jav's expression turned pleading. Supplicant. He was asking her permission to watch this. To want this. He wanted to come, too.

Yes, she thought. *You may come. Come with us. Come for us.*

It was on her then, quick and fast. She pushed up on her hands, pushed back on Alex and let it come crashing down on her.

"I win," she cried out, while Alex finished a close second.

"I lose," he said, collapsed on her back, arms tight around her waist. "And win."

They ripped open the covers and crawled toward the pillows, gasping and reaching for water bottles.

"That was great," Alex said.

"That was sloppy," she said, drawing the word into three syllables. She flopped on her stomach, a leg over his, arm across his chest and head on his shoulder.

"Sloppy's underrated," he said, running his wet mouth over her forehead. "But give me a few minutes and I'll fuck you neatly."

"What, a twofer?"

"I'm not done with you."

"We haven't done it twice in a night in ages. Must've been all that strange chemistry going on."

"Yeah, it was getting weird down there." He rolled on his side and kissed her. "Jav all jealous of my hot wife."

"Think he's jealous of me," she said, her lip caught gently in his teeth. "Or you?"

His laugh curled at her neck, low and sexy. He moved his thumb into the hollow of her throat and out again. "Both of us."

"Would you ever share me with anyone?" she asked. She could because he was high and freshly laid. Sex made him secure. Pot made him expansive.

"No," he said. "I'm too greedy."

She held his head. "No threesome fantasies? Ever?"

"Sure," he said. "But usually it's another woman in the scenario."

"Like who?"

"Your sister."

She laughed. "I'd swat you except it's too impressive a feat. I can't even wrap my mind around Trelawney in the sack."

"I can't either. It's a pathetic fantasy. Turn over..." He slid his hand around her shoulder and gently rolled her to lay on her stomach again. His mouth moved in long strokes up and down her back. Her toes curled. She loved having her back kissed.

"So who do you have in bed with us?" he asked.

"I may have invited Jav once or twice."

"And what's he doing?"

"Oh... Stuff."

He moved the hair off the back of her neck and touched his tongue to her nape. "Like what?"

It was one thing to fantasize, another to tease. But the actual out loud reveal was like getting naked when you were already nude. Peeling your skin off and showing your bones. She didn't quite trust this invitation. "Um..."

His voice was low and husky down her spine. "You do both of us? One after the other? Or both of us at the same time?"

"In my head, I've done it all."

His mouth traveled across the back of one knee. "Tell me."

"I love it in my head," she said, picking words one at a time. "Nothing's awkward, nothing's clumsy. The lighting is perfect, everyone says exactly the right thing at the right time. Nobody's afraid or weirded out. It's like world peace. And no morning after."

"Keep going," he whispered.

She closed her eyes. "I only like you inside me," she said. "While Jav does some other stuff."

"Mm."

"Or takes over if you get tired."

His laughter tickled. His hair was soft on her skin, followed by the rough scratch of his cheek. His tongue laid warm trails on the insides of her thighs and his breath cooled them off. His hand caressed circles on her ass.

"I'll never get tired of making love with you," he said. "It's literally my favorite thing to do."

"It's what you do best."

"Sometimes I think…"

She looked back over her shoulder. "What?"

Lying between her calves, he was gorgeous. His palms spread wide around her legs, thumbs moving back and forth. "It would be a turn-on to have someone watch what I do best."

"Any someone?"

He smiled. "I may have invited Jav once or twice."

"Just to watch?"

"Most of the time."

"What about the rest of the time?"

Alex drew a deep, measured breath. Loosening his skin, getting ready to show some bones. "Well. Sometimes, I—"

Downstairs, Roman and Sheba barked, followed by the sound of the front door opening and closing. Footsteps like a wagon train up the treads, dog tags jingling down the hall. Alex rolled away and Val sat up on an elbow.

"The fruit of thy womb hath returned," Alex muttered, crawling toward his pillow.

"Wearing her weighted shoes, I see."

The doorknob gave a rattle, followed by a rap of knuckles. "I'm home."

"We're fucking, dear," Val murmured. Alex clapped a hand over her mouth and called, "We're going to sleep, babe. Goodnight."

"'Night."

Alex took his hand away and kissed Val. "I can't take you anywhere," he whispered. And kissed her again.

"I love you tonight," she said.

His hand slid between her legs, fingers slipping inside. "You love me always."

"But especially tonight." She closed him up in her fist. Usually the round two erection wasn't as enthusiastic as its predecessor, but Alex was sporting the wood of a sixteen-year-old.

"What should we do with this?" she asked.

"Come here."

He took her over to the chair in the window. He sat and she crawled in his lap, guided him inside. Her thighs enclosed him like a second pair of armrests.

"God, I love you," he said. His hands moved in slow circles around her breasts, down her sides, caressing the planes of her legs.

"You're so good," she said. Her fingertips slid over his skin. She traced the lines of his face, touched his tattoos and his scars.

"So what would he be doing now?" he whispered.

She closed her eyes and turned her head up to the side, looking into the past. Remembering. "He's kissing me."

"What else?"

"All four of your hands. Both mouths on me at the same time."

"That would feel good?"

"Mm-hm. While you do what you do best."

She opened her eyes. His arm muscles flexed and squeezed as his hands raised and lowered her along the length of him. Her mouth played with the memory of Jav's kiss a bit. Then imagined him walking around to the back of the wing chair. His eyes asked permission.

Can I? Please?

Val nodded the slightest bit. Jav leaned over the back of the chair, took a gentle but firm grip on the hair at the back of Alex's head and tilted it up. Alex's throat and jaw rippled as he was kissed. His mouth opened. His tongue reached. His hand went up and around the back of Jav's neck, pulling the kiss in closer.

Val's insides contracted down hard at the visual.

Jesus, that's hot…

Another rattle of fingernails on the door. "Mom?" Deane called gingerly, as if touching an open wound.

Val set her teeth and rolled her eyes to the ceiling. "Yes, Deane?"

"Where's the bag from CVS?"

"On the dining room table." She looked down at Alex and mumbled, "Right where you left it, you stupid child."

He gazed up at her, eyes bright and wide, and a smile filled with wicked, complicit joy. He took Val's head, brought her mouth to his and whispered, "I fucking love being married to you…"

JUST OUT OF REACH

1 F MARRIAGE WAS a prison yard, your spouse was the inmate who had your back. Together you were a devoted Gang of Two, each making sure the other didn't get shanked or shivved.

You are my wife, Alex thought, letting the word unfold and open up to show all its facets. *You're my wife, you're my best friend. My partner, my lover, my gang member. The mother of my spawn who won't leave us in peace when we're trying to fuck. You drive me crazy.*

And I don't need anything else but you.

A third presence shimmered beyond his consciousness.

But right now I think I want more than you.

"What's he doing?" Val whispered.

"I don't know," Alex said. "I'm no good at this, I don't know where to put him."

She got off his lap and turned around. Reached back to guide him into her heat. He held her hips and moved in her, feeling caged in his desire now, and desperate. Reaching for a maddening itch just out of reach of his fingernails.

"See, now," she said, "if I had the two of you…"

He ran his palms up and down her back. "What," he whispered.

"I could be on you like this. But Jav could be kneeling in front of us."

Alex's calves prickled. A hand reached through the wall of his chest and started stirring things around. Heat coiled up tight in his belly, then started uncoiling as he imagined Jav sinking onto his knees between Alex's feet.

"His mouth could be on both of us," Val said.

Alex jerked up harder inside her as he felt Jav's hands slide along his twitching quads. Jav's head bending and his lips opening. His tongue only looking for Val at first. Just accidental contact with Alex. Then incidental contact. Then intentional. Giving them each a turn.

The air turned thick and hot in Alex's throat. His foot lifted off the floor a little, brushing his calf against Jav's invisible hip. Warm, smooth skin over taut muscle.

Fuck, I can feel him.

I want to feel him.

"How's that work?" Val whispered. A flick of her head and her hair swept across her shoulders. The shadow in the arch of her back as she leaned on the armrests for leverage. The hard, tight line of her thighs flexing. Jav's hands sliding beneath her knees and curling around Alex's legs. Holding him. Spreading both of them open and apart so he could get in, go down, go *there* and get a taste of their love.

"It works," Alex said, his mouth dry around inhaled breath and then damp with each heaving exhale.

"I'm so turned on."

"So am I."

"We making you feel good?"

"Don't stop."

In the reality of the night, Val rode him, hard and fast. Deep in Alex's wasted mind, she was wrapping her hand around his erection and guiding it into Jav's mouth. Then putting it back in her. Then in him. In her. Letting Jav have longer and longer turns. Calling the shots. Holding both of them exactly where she wanted.

And Christ, Alex was *into* it.

"Don't stop," he whispered. His fingers curled down on the armrests. His nails dug into the skin of the image and started scratching. A fuzzy static rippled down the center of his perception—like the soundless apex of a yawn, or the limbo of nodding off before bolting awake again.

"Christ, I can feel both of you," he said through the wall of his teeth.

"Come then," Val said hoarsely. "Come for us."

He came in his head before his body joined in, his cells peeling opening layer by layer, heart pounding thick and hard in his chest. He came in his wife's body, came in his friend's mouth. He came forever, flung from the edge as his brain turned inside-out. He came so hard he drooled, sucking wet air between his teeth, cells detonating in feathery white shivers as he shot into a dark, wet warmth that had two names.

⌒

WALKING THE DOGS the next morning, Alex turned off Bemelman onto Main Street. When he saw Jav coming out of the Lark Building, he pulled into the recessed doorway of Murphy's, hiding under the awning until Jav disappeared into Celeste's.

Hiding?

The hell is wrong with you?

Last night, that was what.

Big deal. You and Val were stoned and messing around with a threesome scenario. Who cares?

True. But.

It's nothing he's ever going to know. It was behind closed doors, where anything goes.

He kicked himself in the ass and started down the street again. Jav came out of Celeste's with a cup of coffee. Shorts, rumpled T-shirt, flip-flops. Unshaven, his hair undecided. Even hungover he managed to exude a fuckable vibe. It wasn't fair the man had to work so hard to look like shit.

"You look like shit," Alex said.

Jav swayed sideways and leaned on the building's brick wall. "You look like you got the shit fucked out of you."

"You have no idea."

And by the way, you blew me. I rather enjoyed it.

Did you?

Nodding the tiniest bit, Jav's bloodshot eyes held Alex's. "¿Por qué te estás sonrojando?"

Goddammit, Alex *was* blushing. His face burned. All of him burned, his mind's needle stuck in the groove of last night. How vivid and real it had been. How his calves sensed Jav kneeling between them and how his quads sighed under Jav's palms. His imagination made a clear distinction between inside Val and inside Jav's mouth. It was utter craziness.

"Ever come so hard you drooled?" Alex said.

"No. Describe it to me." Jav's mouth settled on the rim of his coffee cup and took a sip, his eyes still looking Alex up and down. Appraising. Or perhaps waiting. The moment swelled. Pulsed faintly. It took a moment for Alex to identify the coiled, purring energy around them as chemistry.

Jesus, if he were a woman, I'd be going for it.

"If we're done here, I'd like to go back to bed," Jav said.

"We're done."

"Then move, fucky."

Alex moved and Jav shuffled inside. "I'll call you later," he said over his shoulder.

Alex stared through the glass of the door, following Jav in his mind. Back to his bed. He thought about all the beds Jav must've been taken to in his life. Hundreds. Women paid to fuck him. He was a man in high demand. Yet he slept alone.

The doorknob hummed with a magnetic temptation. Luring Alex. Attracting him.

I'm attracted to Jav.

"Hey, Alex, how you doing?" The manager of Lark's winebar walked by, juggling coffee, laptop and keys, on his way to work.

"Hey," Alex said, blinking back into the present. Back into himself. He hustled the dogs through the rest of the walk, went home and attacked Val in the shower.

"Jesus, what's with you?" she said, laughing as she slipped and slid in his arms.

"Aftershocks." He closed his eyes as he tore at the itch and reached for the images of last night.

He couldn't get hold of them.

Thank God.

MILAN-LIVERPOOL

"**Y**OU FEEL ALL right?" Val said. "You don't seem yourself."

"I don't feel like myself, no," Alex said.

"Anything specific going on? Or just general meh?"

"General meh. It'll pass."

He hoped.

This morning, for the third time since Armchair Night, Alex woke up in the throes of a wet dream. *Three* times in a week. Even at the apex of puberty, he didn't have that kind of track record. Maybe the fantasy was a flick of the faucet for Val, but Alex was a deluge, spilling out and flooding everything.

Literally, he thought, throwing the sheets in the wash.

What would Val say if he confessed he was a little infatuated with Jav?

"A little," he said, snorting to the shower tiles. "More like I have a man crush."

That's what Deane called it.

"It's adorable how you and Jav flirt," she said the other night.

"We don't flirt."

"Dad, you *totally* flirt. You have a man crush."

Shaving, Alex thought about crushing on girls in school. Most of the time it was a one-sided experience. You spent more time observing your crush than you did interacting. And interaction was mostly feeling like a moron, and only occasionally feeling you were making a good impression.

Why am I trying to impress Jav?

He rinsed the blade, digging into the strange nervousness that piggybacked on his shoulders every time he saw Jav these days. The weird need to be...

"Liked?" he said to the mirror. "You know he likes you."

His forearm tingled, remembering the glide of Jav's palm along it. Jav's fingers sliding between his, curling down and holding on.

I'm attracted to him. This literally happened overnight.

He tried to dismiss the idea as literal bullshit but found he couldn't. He and Jav shared their 9/11 stories on the drive home from Vermont. They held hands on the steering wheel for a minute. (*Or a minute and a half,* Alex thought). That night in bed, dragons attacked Alex with thoughts of airplanes and his parents. It took Val, a Xanax, and thinking about holding Jav's hand to send Alex to sleep, where he dreamed of many things. Jav leading him, guiding him, following him, assuring him. Jav holding Alex's hand. Jav against Alex's back.

It's no wonder we kept finding each other.

Alex woke up the next morning with a need to hold his own hand on the steering wheel. Thinking about Jav for long minutes and half minutes. Thinking about his touch.

I woke up changed. I'm attracted to him now.

Every night in dreams, Jav's hands were on Alex. Not in a way that was particularly sexual. Technically he was just hugging Alex. Wrapping arms around from behind and crushing Alex tight in the fist of his body. Hard muscle and immutable strength. Ruffling Alex's hair and kissing his head.

Is it a father's embrace? Alex thought. *Is this nothing but a gigantic Freudian analysis? I'm looking for my Dad? Or even my lost sibling?*

If that was the case, what about the dreams where Alex turned around? Turned in the circle of arms, turned to face the broad plain of Jav's chest and feel his hands ache for it. His watering mouth open for it. His cock stiffen and rise up to meet it. Until he woke up coming for it.

Alex looked at his reflection a long time. "You're not gay," he said. "Don't be fourteen about this. He's a highly sexualized person. Sex is his business, for fuck's sake. It's his job to be crushed on. Chill and ride it out. Crushes never last forever. Have some fun with it."

It certainly wasn't doing Alex any harm in the bedroom. Threesome thoughts had him continually worked up these days, and he made love to Val like the world was ending. Every wild night gave him the opportunity to fit Jav into the action, any way his masculinity would permit. Sometimes Jav just watched. Sometimes he and Alex went to town on Val. Sometimes she took both their asses to church. On adventurous nights, Alex let Jav hold him from behind and press his chest against Alex's back, while Alex gave Val his best. And if Jav happened to be sporting wood while he was doing his job—hell, that wasn't Alex's fault. Nor was it anything close to unpleasant.

I like feeling him there.

It was hot. It turned him on, fired him up. He took everything in his head, flung it into Val and made her come like a freight train to Crazytown.

He should be thanking the guy.

Or paying him.

"Will you relax?" he muttered inside a towel. "Quit picking it apart."

He couldn't. Any time his phone pinged, he hoped it was Jav, wanting to hang out. Then they'd hang out and Alex's mind turned into a team of statisticians, analyzing every word and thought and look. And why did Alex *look* at Jav so much? How much was too much? Jav made real intense eye contact when he talked. Did he always do that? Why did holding his gaze feel like playing chicken?

What the fuck is happening to me?

"You all right?" Jav said. "You don't seem yourself."

It was Memorial Day, and they'd met up at a sports bar to watch Milan play Liverpool in the UEFA Championships.

"I'm good," Alex said around a mouthful of Buffalo wings. "Tired."

"Val keeping you up nights?"

Alex smiled. "I call her fucky for a reason."

On the TV, the network cut to sports news. A clip of an interview with John Amaechi who'd come out as gay the previous February: the first former NBA player to go public with his sexuality.

"I underestimated America," the athlete said. "I braced myself for the wrath of a nation under God. Instead the support has been overwhelmingly positive."

"Huh," Jav said. "He should try the wrath of a household under Tío Miguel."

Alex regarded what seemed to be a baited hook. He tore a wing into two sections and took a casual bite. "Tell me about your cousin."

"Nesto?" Jav chewed and swallowed, then took a long, thoughtful pull of his beer. "We grew up together," he said. "We were born days apart. His mother had some problems afterward so my mother took care of both of us. We were like…boobmates."

Alex laughed.

"There's a word for it," Jav said, laughing along. "Some slang expression for two kids who nurse from the same woman. I know I've heard it but I can't remember. Anyway. Literally we ate together, slept together, played together. Had chicken pox together…"

Jav wiped off his fingers, crumpled the napkin and tossed it aside. He grimaced against a fist, shaking his head. "I used to be able to eat three dozen wings and not even belch. Now I look at them and get heartburn."

"How you guys doing?" the waitress said, looking only at Jav. "Can I get you another round?" She made it sound like a proposition.

"I'm good," Jav said, looking only at Alex. "You want more?"

"If it's good, I want as much as you can give."

Upstairs, the statisticians were having a meltdown. Jav kept looking at him, ostensibly to ignore the waitress but Alex could feel his face starting to burn.

"Te estás sonrojando," Jav said. "Again."

"It's hot in here." Alex glanced at the waitress. "Is it hot in here, or is it him?"

She giggled. "Oh, I think it's him. Although you're easy on the eyes, too. You guys brothers?"

"Boobmates," Alex said.

"Ignore him," Jav said. "You can take that." He slid the plate of bones and crumpled up napkins over. "Please." The waitress blinked at the dismissive tone, took the plate and left.

"Meanwhile," Alex said. "Back in the playpen."

"Hm? Oh. So we grew up together and... Ever since I can remember, Nesto was always hanging on me. It's one of my earliest memories, actually. Napping with him and he was jammed tight into my side. He was touchy-feely. You know the type."

"Nobody questioned it?"

"Between family? Why would they?"

"So the night up on the roof was the first time it went beyond family affection."

"Yeah." Jav ran his hands through his hair, held them there a moment then put up one index finger. "I'm getting my thoughts together. It's easy to see a lot of things now that I didn't then. It's not so easy to get back into my teenage head and remember the narrative."

"Plus you were drunk."

"That, too." He rolled his beer bottle around on its bottom. Let go a second as if to balance it. "I remember... My mind kind of splitting straight down the center. One half thinking, *This is nothing I am.* The other half thinking, *But it sure feels good.*"

Jav's tone had dropped and his cadence slowed down. Each word parceled out.

"What were you doing exactly?" Alex said.

"Well his finger wasn't on my prostate but—"

Alex threw a stack of napkins at him.

"Nice," Jav said, laughing. "We were just jerking each other. Kissing. And... It felt like a natural extension of all the other contact. It didn't feel wrong. I was into it." He smiled. "I know I definitely had the thought, *Um, maybe this isn't a good idea.* But it wasn't… Shit, this is hard to put into words."

"It sounds like you weren't exactly shocked by it."

"Right," Jav said. "I wasn't. And look, maybe that was the booze, who the hell knows? But once it was happening, I didn't try to stop it. He kissed me and I kissed back and it felt good. He touched me so I touched him. My body thought, *All right, this is interesting. Let's check this out.*"

Once again Jav was pushing chips onto the table. Anteing up and Alex couldn't match the bet.

"Sounds like it felt safe," he said. "Not only because it was him, but because you had the excuse of being drunk."

Jav nodded, a smile lifting one corner of his mouth. "I guess at a time when we were both experimenting with girls and not getting far, we were kind of a sure thing with each other." He exhaled heavily. "And then my uncle walked in. Game over. The rest is history."

"You never saw Nesto again?"

"Oh I saw him plenty. When he and his buddies were beating me up and down."

"What about your buddies?"

Jav gave a bitter chuckle. "All of a sudden I didn't have any. Funny how that works."

"Jesus."

"Eventually Nesto's father, my Tío Enrique, moved them to Manhattan. After that, no, I didn't see him again. Didn't talk to him, didn't hear about him. Not until I found out he was dead."

Alex hesitated. "What happened?"

"He jumped off the GW Bridge."

"Are you shitting me?"

Jav shook his head.

"Why… What would've made him…?"

"I think because he was gay," Jav said. "I mean, I'll never know. But when I fit the pieces I have together, it seems to be the picture that emerges. He was gay. He got caught and let me take the fall. He went on to live a lie until he couldn't anymore." Jav shrugged. "It's the story I tell myself, anyway."

"I wonder if what he did to you haunted him."

Jav's shoulders gave a flick up and his jaw hardened. A man's instinctive clench against intense vulnerability. Refusing to believe it was that bad when in brutal fact, it was.

"Your cousin really broke your heart," Alex said. "Your entire family, every one of them, just smashed your fucking heart to pieces."

Jav rubbed his fingertips across his forehead. "Yeah."

Their eyes held across the table, both of their chins raising and lowering. Alex swallowed and his instincts told him to look away. He held instead.

All right, this is interesting. Let's check this out.

"It's safe telling you stuff," Jav said. "I mean right from the start, at Morelli's Diner, when I told you my weird thought about the World's Fairgrounds and the Unisphere. A giant's abandoned plaything."

"I remember."

"The minute it was out of my mouth, I was braced for ridicule. But you didn't laugh. You kind of felt the same."

"Everything about that place says *don't you love me anymore?*"

Jav nodded. "And all jokes aside, that's why I gave you my card."

For a moment the world stood still as Alex stood at a crossroads.

I'm attracted to him.

Jav was holding his gaze and not letting go. Alex could either see this through or joke it away.

He counted to five.

And chickened out.

"Well, we all know you wanted Val's business, too," he said.

Jav's entire expression tripped. He blinked around the confusion in his eyes. "Well…"

"An escort has to make a living."

"Right."

"It's cool, it's in the past. We're civilized people."

Jav looked away, shaking his head. "You Larks are going to be the death of me."

The waitress appeared, lipstick fresh and glistening and an extra button in her blouse undone. "How are you guys?"

"At what?" Alex said.

Jav kicked him under the table. "We'll take the check, thanks." As she walked off, pouting, he kicked Alex again. "I can't take you anywhere."

"C'mon, I'm an excellent wingman."

"Oh yeah, you got all the good lines. 'Someday I'll be able to check you for worms.'"

Alex groaned. "Jesus."

"You must've gotten a *ton* of chicks with that one."

Alex slapped the table, laughing. "I can't believe you remember that."

"It was kind of unforgettable."

"I was such a dork."

"Was?"

The waitress came back with the leather folder. "Who's the lucky man?" she said, holding it out.

Jav closed his fingers around it but didn't take it. "May I?"

"Will I have to put out later?"

"Yes."

Alex gestured assent. "By all means then."

This is nothing I am, he thought, watching Jav sign. *But it feels all right.*

It's stupid fun.

That's all.

"What's going on this week?" Jav asked as they walked across the parking lot.

"Got a transport of pups coming in tomorrow, adoption event on Thursday. Four spays. Six neuters. One hip dysplasia. Other assorted pleasantries."

"Worm checking?"

"Worm checking. Anal gland expressions. Rabies shots. Blah blah."

"Your career turned out far sexier than mine."

"Hardly."

"Telling you, on my next date, I'm definitely trying an anal gland expression."

"You may have to raise your rates."

"Five hundred for a minute and a half."

"Jesus Christ, are you ever going to let that go?"

"Um. No." Jav reached and ruffled Alex's hair. "You good to drive?"

"Yeah, I'm fine."

"Adiós, mi compai." Their right palms smacked together and they pulled in for a hug.

The broad plain of Jav's chest settled against Alex's heart. Jav's hands patted his shoulders. Rubbed in a circle. Both of them sighed and held still.

This was interesting.

No, this is nothing I am.

"All right, break it up," Alex said.

"You first."

Alex pushed him away. They grinned as they stepped back, but the night slumped, looking from one man to the other, disappointed.

"You're killing me," Jav said, and punched Alex's arm.

"What?"

"Nothing, I'm an idiot." Jav opened his car door, put a foot into the well and paused. "What, are you watching me drive away?"

"Yeah," Alex said. "Actually." He crossed his arms on the roof of his car, rested his chin on top and watched Jav back out. Long after the taillights disappeared and the last honk of the horn echoed in the car's wake, he kept staring. Kept wanting.

What I want is nothing I am.

NOT FOR SALE

*T*HE FIFTEEN-MINUTE DRIVE home was enough time for Alex's euphoric buzz to wear off and a confused headache to take its place. Plus a delayed case of Sunday Blues. The holiday weekend was over and tomorrow was back to the grind.

Hoo. Fucking. Ray.

He trudged upstairs to his bedroom. He could hear the shower running. Deane, for some reason, was standing by Val's side of the bed, looking at Val's phone.

"What are you doing?" Alex said.

Deane looked up, pale and wide-eyed. "I…"

Annoyed, Alex put his hand out. "Give it. We snoop on you, you don't snoop on us."

"Sorry, I…"

Alex crossed his arms, the phone tucked in his hand. "Did anyone walk the dogs?"

"Not yet."

"Go walk them. And mind your business."

He shook his head as she split, muttering, "Nosy little shit."

He looked down at the phone, which showed a text from Jav: **Did u tell Alex about us?**

For a moment Alex was confused, thinking he was looking at his own phone and the text was missing some punctuation.

Did u tell, Alex? About us?

His other hand checked his back pocket. His phone was there. Val's was in his hand. With a text from Jav.

Did u tell Alex about us?

He read and reread the text. Of all the words, *about* was the most puzzling. The most loaded and sinister. Staring at the display, Alex walked toward the bathroom, intent on finding out what this was *about*.

Val was singing in the shower. He looked through the steamy gap between the curtain and the tiled wall. She turned in the spray, rinsing the last suds out of her hair. Eyelashes wet on her elegant cheekbones. Water dripping down her breasts and off her nipples. Steam wreathing the body Alex knew by sight, sound and smell. His hands knew the feel and his tongue knew the taste of every inch of her skin. They were each other's bank vault, guarding secrets and fears and pain and dreams. One thought it, the other said it. So connected, they barely needed to speak out loud.

Did u tell Alex about us?

Val jumped when Alex pushed the curtain aside, the metal rings squealing across the rod.

"Jesus, you scared me," she said, and spit some water.

He stared at her. Her chin tilted, eyebrows coming down.

"What's wrong?"

He turned the phone toward her and asked, "What's this *about*?"

She read the text. He watched the color drain out of her face. Watched her skin rise up in a grid of goosebumps. Watched her chest expand and contract as she took a slow deep breath through her nose. She turned off the water. Her hand reached for a towel but Alex took hold of her wrist, stopping her.

"What *about* you and Jav are you not telling me?"

He held her wrist, making her stand there naked and wet and cold to answer him.

Her shoulders trembled but her eyes met his and held still. "I used to hire him."

His fingers tightened. He felt the roll of her bones and a crunch of a tendon.

"Twenty years ago," she said. "While you were out in Colorado."

They stared. The fan hummed, cocooning the bathroom in white noise.

"You paid Jav to fuck you," he said.

Her chin raised a hair. "I paid him for his time. You're hurting my wrist. Please let go."

His fingers loosened. Her eyes didn't leave his as she took the towel and wrapped it around her body.

"Why didn't you tell me?" he said.

"Alex—"

"All this time," he said. "All this time you were…"

"No, not all."

"You and him were—"

"It was twenty years ago."

"I'm supposed to believe that?"

Her eyes widened and blinked twice. "Yes," she said. "You are."

The two-decade narrative whirled like a carousel in Alex's head. "I don't believe this," he said. "I don't fucking believe you lied to—"

"I've never," she cried out. "Tell me one time I ever lied to you."

"One time? How about the past twenty goddamn years?"

The disbelief was morphing into anger and the anger was primed by his utter stupidity. He'd been making a fool of himself. Nurturing a misguided infatuation. Trying to flirt like a pathetic twink. Staining his sheets for some guy who didn't give a flying fuck about Alex.

He wants her.

"I didn't know how to tell you," Val was saying. "After so many years went by, I didn't see the point in telling you. Then you and Jav became such good friends that I…"

The phone dropped from Alex's hand and clattered to the floor. He dragged his palms along his head. The carousel whirling, pieces falling into place, history rewriting.

He doesn't want me, he wants her. Again. He's using me to get to her. And she's…

"Oh my God," he said, fingers digging into his hair. "I'm such an idiot."

"Alex, I'm sorry," she said. "Let me get dressed, we can—"

"No," he said. "We can't." He walked out of the bathroom, then out of their room. Along the hall toward the stairs.

"Alex," she called after him.

He went down, each foot on a tread making his spine vibrate. Deane sat on the bottom step, tying her shoes. The dogs sat nearby, leashed and ready to go out.

"Alejandro," Val said from the top of the stairs.

Alex looked back and up. "Don't fucking talk to me." He turned and Deane was staring at him, mouth open in an O of shock.

"And you mind your business," he said. He banged out of the house, strode down Bemelman and turned onto Main Street. He walked past big stores and little houses. Battle-ready, confrontation prepared, he had a hand on the knob of the red door leading to Jav's apartment when he remembered something.

Ari might be home.

His eyes closed.

"Oh for fuck's sake," he said under his breath. "Ari."

He stepped back, looking up at the second story windows, as if the way they were lit up would tell him who was inside. He didn't want to do this in front of Ari. Deane would never forgive him.

Of course, Deane snooping around started this whole mess.

It would serve her right.

"Looking for someone?"

Jav had come out of Celeste's, laptop under his arm, a cup of coffee in his hand. He leaned a shoulder into the brick wall and his eyes gave Alex an up-down. The statisticians in Alex's head crossed their arms and narrowed their gaze.

Jav's crooked smile slowly straightened. "You all right?"

"No."

Jav's eyebrows came down. "What's going on?"

"I saw the text."

The eyebrows went up. "¿Qué?"

"The text you sent Val, asking if she told me. The answer is no. She didn't."

Jav took his shoulder off the wall and stood up straight. The cup in his hand trembled the littlest bit. "Alejo…"

"She never told me. Here we are, the three of us such close friends, our kids are dating. And she never once told me she used to hire you."

"Oh Christ, man, I…" Cup still in hand, Jav pressed his thumb knuckle between his eyebrows. "I'm sorry."

"What you are is one arrogant son of a bitch."

"Look, it's not what you—"

"I know what it is, Jav. I get what you've been doing. I may be a little slow and a little too trusting, but I'm not a complete idiot."

"You got it all wrong. Dude, you're my best friend."

"While my wife's your best client."

"It was twenty years ago. I have no idea why she didn't tell you about it, but was I supposed to? It wasn't my story to tell."

"Oh, I got one to tell," Alex said. "Once upon a time, you keep the fuck away from my wife. You keep away from all of us, you understand me? My family is not for sale. You come near me, near Val or near my house ever again, and I'll fucking kill you. End of story."

BREATHE
ONE BREATH

DAY ONE

*V*AL LOOKED AT the clock. It was a minute since the last time she looked at the clock.

I'm never going to make it.

She'd been afraid to come to bed. Alex came home and went straight upstairs. Without a look, a word or a fight. Nothing but footsteps up the treads and the bedroom door closing. Not with a slam, but a definitive "keep out" click.

Am I allowed to get into my own bed? What's the protocol here?

She stayed in her office, tackling paperwork she typically avoided until the last minute. She kept glancing at her phone, waiting for a *please come upstairs* text she knew wouldn't be coming.

They'd never gone to bed angry. Maybe irritated and annoyed, bickering about something stupid. But they'd never gone to bed not speaking.

She put down her work, drawing a deep breath past her tight throat. She'd act normal and go to bed. They'd sleep on it. Everything wouldn't be fine in the morning, but it would be a little better.

It couldn't possibly be worse.

She turned out lights, locked doors and brushed her teeth. She didn't so much get into bed as insert herself between the sheets with as little noise and disruption as possible. Alex lay on his side, his back to her.

"Goodnight," she said.

The dark silence rolled its eyes.

Moments squeezed by. Val's heart pounded loud in the ear pressed to the pillow. She felt she was in one of those recurring nightmares when you were back in high school, sitting a final exam for a class you'd never taken.

Her hand reached across the desert of mattress between them. Her fingers tingled as they neared the back of his head, not in a pleasurable tickle but a sinister warning. Alex had an electric fence around him tonight. A force field impervious to her.

"I'm sorry," she whispered.

"You don't ever fucking talk to him again."

She could hear the clench in his jaw: every word forced out sideways through his teeth. She withdrew her hand and took a deep, careful breath. "All right."

She rolled on her other side, putting her back to the black, crackling energy radiating off Alex's shoulder blades. She inhaled and exhaled without making a sound, staring at the clock.

I'm sorry.

She closed her eyes, dividing and subdividing her offense, sorting and resorting.

She hired a man for sex. *I'm not sorry about it. I was a young, single, independent woman. What I did with my time, money and body was nobody's business. Hiring Jav hurt not a single person.*

She didn't tell Alex about it when they started dating. Or when they got engaged. Or at any time during their marriage. *Well, how the hell does that come up in conversation? "Hey honey, what's the craziest thing you've ever done? Bet I can top it." And what for?*

She didn't tell Alex when Jav did show up again.

And that was stupid. I regret it. I was wrong.

"I'm sorry," she mouthed. Her throat burned and ached. The tears leaked sideways, sliding into her nose. She didn't sniff. She didn't want Alex to hear her cry. She only wanted to be invisible, while at the same time her back screamed across the great divide of their bed, reaching pleading hands out to her husband. The man who never fell asleep without kissing her. The man who always made an optimistic pass at her when the lights went out. Or, at minimum, pulled her into his arms, pulled her against him and told her he loved her.

She looked at the clock and thought about going to sleep in the guest room. She stayed where she was. Sleeping next to him was both her right and her punishment.

If I don't do something, this is going to be the longest, loneliest night of my marriage.

"Alex," she said to the wall.

Not a rustle from behind her. The mattress didn't shift a millimeter. But she knew he wasn't asleep. He was her husband. She knew his sounds of slumber.

"I love you," she said.

A faint, measured inhale. "I am really angry right now, Valerie." His voice was tight and stiff, as if stuffed into a too-tight suit of armor. The V of her name slid into a B—something that only happened when Alex was upset.

"I'm so sorry."

"Fix it with Deane."

"I will."

"It affects all of us, you know."

"I know." His words piled up in her arms. She juggled them frantically, not knowing what to do with this box of anger, this bag of disappointment and this jar of disgust. *Mine? You're giving these to me?*

"Now I feel like I don't even want to see Ari in this house. Jesus fucking *Christ*, Val."

"I'm sorry, I didn't envision this happening."

"You didn't? Right in front of your face you saw I was getting tight with Jav. Ari empties our goddamn dishwasher three nights a week. You didn't think *once* that finding out about you and Jav would blow up three different relationships? Jesus, you're an idiot."

She flinched, screwing her face up tight. Her arms were laden with guilt and shame and she staggered under the load. Panic began to fill her veins, followed by a surge of anger as her mind immediately went on the defense. *Don't you fucking lecture me.*

She clenched her jaw hard. *Just listen. Let him dump it on you. You wronged him, he's hurt and angry. Acknowledge the emotion. Let him get the worst of it out.*

"It was stupid of me," she said, trying to keep her voice steady, but let the remorse come through. She was nauseous with sorrow. It wasn't merely lip service.

"You got that right," Alex said. "Stupid's only the beginning." All at once he was on her, right up against her back, extending his arm over her shoulder and pointing to the chair in the bay window alcove. "What happened over there? The other night? Remember?"

She nodded.

"It was fantasy. Except it wasn't. You really had him in your head the whole time. You knew exactly what it was like fucking him. For all I know you were *remembering* fucking him."

"No, that's not true."

"And I'm supposed to believe you?"

Her mouth opened but nothing came out. She slowly shook her head, letting everything fall out of her arms into a pile on the floor. "I can't make you," she said. The words couldn't get past her thick throat so they crawled out through her running nose. "I can't make you believe I don't want anyone but you."

"You lied to me," he said. "You were riding my cock and lying to me."

"Alex, please. It was twenty years ago and I don't *want* him."

He moved away from her, throwing himself down on his pillow again. "Fix it with Deane. I don't know what the fuck I'm going to do about this."

"I'm sorry."

"Just…go to sleep."

A hoarse laugh tumbled out of her chest. She couldn't help it. Go to sleep. Sure. Flip the "off" switch and pause all this until the morning. No problem.

I can't stay here.

The bed felt poisoned. Sullied and soiled. Such ugly words had never been exchanged in this space. Only love.

She'd ruined it.

Her teeth chattered. She pulled in breath after breath, trying to find a safe place, a haven, a comfortable position for her thoughts to lay in.

Stay here and own it. It's a test.

Vamos a sobrepasarlo.

No.

Vamos a superarlo.

I won't evade or avoid or get around this. I will get through it.

We will…

<hr>

HER EYES OPENED and her first thought was, *I slept?*

Holy shit, she slept.

Before she could congratulate her brain for shutting off, the bedroom door opened briskly and Alex put half his head in. "I'm leaving now. I made coffee."

You made coffee? That means you like me.

She snatched the gesture and gobbled it down. *You made me coffee. You offered me the elixir of life. All is not lost. It's going to be all right. We're going to get through this.*

"Thank you," she said, while her heart kowtowed, *Yes, thank you. I am most humbled and grateful for this generous gesture.*

"You need to talk to Deane before she leaves for school."

The pure nag in his tone tripped her gratitude and made her eyes roll. *Gee, thanks for reminding me. I would've surely forgotten.* "I will," she said evenly.

"What are you going to say?"

She sat up and faced his gaze. "I'm certainly not going to tell her that her boyfriend's uncle used to be an escort. If you would like to tell her, *you* instigate that conversation." It was an effort keeping the snark out of her voice before she'd even brushed her teeth.

Alex stared back and his chin raised up and down in the bare minimum of agreement.

"I'm going to explain you're angry at me for withholding information. I haven't yet decided how much information I'm going to give her about the information. I'll need a cup of coffee first. Thank you for making it."

He closed the door.

Val exhaled, folded back the covers and put her feet on the floor. "Day one of being on the shit list." She dug her fingers into her hair, scratching vigorously. "And I haven't a thing to wear."

Get up. Move. Game on.

It was cloudy and gloomy out. Of course. Even the sun was pissed at her. She washed, dressed and drew three deep, fortifying breaths before heading downstairs.

Deane was one of the few teenagers on earth who ate breakfast every single day. She had a cup of coffee and some homework in front of her, and a scrap of toast held in her teeth.

"Good morning," Val said.

Deane made a vague noise. Val poured a cup of coffee.

"I apologize for how ugly it was last night," Val said. "Dad and I have some things to work out and I'll expl—"

"I really don't want to talk about it."

"Good, you don't have to." Val pulled a chair out and sat. "It's awkward for everyone so I'll keep it simple. I used to date Jav. Dad and I weren't a couple yet, we weren't even living in the same city. Jav wasn't a serious romance, but it was a relationship. It ended on difficult terms which is why we lost complete touch for almost twenty years. I didn't tell Dad about him when he and I started dating, which was a mistake. And I didn't tell him when Jav randomly showed up in Guelisten and ended up staying. That was a bigger mistake and Dad is incredibly angry with me about it. I don't blame him. I was wrong."

Deane's face was an empty plate. She chewed slowly, tapping the point of the pencil on the notebook.

"I'm sorry," Val said. "I've upset both you and Dad. I've upset the house. I feel like shit and I'm going to do whatever I can to put things right."

Now Deane's eyes circled the universe as she crammed the last bit of toast in her mouth. "Whatever," she said around it. She collected books and papers and shoved back from the table hard enough to make coffee slosh in the cups. "I gotta go."

"Have a good day," Val called. After the front door slammed, she sat and drank her coffee, staring at nothing, thinking about nothing. Sheba padded over and put her muzzle on Val's knee.

"What do you think?" Val said to her. "Did I handle that all right? Short and to the point. I told her what she needed to know and I apologized."

Sheba yawned and blinked at her.

"Yeah, I suck." She ran her hand along Sheba's inky head and sighed. "I suck here so I'm going to work and not suck at my job."

DIFFICULT TERMS

"**1** DON'T HAVE A tissue or anything," Ari said. He stretched out the hem of his T-shirt sleeve and gently dabbed at Deane's face.

"Sorry," she said, blowing the air out of her lungs.

"Don't be sorry. You're upset."

"Everyone's parents fight. I don't know why I'm being such a baby about it."

"I think your parents fight on the same schedule as Halley's Comet," he said.

She pressed her forehead to his shoulder. "I can't deal. The air in the house is changed. It's *gone*. All night long I couldn't catch my breath."

"I'm sorry," Ari said, smoothing her hair and kissing her temple. "Come on, let's get out of the sun."

He put his arm around her and walked her toward the bleachers. It was cool beneath. And private.

"Tell me what happened," he said.

"I don't even know how to start. Did you know my mother and your uncle used to date?"

The strap of Ari's backpack slid off his shoulder and the bag hit the ground in a puff of dust. "I'm sorry?"

"Jav texted my mom yesterday and it said, 'Does Alex know about us?' Now Dad's pissed at Mom because she neglected to tell him she and Jav dated a bunch of years ago. Which makes things fucking *awkward,* to say the least."

Ari's mouth was slightly parted and he stared off over her shoulder.

"What a bitch thing to do," Deane said. "Why in hell would she keep something like that a secret? My dad is so upset and I don't blame him."

Ari's eyes slowly blinked. He looked like he was doing mental math problems and not digging the answers.

"What are you thinking?" Deane said, alarm coiling around her stomach.

Ari slowly sat on the ground, put his elbows on his shins and his chin on his hands. Now his lips were moving faintly.

Deane sat as well. "Ari?"

He shook his head a little and came back. "I'm sorry, I was putting together a lot of pieces of…" He stared off again, an index finger raised. "You're going to think I'm crazy, but this sort of makes sense to me."

"What do you mean?"

"Jav told me… Look, this stays between us, all right?"

"Of course."

"After Jav's parents threw him out, he had nothing. Nowhere to go. He was sleeping in a stock room for a while. He said he once won some cash in the lottery but he socked it all away as an emergency fund and lived hand to mouth waiting tables and shit."

Deane raised her eyebrows, not sure where Ari was going.

"He told me once, 'I did some stuff I'm not too proud of. But I did it to survive.'" Ari ran his hands back through his hair. "I kind of dismissed it, but then I heard him and your dad talking on the drive up to Vermont. I can't go to court with anything I heard. It was all in Spanish and Jav speaks so fucking fast, I can only pick up a few things. I understand your dad better. And I heard something that made me think…"

"What?"

"That Jav might have used to…you know. Turn tricks. Or something."

Deane's stomach felt hollow. "You mean have sex with people for money?"

He nodded. "Did you read *Client Privilege?* His short stories?"

"No, I only read *Gloria.*"

"All those stories are told from the point of view of a male prostitute," Ari said, just as Deane recalled how *Gloria in the Highest* was filled with whores of all persuasions. How gritty and raw the details of their lives had been depicted. Deane would close the cover and unconsciously wipe her hands off, as if they were coated with coal soot and cheap sex.

"Holy shit," she said softly.

Ari shook his head with a small groan, the lines of his face etched in misery. "I feel like shit discussing this. I can't prove it and it's not something I'd ever ask him or confront him about. I mean, Jesus."

"I know."

"Maybe it was something else. Selling drugs or whatever. I'm reaching here. The point is he went through a really fucked-up time. The bigger point, and this brings it back to your situation, Jav also told me a woman helped him get his act together." Ari exhaled roughly and looked at Deane. "Maybe that woman was your mom?"

"Huh."

"I don't know if it means she literally helped him, or if losing her was the catalyst to him getting his act together."

Deane's gaze wandered off in the distance. "She said it ended on difficult terms and they fell out of touch."

"If she kept it from your dad, it couldn't have been good. Maybe T broke her heart. Or his behavior broke her heart?"

"Maybe," Deane said, trying to make the two-dimensional pictures she'd seen that morning flesh out into a story. She was confused now.

"I'm sorry," Ari said. "I don't know if I'm any help, but what you were saying kind of clicked with some stuff I knew and some other stuff I wondered about."

"No, no," Deane said. "It's… God, this is fucked-up. And if you're right about Jav, then it's fucked up and *sad*."

She tried to picture Jav in that time of his life: younger, thinner, hungrier. Alone and desperate. Standing on a corner, a cigarette held tight in his mouth. Sole of his foot against a lamp post, looking up and down the street. Looking for work. For business. For money. For women.

For men, too?

Her mind flinched from the imagery, shivered it off and away. Maybe this was why gorgeous Jav had no one special in his life. Maybe he'd sold himself so many times, sex ceased to mean anything. Maybe it was such a horrific experience, when he finally achieved success in his writing, he decided people could look at him all they wanted, but nobody—*nobody* would ever touch him again.

"Poor Jav," Deane whispered.

"I know. You can't tell this to anyone. It's so empty, it has no legs, it's totally shitty and…"

"Oh, God, no. I won't."

They got up, brushed off their butts and picked up bags.

"You done for the day?" he asked.

"I have a free period then I have English. I'll go home and make a sandwich. See if the air's any different."

"Be careful, all right?"

"What do you mean?"

His hand caught hers, fingers twining. "Sometimes you get the answer to a question and it makes everything worse. Sometimes not knowing all the gory details is better. Your parents love each other. And that's probably why this sucks so bad."

Deane nodded. "They don't know how to be mad at each other."

He pressed his lips above her eyebrows. "Call me later."

She wasn't off school grounds when he pinged her phone: **Watched you walk away. Miss you already.**

She breathed easy going down Courtenay Avenue, Ari's story sliding into place and creating a scenario that made more and more sense with every step. Her mother did something foolish that hurt Alex, but Jav was really to blame.

Then the picture of Jav on a street corner jumped into Deane's head again and she felt bad for blaming him.

Goddammit.

Sometimes not knowing is better.

She got home more confused than ever. Alex was making a sandwich at the kitchen counter.

"¿Qué onda, cosita? You all right?"

"Yeah."

"Sorry it got so unpleasant last night."

"No biggie. I'd be pissed too if I found out my wife used to fuck my best friend."

She meant it to be flip, but as the words left her unfiltered mouth, she knew it was mistake. A split second when both her father and the entire kitchen whirled around, aghast.

Then Alex hit her.

It wasn't quite a slap. She sensed he checked it at the last second and only his fingertips cuffed her chin hard. A burning, embarrassed shame swept from her scalp to her chest. Other than a stinging swat on the butt when she chased a ball into the street at age five, her father had never hit her. Never.

"You watch your mouth," he said. "Just because I'm pissed at your mother doesn't give you carte blanche to be a bitch. Cachai?"

Her stomach turned over. "I'm sorry."

His finger pointed in her face. "If you hadn't been snooping around this wouldn't have happened."

"Dad, I'm sorry," Deane whispered, terrified of the rage in his eyes. The same anger he'd flung at Val last night.

He wiped his hands on a dishtowel and threw it on the counter. He left, abandoning his sandwich. The kitchen door slammed. Deane stood, trembling and mortified, her fingers pressed to her mouth. The kid who'd gotten spanked in front of her friends now looking for a victim, someone or something to make hurt as much as she did. Preferably more.

I hate you, she thought. *I fucking hate all of you.*

BURN THE HOUSE DOWN

"*T*HANKS FOR SEEING me."

Gloria put her chin on her hand. "You make it sound like I'm your therapist."

"Aren't you though?"

She touched his cheek. "I worry about you."

He sighed.

"And you sigh a lot when no one's looking. I wish you wouldn't, it makes me feel old."

He took the wine out of the ice bucket and topped their glasses with the last of it.

The waiter materialized and cleared their plates. "Can I interest anyone in dessert?"

Jav glanced at Gloria, who mouthed *coffee* as she opened her compact.

"We'll have coffee, thanks," Jav said.

Gloria fixed her lipstick and put her purse away. "Have you apologized to your friends?"

"I tried with Alex but he's...pretty pissed."

"Can't really blame him."

"And I called Val but didn't do much apologizing. She was screaming at me and it was hard to get a word in."

"I can't blame her, either."

"Not my finest moment."

"Think before you speak, Javier. It's the first thing I taught you."

"And the first thing I forgot."

She put her hand on top of his. "At least I know you don't make the same mistake twice."

"God, I wish I'd left well enough alone," he said, staring at the charred beams and smoking struts of his house.

They separated their hands so the waiter could set down coffee cups, cream and sugar.

"Are you in love with him?" Gloria said.

He opened his mouth, closed it, then exhaled. "I wouldn't know love if it knocked on my door," he said. "But he's all I think about. I know that much. Is it love or obsession? Do I love him, or do I love the idea of being able to love him because he's straight, married and safe?"

"You flew across a continent for his daughter," Gloria said. "I call that love."

"I do love Deane. I love all of them, Glor. It's such a tangled mess of feeling. He's like a brother to me. And I want him so goddamn bad at the same time." He pressed the heel of his hand into his forehead. "It makes me make really stupid decisions."

"Bad choices make good stories."

He laughed down at his lap. "Maybe I'll get a book out of this. It's some consolation."

She took both his hands now. "You lost everything once before and survived. You'll survive this."

Her love came through her squeezing fingers and soothed the most raw, stinging parts of his conscience. As he drove home from Manhattan, it was less *you fucking idiot* and more *perhaps we'll treat this as a teachable moment?*

"You fucking idiot," he mumbled. It was easier.

The past five days had been pure torture. Five days of Alex not speaking to him. It was like someone had removed one of Jav's leg bones and was forcing him to run a marathon. He didn't realize how invested he was in the daily contact with Alex until it ceased. The texts, calls and stop-bys were like oxygen, and now the supply was abruptly and angrily cut off. Jav suffocated through the hours, smothered by a self-loathing misery that made him ache to his bones. He could kick himself to death for firing off that text to Val.

With a groaning grunt, he slammed the steering wheel with both hands. That stupid, spontaneous, passive-aggressive high school drama club text. No hesitation before hitting the send button. He didn't even think about thinking it through. He thought about it plenty now, though, and every time it made him cringe.

"Idiot," he yelled at the windshield.

He turned on the radio. Turned it off again and scrubbed at his hair. Yawned. The drive to and from the city was getting old. But he didn't get to see Gloria much these days and he missed her. Right now he flat-out needed her. So when

Ari went with the shelter staff on an emergency rescue in Ulster County, Jav took advantage of the free night to meet his mentor for a late dinner. It was worth driving back at two in the morning.

He came around a bend of 9D, outside Hudson Bluffs. High beams from the other direction stabbed his eyes before dimming. Then Jav saw the dog, five feet from his front bumper.

"Cabrón," he cried, hitting the brakes. A squeal of locked tires and burning rubber and a flash of buff and white fur as the dog careened off the hood of the oncoming car.

"Jesus," he said, pulling onto the shoulder. The other car pulled off as well. It was full of teenagers, piling over themselves to get out.

"Are you all right?" Jav called, crossing the road. "Anyone hurt?"

"We're fine, we're good," a tall boy in a baseball cap said, breathing hard. "Holy *shit*, what did we hit? Was it a deer?"

"It was a dog," Jav said, brushing past him. He turned back and pointed a finger around. "Is anyone drinking? Say it now."

"No, man," the boy said, wide-eyed. "I swear."

"Good." Jav hustled over to where two other boys were crouched down over the dog.

"Oh fuck," one of them muttered. "Oh fuck this isn't good. Fuck."

It wasn't good. Jav took the panting, yelping dog's head into his hands. "Get my phone out of my jacket pocket," he said to one of the boys. "I have the Hudson Bluffs Animal Shelter in my contacts. Call them first, say we're ten minutes away. Then call 911 and ask for Animal Control. Go."

"I didn't even see it," the other boy said, on the verge of tears. "I had my eyes on the road, I wasn't texting or anything, I swear. I didn't even see it."

"It's all right, it was an accident," Jav said, trying to keep his voice calm above the dog's keening howls. "We have to get him to help now."

"Her," the boy said in a strangled voice. "And I think she's pregnant."

The first boy came back. "Shelter says if we can get her there it'll be faster. They're paging their on-call vet right now."

They put the seats down in the back of Jav's SUV. The teens had a blanket in their trunk and the driver crawled in to sit with the dog.

Jav felt a twist of nerves in his gut as they pulled into the shelter lot. *Alex went with the rescue*, he told himself. *He's not even here, so knock it off.*

But when the on-call vet hurried out to help them, Jav's stomach dropped to his shoes.

"Maldita madre," he muttered, cursing fate as he opened the hatch.

"Let me in, boys," Alex said, brisk and efficient. "Out of the way, please." His hands moved in a swift assessment before he caught Jav's eye. If he was surprised, he didn't show it. His game face was latched down tight.

"We're going to take her in, blanket and all," he said, gathering edges and corners. "Straight through, first door on the left. On my three. One, two..."

Jav shut his mouth and his feelings down, following orders and keeping the teens out of the way. His head spun from all the yelping and crying and keening, undercut with the fast, jargon-laced decisions Alex and the vet tech were making. Jav's tired eyes filled with protruding edges of bone, his nose breathed blood, wet fur and urine.

One girl was losing it, hellbent on making a situation that had nothing to do with her all about her.

"Put her down," she screamed over the dog's screams. "Put her down, make it stop."

The dog convulsed and the girl started gagging.

Pale and haggard, blood on his gloved hands and his scrubs, Alex didn't look up. "Javito, get her out of here," he said in Spanish.

Jav grabbed the girl and hustled her out, barely getting her to the small lavatory in the hall where she was dramatically sick. When he emerged, all the kids were in the waiting area, trembling and upset. Jav got some waters from the vending machine and calmed who he could. When parents showed up, he assured them it was a tragic accident and their kids had done all the right things.

Once the last family left, the bottom fell out and Jav dropped into a chair. *Holy crap.*

HIS CHIN JERKED up. He'd dozed off. Checking his watch, he saw it was nearing five in the morning. Lisa, the vet tech, came behind the reception desk with some papers and did a double-take. "Oh, Jav. You're still here?"

"Yeah, I fell asleep." He stood up stiffly and walked toward the counter. "What happened?"

Lisa shook her head. Her eyes were red-rimmed and puffy. "She had five puppies. Four were dead. The fifth was alive, but barely." She put her elbows on the counter, fingertips at her brow. "It rallied for a little while, seemed to stabilize. Alex put it with a German shepherd who whelped this week. She couldn't get it to eat though." Lisa glanced up at the clock. "Died about twenty minutes ago."

"Shit."

"Yeah."

"Where's Alex?"

"Cleaning up."

"I thought he went on the thing in Ulster County."

"No, our regular on-call vet is sick so Alex stayed behind to cover."

"Is he all right?"

Lisa's tired, swollen eyes blinked as she slowly shook her head. "He's...not handling it well tonight. For some reason. Want me to tell him you're still here?"

"No. Leave him be."

She got Jav some paper towels and cleaner and he wiped out as much piss and blood from the back of his SUV as he could. He'd do a more thorough job in the morning. He returned the spray bottle, washed his hands and headed back to his car.

"Don't make this about you," he said, paused with his hand on the door latch.

I'm not. I just want to make sure he's okay.

"He's fine. This is his job. Leave him alone and go home."

He turned around, put his back to the car and crossed his arms. He waited, staring at the clinic. Time dripped by. Jav was patient. Finally, Alex came out the back doors. He'd changed out of his scrubs into jeans and a T-shirt. Instead of walking to his car, he sank down onto the concrete steps and put his head in his hands.

Jav hesitated only a moment, then walked over. As his footsteps echoed on the concrete, he expected Alex to look up. He didn't. Coming closer, Jav saw Alex was practically hyperventilating.

"Alejo," he said.

Alex's fingers clenched tight in his hair and he kept looking down between his feet. "I told you not to come near me."

Jav ignored the threat and crouched down. "You all right?"

"I'm fine. Get lost, will you? Shit..." Alex curled tighter in on himself, head to his knees now.

"Take it easy."

"Fuck off."

"You'll pass out if you keep it up. Take a breath in and hold it," Jav said. "Let it out slow through your nose. Breathe slow through your nose, not your mouth."

Alex stayed slumped over but seemed to be listening. His breath slowed down and his fingers let up. Jav stayed crouched at a distance, measuring inhales and exhales.

"Better?"

"Christ, I need a drink."

"Be right back." Jav's birthday gift from Talin Trueblood every year was a bottle of Appleton Estate Rum. He had it in the car because he didn't like keeping booze in the apartment with a teenager around. He fetched it, using the penknife on his keychain to cut the foil.

"Here," he said, unscrewing the cap.

Alex looked up, like a man emerging from sleep to find a quarter century had passed. His eyes met Jav's in bewilderment, which gave way to a slow nod as his hand reached.

"Thanks," he said hoarsely, and took a slug. He screwed up his face as he swallowed, shaking his head hard. He looked at the bottle label in the dim light, then took another swig and handed the bottle back.

"I really don't want to talk to you," he said.

"We're not talking, we're drinking." Jav took a healthy chug, letting the oaken vanilla flavor fill his mouth before slipping in a fiery kiss down his throat.

"Shit," Alex said, hands in his hair again. "Jesus, it doesn't always bother me this much. I mean it *bothers* me, but you learn how to distance yourself from it. But sometimes... Man, it's when they're howling like that. When a dog *cries* in agony like that." Alex reached for the bottle and took another swallow. "Plus I'm not good when I'm woken up in the middle of the night. By a doorbell or a phone ringing. It kind of rattles me. I mean, it...reminds me."

"Of what?"

"The night my mother disappeared."

Jav crouched down, listening.

"The police arrested my father first," Alex said, turning the bottle over and over in his hands. "Burned the bookshop and took him in. About four days later, they took my mother..." His voice dissolved and he put his forehead into a palm a moment, taking a deep breath in. "They came around three in the morning. They rang the doorbell and woke us up. My mother pushed me into her closet and went with them. I never saw her again."

Jav slowly leaned back and rolled down onto his butt.

Alex took another chug of rum and handed the bottle over. "I was alone in the apartment for nearly a week. Hiding in the closet. And outside the window... The window I showed you in Santiago was my parents' bedroom. The window was open and out on the streets the dogs were barking. Until the soldiers started taking pot shots at them. Then the dogs started howling." He jerked his head over his shoulder. "Exactly like that one was."

Jav slowly nodded, as two pieces of a puzzle joined hands and gave a sly, mean glance his way.

"They shot one right by my building. It was screaming and crying and howling and I could hear it through the window. But it wouldn't die. It went on crying and crying. I couldn't take it after a while. So I got my father's knife."

"Oh Christ," Jav said into his hands, more puzzle pieces falling into place.

"And I went downstairs and cut its throat."

Jav went on nodding into the steeple of his fingers, remembering Alex crouched down by the front wall of the apartment, touching the sidewalk as Val asked, "Here?"

It's where he killed the dog. To put it out of its misery.

He was eleven years old. And the misery didn't stop because thirty years later, he cut himself with that same knife...

Alex was staring off across the parking lot. In the dim orange light he didn't look like a man who had unburdened his soul. He kept licking his lips and starting to speak, then his eyes would close and he'd sigh hard, trying to expel the last secrets lingering in his heart.

"There's more," Jav said. "Something else happened."

Alex nodded. "They gutshot her."

Jav leaned forward slightly. "¿Y estaba embarazada?"

Alex nodded, his lips curled in so tight they were invisible.

Jav looked down at the pavement. The dog was pregnant. And gutshot. Innards and dead puppies on the sidewalk. She was crying for her babies. No wonder tonight kicked Alex's ass.

Alex's breath was growing choppy again, his shoulders twitching. "So was my mother."

"Your...?"

"My mother was pregnant when they took her."

Jav swallowed. "How far along?"

"Seven, eight months."

"Jesus Christ."

"I can't think what... I don't talk about it. I can barely think about what they might have done to her and the baby." He swallowed. "And I can't not think about it."

Jav closed his eyes.

"I've read eyewitness accounts of pregnant women being pushed out of those airplanes," Alex said.

"Oh God, man, don't."

"I've read other testimonies of babies being born in prisons and detention centers and dying there. Accounts of babies taken from detained mothers and smuggled to Peru or Argentina. Adopted out of orphanages and growing up with no idea who they are. I could have a brother or sister out in the world. Or maybe he or she died with my mom. Maybe they shot her stomach open and she cried to death with her baby on the bloody ground. Or both of them could be rotted bones at the bottom of the Pacific—"

"Stop," Jav whispered.

"I can't stop," Alex cried, his voice echoing across the parking lot. "I'll never know what happened, so I can't fucking stop and neither can you. Don't sit there and tell me you don't dwell on the last minutes of Flight Ninety-three. Don't tell me you haven't imagined twenty-seven ways Flip died. His last words. His last thoughts. Whether he was on his feet or on the floor. If he was holding someone's hands praying or if he was alone in a ball screaming for his mother. Hoping to God he was dead of a heart attack before the plane hit the ground. How the impact must've torn him into *pieces*. Don't fucking tell me you don't do it."

"I do it," Jav said. "You're right. I do it all the time."

Alex gave a final exhale and crumpled, exhausted and drained. "Well, you got to see the show," he said around a terse chuckle. "Phone call in the middle of the night and a screaming dog who was pregnant. The perfect storm to make me lose my shit." His knee joints popped as he got up. "And I'm spilling it to the guy who used to get paid to fuck my wife. Christ, could my life be any weirder?"

Jav stared as Alex started walking away. Not to a car but an airplane.

Then he heard his own voice calling after.

"You want weird? The guy who used to fuck your wife is in love with you."

A sick thrill surged through him. Slightly triumphant. Almost holy. The martyr with nothing more to lose, willing to concede the war if he could win this battle. Die for his cause in a blaze of glory.

"Come on, man, let's make this really interesting," he said. "Why strike a match when you can burn the house down?"

Alex stopped. "The two of you are playing me for an idiot."

"I want you so bad I don't know what to do with myself. Who's the real idiot in the parking lot?"

Alex looked back over his shoulder. Jav got up.

"Let me tell you a story," he said. "I came around Morelli's Diner all those months because I liked you. I liked looking at you, watching you interact with people. Wishing I were one of them. I gave you my card the first time because you asked for it. I gave it the second time because I trusted you with my weird thoughts. I thought maybe you'd call. Just to hang out, you know? But when the phone rang, it was Val. I didn't know who she was to you but figured if she was calling me for a date, it couldn't have been that serious. Besides, I'm an escort, not the morality police. She called me and I had the time. It was a walk. Walks are easy, you just have to pay attention and give a shit. Then one thing led to another and—"

"I really need you to stop talking now."

"She hired me six times. I liked her. She was my favorite client. For a while I thought it could be something more but she was too smart for my baggage. She knew I didn't trust love, certainly not enough to give up the work. And she knew I liked men but I wouldn't admit it. No, that's not true. I admitted it, but never did anything about it. I was content to be bi-curious and bi-cautious."

"I'm going home," Alex said, and didn't move.

"I got too attached to her and she stopped hiring me. I sulked for a few months but soon enough, I got dopey about another client and she was my new favorite. I realized Val was right. Escorting is the work I do best. It's a sweet gig. I don't want to quit, why the hell should I?

"Then a bunch of years go by and I meet this guy, Flip Trueblood. He likes me. And I like him. I like him a whole fucking lot and I think, *Yeah, this could be it. This could be the one.* But he got on a plane on Nine-Eleven and my life turned into that picture you told me about. Jagged metal, rubble, smoke and apocalypse. I thought, *Never again. Forget it. Love and me aren't friends. I'll stick to escorting. That way lots of women love me, I don't have to love anyone in return, and nobody leaves me. I don't want and I don't lose. It's perfect.*"

Alex had turned all the way around now but Jav kept talking past him.

"Then I get a phone call one day," he said. "My sister's dead and I have guardianship of a nephew. In Guelisten. Like fate playing some practical joke, I see you on the street and it starts all over. I like a guy again. Except this time I want to make him miss his plane. I want to grab onto him and not let go. I don't want to talk him down to death from the sky, I want to talk him into my bed and never shut up because…"

The Earth was utterly still and silent. No traffic. No crickets. No hum of streetlights or rumble of A/C. Only Jav's voice, weaving through the quiet like a thread, sewing the pieces together.

"Because I love him," he said. "And I never get to say so. Fuck it, I'm saying it now. I love you, Alex. It started outside the embassy in Santiago. When you were between me and Val and we were holding you. I don't know if you remember, but for me it was unforgettable. It was a pure moment, nothing to do with sex or attraction. It was when you became my best friend. But it was also a match. Flame took hold around Thanksgiving. Then it exploded the day Pinochet died and I've pretty much been a forest fire since."

"Jesus Christ," Alex whispered.

"I love you. I love all the weird coincidences and random meetings and crossed paths. I love how my tiny little family got tied up in yours. I even love that Val…"

He finally looked at Alex. "I don't care anymore. I blew it all to hell with one stupid text. I might as well throw it all out there now. I love Val to pieces, but I don't want her. I want you. Now go home."

Alex swayed on his feet. "Jav, you and I—"

"Go home, man. Go home to Val. She loves you so much it's ridiculous and she's been your home since you were eleven. Don't hold this over her head. It was my fucking fault, my stupid text. Go home. You're straight, she loves you and I'm the idiot. Let there be one idiot, all right? Me. I'm good at it. I'm excellent at this job. You're excellent at being her husband. Let's just go do our jobs."

He pushed the rum bottle against Alex's chest until it was taken, then he walked away. Without looking back, he got into his car and drove home.

I'll leave, he thought. *I'll lay low and stick it out until Ari graduates. Then I'm going. For good. I'll get a place in the city with room for both Ari and Roman. It will be all right. I'll get over it. At least he knows.*

Alex knew. Jav wasn't choking down the truth anymore. Strangling on his own desire. He'd let it be known. A small step of progress.

"I'm bisexual," he said. He took a breath, let it out and came out. "I'm bisexual. I'm done being just cautious and curious. I like women *and* men. I like sleeping with women for money and sleeping with men for love."

He inventoried all four limbs and his head. Still here.

All things considered, he felt pretty good.

Maybe next time I'll put it all together, he thought, turning into the small lot behind the Lark Building. *Maybe there'll be a next time. A third chance.*

He was so lost in thought, he didn't realize Alex had pulled in next to him.

GROUND TO A HALT

*A*LEX CAME AROUND his trunk and stood between the rear tires of both cars, blocking all egress.

"You ruined my dramatic exit," Jav said, closing his door.

"Shut up," Alex said above the thud of his heart.

Jav crossed his arms. "My silence is expensive."

"Shut the fuck up."

Jav closed his eyes once and opened them again.

"We're so alike, you and I," Alex said. "With our missing families and our Nine-Elevens—"

"Yeah, yeah. Tell me what I don't know."

"When I called the hospital in Santiago to tell them you were coming, you know what I said?" Alex didn't wait for an answer. "I said my brother was coming. Those exact words. I said, 'My brother Javier is coming, and you tell him anything you would tell me. He acts in my stead. Until I get there, he is me.' You said I became your best friend outside the embassy. You were mine before I even got on the plane."

The wind blew through the lot, scattering a bit of litter and single tin can.

"I quit believing in God a long time ago," Alex said. "But when I saw you on the street with Trelawney last year, I had this crazy idea God or fate or something was saying, *Here, you lost your family, so I'm putting this guy back in your life. He's supposed to be here. You're meant to be around him. He's not Roger who comes and goes. He'll always be close. A friend who speaks all your languages. The guy who's always where you need him to be. When you need him.*"

Jav shrugged. "I'm an escort. I get paid to be where I'm needed." His eyes narrowed at Alex. "Now are you getting out of my way? Because if not, my time is fifteen hundred an hour. Up front."

"You're worth more than that to me."

The space between them stretched and contracted, like a pair of lungs. Dawn was beginning to turn the sky pale grey, yet time disappeared. As daylight emerged, layers of defense dropped from Jav's face. Atom by atom he unfolded, his shoulders sinking, arms dropping to his sides. Light began to fill the angles and planes of his face, his gaze filling with a pain that reached arms out to Alex like an old friend.

"What do you want, man?" Jav said, his voice hoarse. "I just came out and put my dick at your feet. I get you don't feel the same. But being told I'm your best friend isn't much consolation right now."

"I'm trying to tell you I do feel the same."

"I'm not *crushing* on you Alex. I fucking want you."

Alex moved a step closer. "The night you told me about Flip calling from the plane, I dreamed about you."

"Don't," Jav whispered.

"You were up against my back. All along my back. I was between you and Val. Exactly the way we were outside the embassy. I remember it. I relive it every night in my sleep. And every time I drive somewhere, I can feel your hand running down my arm."

"Stop telling me this shit."

"No. It's blown to hell so might as well throw it out there. I don't know what this is. I've never been attracted to a man in my life, but ever since the drive home from Vermont, I don't stop thinking about you. Jesus, I haven't fucked my wife since this shit went down but *you're* still in my goddamn dreams every night. All you do is hold me and I wake up coming. I get a hard-on any time I think about your fingers in between mine."

Jav's voice was a like a bottle breaking on the pavement. "Don't do this to me."

Alex never knew what made him do it. Maybe the sadness of living a good life when those you loved were pushed out of airplanes for someone else's cause. Maybe the struggle to be excellent at a job you never asked for. Or maybe it was simply the tiger filling up his eyes. Whether a momentary insanity or an impulse of the heart, he closed the last bit of space between them and put his mouth against Jav's.

Jav's body bucked, as if touched with a current, then, with a ragged exhale, he went still, his breath blowing warm against Alex's face.

The machinery of the universe ground to a halt. Bucked once, like Jav had, then settled.

Alex closed his eyes.

And breathed.

They didn't touch, except for their mouths. They didn't move, except for their breath. The inhale of one became the exhale of the other. Alex felt the Earth tilt and adjust beneath his feet. The odd proximity of rough, male skin and its beard growth became ordinary. The strange desire in his chest and groin became normal. The world was surreal but he felt himself present in it.

"Open your mouth," Jav whispered.

A jerk and a tug behind Alex's ribcage. A stab of adrenaline and his limbs were on fire, fingertips prickling. His eyes still closed, he let his lips part, tasted cool air across his teeth and tongue. Tasted oak and molasses as Jav slowly curled his mouth around Alex's bottom lip. Then the upper. Then he rested his eyebrows on Alex's and took a shaking breath. All of him was trembling.

"Do that again," Alex said.

Jav did. Slower. His lips releasing their hold with an agonizing reluctance. As he drew back this time, his hands came up and rested on Alex's shoulders. Warm and heavy. He didn't caress or pat. Only pressed, as if pinning them both in place.

"If you're going to walk away, do it now," Jav said.

"I'm staying here," Alex whispered. He was so hard, it hurt. So confused, he couldn't get one thought to hold still. His hands itched. He didn't know what to do. If Jav were a woman, Alex would have her up against the building now, his fingers plunged deep in her hair, turning her face around his kiss and pushing into her softness. If Alex were a woman, he imagined his back would be against the bricks, his hands pulling Jav's hardness closer.

Who was hard and who was soft here?

Who was pulling and who was pushing?

"Man, say something," Jav whispered.

"I want…" Alex swallowed, shivering under Jav's hands. "I want…you not to laugh at me."

"Do I look like I'm laughing?"

"*Fuck*, you always made me act like such an idiot."

"Hey." Jav took his head. His thumb touched Alex's bottom lip. "I'm the idiot, remember?"

A rush of cold air in Alex's throat as Jav leaned in.

What I want is nothing I am.

And then Jav's warm, rum mouth was on his.

Nothing I am.

Yet it was everything. Jav was kissing him and he was kissing back. Open-mouthed and hungry. His hands slid along the back of Jav's jacket and held on tight as he pulled hard and pushed soft.

He was a foreigner in his own skin and couldn't remember a time he felt more human.

Polarity reversed. Gravity resigned. The natural laws of the universe threw up their hands and surrendered as Alex threw everything he had at Jav, who caught it and threw it back. He kissed Jav, sinking into his mouth, holding Jav hard up against the brick wall. He felt edges of teeth along his tongue, rough stubble along his lips. It was all wrong, yet his body scooped it up and dumped it over his head, soft and wet and hot and melting and *right.*

"Jesus, I can't breathe," Jav said, breaking away, breathing hard. He was shaking.

Alex's teeth chattered as he pulled Jav back.

"Let go of me before I do something stupid," Jav said.

"No," Alex said, the world tilting and wobbling under his feet, his chest torn apart with desire that flooded his mouth like rum. He swallowed and swallowed, afraid it would go further. Terrified it wouldn't stop.

"Trelawney's coming any minute to open Celeste's. She'll find two idiots in the parking lot."

"Then let's go be idiots upstairs," Alex said.

Jav stared at him.

"Ari's on that rescue, isn't he?" Alex asked. "He's not home."

Jav shook his head, licking his lips.

"Come on," Alex said.

Jav reached behind him and peeled Alex's fingers off the clench on his jacket. He twined them with his, holding both their hands behind his back. "If you come up," he said, "if you put a foot over my doorstep, if you breathe one breath into my house... Then I'm locking the door behind us. Cachai?"

"Let's go."

"I'm not even close to kidding. You walk into my house and I will be on you."

"I know."

And it was Alex who led the way, walking past his wife's dress shop and opening the narrow red door between Celeste's and Lark's. Without looking back, he started up the stairs, breathing deeply. Filling the space with his air.

Behind him he heard the door close and a bolt slide. The snap of a light switch. Then footsteps up the treads. Following him.

On him.

THE MOST NORMAL THING

*A*LEX TRUDGED UP the front steps of his house, returning from a long journey as a changed man.

Sheba looked at him as he came into the front hall, her liquid eyes full of reproach.

And where have you been?

He walked past her, lurching toward the kitchen like an automaton with a few wires yanked out.

Already the memory was fading, replaced by a surreal doubt it even happened.

From the open basement door, Alex could hear the rhythmic cadence of feet on the treadmill. Val was working out. She had made coffee. He poured a cup, then left it forgotten on the kitchen table and went back toward the front hall. Heeling off his sneakers, he bumped the little table and knocked over a stack of magazines.

His memory focused, obliterating doubt.

The apartment door hadn't yet closed when Jav was on him. All three of them— the door, Alex and Jav—slammed. They crashed like a wave against the wall, careening against a little table and knocking things to the ground. Heeling off shoes, tearing arms from jacket sleeves and seizing each other again. They kissed like the world was ending. Like La Moneda was bombed, the Twin Towers were falling and the plane was in a nosedive. Neither was soft in the dark or pulling at the desire. They were both hard and pushing harder…

Alex went upstairs and started the shower. Waiting for it to warm up, he stood at the sink, running fingers over his mouth. Jav's kiss echoing there. He leaned forward, a hand on the wall on either side of the medicine cabinet, his forehead pressed to the cool glass. Remembering.

In the bedroom, Jav took Alex's wrists and pressed his hands to the white sheet-rock. As if Alex were under arrest.

"Hold still," Jav whispered.

Alex set his forehead to the wall, fingertips curling and digging but finding no purchase. Jav's palms were warm on his head. They slid down to Alex's shoulders, glided warm down his back. Stopped at his sides, fingers spreading, fitting into the indentations between ribs. Jav's mouth touched the back of Alex's neck.

"All right?" he whispered.

Alex nodded, his skin a raised matrix of bumps, his teeth faintly chattering.

"Hold still," Jav said again. He took one of Alex's arms, worked it gently out of a T-shirt sleeve and then replaced the palm on the wall. Repeated with the other sleeve. Then drew the shirt over Alex's head.

Jav's hands followed the same path now: head, shoulders, back and sides. On Alex's skin this time, warm and dry and strong. His breath a little choppy within the measured inhales and exhales. He touched the inked Unisphere. The long scar from Albacete. The band of Valerie and Deane around Alex's right arm. The band of The Disappeared Ones around his left.

"Your whole life means something to me," he whispered. His arms slid around Alex then. His chest glided warm and wide against Alex's back. A sound came out of Alex's throat, something between a cry of mourning and a sigh of relief.

Jav's fingers dug into Alex's hair. The edge of his teeth gently ran along the two 9/11s between Alex's shoulder blades. His mouth closed again on Alex's nape and his hands slid down, pulling the tail of Alex's belt free from its loop.

Alex's hands went to fists and the sound out of his chest had the tiniest echo of a howling dog. Jav's mouth slid along his spine. The floorboards creaked and tilted beneath Alex's feet. Jav was kneeling, his hands on Alex's hips, soft hair in the small of Alex's back. A long exhale.

"Alex, turn around."

Alex turned around. The bathroom was filled with steam now. He took his shirt off. Unbuckled his jeans. And remembered.

Jav touched Alex's belt buckle. Swallowed. "Are you scared?"

"No."

"I am." His fingers worked the buckle open. The air was heavy and thick as Alex moved his hand through it, pushing molecules and atoms aside to lay his palm on Jav's head. The spring and give of his thick hair. The shape of his skull beneath.

Button. Zipper. Jav pulling his jeans and shorts down. Off one ankle along with that foot's sock, then the other. Then his hands were on the map of Alex's body, looking for him. Finding him…

Alex found the soap and scrubbed as he usually did. Another ordinary day. His same bottle of shampoo, his same bar of Dial. His shower in his bathroom in his house where he lived with his wife. Her mouth had been the only one to touch his, and her hands had been the only ones on his body for the past eighteen years. Now Jav's hands had been on him. Today was eighteen years plus one day.

He shut off the water and dried off. His body cried to lie down but he went to the armchair in the bay window instead and sat. He thought about Val's beautiful back to him in the moonlight. The sucking pulling warmth up and down the length of him. The memory of Jav's hands and mouth in her head. Riding Alex's cock and lying to him.

Raindrops began to plink and plunk against the windows, beading up. Alex's hands ran up and down his bare legs. Remembering.

Jav ran his hands down Alex's quads. Then his arms circled Alex's legs and his cheek pressed down low on Alex's belly. Alex's heart pounded slow and thick but not out of fear. Not even in surprised wonder. As if standing here naked with his erection snugged up under Jav's chin were the most normal thing in the world. The air in the bedroom cloaked him in a cape of certainty. He wanted what he wanted.

His hands fisted around Jav's T-shirt. "Stand up."

He pulled Jav's shirt off, then went for his belt buckle. Jav stepped out of his pants and Alex reached for him. Facing the dream, pulling it against him, testing its strength. Testing his own desire.

Are you in? Are you breathing this breath? Walking this walk?

Jav planted one forearm on the wall and put his weight on it. The other open palm made slow circles around Alex's heart. "Feel good?"

"Yeah."

Jav moved closer. His hands slid around Alex's head. Then they were going at it again, kissing like tigers. Sighing and growling. Tumbling like felled trees onto the bed. Skin on skin. Pain on pain. Hard to hard and soft to soft. Neither above nor below, only face-to-face, four hands wrapped around two needs and rum-sweet breath in their mouths and noses and lungs. Spanish words. English words. Wordless words.

"All right?" Jav said.

"You don't need to keep asking me," Alex said, holding Jav's face in his hands. "I'll tell you when it's not all right."

Jav rolled on him, pushed him down and pinned him tight. This kind of loving felt like fighting. Their bodies crashing together like two rutting bulls, locking horns and twisting, trying to see who would break or back off.

"Give me more." *Alex shook with hunger. He was a ravenous hoard, starving, ready to fight to the death for this meal.* "More than this, I know you have more. Come on, Javi, I can take a lot more than you think."

"I know." *Jav's voice chiseled away at the dark.* "But can you take me, Alejandro....?"

"Alejandro?"

Alex blinked and came back to the present. His bedroom in his house. His wife standing in the doorway. Pink-cheeked and sweaty from exercise. His fierce tigress. His beautiful lark.

"When did you get home?" she said.

"Just now."

"Was it horrible?"

He looked at her, unable to answer.

Because it was ridiculous.

From the floor, inside a pocket, Jav's cell phone rang. They both froze up, panting. Listened through four shrill demands for attention, and then a silence that screamed. Jav reached to put his palm on Alex's head, his thumb running along Alex's eyebrows. The pained desire in his face beautiful in a way Alex couldn't articulate aloud, only feel in his bones and recognize in his heart.

Now the house phone rang, loud and jarring from the night table.

Alex swallowed. "Answer that?"

"No." *Jav kissed him, crushing him into the mattress. His skin fiery and his weight pinning Alex down. The moment swelled, buzzed like a hive of bees.* "I want you so fucking bad," *Jav whispered.*

Alex grabbed at Jav's kiss like it was honey, gulping and greedy. He barely recognized himself—his arm hooked up around a man's neck, his fingers sliding over sideburns and digging into short hair and liking it. Thrashing and snarling inside this alien desire. Groaning as Jav kissed his way down Alex's chest, his biting mouth finding places Alex didn't know existed. An electric current in his cock, so full of blood and want. He arched into the ruffle of Jav's breath on his stomach, looking for the remembered dream of Jav's mouth.

A cell phone pinged an incoming text. Then another.

"Jesus fucking Christ," *Jav said, falling to his back.*

"Someone needs you," Alex said, *giving Jav a shove.* "Go."

Jav slid off the edge of the bed and went crawling around in the dropped and flung clothing. "Shit," *he said with a groan.* "It's Ari."

"*What?*"

The phone arced up from the floor and landed next to Alex on the mattress. A series of text bubbles from Ari were on the display:

You there?

T, I'm downstairs. You threw the deadbolt on the street door. Can't get in.

Mr. Legal Guardian… Wake up. Your guardee is tired. Gotta pee.

Where are you? I saw your car parked in the lot?

"Where is your car?" Val said.

"What?" Alex said. His car was still parked behind the Lark Building. Like a true fleeing lover, he'd made a beeline up a side street and headed straight for home. Leaving his car behind, skirting the parking lot entirely in case Ari was wandering around.

"Where's your—"

"It's fine," he said. "It's in town, I'll explain later."

"You're wrecked." Val folded back the comforter. "Come lie down. Go to sleep."

Alex took two lurching steps and fell sideways across the mattress. A breeze of cool air across his back and legs before the sheet dropped softly on his bare skin. His hand crept beneath his pillow and found his handkerchief. He squeezed it tight in his fingers.

"*What the fuck.*" *Alex's fingers squeezed the phone as he stared at the texts.* "*I thought he was on the rescue in Ulster.*"

"*So did I.*" *Jav was stuffing one leg, then the other into his jeans, hopping around and pulling them up.* "*But now he's home, the punk. God motherfucking dammit. Give me the phone.*"

"Jesus Christ." *Alex tossed it to him, seized his own clothes and pulled them on.*

Jav was texting. "*He has to be tired. He'll come in and go crash. Just stay in this room.*"

"And what, hide in the closet? Your shirt's on inside-out."

Jav's laugh had an edge of hysteria as he yanked the shirt off and put it on properly. He dashed out to the living room, grabbed Alex's jacket and sneakers and threw them into the bedroom. "*I swear, someone up there hates me.*"

"What if he doesn't crash?"

"He will."

Alex jammed his right foot into his left shoe. "*I don't know. At that age I needed four bowls of cereal and an hour of cartoons to unwind.*"

"You're right." *Jav pointed to the window.* "*Fire escape.*"

"I'll see myself out."

"I can't think when I had a better time," Jav said, shaking his head as he pulled the bedroom door shut.

Alex opened it. "Listen—my wife doesn't know about us. Don't send a text asking, all right?"

Jav looked back from the front door. "Where the fuck you been all my life…"

Alex opened his eyes and Sheba looked up at him from the floor, wanting to know where he had been.

FAITHFUL
ANOTHER YEAR

PARALLEL TO NORMAL

1 *I*F A MILLION dollars were in it, if a gun were held to his head or his daughter dangled off a rooftop, Alex would not be able to say what happened the rest of that Sunday. Whatever transpired, whatever he did and said and thought, his subconscious studied it and made an executive decision: *Let's put this day away and pretend it didn't happen.*

Monday dawned cool, clear and bright like a promise. It was Alex's day off and he bashed through a to-do list of errands, household chores and yard tasks. His body crackled with productive energy as he put his world in order. Getting shit together where it belonged.

He didn't text Jav, who didn't text him. The desire seemed far away. A garment he'd ordered online, tried on, found not to be a good fit and returned.

It really is like a dream already, he thought. *Maybe it'll just be a weird, random thing. A crazy moment between friends. Like Roger and I jerking off to porn. We'll let it go and let it be. And laugh someday, about how I left via the fire escape.*

In the late afternoon, he was mucking around in the shed when a hand grabbed his arm, whipped him around fast. His shoulder blades hit the wall, the breath collapsed out of his chest.

"Where were we?" Jav said, and kissed him.

It was no dream. It was right here, right now. And it fit perfectly.

Jav's mouth was hard but his tongue was soft. A sweetness with a tannin edge was in his breath and it exhaled warm on Alex's face.

They stopped, breathing hard, Jav still holding Alex's head. Alex's fists clenched tight around Jav's T-shirt.

"Scared the shit out of me," Alex finally said.

"Sorry."

"No, you're not."

"You're right." He kissed Alex again. His weight shifted onto one leg and with the other he kicked the shed door shut.

"Nice afterthought," Alex said in the dark.

Jav tugged Alex's shirt up and over his head. "I get kind of stupid around you."

"Sorry."

"No, you're not."

They kissed. Alex pulled Jav in tight, gripped in an alien physical desire he thought would suck out his soul. Jav's hands slid down his chest, then around his back. An involuntary groan tumbled out of Alex's throat, the iron rod of Jav's erection against his making him remember unfinished business. Jav pushed against him harder. The dark wrapped him in a hot cloak. Alex didn't like the dark. Didn't like small tight spaces, either.

But he liked this.

He pulled Jav's shirt off so he could get closer to it. Opened his mouth to bite and lick at it. Dug his nails into the itch and scratched hard.

"I swear I could fuck you right here," Jav said, his hand stroking the front of Alex's jeans.

Alex laughed against Jav's mouth. "You're not fucking me in the *shed*."

Jav laughed too, holding Alex hard, but then Alex's hoot dissolved into a nervous chuckle. Jav was popping the button on Alex's jeans with one deft, practiced hand. His mouth was on Alex's neck and the dark's soft cloak turned rough and scratchy. Anxiety began curling around Alex's heart, siphoning off his breath. Jav picked his head up, inhaling deep and putting his hand flat on Alex's chest. He exhaled and pressed it.

"I swear this isn't blind, reckless curiosity," Jav said softly. "I'm not out to just fuck you for the experience. I meant what I said, Alejo. You mean something. Your whole life means something to me."

"I know."

"Breathe. Cálmate. Please..."

Alex let the shoulders up around his ears fall. Jav's palm rubbed a circle on Alex's heart. His other hand slid to the back of Alex's neck, then kept sliding until Alex's head was cradled in Jav's elbow. Jav kissed him. Pressed and pinned him. Muscle and bone and skin. All that lean power and strength holding Alex safely in place. All the desire and hurt and passion mirrored back, revealing some essential core truth.

He acts in my stead. Until I get there, he is me...

His hands reached for Jav's fly. Jav was unzipping Alex, their mouths twisting and grabbing, opening and closing. An identical groan in each chest as their hands dug in and took hold.

"Jesus," Jav said, gasping and laughing. "Val was right."

"About what," Alex said, his hand gripping, squeezing, moving up and down as he pushed his hips further into Jav's fist.

"About you being hung like a horse."

"She told you that?"

"Yeah." Jav's mouth closed around Alex's bottom lip and let go. "I made her tell me everything about you."

"This is so fucked-up."

"I want you back in my bed," Jav said. "I want to make you come. It's all I think about. Wanting to feel you come in my hands..." Those ravenous, demanding hands went down the back of Alex's jeans now. Inside his boxers and on his ass, pulling Alex in tight, grinding their hard dicks together and God, it felt fucking good.

"Let's go," Jav said. His smile curled against Alex's mouth. "Ahora. Before Val kicks the shed down."

Alex tensed up, his head full of a remembered splintering noise. The crash of a foot connecting with wood. The squeal of a door torn off its hinges to reveal Val, angry-eyed and breathing smoke, coming after what belonged to her. Only a split second of shock before Alex realized he'd expected nothing less. A locked door wouldn't stop her. Wild, well-hung horses couldn't stop her. She'd tear an embassy gate down to go after the things she loved. She got on the fucking train to Crazytown to make sure her man came back to her.

I'm her man... Oh, Christ, what am I doing?

"Basta," he said. "Jav, hold up."

"What's wrong?"

"I can't breathe." Panic filled the back of Alex's throat. "I mean, I don't know what I'm doing."

"It's all right, neither do I." Jav's hands ran up Alex's chest. "Come on, let's go home."

"I *am* home." Alex's hands found Jav's shoulders, dug into his skin even as he was trying to push him away. "This is my... I can't."

He couldn't see Jav's face in the dark and he was glad of it. He needed to get out of here and out of this. He wasn't striking matches. He was burning his house down. Worse, he was letting Val think she was the sole arsonist.

The realization punched his stomach. He wasn't just cheating on Val. He was torturing her. He was staging a coup on his marriage and violating his own Geneva Convention.

"I can't do this," he said, in a cold sweat. "It's too much to lose." He felt around on the floor for a shirt. He pulled it on, hoping it was his.

"Alejo, don't," Jav said.

"I'm sorry." Alex tucked himself back into his pants, zipped and buttoned. "I love her. She's my life, this is my life. You know this. It isn't…"

"Hey, cálmate," Jav whispered, but *cálmate* was the wrong thing to say. Bad things happened when Alex calmed down.

"We can't be here," Alex said. "Deane's coming home from school any minute. Ari will probably be with her."

As he zipped up, Jav gave a sharp exhale out his nose. "Story of my life."

"Jav, I can't sneak around like this. I'm too fucking old."

And too fucking married.

He went out of the shed. And when he saw Val on the back porch, shaking out the kitchen rugs, it was with a mixture of sickening dread and abject relief. And no small amount of absurdity.

Hi honey, he thought. *Jav was just borrowing the hedge clippers.*

Roman and Sheba trotted over barking, as Val stared at Alex and Jav. Two cats trailing canary feathers. Tousled and sweaty, eyes glazed. A suspicious bulge in each pair of pants. Jav's shirt on inside-out and backward.

Alex watched his wife's face go from surprise to realization, then slowly fill with rage.

I. Am. Fucked.

Deane and Ari came around from the side porch, hand-in-hand and laughing, followed by Stella with Henry.

"Christ, es una fiesta," Jav mumbled, jamming his hands in his pockets.

"Whoa, is this an intervention?" Deane said.

"Deane, we're here because we love you," Ari said, crouching down to hug Roman.

Val looked at her daughter and gave a weak laugh. She gathered her rugs and went back inside, closing the door gently behind.

From the windows on either side, Alex saw flames.

"Hey, Mr. Landes," Stella said. "How are you?"

"Leaving," Jav said. "Sorry I can't intervene. Got shit to do."

"I have to go to work," Deane said.

"Big math test tomorrow," Ari said.

"God, who planned this intervention?" Stella said.

Alex walked away from all of them and went inside. The kitchen was empty. The downstairs quiet. "Val?" he called.

He went toward the stairs. "Valerie?"

He looked up to the landing. Never—not in the closet in Santiago, not when he cut a dog's throat, not on his second 9/11 and not at Deane's hospital bedside—had Alex been so frightened.

Get your ass up there now.

Going up the steps was like walking through water. His heart pounded slow and heavy. Strikes on a gong, making his limbs and fingers vibrate.

He found Val in the bathroom, throwing up.

"Oh, honey," he said, crouching down.

"Fuck you," she whispered. And heaved again.

He raked her hair off her neck, gathering it into his fingers. "I'm sorry."

"Don't touch me," she said.

He pressed the handful of hair against the back of her head and slid his other arm across her chest, holding her steady. The way she needed to be held when she was puking. This was his job. And he was excellent at it.

"It's all right," he said, feeling sick himself.

I fucked up. Oh God I fucked this up bad.

She gagged and spit. "I hate you."

"I know."

She bucked and dry-heaved, but didn't fight off his arms. When he wet a washcloth, she turned her face into its soothing damp. Then she put her forehead on the rim of the toilet and wept.

"Val," he whispered. "I'm so sorry."

"You lied," she said. "In that chair, when you were fucking me and in our *bed*. You lied to me. You threw me over the side and let me suffer through the worst night of my life when we could've had a conversation about who he was to *both* of us. You lied and let me suffer through these past few days, thinking I'd lost you."

"I'm sorry," he said, wanting to die.

"Did you sleep with him?"

"It's over. Nothing even started but it's over. All of it. I swear."

She picked up her head and slapped him. An open hand straight across his jaw, her face contorted with fury. "You son of a bitch," she said through her teeth. "You wanted him all this time—"

"I don't want him. I want you."

She slapped him again, on the same side of his face, making his teeth rattle. "Who the *fucking* hell do you think you are?" she cried.

"Val…"

Her hand hung in the air, then slowly curled into a fist with one finger left pointing. "You," she said. Her hand dropped in her lap as a fresh stream of tears fell from her swollen eyes. "I don't know you…"

Not knowing either, Alex braced himself for the verdict as the flames rose up. Thick choking smoke burning his eyes and searing his lungs. Timbers cracking and collapsing. The roof caving in. It was over. All of it. He wouldn't be sleeping here tonight. He'd be the one fixing it with Deane in the morning.

I've lost her.

"Valerie, please."

"Don't touch me." She rolled off her knees, onto her butt and slumped against the side of the bathtub, a cheek against the cold porcelain. "The other night I begged you, *please,* and you…" She curled an arm around her head and dissolved into weeping.

Alex reached and flushed the toilet. He ran the washcloth under cold water again and laid it on the ledge of the tub. "I'm sorry."

"If you gave me shit about sleeping with him twenty years ago when you were fucking him in our back yard, I swear to God, Alex—"

"I didn't fuck him," he said.

Things you never imagined saying to your wife, he thought, floating in some surreal dimension running parallel to normal.

"I don't believe you when you said nothing started," she said. "Something's been going on and it didn't start today. It was all over you when you walked out of the shed. You think I can't read your shitty poker face? Think I don't know you and your moral compass that only points one way? Think I don't notice when you're *considering* getting a hard-on?"

He wrapped his arms tight around his knees, trying to squeeze himself into nothing. "Yes."

"Yes what?"

"Yes, something's been going on and no, it didn't start today."

A cautious knock on their bedroom door. "Mom?"

When Val answered, "Yes, Deane," her voice calm and steady, Alex thought he'd never loved her more and liked himself less.

The click of a locked doorknob being tested. "Are you all right?"

Val glanced at Alex. "I'm a little sick to my stomach, honey."

"Where's Dad?"

Her gaze intensified. "He's in here with me. Cleaning up."

"Oh. I'm sorry. I'm going to work. Feel better."

Val picked up the wet cloth and pressed it to her face. "Start from the beginning. And I don't care if it was when you were waiting tables in eighty-six, or if it was last night."

Alex started with the drive home from Vermont. When he was finished, Val took a deep breath and weakly threw the washcloth at him. "That's everything that happened?" she said.

"It is. I swear. Val, I'm sorry."

"I know," she said. "You really are the sorriest man sometimes, Alex."

She got up, holding onto first the tub, then the sink for support, and lurched into the bedroom as if one leg were shorter than the other. She pulled a tote bag out of the closet and started opening drawers.

"Where are you going," Alex said.

"I'm going to my sister's," she said. "I can't sleep next to you tonight. I don't want to see you. You can explain to Deane."

"Val, please. I didn't mean for this to happen. I never saw this coming. I'll do anything—"

"Good. You can start by leaving me the fuck alone."

MASTERS IN HUMAN SEXUALITY

"**F**EEL BETTER?" TRELAWNEY asked.

Wrapped in a robe, her head swathed in a towel turban, Val shrugged. "No, but I feel cleaner."

"I'll open a bottle of wine," Trelawney said. "Unless you prefer the harder stuff?"

"I need to get something in my stomach first."

Trelawney put out her hand and Val took it, let herself be led into the kitchen, grateful to be the little sister now.

"Your phone pinged a few times," Trelawney said, flicking her chin to the counter where the phones were charging. Val picked hers up. If it were Alex, she wouldn't answer. But she had two texts from Deane.

Mom, I don't understand what's happening. I'm really scared.

Mom, are you coming home?

Val sighed. "What do I tell her?"

"The truth," Trelawney said.

"That her father's screwing around with her boyfriend's uncle?"

"No, no. The other truth."

"I'm having a sleepover with my sister, we're going to get drunk and dish and I'll be back in the morning?"

"Perfect. Don't text. She needs a voice."

Val called her daughter's phone. "Hey, baby."

"Mom, what's going on?"

"Nothing you need to make into a worst-case scenario, I swear."

"Are you in love with Jav?"

"No," Val said. "I wasn't then, I am not now. What I am is upset, so I'm hanging with my sister."

"Can I come over, too?"

Val bit her lip. "Not tonight, but you know, I like that idea. We should do it soon. The three of us could have movie night or something."

"Are you coming home?"

"Of course I'm coming home. Look, remember when Stella came over after Casey dumped you? Two pints of ice cream and sympathy? That's what this is. I need my Stella."

"All right." Deane's voice wasn't putting any money on this.

"I'm not leaving you or Dad. I promise. This is not divorce. All will be worked out, but I need tonight here. If you don't hear from me in the morning, call Weight Watchers."

Finally, Deane laughed. "Oh my God, Mom."

"I love you. I for to text you before I go to bed."

"I for to love you as well."

"Oy God," Val said, tossing her phone aside and sinking onto a stool.

"Here." Trelawney put down a bowl with some plain pasta. "Line your poor stomach with that."

Val forced a few bites down. "What am I going to do?"

"What are your options? Start with the obvious."

"Leave him?"

"Any self-respecting woman with zero tolerance for infidelity would."

"I'm a self-respecting woman, sure."

"He cheated on you. He had sexual contact with someone else. Gender is irrelevant. Gratification is irrelevant. That he didn't get off is no excuse. He gave and received pleasure. He's out." Trelawney cocked her head. "Is any of this working?"

Val slowly shook her head. "I don't feel cheated on. I feel *shit* on. He threw me under the bus, then put it in reverse and backed up to finish the job."

"Who are you and what have you done with Alex?"

"Right? He's unrecognizable to me."

"Which tells me his own mental state is a disaster area."

Val ate a few more bites. "The thing is," she said, "I get it. I completely understand Alex and Jav being attracted to each other."

"And a bit of you is turned on by it, I bet."

Val put her fork into the bowl and pushed it away.

"Shit, I wouldn't kick it out of my bed," Trelawney said. "Purely from an aesthetic viewpoint."

Val unwound the towel from her head and tossed it onto another stool. "Alex and I... We fooled around with the idea. Couple weeks ago, we were stoned and having magnificent sex. Inhibitions gone, minds open and we fantasized a little about Jav being with us. Together. It was hot."

"That's bold," Trelawney said. "If I didn't know then what I know now, I'd be shocked Alex entertained another guy in the scenario. Usually with men's threesome fantasies, it's another woman."

"The idea of it is a total turn-on. Having both of them at the same time is like número uno in the spank bank. I pitched it one night and I was amazed he played along. We shared a crazy fantasy. It was *fun*. We came our brains out over it. How the hell was I to know...?" She turned her hand over, cupping it toward the ceiling. Looking for an explanation but seeing only the silver bands encircling her fourth finger and an empty palm.

"How were you to know he'd take it out of fantasy," Trelawney said.

"But he said it started in Vermont for him."

"What? He and Jav fooled around in Vermont?"

"No. He said on the drive home from Stowe, it started to get into his head that he was attracted to Jav. He already had something cooking in his brain." Val pressed her lips hard as her eyes welled up and overflowed. "What the fucking hell. Telling me I was riding him and lying when he was doing the same goddamn thing. He was..." She was crying too hard to finish. Trelawney came around the corner and put arms around her, crossed them tight around Val's head and rocked her back and forth.

"I'm so sorry, honey."

"I don't understand," Val said between sobs. Over and over. "I don't understand. I don't know who he is."

"I know. I don't either. I mean, I understand *how* the attraction could happen. But I don't understand his actions."

Val reached for the towel to wipe her face. "If he'd only *said* something sooner. If he'd brought it out when he found the text, found out Jav and I used to sleep together. We would've been on equal ground and we could've had a conversation. I am so *pissed*, Trey. I withheld information but so did he. Making me feel like shit while he's making out with Jav in the fucking shed..."

Trelawney stepped into the little bathroom off the kitchen and came back with a comb. She started working it through the wet tangles of Val's hair.

"Maybe I'm biased," Val said. "But his was the shittier transgression. Or hell, maybe we each drew blood. Game ends in a tie. We can reset and move on."

"Can you?"

"I don't know."

"You can't make decisions when you're this emotional. Right now you have to sit here and be hurt."

"The fucking goddamn *shed*, Trey." Val leaned back against her sister, reaching for Trelawney's wrists and pulling them around to hold her. "It hurts so bad."

"He loves you. And I know he's dying right now. He couldn't have seen it coming, either. When everything you thought you knew about yourself is suddenly different, you make lousy decisions. You make self-preservation decisions. Hide your bad qualities by ripping open someone else's. Who knows, maybe he dumped on you the other night in a desperate attempt to be the man of the house. Masculinity fire drill."

"If he just *told* me."

"Well, to be fair, when I counseled you to tell him about Jav, you balked. Why? Because, quote, how the hell do you bring *that* up in conversation?"

Val squirmed in the circle of her sister's arms. "Who's side are you on?"

"Yours."

"I hate what Alex did, because I know he's not an asshole," Val said. She exhaled. "And I'm not a bourgeois twit."

"No, you're not."

"Where did that even come from? Bourgeois twit. I've been saying it all my life and I don't even know where I got it."

"Don't you remember? Mom read it in one of those Rosamunde Pilcher novels she loved. A woman's drip of a husband is at war, and she's falling for the handsome American ranger stationed in town. She tells her father she's worried she'll get involved and he says to her, 'So get involved. You're a married woman, but not a bourgeois twit.'"

"I think I'll tattoo that on my face."

"How about that wine?"

"Big glass. Fuck it, give me the bottle."

"Eat some more. Choke it down."

Val choked down a few cold mouthfuls of pasta. Her phone pinged. She knew before looking it was Alex.

Val, I'm so sorry. Please come home.

The pasta felt like glue in her mouth as she chewed and texted: **What did you tell Deane?**

That I was an asshole.

Good. Leave me alone now.

"He's sorry," she said, sliding the phone away.

"Of course he is," Trelawney said.

"God, if I were twenty-something I'd be milking this one out for a week."

"It's prime drama, baby. You could get… I don't know, jewelry or something."

"Fuck drama. I don't want jewelry. I'm forty-five years old—I don't have time for this shit."

Her phone pinged again.

Val, I love you. Please come back and talk to me. I need you so much.

She typed back, *I needed you the other night, you know.*

I'm so sorry.

She should be cool and distant. Make him suffer as she had. Teach him a lesson. But it wasn't her. She relied heavily on comic relief in a tense situation. Her way of diffusing stress was to find the funny in it.

Or at least snark.

You fucking hurt my feels, dude, she typed. *I'm sleeping over my sister's. We're going to make popcorn and talk about you. I'll be home tomorrow. Or the day after. And we'll do whatever couples do in this situation. Right now I'm pissed off and it's your turn to suffer through a long night.*

She put the phone down and picked up her wine. "Twenty bucks says he'll be throwing pebbles at the guest room window tonight."

"Fifty says he'll be ringing the doorbell in an hour."

⟜

TRELAWNEY MADE POPCORN on the stove with an obscene amount of butter and salt, the way Roland Lark had always made it. The sisters took the giant bowl and two dish towels into the living room.

"Have you said anything to Jav since this shit went down?" Trelawney asked, pouring more wine in their glasses.

"Said? No. Screamed? Yes."

"And what did he say? Or scream?"

"I didn't give him a chance to do either, frankly. His side of the story wasn't relevant at the time."

"Fair enough." Trelawney donned her reading glasses and opened a book.

Val flipped through a magazine with greasy fingers, pictures and text blurring together. "This changes everything," she said, closing her eyes. "I don't mean just

Alex and me. We'll work it out. I'm angry and hurt but I don't want to leave him. This is marriage. It's my marriage and it's worth fighting for. At the same time…"

"It changes both your relationships with Jav."

"And I *like* Jav. I want to throw him off the bridge at the moment, but that man flew to Santiago for my daughter. Twice he got her down from the mountain."

"He's a lovely man. Damaged, but lovely."

"He got dealt a shitty hand in life and he wants to be everything his own family wasn't. And as much as he denies it, I think he desperately wants someone to love."

"All of which tends to color the decisions he makes. Parts of him still make the choices of an abandoned teenager."

"Now it's all going to be tense and awkward, at best. Estranged at worst. And that sucks. He'll feel kicked out again. I liked having him around. I liked seeing Alex be friends with him."

"Until the attraction part kicked in. Who saw that coming?"

"Me, dammit." Val threw the magazine and put her head on the back of the couch. "I should've known he hadn't worked it out yet."

"Who hadn't worked what out?"

"Jav. Twenty years ago he was on the fence about being bisexual. He had a thing for guys he didn't know what to do with. Guys in general and Alex in particular." She scratched at her scalp, trying to dig answers out of her head. "But it was twenty years ago. I can't believe Jav flew to Santiago for a second chance to get in Alex's pants."

"No," Trelawney said. "That kind of thing, you do for love."

"He's become like family. Same way Alex became part of our family."

"And you blew him in the back room of Grandma's shop."

"*Once*," Val said, but she was laughing. "Oh my God, maybe this is the Lark destiny."

"The exaltation of Larks."

"Shut up."

Trelawney sighed into her glass. "It's certainly complicated."

"Thank you, Madame Obvious."

"Alex was jealous you got to sleep with Jav and he didn't. Now you're jealous Alex got to mess around with Jav and you didn't."

Indignant, Val coughed through a swallow of wine. "I am not."

Trelawney lowered her glasses. "And I don't have a master's in human sexuality studies."

"*Fine.* Yes. A little."

"A lot."

"Whose side are you on?"

"Yours," Trelawney said, smiling.

"Look, I admit Jav was an amazing experience. It doesn't suck to look at him and walk down memory lane. He hugs me hello or goodbye and it feels like a private joke. It should be illegal for a man to smell that good. But I never intended on acting on it. If Alex is going to pursue some homoerotic wet dream, it's going to be…"

Trelawney blinked through the silence. "Be what?"

"Nothing."

"No, go on. It's going to be what? On your terms?"

Val filled up her lungs and slowly exhaled. "What if I hired him?"

"For Alex?"

"For both of us."

"To what purpose?"

"Pure entertainment."

The sisters caught eyes and held. Then, at the same time and at the same cadence, shook their heads.

"Probably the greatest terrible idea I've ever had," Val said.

"It would not end well," Trelawney said.

"And Jav doesn't do couples anyway." Val blew her breath out and buried her head in her palms, fingers scratching at her scalp. "I love you."

"I love you."

"I want to go home," Val said to her lap. "My whole life, whenever the shit went down or it got to be too much, I'd always think, *I just need to go home.* And whenever I did, Alex was always there. After Mom and Dad died and I finally broke down, I went running from town back to the house. Falling down sobbing. Alex was there and he caught me. He's home to me. Getting out of New York on Nine-Eleven, all I kept saying to myself was *Get home, just get home. Get back to Alex, go back home…*"

The doorbell rang. The Lark sisters looked toward the front hall, then at each other.

"Your ride is here," Trelawney said.

Val sighed, but didn't move.

Trelawney leaned forward. "My front door is fumed oak and extremely expensive," she said. "And I will send you the bill if Alex breaks it down."

The doorbell rang again. Val uncurled her legs and got up to answer it.

COHERENT ANSWERS

*V*AL CAME HOME and accepted his apology.

"Please forgive me," he said.

"I will," she said. "I want to. Right now, I'm still hurt."

Tender, fragile days turned into anxious nights.

"I don't feel like making love," she said, when he reached tentative hands toward her. "I'm not punishing you. I literally don't feel like it."

"I understand," he said, desperate for her and feeling punished. He barely recognized their relationship without its sexual current. They moved through the house like cordial roommates, giving short bulletins on their whereabouts. Val was busy with a wedding order and worked late into the night. Alex had rescues and adoption events. Graduation loomed. Dogs had to be walked, bills paid, dinners cooked.

Life went along on its routine, but the comfortable, perfectly-broken-in jeans of their marriage had fallen to threads. Now Alex was walking around in stiff, scratchy denim, the inseams chafing him. They'd feel good one day. But not today.

Hey, Jav texted once.

Hey, I know we need to talk, Alex typed back. **But right now all my time, energy and attention is here. I need to be here.**

I know. I'm sorry. I'll leave you guys alone.

Alex almost deleted the exchange, but after consideration he left it, and left his phone on the kitchen counter where anyone could look at it. Transparency was key right now. He'd be an open book.

Besides, he had a shitty poker face.

And he still wanted Jav.

In the immediate aftermath of the garden shed bust, his thoughts flinched away from Jav and stayed far away. By day, anyway. He couldn't control the dreams at night. The weight on his back, the tattooed arms pinning him safe and Jav's voice on the nape of his neck.

I walked into your house. And now I'm on you…

Then Alex would wake up with a throbbing, guilty erection and Val's back turned on him.

Jav was right, he thought. *Three in a bed is too complicated.*

His thoughts were a tabloid scandal but Alex kept his behavior unimpeachable. He didn't call or text Jav, didn't casually wander down Main Street or into Celeste's where he might see him. He kept up a calm, amiable front for Deane. He paid special, solicitous attention to Val. He not only made coffee in the morning, but brought her a cup in bed. Took a sandwich to her if she was bogged down at the shop. Texted her often. He kept reaching out to touch her. She didn't shy away, but didn't lean into him either. He refused to let it make him complacent. He had to own this, and he couldn't own it without putting his hands on it.

At the end of the day, they said goodnight and lay down. The "I love yous" sounded perfunctory. Sometimes they held hands. Most nights they didn't touch at all. The dreams came then, and Alex exploded in happiness and imploded with desire as he was pressed tight between the two things he wanted most in the world.

I want him, he thought. Some days he could sit it down in a chair like a child who needed a talking-to. Elbows on knees, fingers laced and expression firm, he looked it in the eye. *I want him. But I can't have everything. I'll just have to want it until I don't anymore.*

Other days, he thought he was losing his mind. Then more anxiously juvenile thoughts came for lunch.

Am I gay?

He had no one to talk it out with. He wanted Val desperately, and not just to prove his masculinity—he needed her head, her insights and her patient ear.

"Please can we talk," he said. "I love you and I want to work this out."

"I know," she said. "I'm just tired, Alex, and I have nothing to say right now."

His finely-tuned antenna could feel the sad tension radiating off his wife. It wasn't angry. It was depleted. Being his rock had exhausted her. Somehow, her ambivalence hurt more than a screaming rage. More than his own shame. Her abstracted demeanor was a wrecking ball into his spiritual house. Being so disconnected from her was like trying to drive around town with the car in reverse. Like walking backward through life—not knowing what was coming next, only what had already occurred.

What have I done? he thought, while his thumb ran over the keyboard of his phone, itching to connect with Jav.

An evening came when Alex was watching Val mix ground beef with Worcestershire sauce and spices, molding it into burgers. Water was boiling for corn, and tomatoes were sliced and fanned on a plate, sprinkled with salt and pepper.

"Our anniversary's coming up," Alex said.

"I know."

"Do you want to go out?"

"Don't we always?" She gave him a closed-mouth smile and flicked the faucet on with her elbow. She washed her hands, then took a small toothbrush to the corncobs, getting rid of the silks.

"Have you ever felt anything was missing in our marriage?" Alex asked.

"Never," Val said, without hesitation. "Is there any white wine in the fridge?"

Alex found half a bottle of Cono Sur. He poured it out into two glasses. "I never felt it either," he said. "I've been happy with you. And Deane. And this life. I never needed anything else."

Her eyebrows raised.

"So why is it I wanted something else?"

She took a long drink of wine. "Ah," she said.

"And why with a man?"

She drained the glass and reached for the bottle. "Why indeed." As she filled her glass, she drew in a deep, preparatory breath that made Alex instinctively brace. "What I still don't understand," she said, "is why you didn't tell me about it."

"I didn't know how."

"Same reason I didn't tell you about him and me," she said. "How do you bring it up? And what for? It has a better chance of being hurtful than an interesting topic of conversation. Why risk it?"

He nodded, mute and answerless. Pinned down in a lab tray for dissection but he was empty inside.

"That night in the armchair," Val said. "We both had an opening. What would've been worse? That I wanted him once and remembered? Or you wanted him now and desired?"

"Would you have understood?" Alex said. "Or is it easy to say you would in hindsight?"

Val ran the back of her hand along her forehead. "I saw you through the dark after Nine-Eleven. I understood when you could barely leave the house. Understood the anxiety when Deane was out of your sight and the panic when I was late to show up somewhere. I know when you cut your arm, you were cutting a throat. I know why you have both Nine-Elevens tattooed on your back. I know why that handkerchief has to stay under your pillow. I know why you're afraid of the dark. Why would I understand all that but not understand this?"

Alex stared off at some invisible horizon. "Maybe because it's about sex," he said, flipping the cruise-control switch on his consciousness and taking his hands off the wheel. "It hits below the belt. It upsets what I think of as being a man. It alters the man I am. Or the man I think I am."

"All the reasons Jav's family threw him out."

"It's not about sexual persuasion, Val, it's about being weak."

Out the corner of his eye he saw Val's gaze widen and her head tilt.

He gave a laugh under his breath. "Aren't I weak enough?"

"I've never thought you were weak," she said. "Is that really what you think?"

"I don't know," Alex said. "I don't know what I'm saying. I was attracted to Jav and I don't have one goddamn theory for it that makes sense. The point is I pursued it. I went for it. Why, just because it was new and different and wild? Because it was Jav? Because I could?"

"Because you never royally fucked up anything in your life before now?"

Alex looked up at her. "Yeah, I have."

"No. You haven't."

Val slid her butt along the lower cabinets and sat on the floor. Alex followed. Sheba put her head in his lap. Roman sat by Val. Two referees.

"Look, I don't want to tie everything back to your childhood," Val said.

"Except everything *does* tie back to it. Come on."

"You never got in trouble. All your life, you've never been in trouble. You lost your parents and with them, you lost the rite of passage of pushing boundaries and suffering the consequences. You never crossed swords with Felipe. You never butted heads with my parents."

"Only you," he said.

Her finger came off the wine glass and pointed at him. "Exactly."

He tilted his head, eyebrows wrinkled. "What, you've been my mother?"

One of her shoulder shrugged. "I've been friend. Sister. Lover. Caretaker. Wife. Soulmate and fucky. I'm sure part of you still wants a mother. Shit, I still want my mother."

"So I never got in trouble."

"And now you're grounded." She got up.

"Kind of makes sense," he said. "Except I still don't have coherent answers for why I felt this way about Jav."

"Feel," Val said.

He blinked, not understanding.

"Feel," she said. "You're speaking in past tense but it's still present. You want him."

"Yeah." The word burned his throat as he pushed it out. "I'm sorry."

"Alex." Tiny muscles in her face twitched as she looked down at him. "Deep down in my heart, I truly believe wanting isn't something to apologize for."

Slowly Alex put his arms around his knees.

"I go through phases of wanting all the time," she said. "Wanting isn't having. Wanting isn't doing. Wanting isn't making come to fruition. Everyone wants. I want. It's the human condition."

"I want you back," he said softly.

Val crossed her arms. "Problem with wanting… Even when you do the right thing and don't put anything in motion? You can't switch wanting off. This is an emotional flu you have to suffer. And I have to live with you until it passes."

He got up from the floor. "Do you want to live with me?"

Her hand reached and brushed his face. "I've liked having you around since I was twelve."

"Even though I'm a train wreck?"

"You're my train wreck. And all tickets to Crazytown are round trip."

He turned his mouth into her palm. Her skin was cool and damp from the wineglass and smelled like lemongrass soap. "I love you."

"I know, and you're still grounded." Val handed him the plate with the burgers. "Put those on the grill please?"

He did as told, wanting her badly. *I don't want to eat. I want to go upstairs. Please let's go make love. I need to be inside you. I need you so bad.*

For the first time in his married life, he felt he didn't deserve to ask.

FIVE

*J*AV LAY DIAGONALLY across his bed. Sprawled on his stomach with one arm around the pillow, the other outstretched on the mattress. The sunlight sliced through the window and eased between the spaces of his fingers. He turned his hand over, then back again. Looking at the light coming through the gaps where Alex had slipped away.

All of him. His love, his friendship and his family. You've lost it all.

Again.

But you knew you would. You knew what you were doing. You knew you were setting the house on fire.

His hand turned palm down, moving through the air as if running over Alex's head. He could still feel the roll of Alex's jaw in his palm. The close of his teeth around Jav's thumb. How he pulled his arms from his jacket sleeves and flung the garment aside. Threw himself against Jav's body and pushed up hard and tight, groaning in his throat. The two of them bouncing off walls, kissing and seizing as they ricocheted into the bedroom.

Jav's hand pushed through the dusty sunlight. Remembering the heave of Alex's chest, yanking breath between kisses that bit and sucked and pulled at Jav's mouth. His passion was a punch straight from the shoulder. No uncertainty in his touch. Nothing shy or hesitant. Not a shit or giggle as he slid a hand between their bodies, folded it around Jav's erection and gave it two long, expert strokes.

Come closer, he said. Jav did and Alex gathered both of them into his big hands, unleashing a moan into Jav's mouth. Jav bit the cry in half and swallowed it down. He dug his fingers into Alex's hair, held his head immobile against the wall and kissed him. Crazed, on fire, burning to death and unable to stop.

Want you so fucking bad, he said against Alex's throat. *I always did. Starting back at the diner, when I didn't know what the fuck it meant.*

No wonder you always made me act like an idiot, Alex said around a small, wicked smile.

Jav grabbed Alex's shoulders and shoved him toward the bed. He dove after, wrestled Alex down into the sheets and kissed the grin off him, slid his tongue into Alex's mouth and shut him up good because there could only be one idiot in the room.

Now Alex's fingers dug into Jav's hair as his body bucked under Jav's crushing weight. He pushed up into the kiss, sliding his cock against and along Jav's. His ribcage rose and fell like a wave and Jav, out of his mind now, surfed its crest as he slid down the mattress. Running his face over Alex's stomach, following the inverted parenthesis of iliac lines pointing the way. An elementally male scent rising up to meet him, making Jav's mouth water.

Jesus Christ, Alex howled in a whisper as Jav's hand closed around that pulsing hardness, filling up his fist and bringing it to his tongue so he could—

"You feel all right, T?"

Jav closed his mouth, counted to five and opened his eyes. "No," he said. "I've got a headache. I think I'm coming down with something."

"Can I get you anything?" Ari said. "Couple aspirin?"

You can get out and stop interrupting my life. If it weren't for you, I wouldn't be in this shitshow.

He closed his teeth down on the tip of his tongue, curtailing a dozen other cruel replies the boy didn't deserve. Full of misery, guilt and uncharitable thoughts, Jav swallowed hard, counted to five again. "No, I just want to sleep. Can you close my door?"

"Sure. I'm going to work. Feel better."

"Thanks, sobrino."

With a quiet click, Jav returned to being the idiot in the room. He dragged his wet face along the pillow and tilted his fingers into the sunlight again. Squinting between them and looking for Alex.

I'm sorry, where were we...?

Speed-Dialing My Lawyer

"**W**ELL, THIS FEELS familiar," Val said.

From his place in line at the deli counter, Jav turned around and, as he did twenty years ago, he looked a little horrified.

Goosebumps swept up Val's arms, not only from the grocery store's refrigerated chill, but from the swift passage of time. "I've definitely been here before."

She was twenty-six on that hot summer day. Dewy-skinned and bright-eyed, fresh and energetic and determined. As she looked at Jav, mental calendar pages began to fall away. She was sorting out her parents' house after their death. Leading Alex down a hallway in Vermont. Standing before a judge to be married. Opening her arms to clasp the squalling, bloody miracle of Deane to her chest. Moving to Guelisten and starting two businesses while raising a child. Working and worrying their asses off. Making love to recharge the batteries. Deane growing up. Alex breaking down. Work and worry and love and life. And now she was forty-five, a wife and mother with a grocery basket on her arm, staring at Jav again.

"Is it just me," she said, "or did two decades flash before your eyes, too?"

He nodded. His shoulders were tense and his weight shifted from foot to foot, poised to flee.

"I'm not going to hurt you," she said.

"You should."

"I wasn't prepared for this today, but…" She set her basket down. "This is me attempting to be hip and civilized, and inviting you to a conversation. In public. Where I can't make a scene or kill you."

He thought a minute, then slowly nodded. "There's a Starbucks next door."

The coffee shop was cool and quiet, and mostly empty. They took their cups to the most remote table possible and sat.

"Val, I'm sorry," Jav said. "I ruined everything."

"As I recall, you're in the business of ruining people."

"I feel like shit. I'm sorry."

"Can't say I'm surprised at all this." She shrugged and blew across the surface of her drink. "I mean, I told you Alex had a really big dick."

Jav's eyes widened, then he leaned on an elbow, two fingers touching between his brows. "I swear to God," he said. "You Larks are going to be the fucking death of me."

"You know, when you look at the arc of our friendship." Val's hand drew a generous arch in the air. "It's really rather funny. But it also feels sort of fateful."

"I'm sorry," he said. "Barely anything happened, I swear. It's over and after Ari graduates, I'm leaving Guelisten."

"And we'll miss you," she said. "Which is so fucked up."

Jav's laugh was a bitter bark.

"I'll be brutally honest," she said. "Because I'm exhausted and I have no filter. A part of me is extremely aroused by the thought of him being aroused by you."

"I find that arousing."

"It's put a lot of deposits in the spank bank."

"I'm glad to know that."

"Should I not make jokes? It's how I deal."

"I love your jokes. I love you. I love this town. I love your family. And I love Alex." He drew in a deep breath and it trembled out of him.

She took her own bruised breath. "What if I were there too?"

"Where?"

"With you and Alex. What if I gave permission, for want of a better word, but only if I was there?"

He blinked at her. "You're seriously considering this?"

"I'm considering everything. This is called having coffee. Play along."

He stared at her a moment with narrowed eyes. "I told you once I don't dig fucking another man's wife in front of him."

"I think in this case you'd be fucking another woman's husband in front of her."

"Val, I'm sorry. I got caught up in the heat of the moment and I grabbed for it. I had no right, I knew it was wrong and—"

"And Alex was pissed at me so it gave him justification to even the score," Val said. "Blah, blah, blah. I should be screaming threats at you while speed-dialing my lawyer to file divorce papers. Fuck that. I love Alex more than anything in this world. He's my husband and you can't have him. I can pee on what's mine, no problem. But it's hard to see you as a threat when I love you so goddamn much. When you're part of my family and you belong to our story."

"I'm not your family," he said dully.

"Oh? You left a job and flew to Santiago for my daughter. Was that for shits and giggles?"

Jav didn't answer.

"Jav, I'll never forget or dismiss what you did that day," Val said. "You were one of us afterward. I'm not happy with you right now. I am pissed as all hell. But I *cannot* throw you down the stairs of my house. It's not me. It's not the family I was raised in. And the people that raised you were wrong. Flat-out fucking wrong."

He sank his face into his hands. Hunched over, he looked younger than Ari.

"I'll ask again," Val said. "What if I were there?"

He chuckled through his fingers. "And then what, we go on being friends? Hanging out and taking ski trips to Vermont because we got it out of our system? Christ, Val, if I want a gay experience for my resume I'll hire someone. I *love* Alex."

"I'm just—"

"I know." He put up his palm. "I know you are. You're hurt and betrayed. You're being supernaturally cool when I should be floating in the Hudson by now." He exhaled and looked up. "If you were there… I don't know. I guess."

"What if you were paid?"

His head flicked to her. "What, you're hiring me? Not asking me?"

"I'm not doing either. I'm throwing shit on the table. You know, I could do this the easy way and tell you to stay the fuck away from Alex. Vaya con dios and don't come back. Throw you down those stairs. I could be a real vindictive bitch and ban Ari from the house. Would you rather? For fuck's sake, tell me now."

"I'm sorry."

"My daughter's in love with your nephew." Her voice was starting to dissolve. "You're in love with my husband and I'm *trying*, Jav." She sniffed hard. "You don't want to see my ugly cry. It's worse than the drunk cry."

Her hand itched for a handkerchief as Jav slid a napkin toward her, then folded his fingers around hers. "I'm sorry," he said. "If I could pull wires out of my head and disconnect these feelings, I'd do it yesterday. I don't want this. I don't want to want what I'll only lose. I don't want to ruin your life. I don't want to break up Deane and Ari. I don't want to be with Alex in front of you and I don't want to be paid."

"What do you want?"

"I want what's impossible, I want what's not mine and I have to figure out how to deal with it."

"All right, then."

They sat in silence a while, still holding hands.

"Alex told me about your friend," Val said.

"Yeah."

"I'm so sorry. I can't even imagine how it haunts you."

He sighed. "Yeah. Five years and part of me is still waiting for him to come back and have a conversation."

"Were you in love with him?"

Jav took a deep breath. "It was still new when he died. A more honest answer is I could've been."

She squeezed his fingers. "I can see how it would make you feel more reckless with Alex. Not reckless. Daring, maybe. Aware of how tenuous life can be. How too many things go unsaid or undone. How we wait too long and miss the chance."

"Miss the chance to make someone miss their flight," he said. He stared at her a long time. "I'll think about it," he said softly.

"It would be for him," she said. "I'd be doing it for him. Paying for it makes me feel part of it. In control of it."

He nodded. "I know."

"And I know it's the part you like least. But I'm trying to think of how everyone can get some of what they want."

"Want some, lose some."

"Better than all," she said. "And better than you sneaking into the garden shed behind my back. Like you tried to sneak into me without a condom that last time. It was sloppy then and it was sloppy now. I love you awful, Jav, but both you and Alex need to grow the fuck up." She rose from her chair. "Whichever way you decide, you tell me first. Not him. Me. Agreed?"

"Agreed." He huffed out his breath and ran hands through his hair. "I'll go somewhere else if you still need to food shop."

"No, you have a growing boy at home. Feed him."

JUST ONCE

*T*HEY MET DOWN at the waterfront.

"I promise I have no matches," Jav said.

Alex shrugged and gestured toward the Hudson. "First sign of smoke and I'm jumping in."

They walked along the rec path, heading for the marina docks.

"Ari got into that summer program," Jav said. "In Vancouver."

"I know, I heard. Good for him. Roger always had great things to say about Vancouver."

Their feet fell into step down the long pier, elbows occasionally bumping.

"Everything all right at home?" Jav said.

"Getting there."

"Feels weird not to call you every day."

"I know. I miss it."

"Do you?"

"I wouldn't say it if I didn't." Alex leaned elbows on the wooden railing. "I'm not going to bullshit you and I'm not going to lie to you about anything."

Jav leaned as well, their upper arms grazing. Boats chugged in and out of the marina. The hum of bridge traffic was a dull roar in the distance. Seagulls cawed their harsh lament.

Jav gave a single, snorted chuckle. "You know, I've never been dumped. This is a first."

"I've never dumped a guy."

"Couple of forty-something virgin fags."

The water slapped against the pilings.

"Sorry," Jav said. "That was…stupid. And inaccurate."

Alex cleared his throat. "No puedo seguir con esto."

"I know."

"I want it," Alex said. "But I have too much to lose, man. I can't."

"And it's not you, it's me."

"Knock it off. Do I look like I'm enjoying this?"

Jav stared out over the Hudson. "Te amo, Alejandro."

Alex pulled in a tremendous breath and let it go. "I know you do," he said. "I know. I'm not dismissing it."

"I'll be fine."

"Will you?"

Jav shrugged. "It's par for the course."

"And that's what I hate."

"Why?"

"Because I fucking care about you, Jav. Jesus, you know, the way I feel about you is so many different things."

Jav didn't take his eyes off the water. His silence wasn't hostile. It beckoned like an open hand.

"My daughter crashed on the other side of the world," Alex said, "and you got to her first. She froze up on the mountain and you got her down. You being there for her… I can't even tell you. I love that she has you. I love that Ari has you. I love that I have you and I'll fucking miss it."

"Will you miss me touching you?"

"Yeah. I will."

Jav ran a hand through his head. "Look, whatever you can give me, man. It's enough for—"

"Oh come on, what are you going to do? Stick around Guelisten and wait for me to get weak? Come to you desperate, sneak to your place for an hour or grab five minutes in the shed? Then sneak off again? A rest stop, fast food relationship, is that really what you want, Jav? Is that what you think you deserve?"

Jav pushed off the railing as if he were going to walk away but Alex grabbed his arm. "Get back here. Look at me." He took both Jav's upper arms now. "Hold still. Look me in the eye and tell me it's what you deserve."

Jav met his eyes a second then moved away.

"You're worth more," Alex said. "You're worth more than all the money you've made escorting. Those women needed what you had and you made a career, you made a *life* being everything to them. Who was your everything?"

"You."

"I'm not free and you deserve *more,*" Alex said, digging his fingers in. "I want you to be all right. I wanted that long before all this other stuff showed up. I wanted you to stay in Guelisten, I wanted my home to be your home. A place where you feel good. A place you can come as yourself and bring along your happiness and your pain. I wanted you around since the beginning. I told you. It was like finding a brother."

Jav glanced up, a small smile playing around his mouth. "Falling for your honorary siblings. This is like a thing with you."

"I know." Alex let go Jav's shoulders. "No shock I didn't look outside the nest to find a mate. When the Larks took me in, I imprinted like a little bird."

"Same," Jav said. "It's not the Larks that kill you. It's the exaltation."

"Christ..." Alex pulled Jav back in, hugged him hard. Jav held on for one deep inhale and exhale before stepping back.

"Don't," he said, putting his back to the dock railing and crossing his arms. "I can't stand it."

"I want you to know this isn't easy for me. I don't know how I got here, I never saw it coming. But let the record show...for what it's worth... I wanted it bad and letting go of it is fucking tearing me up inside."

"Yeah," Jav said, his voice thick and tight.

"I want it. Bad. And I could take it, but I'm not going to. Cachai?"

Jav slowly nodded, pulling at his bottom lip. "My dad always said second chances are given or made."

"I wonder," Alex said. "If my old man and your old man found each other on the other side."

Jav laughed. "It's no wonder." His chuckling died down and he looked at Alex a long moment. Alex held still, letting Jav fill his eyes. Tasting it. Touching it. Pressing it into memory and letting it be all right.

"It felt good to me," Alex said. "It made no sense but it felt like me."

"Goddammit..." Jav pushed off the railing, took Alex's head and kissed him. Alex tried not to kiss back and, when that failed, tried to let it fill him to some spiritual brim so he could take it along after he said goodbye.

"Come home with me," Jav said. "Just once."

"I can't." Alex turned his head away, rested his temple on Jav's lips. "Come on. Don't make this harder."

Jav's palm slid along the front of Alex's jeans. "Too late."

"Don't," Alex said, but he didn't move from the stroke and squeeze of Jav's hand.

"Maybe I should stick around Guelisten and wait for you to get weak," Jav said. "Something tells me I wouldn't wait very long."

"Fuck you." Alex shoved him off, the blood pounding behind his eyeballs. Jav started walking backward, a curl in his lip and the barest trace of arrogance in his eyes. Turning on the full power of his appeal and letting Alex take a good look at it.

For the first time, Alex saw the tiger.

Torn apart with anger and desire, he saw the walker and the nephew.

Watching Jav turn and stride down the dock, Alex saw the assassin.

ALONDRA

I, **WHERE ARE YOU?** Ari texted.

Celeste's, Jav replied. **Bad creative mojo in the apartment today, I needed a change of scene.**

Is it working?

No.

LOL. Where's my birth certificate? I need it to get a passport.

Strong box under my bed. Key's in a little envelope in my top desk drawer.

Thanks. I'm running to get pictures at CVS. Then I'm going to bed. Wiped out.

Night. Sleep well.

Need condoms?

Ha ha. No. Smartass.

Jav pounded at the keyboard until the barista cleared his throat. It was five of midnight, the place was empty, chairs turned upside-down on tables. Smiling a sheepish apology, Jav shut down his document without saving. It was shit anyway. All of him was stuck, stoppered up in a writhing frustration. His bones ripped apart with longing again. Lonely and aching and wanting, but none of it wanted to get out of his skin and get into words. Sons of bitches.

He wished he had a date.

Maybe I should hire someone…

Wouldn't that be something?

You're worth more.

He trudged upstairs, weary, but when he lay down in his bed, sleep refused to come. He turned over and over, rolling from one side of the mattress to the other. Finally around quarter of three, he gave up and got up. If he was going to brood, he may as well pace and brood.

Setting the carton of orange juice on the counter, he knocked off the bundle of Ari's papers. He collected them back into order: the passport application, the photos taken at CVS and the copy of Ari's birth certificate.

Or rather, certificates. Both were on the counter. Ari's original birth document and the amended one from when Nick Seaver adopted him in 1997.

Jav's eyes lingered curiously on the original, momentarily taken aback as he remembered he and his nephew shared the same surname at birth.

Child's name: Aaron Rafael Gil deSoto.

"Huh," he said, a fingertip touching the typed letters, seeing both his father and his pen name within them. His gaze moved down the fields.

Mother's maiden name: Naroba M. Gil deSoto

Father's name: Rogelio Alondra.

"Rogelio Alondra," Jav said under his breath. "So who are you?"

He set the paper aside, thinking. Lining up the timeline in his head. Ari was born in 1989. Naroba was twenty-seven. Long done with nursing school and working. Somewhere.

He remembered meeting his nephew for the first time at Lark House. *I think my mom worked here for a little while,* Ari said.

Jav picked up the certificate again.

Rogelio Alondra.

He blinked. Then slowly his fingertip reached out and covered up the *-elio* of the first name.

"Alondra," he said, louder now.

Was it a word?

His face felt hot and his heart thumped loud as he went online to a translation tool.

"Oh, Jesus Christ," he whispered.

Ari's a great kid, Roger said at Thanksgiving. *He's going places.*

Man, I like that kid, he said up in Vermont.

Hey Schnozz.

You're no slouch in the honker department either, kid.

"No," Jav said, staring at Ari's bedroom door. "Roger is your... No."

Impossible. The name was just a coincidence. Pure chance. Like everything else in this fucked-up story.

No wonder we kept finding each other.

Jav closed his eyes, seeing Roger's hand reach to ruffle Ari's hair. The long scar from when he broke his arm. It was one of the Lark legends. Jav himself heard it at Thanksgiving. Rog worked on the tree fort at Lark House in the late 80s. He toppled off the edge of the main platform and fell ten feet to the ground. He was lucky he only broke an arm. When he came to and saw the bone poking through his skin, he threw up on the resident nurse.

The punch line, wait for it... He got the nurse's phone number. They dated a little while. Great story.

"He was sitting right the fuck in front of Ari," Jav said, pulling his hands back through his hair. "At the table. Skiing. At the fundraiser at Lark House..."

I think my mother used to work here, Ari said, sitting on the platform of the tree fort, seventeen years after Roger fell off it. *She said she worked at a private group home. In some rich little town on the other side of the river...*

"Holy shit," Jav whispered as pieces fell into place. As branches bloomed on an intertwined family tree. As Roger's scar was tattooed over with a compass rose. A single letter "N" at its point.

Roger was Ari's father.

Which meant Ari was Val and Alex's nephew.

Which meant Deane...

Jav was on his feet and pacing again, the truth clutching at an ankle, trying to bring him down.

They're cousins.

In a sickening backward jolt through time, Jav was up on the roof, drunk on mamajuana. Nesto hard in his hand, his mouth full of daring sweetness.

We're blood. This is nothing.

It was just some fun.

It didn't *mean* anything.

He winced, remembering the hard shove between his shoulder blades, followed by the pinball crash of his young, drunken body down the stairs.

The treads catching his knees and hips, the stairwell walls catching his elbows. The final slam on the landing and Miguel rising up over him, fists clenched, breathing fire.

Stop, he thought. *Don't twist this into your story. Ari and Deane aren't you and Nesto. Alex and Val aren't your uncles. This is different.*

Isn't it?

He walked over to Ari's bedroom door and set his fingertips against it a moment. He took a deep, deciding breath. He wouldn't tell Ari tonight. No. It could wait until morning. Tomorrow Jav would break it to him. Break his heart.

I'm sorry, he thought. *I know you love her. Believe me, I know.*

He carefully and quietly turned the doorknob. He needed to look at his sister's son, this boy who never did anything to hurt anyone.

Aaroncito, sobrino, I'm so fucking sorry.

He peered into the dark, then opened the door wider. His hand slid along the wall, found the light switch and flicked it.

Ari's bed was empty.

THE ELEMENT OF SURPRISE

*T*HE DOORBELL RANG at three in the morning.

Val lifted her head off the pillow.

"Was that the…?" Beside her, Alex went on sleeping, undisturbed. His chest rose and fell. Deep and even, like an ocean at peace. Val laid her head back down. She must have been dreaming.

Then the doorbell rang again.

Alex exploded awake, sitting straight up. "¿Qué mierdas pasa?" He flung the covers back and put his feet on the floor.

Deane, Val immediately thought. But no, Deane was home. She'd said goodnight to them, she was safe in her bed, thank God.

Alex stood up, ready to fight or flee.

This can't end well, Val thought, throwing her side of the covers open.

"Stay here," Alex said.

Her pulse loud in her ears, Val followed him. Together they moved past Deane's bedroom door, down the stairs as the doorbell rang a third time.

Val's mind whirled in dire scenarios. *My sister? Did something happen to Trelawney?*

Alex fumbled on the stairwell wall for the porch light switch. Val braced to see police officers through the front door's glass panels and put a steady hand on Alex's shoulder. Doorbells in the night and uniformed men. This could be ugly.

The light clicked on. Val saw Jav on the porch and the bottom fell out from her stomach.

Her heart thudded against her breastbone as Alex unlocked and opened the door. Cool air swirled around Val's bare arms while an anxious heat swept down from her scalp.

We had an agreement, she thought, clenching her teeth hard. *You promised you'd tell me first.*

The porch light fell golden across Alex's bare torso as he looked at Jav. Val's hands fisted at the unfair disadvantage. Alex woken from sleep, full of adrenaline and uncertainty, with nothing but a pair of scrubs for armor. Squinting because he didn't have his glasses.

How dare Jav pull a move like this? And pull it by ringing their bell in the middle of the night, when he knew damn well what it could do to Alex.

I should throw you down the stairs, you son of a bitch.

Jav stood feet apart, fully dressed and armed for battle. Up on the high ground with the element of surprise on his side. His dark, handsome face a stone as he looked from Alex to Val, and back to Alex again.

Nobody spoke. In the distance, a car drove by. From the yard, the spring peepers continued their incessant chorus.

Life has rules, Val thought. *And you cannot come in the middle of the night and take what we agreed isn't yours.*

Her throat constricted with betrayed rage. "Jav, what are you doing?"

Arms crossed now, Alex turned his head to look at her. The faintest trembling in his shoulders indicated his body was still dealing with the shock, but his eyes were sober and resigned. *You know what he's doing,* they said. *You knew it was coming.*

Val moved closer to Alex's side and slipped her hand into his. He pressed their linked fingers against her leg, moving her slightly behind him.

"It's too late for this, man," he said.

Jav stared over their touching shoulders.

"You have something I want," he said.

RUNS IN THE FAMILY

*J*AV DIDN'T HAVE to ring the doorbell. He had walk-in privileges at Tulip Street.

He rang it. And enjoyed seeing both Alex and Val come to the door, wild-eyed and shook up. He waited through the moment of triangular staring on the threshold. Relishing the confusion.

"You have something I want," he said.

He let Alex think it was love.

He let Val think it was money.

He gave them a long moment to ponder before he lifted his chin and shifted his gaze higher over their heads. "Actually, Deane has it."

Alex and Val looked back together. Their daughter stood on the stairs, her arms crossed tight over her middle.

"Send him down, honey," Jav said.

Ari was already coming. Tousled and rumpled, his sneakers in one hand. The other slid over Deane's shoulder a brief moment before he came the rest of the way down. He looked at no one. Only whispered, "Sorry," as he squeezed past the adults.

Jav gave a brief nod to the Lark-Pendas. "Sorry to wake you. But life has rules."

He followed his nephew down the porch steps. Ari said nothing on the walk toward town. He was still barefoot and his shirt was on inside-out.

Runs in the family, Jav thought sourly. *Gil deSotos are good at getting our clothes off but we suck at getting them back on.*

"We need to talk in the morning," Jav said as they turned onto Main Street. He tried to get a hand on his nephew's shoulder but Ari shook it off.

"Did you have to embarrass Deane like that?" he said in a hiss. "Jesus Christ, T, if you'd fucking texted, I would've come home."

"You shouldn't have been there in the first place."

You're not allowed, Jav thought, gritting his teeth. *And even if you were, you don't get to make love in that house where I can't. You don't go up the stairs I was thrown down.*

"You're not my fucking father."

"No shit, but I'm your goddamn legal guardian. I'm paying the rent, paying your expenses. I'm responsible for you."

"Jesus Christ, I went over for a minute. We fell asleep."

"Bullshit," Jav said, taking a bit of Ari's T-shirt and turning it up to show the exposed seam.

"So?" Ari yanked away again. "The fuck do you know anyway?" He stomped up the stairs to the apartment door, Jav following.

"I know you're not allowed to be at her house when her parents are asleep," Jav said. "I turn more of a blind eye when you're sneaking into our apartment to screw. Oh, don't look at me like that. You think I was born yesterday? Hide your condom wrappers deeper in the trash next time."

Ari banged the door open with his shoulder and chucked his sneakers aside. "This is bullshit."

"These are the rules, kid. And they suck sometimes but they keep you safe and they keep the world in order."

"You fucking ruined everything." Ari slammed his bedroom door. Jav almost slammed his but remembered his age and closed it quietly. He leaned back against it with a pained exhale. "I'm only starting to ruin your life, kid."

❧

EARLY THE NEXT morning, Jav sent a group text to both Alex and Val:

I have to talk to both of you. Not about us. It's about Ari and Deane. I found something I need to show you. Please give me 10 minutes in Celeste's.

He brought the papers downstairs, ordered coffee and took a small table. When Alex and Val arrived, he got straight to the point. He gave the certificate to Val, who passed it to Alex.

"Exaltación de las alondras," Alex said. "I would've seen it right away." He folded the document along its creases and put it on the table. "Holy. Shit."

Val was pale, her eyes circled. "What do we do?"

"Where's Roger?" Jav asked.

"Nova Scotia." Alex looked around the table, chewing on a lower lip. Then he took out his cell phone. "Fuck me," he said, dialing. He put the phone to his ear and crossed the other arm tight over his chest. "Hey man. Yeah, I know it's early, I need to talk to you. No, nobody's dead. Fine, go pee. I'll wait."

Val took out her phone and snapped a picture of the certificate. "I'll email this to him so he can see."

"Hey," Alex said into the phone. "So... Weird question, but it's important. The nurse from Lark House. The one you puked on when you broke your arm. Yeah. You had kind of a thing with her, right? Yeah, and then you headed out. Okay..." He glanced at Jav, then looked up at the ceiling. "Do you remember her name?"

Jav's heart was throwing itself against the wall of his chest.

"Naria?" Alex said, looking at Jav.

Jav closed his eyes and nodded into the dark.

"Do you remember her last name?"

Jav opened his eyes. Alex was nodding. "Naroba Gil deSoto. Yeah, it's pretty. Listen, Rog... Val just emailed you something. Go look at it."

They waited, drumming fingers, jiggling knees. "You see it?" Alex said. "Alondra means Lark. Yeah. I know. Jav figured it out. I know. It's crazy. Look. Rog. You need to come home."

A few more words were exchanged then Alex hung up. "He'll wrap a few things up then come home. It was her. He's shocked. Said he had no idea. None."

"He and Ari met at Thanksgiving," Val said. "Then all the time up in Vermont. Either Roger didn't know or he's the greatest actor in the world."

Alex shook his head. "Rog is many things but he's not an actor. He just doesn't...do that."

"I don't think he knew," Jav said. "Why else would my sister have disguised his name?"

"Why didn't she tell him?"

Nobody ventured an answer. Air dwindled out of three pairs of lungs.

"Shit," Alex said.

"Talk about staging a coup on someone's life," Jav said.

Alex took off his glasses and tossed them on the table. "This is unbelievable," he said, rubbing the bridge of his nose.

Jav saw no need to prolong things. He gathered up the papers. "I guess I'll go break the news."

"Shouldn't we wait for Rog?" Val said, looking between the two men.

"No," Alex said. "He said Jav should tell him. And I agree." His eyes met Jav's. "Ari belongs to you."

Jav drew a long breath. "Listen, about last night."

"Right," Alex said, taking a sip of coffee. "We had it out with Deane already. She and Ari broke rules. He'll be restricted from coming over for a week."

"Does it even matter now?" Val said.

"Yes, it does. The cousin thing...will be a separate issue." Alex looked at Jav. "A separate coup."

"That's fair," Jav said. "But I wanted to say..."

Both Lark-Pendas stared at him now. "What?" Alex said.

"I rang that bell to upset you. I knew it would. I could've waited until morning but I didn't. It was...shitty of me. And I'm sorry."

"Yeah," Val said, her circled eyes narrowing. "It was shitty."

Alex put his hand on Val's wrist. "One coup at a time. He didn't shoot the dogs. Nobody disappeared."

Val exhaled roughly. "And nobody got thrown down the stairs."

"Today's going to be a shitty enough without piling on all our other shit."

"Our shit," Jav said, rubbing his forehead.

"I told you, he does *we*," Val said.

Alex stood up. "I'll punch you out later if it makes you feel better."

"A two-by-four might do the trick." Jav stood as well. "Into the shitshow we go."

"Good luck," Val said. Her eyes were soft on Jav now, slightly ironic and resigned to a greater cause.

"Thanks," Jav said. "You too."

MAGNIFICENT SISTER-SON

*J*AV MADE MORE coffee—platinum strength. When Ari shuffled out, silent and sullen, Jav poured his nephew a cup, showed him the papers and translated the name Rogelio Alondra.

Still sleepy, Ari shrugged and tossed them back across the table. "I don't get what you're saying."

"Roger Lark is your father."

Ari stared. "Bullshit," he half sang. "Are you fucking with me, T?"

"Alex called Roger. He confirmed it."

Ari dragged the birth certificate toward him again, squinting at his fingertip on the names. A hundred different things went through his face. Jav waited it out.

"He's my father? For real?"

"For real."

"Fucking A." Ari's mouth twisted. "Wait, he confirmed it? He *knew*?"

"No—"

"The whole fucking time at Thanksgiving and then skiing, he knew?"

"I'm telling you everything I know. Alex called him. I was sitting right there. Alex didn't tell Roger what we'd found, he only asked if Roger remembered the name of the nurse he used to date at Lark House. And he did. Then Alex explained the rest. Rog was shocked."

"Or acted shocked," Ari said, crossing his arms.

"He didn't deny it. And he's coming here to talk."

"What if I don't want to talk to him?"

"You don't have to. But he's coming. Look, I don't know him all that well, but from the little I do know, I'm inclined to give him the benefit of the doubt. But if you don't want to see him, you don't have to."

Ari scrubbed his face vigorously. "Jesus Christ, this is like a bad soap opera."

"I wouldn't make it up in a book."

"Rog is my father?" Ari picked up the certificate again. Put it down again. "So... That means... Val and Trelawney are my aunts?"

Jav nodded.

The twist became a tentative smile. "Oh. Well, that's cool, I guess."

Jav's nodding head slowly became a side-to-side shake. "It's kind of a problem."

Ari's chin tilted, his eyebrows furrowed. Then his face smoothed out, expanded with alarm.

"No," he said.

"Ari, I'm sor—"

"No."

"Deane's your cousin."

"No." Ari's hands went for his head, raked back through his hair, pulling the follicles tight along his forehead.

"I'm sorry."

Ari got up. "No. No, I don't care. No." He paced around the apartment, much as Jav had paced the night before. "God fucking *dammit*..."

"I'm sorry, Ari."

"Why'd you have to tell me? I swear to God, you ruin everything. *Fuck*..." Ari swept a side table and sent a stack of books to the floor. "I don't care, T. I don't. I didn't know. I'm in love with her. I can't switch it off."

"I know you can't."

"What am I supposed to do?"

"I don't know."

"Great. Thanks. Ruin my life and tell me you don't know."

"I couldn't not tell you."

"Sure you could. What difference does it make?"

"It makes a huge difference if you get her pregnant."

"I have no intention of getting her pregnant. Different condom every time, remember? Jesus, I may be eighteen but I'm not an idiot."

"Exactly. You have a whole life in front of you."

"I don't care what's in front of me. I want what I have now and I want it with Deane."

"You're too young to know wh—"

"Don't fucking tell me what I know and want. I don't take life advice from a whore."

Everything froze, even the air.

Jav stared at his nephew a long moment. "That was a heavy-duty line," he finally said. "How long you been saving it up?"

Ari stared back, open-mouthed like he couldn't believe what came out. "T…"

"Twenty-three years," Jav said. "No one ever called me a whore. Not to my face, at least." He shrugged with a chuckle. "I guess it's a small but significant accomplishment."

"T, I'm sorry."

"What for? I am a whore. You can dress it up as escort, but whore's accurate. I sleep with women for money. Been doing it since I was twenty-one."

Jav crossed his arms and leaned against the counter, feeling strangely liberated. "You know, you're right. Don't listen to me. I've never been in love. My cousin put his hand down my pants and before I could figure out how I felt about it, I got thrown out of the house. A woman liked the way I behaved with people and she paid me to come home with her. Love and I were never friends. Cash was my friend. I needed money and all I had for sale was myself. Women wanted what I was selling. I did this and they gave me that. It's made me who I am but that was my choice. You have a choice, too. I don't know what to tell you, kid. All I can do is promise that whatever your decision, I won't throw you down the stairs or cut you off. I might not know much about love, but I know it means you don't turn your back on family. Not in my definition."

"I never judged what—"

"Forget it, we're not talking about me anyway. I've said my piece and I've got editing to do. Where's my hat?"

Ari blanched. "I left it at Deane's."

"Oh, now you're pissing me off."

"Calm down, it's just a hat."

"You think? I was in love with the guy it belonged to. I let him slip through my fingers because I thought there was time. Instead he boarded an airplane on Nine-Eleven, crashed in a field in Pennsylvania and we never got to talk about it."

Ari stared.

"When I flew to Santiago, I didn't do it for Alex and Val. I did it for *you*. To make sure Deane came back to talk about it the way Flip didn't. I didn't let you wear his hat just because you looked good in it. I did it because you got your conversation. You got the second chance I didn't."

"T," Ari said. "I…"

"Look at me." Jav stepped up and put his hands on Ari's shoulders. "I love you from the bottom of my heart. I'm on your side. And if you lose that hat, it's going to be really fucking unpleasant around here. So I suggest you man up, take your ass over to your aunt's house and *get it*."

Ari manned, took and got. Jav poured his third cup of coffee when all he wanted was to lie down and pass out. But he manned up as well, took his ass to the computer and got some words down.

Ari came back in and set the hat on the desk by Jav's elbow.

"Thank you," Jav said, putting it on. "Sorry I brought my shit into it. It's an emotional subject. I probably should've told you the first time you borrowed it. I should've told you a lot of things, I guess."

"No, I get it. Sorry about the whore…thing."

Jav went on typing but Ari lingered.

"Don't read over my shoulder," Jav said. "You make me nervous."

"I'm not." Ari picked up the framed picture of Jav and Naroba as children in Queens, studied it, then set it down again. "I was thinking… I mean, it kind of hit me… I've never heard a male relative say I love you."

Jav smiled at the screen. "I'd bet all my money Nick Seaver loved you."

"Yeah, but…" Ari's voice fractured. "It's different. Because…"

Jav took his glasses off and set them down. "Y tú eres mi verdadera sangre."

"Truth of…my blood?" Ari said. "Blood truth?"

"Trueblood."

"Yeah. You're my Trueblood."

His face crumpled. Jav got up so fast, the chair fell backward and the hat fell sideways. Ari stumbled against Jav's chest and Jav held him tight. "I got you," he said.

Ari shook in his arms. Into Jav's shoulder he pushed the heartbreaking sob of a boy who didn't want to cry, but couldn't hold it in anymore.

"It's all right," Jav said. "Let it go."

One sob led to another. Then a chain of them. Hard, damp huffs of air gouged out of Ari's throat and flung against Jav's shirt.

"I got you," Jav said.

"I can't take losing anything else."

"I know." Jav kissed Ari's head. "I know."

"I always think…" Ari's voice was bubbled up with pain and despair. "I wouldn't have met Deane if my mother hadn't died. Everything that happened put me on a trajectory to this place. It helped make sense of it. Deane gave me a reason. And if I lose her, T, it's like my mother fucking died for *nothing*."

He cried like a child, his hands scrabbling to hold onto Jav's shirt. Jav's eyes were dry and his arms were strong. His heart full of a fierce love for this tough kid, this vulnerable boy, this magnificent sister-son given into his care.

He's a Lark. But I am his Trueblood. And my excellent job is to navigate him out into the open sea. And if he flies too high, I help get him down.

"It's all right," he said. "I'm with you. No matter what."

SEE WHAT HAPPENS

*D*EANE WAS SHATTERED, but took the week-long restriction on seeing Ari harder than she took the news about being related to him. "A week?" she said. "How does that make any sense?"

"You knew what the deal was," Val said. "You knew what would happen if we found him in the house in the middle of the night."

"But what's it matter at this point?" she cried. "How can you do this to me right now? I need to see him."

No sooner had she calmed down when Ari showed up, pale and anxious, looking for the hat he'd left upstairs. Deane ripped open like a fresh wound when Alex wouldn't let Ari in, and she sank on a kitchen stool in a sobbing rage while Alex went upstairs and got the hat.

This is ridiculous, he thought, brushing the brim off. *He's my nephew. This is Roger's child. How can I not let him into my house?*

He sighed and looked at the window. A smile twitched at the corner of his mouth and he had a hard time holding it back. "I'll be damned," he said under his breath. He leaned on the sill and scanned the yard, mapping how Ari had scaled the oak tree to the top of the porch, then climbed up onto the main roof, slipping past the gables and through Deane's window.

If that wasn't love, what was?

He turned to look at his daughter's bed. A strip of red paper lay on the floor by the wastebasket: the unmistakable ripped-off top of a condom wrapper.

He's my daughter's lover. Which isn't allowed in my house after lights-out.

"You were her lover first," Alex said, sighing. "So that rule comes first."

Out on the porch, Ari took the hat and even managed a second of respectful eye contact. "I'm sorry," he said.

"It's purely for breaking one of our rules," Alex said. "It has nothing to do with what we've just found out. I don't even know what the rules are for that yet."

Ari gave a short nod and went down the porch steps. Alex returned to the crime scene in the kitchen.

"This is so *stupid*," Deane said through her teeth, clenched fists hitting her legs. "Dad, you don't understand."

"I do," Alex said, trying to reach for her but she was having none of it. "Nobody saw this, cosita. Nobody guessed, nobody had any idea. We're all stunned. A little bit of distance will be good."

"No, it *won't*," Deane said, her voice soaked and mushy. "You don't have a fucking clue what's good for me."

"Hey," Val said, getting an arm around Deane's shaking shoulders. "It's all right."

"No," Deane said, chopped apart with sobs. "No, it's not all right. I won't let you... I'm going to see him. I'm eighteen. You can't stop me."

Alex felt his temper flare behind his eyes as he stared her down. "Soy tu padre y puedo. Cachai?"

"You," Deane said, spitting the word at Alex's feet. "You're the one who—" The breath squeaked out of her as Val's hand closed around her upper arm.

"Don't even," Val said. Her face was composed, her tone pitched low, but her fingers pressed indentations into her daughter's bicep. Deane gulped and sniffed back whatever she was going to say.

"I know you're upset," Val said. "But if you disrespect your father, you'll lose your phone and your car keys. Do you understand?"

Deane nodded, her mouth a tight, crooked line.

"Go put cold water on your face. Take a few minutes alone." Val released Deane's arm and the girl ran out of the kitchen.

Val slumped on a stool. "This is surreal."

"This is fucked *up*," Alex said, slumping on another.

"Parenthood. It ain't for sissies." She rubbed her face hard, then lifted her gaze and looked at Alex a long time. The kitchen clock ticked, followed by the muffled rattle of ice cubes falling in the freezer.

"Hey," she said.

Alex smiled. "Hi."

Chin on her hands, she smiled back. "How about I take your phone and car keys too? Go lock myself in the bathroom."

"I'll just kick down the door."

"What, to get them back or me?"

"You." He brushed her cheek. "I'd jump out of a fucking plane for you."

She reached her hands out and he took them. He pulled her against his body and wrapped his arms around her, exhaling. Letting her fill him up like a rich dessert after weeks of strict dieting.

"Valerie, please forgive me," he said.

"I will," she said.

He buried his hands in her hair. "Soon?"

"We're better off doing this together," she said. "I don't like doing this shit without you."

"Me neither. I suck without you."

She squeezed him, wiped her face against his shirt and then looked up. "I think you should make dulce de leche."

He felt his smile unfold until a chuckle fell out. "You're brilliant."

She touched a fingertip to one of his dimples. "I know."

<hr />

ALEX NEVER HAD a burning need to keep his culinary heritage alive, but after Deane was born, he felt it his fatherly duty to produce dulce de leche. Buying it pre-made in a jar was cheating. He made it the way his father did, by taking a can of condensed milk and letting it simmer in water for three hours, turning to a rich, dark caramel spread. It was Deane's favorite thing in the world. She and Alex ate it on toast. Or straight out of the can, depending on what kind of day it was.

Today called for the can. And a soup spoon.

Alex stayed downstairs most of the afternoon, supervising the milk-and-sugar alchemy and doing odd jobs outside. A luscious, comforting perfume slowly filled the quiet house with sweetness. Alex took the can out of the water to cool, turned off the stove and went upstairs.

Val was napping, which he expected. He didn't expect Deane to be in bed with her. She and Val were spooned up tight under the covers, Val curved like a shield against Deane's back, an arm holding her close. Both Deane's hands were in fists against her collarbones, the crown of her head right under Val's chin. Her mouth was slightly parted and her hairline damp with sweat, the way it always was when she napped as a toddler.

Deane stirred when Alex moved closer to the bed, and Val opened her eyes.

"We for to take leetle nap," she whispered.

Alex heeled off his shoes and lay down. He put his hand at the back of Deane's neck and pressed his mouth against her flushed forehead. She made a little hum in her chest and gave a heavy sigh.

"Hi, Dad," she said softly, taking a bit of his shirt into her fingers.

"Hey, babe."

She put her face into Alex's chest and cried. He dug in his pocket but for once, a handkerchief wasn't in it. He found the one under his pillow and handed it over.

"I don't know what to do," she said, wiping her eyes. "Ever since I can remember, I wanted a love like the one you guys have. I finally found it. And now I'm supposed to walk away and forget it?"

"No," Alex said against her head. "No one's suggesting you do that."

"I think you should love him and see what happens," Val said, running her hand along the long, blonde ponytail.

Deane sniffed, swallowed hard and looked back at her mother.

Val smiled. "You love him. And love isn't something you can switch on and off." Over Deane's head, Val's eyes met Alex's and held a moment. "You're young, baby. And the world is yours. Maybe you'll feel differently when you go to school and you're away from him. Maybe you won't. The only thing to do is find out. Love him and see what happens."

Deane looked at Alex then, as if for approval. He gazed back, seeing his daughter's face morph back and forth between little girl and woman.

What you feel now is all that matters. What you believe and feel right now. Later on, you might feel differently. Later you might be able to explain it better. But it doesn't ever change how you felt at the time...

"Who am I to tell you can't love your cousin, cosita?" he said. "I practically married my sister."

He smoothed her hair, then reached beyond and caressed Val's face. Her fingers crept over and tucked into one of his belt loops. "Rest," she said softly.

But Alex stayed awake, holding his girls.

THAT GIRL

"**D**O YOU WANT me to be here when Rog comes?" Jav asked.

Ari thought about it, already feeling his loyalty was being tested and one answer or the other would be dickish to somebody. "I guess," he said, lobbing the decision back into Jav's court.

Jav closed his laptop and unplugged the power cord. "Tell you what. I'll go sit in Celeste's and write. Then you can have privacy and if shit gets weird, I'm twenty feet away."

"Sounds good," Ari said. "Thanks."

Jav hooked an arm around Ari's neck and pulled him in, rubbing his hair. He was touchy-feely lately, and while the bristly, adolescent part of Ari rolled its eyes, the tender and bruised parts of him leaned into the hugs. He rested a moment against Jav's tall, muscular weight and let it soothe the crackling, confused ends of his nerves.

"Eres el más valiente," Jav said.

"Eres mi verdadera sangre."

Along with accepting physical affection, Ari was attempting to speak Spanish with Jav. It came to him slow and klutzy, simple words and expressions pried from memory. But it made Jav happy, and his happiness mattered.

Waiting alone, Ari tried to relax and draw, but his fingers were trembling around the pencil, which annoyed him. He crumpled up paper after paper, firing it over his shoulder.

Are you nervous? Deane texted.

Yeah. Which is stupid, because come on it's just ROG.

And you've met him before.

Yeah. Which is surreal and stupid.

I miss you.

Ari exhaled. Words didn't exist for the empty place in his heart and the aching need in his hands. ***Soon,*** he typed. ***I'll see you so soon.***

A knock at the apartment door. A stab of adrenaline in Ari's chest, cold like an icicle, followed by a boiling rush down his arms. His damp palm slid off the doorknob once before it could get a grip and open it.

At Thanksgiving, Rog had been soft, tousled and casual. Up in Vermont, he'd been a lumberjack—bearded and rugged. Now he was shaved and combed and sharp. As if for a date.

"What, no flowers?" Ari said, pretending to close the door as Roger laughed out loud.

"Goddammit, I was going to get some, too."

The chuckles died off as they looked at each other across the threshold.

"Hey, Schnozz," Rog finally said. The words were joking but his voice trembled.

"I prefer Son of Schnozz," Ari said. He cleared his throat and reached out. "Hale, hearty handshake?"

Rog's eyes crinkled above big teeth in a big smile. His big hand folded around Ari's and gave it a brisk pump. "Nice lid," he said.

Ari flicked the brim of the porkpie hat. "It's Jav's."

"I brought a friend with me," Rog said, pointing down the stairs. Ari leaned out and looked down. Roman sat at the foot of the steps, his leash looped around the banister bracket.

"I thought we could take a walk," Rog said. "Head up to Lark House. I don't know about you, but I think better on my feet."

They headed up Bemelman Street, making small talk and letting the incline burn off some of the nervous energy. They ambled down to the cool, shady grove. Ari looped Roman's leash around a small beam, then he and Rog climbed one of the spiral staircases to the main platform. They sat, each with a back up against a trunk, and exhaled a sigh.

"I guess let's start with the obvious," Ari said.

"I didn't know," Rog said.

Ari nodded.

"I give you my word, I didn't know."

"I believe you."

"But I'd like to…get to know you."

"I don't know what I'd like."

"That's fair."

The wind blew through, rustling the green leaves, throwing patterns on the wood platform's planks.

"Alondra," Ari said. "Well-played, Mom."

Rog's smile was sad. "Well-played."

"Did you really throw up on her?"

"Full projectile unload," Rog said. "Right in her lap."

Ari laughed. "Smooth."

"And that's how I met your mother."

"How long were you together?"

"Only a couple months." Rog reached into one of the pockets of his cargo shorts. "I have some boxes of stuff in my sister's attic. I went digging around last night…" He handed over a stack of photos.

Ari took them. A young, sandy Roger stood at the base of a tree, a cast on his arm and signs of construction all around him. Safety goggles pushed up on his forehead, sawdust in his hair and joy in his smile as he looked down at the woman at his side. Tucked under Roger's arm, she looked off beyond the camera, laughing.

Ari stared. "Look at her hair," he said softly. It fell nearly to her waist. He'd only seen it short.

"Oh she had some head of hair," Roger said. "Thick. I mean it had *weight*. You'll never lose your hair, kid, I guarantee you that."

Ari glanced up. A quick, two-second look and for the first time, he saw a flicker of himself in Roger's face.

He looked at the next picture. Roger and Naroba, down by the river. He was soaking wet in swim trunks, hair slicked back and water beading on his shoulders. His arms held Naroba from behind, the casted one wrapped up in a plastic bag. His face was hidden in her shoulder while her head was turned to the side. She was laughing at him. Happy and confident in a striped bikini, her hair pulled up in a high ponytail. One arm curved up around Roger's neck.

A third shot, by the river at sunset. Roger and Naroba sitting on a rock, looking out at the water. He was pointing at something and her gaze followed his finger. Then one more shot of them on the rock, sitting close together. Roger's arm around Naroba's back, a hand buried in her thick, weighted hair. Her head lay on his shoulder.

"You looked really happy," Ari said, his throat warm.

"It was a summer love. You find it under H in the dictionary."

"Mm." His eyes kept widening and narrowing, focusing on his mother. So young. So fresh and pretty and full of sass.

God, Mom...

"Naroba," Rog said. "It's pretty. It rolls around your mouth. But she liked to be called Naria."

"I never heard anyone call her that."

"You know, it hit me while I was on the plane: Ari is the three middle letters of Naria. I don't know if it's significant, but it sure seemed like it."

Ari's mouth hung open a little as he envisioned the name, seeing himself within it. "Holy shit."

A long silence passed.

"Was it here?" Ari asked.

Rog wrinkled his eyebrows.

"Here," Ari said, patting the platform beside him. "In the treehouse."

"I don't kiss and tell."

"I think I'm entitled to know if I was conceived in a tree. It would explain a lot."

Rog laughed and bumped his feet against Ari's sneakers. "Let's say it was nowhere near the ground."

The quiet between them was comfortable now and they held still under each other's curious gaze.

I can see it now, Ari thought. *I see me in him.*

"What ended up happening?" he asked.

"It always had a finite amount of time. I was leaving."

"Where?"

"To southeast Asia. To work with Habitat for Humanity. And then my parents died. That turned the world upside-down and I became a...not pleasant person to be with for the rest of the summer."

"I hear you."

"It didn't end badly," Rog said. "It just finished. It was a summer love story and we came to the end of the book, the way we knew we would."

Ari stacked the pictures and extended them back to Roger, but Rog held up a palm. "They're for you. If you want them, I mean."

And all at once, Ari did want them. Wanted more to fill in the gaps, wanted a structure built on this stunted branch of his family tree. "Did you ever see her again? Talk to her?"

Rog shook his head. "No. For whatever reason, we didn't reach out again." He rolled his arm up, showing the rose compass tattoo. "But I never forgot. I always thought about her. There's always a girl, Schnozz. That girl with a capital G. You keep coming back to in your mind. Not with regret. More like she's north, with a capital N. And your memory's compass needle likes to turn toward her and wonder."

"She put you on my birth certificate. Sort of. But I've been wondering why she didn't name you my guardian in her will."

"When you think about it, she didn't have much going on in terms of choice, huh? Name me or name her brother—two men she'd had little to no contact with in years. I guess... Well, no need to guess really. Between the two of us, Jav is the better man."

"You think?"

"I know. We got it all backward. Jav should be your father who looks out for you. I should be your uncle who gets you into trouble."

"Jav kind of saved my life." Ari ran a hand through his hair. "I mean, I don't know what I would've done without him this past year."

"I don't want to upset your life," Rog said. "But I don't want to be a stranger to you."

"What do you want me to call you?"

"Rog is fine."

"All right."

"As for Deane... That's a surreal, shitty situation. Because at the moment I sense she's that girl. Capital G."

"Yeah."

"I'm not one to be giving love advice. Not that you're asking."

"I don't know what to do. Advise away."

"Just love her. You're young. Anything could come of this. First love doesn't always turn into forever love but... I don't know, Ari. I'm not a clairvoyant but something in my gut tells me this isn't going to be a tragedy." He grinned. "I have a nose for these things."

Ari slowly nodded. "Want to come to my graduation?"

Roger blinked a few times. "I'd be honored." His voice faltered and he looked away, a fist touching his mouth, his large nose resting on top. "Holy shit, it's all kind of hitting me. You know?"

"Yeah."

"I remember at Thanksgiving, and again up in Stowe. I kept saying to Jav, 'That's a great kid. I like that kid.' I mean, I *liked* you. Right away. Maybe I'm projecting backward but I swear, some instinctive...something was going on. When I think about the whole damn time at the dinner table and later at my house, my own son was sitting right there… Ah, shit, look at me now." He laughed, pressing the heel of his hand into his eyes. "It's just *crazy*."

Ari took a deep, trembling breath. "I know."

"Oh, hey," Rog said. "There she is. Perfect timing."

"Who?"

Rog pointed down. "I convinced Alex and Val to spring her."

Roman barked as Deane came walking into the grove.

"Dude, I fucking love you," Ari said, scrambling to his feet.

Roger rolled his eyes. "Don't sweet-talk me, Schnozz. Get out of here."

Ari went tearing down the spiral stairs. He took off running. Deane came running, too, and flung herself into his arms. He whipped her around in two whirling circles and then crushed her against him.

"I love you," she said, as they stumbled sideways together and came to a rest against a massive oak.

"I love you." He pulled her in tight. "I swear being cousins doesn't matter to me. Maybe someday it will. But not now."

He closed his eyes a moment, the hot summer day wrapping around him and Deane. Even the trees crept nearer, joining branches to make a green ring around them.

Deane lifted up her head, eyes shining silver and gold. "My dad says how you feel now is all that matters."

She kissed him, and as his mouth opened to hers, Ari felt his inner compass needle spin in a slow, contented revolution. Deane wasn't north. The needle wasn't even looking for a direction. It only wanted to turn around and around, with Ari at its center, the fulcrum for all the directions, all the possibilities and *somedays* the world offered. Ari in the middle of a ring of trees, beneath the spot where he was conceived.

Ari, who was the center of Naria.

BROTHERS

WHO I WANT TO BE

ALEX AND VAL went out to dinner for their anniversary. They had their little cards. And their pens. Nibs poised over the paper and the words prepared: *I'd like to be faithful to you another year.*

"I knew one year it would be hard," Val said.

"Did you?"

"It's silly to think nobody will ever come along who makes the floor rock beneath your feet. Makes you stop and think. Weigh the consequences."

Alex nodded. "I know. It's just…" He rolled his lips in, eyes bright. "This sounds so shitty."

"You didn't think it was going to be you."

He shook his head.

"And certainly not with another guy. Who saw that coming?"

He pretended to jab the pen into his temple.

"At least we're laughing," she said, even though above the laughter they were both tearing up. And still the squares of paper on the table were blank, the pens uncapped.

"So, do we not sign this year?" she said. "Give it a pass? Sanction an affair each?"

He looked a long time at her. "We're better than that."

"This isn't a competition. Not with anyone else. Not even with ourselves." She reached her hands across the table and he took them in his. "I know life has rules," she said. "But the only rules I care about are the ones you and I make for us. And I know now I can handle anything from you except secrets. It sounds crazy, but rather than sneak off to the shed, I'd rather he came into our bedroom as a guest—"

"Honey, no," Alex said, twining his fingers with hers.

"I'd rather you told me you were going to see it through. And then come home to me."

"I don't need to see anything through," he said. "This attraction to Jav is intense and confusing, and it's shaking me up. But coming home to you has never been a question. This isn't coming from a place of dissatisfaction. That's what's so bewildering to me. I'm not unhappy. I don't need anything or anyone else."

She let go one of his hands to caress his face. "Thank you for that."

"I love you. I don't want to share you. I don't want to be shared. I love my life with you. I don't..." Almost angrily, he took his hand away, picked up the pen and wrote out his card:

I'd like to be faithful to you another year.

He slid the card across. "That's who I am. That's who I want to be. Wanting isn't having. You letting me be open about the wanting is enough."

Her throat clenched as she took the cap off her pen.

"The wanting is enough, Val," he said. "It's enough."

She wrote, blinking through tears. "It's enough. But God, it hurts like hell, doesn't it?"

He nodded. "It's hard this year."

She looked at him a moment, then wrote a little more and showed him:

I'd like to be faithful to you another year. (It's hard this year.)

"One day," she said. "We'll look back through these cards and we'll remember this year."

"And laugh?"

"Or cry."

"No," he said. "I think we'll laugh. Not at him. Just laugh and remember."

"We'll think, *Wow, that was tough.*"

"I thought I was gonna die, what the fuck?"

"My heart."

"My stomach."

They both inhaled and sighed at the same time.

"The old man in Santiago said it's a life," Alex said. "Not everyone gets one."

She touched his face, burning to touch him all over.

"And not everyone gets you," he said. He put his hand over hers and turned his mouth into her palm. "You're my life, Valerie. I'm sorry I took it for granted. I'm so sorry I hurt you."

She closed her eyes, feeling his warm breath curl through her fingers. "I haven't made love in a long time," she said softly.

His smile flickered. Sputtered like a damp candle wick. Then it grew warmer. Brighter. One dimple showed, then the other. He gathered the cards together and slipped them into his blazer pocket.

"Let's go home," he said.

MATCH

"**I**'M TAKING MY mother's advice," Deane said. "I'm going to love you and see what happens."

Ari was leaving for Vancouver in a few days and wouldn't be back until August. Then it would be a matter of weeks before they both left for college.

"Are you worried?" he asked.

"I'm not," she said. "It feels like I should be, but I'm not."

Jav already planned to fly to Vancouver mid-July to visit. After some discussion, Alex and Val agreed Deane could go with him.

"So we have that to look forward to," Ari said. "And then..."

"Then we see what happens," she said. "Let's be real: we're both of us heading off. Our relationship had this coming whether we found out we were related or not."

They packed as much time together as they could that week. Made as much love as they could, down by the river or parked in Ari's car.

"You're my cousin," he whispered as they lay under the stars one night. "I keep saying the word but it doesn't register. I don't react to it. You're my cousin."

"We didn't know. We didn't grow up together. We didn't imprint as genetically off-limits or whatever. We met. We liked each other and—"

"But do you ever think part of why we liked each other right away was *because* we're related?"

"All the people in the world," she said, running her hand over his chest. "And it ends up being you."

"I don't know," he said. "Is it a freaky coincidence? Or is it destiny?"

"Lying around talking, I tend to think it's a freaky coincidence." She pushed up on her elbow and looked down at him. "But when you're inside me, I definitely think it's destiny."

"Oh is that so?" He pushed her down on the blanket and slid on top of her.

"I love you," she whispered.

"Put your arms around me," he said. "Put your legs around me too. Hold onto me with everything. Don't let go."

She held on. All through those last days of the last week, she held him tight, pressing him into her body and into her memory.

They hugged goodbye in the parking lot behind the Lark Building, teary-eyed but laughing. Waving after Jav's car, Deane felt happy and brave, but later in the day it started to hurt. Lying in bed that night, it *really* hurt. Enough to make Sheba leave her post outside the master bedroom and come hop up on Deane's bed.

"This sucks *ass*," Deane cried into the smooth, black fur.

She crammed her days with work. She was assistant coaching a girls' lacrosse clinic, which meant long hours of physical activity in the sun. In the evenings, she went to the gym or ran with Alex. On Saturdays she worked double shifts at Celeste's, both for the money and to wear herself out. She slept late on Sundays, then hung around in Val's workroom, being crafty.

Her parents acted less tense around each other these days, but the air in the house stayed still. They hugged in the kitchen and held hands in front of the TV. But no soft laughter or little noises from behind their bedroom door at night. Once this would have filled Deane with a nervous upset. Now she could only hope they were loving each other and seeing what happened.

They had a beautiful Fourth of July, then rain hit Guelisten. By the third day of the deluge, the athletic fields turned to swamp and the clinic was cancelled until the weather cleared. Deane slept until eleven, woken when Val brought in coffee and toast with dulce de leche.

"Mumsy," Deane said, sitting up and stacking the pillows behind her. "You shouldn't have."

"You for to work hard," Val said, kissing Deane's head. "I for to make you break the fast."

Deane lay around, eating and reading until she dozed off again. This time she was woken by the slam of the front door, followed by the dogs barking and footsteps pounding up the stairs and down the hall.

"Val?" Alex called.

A door was flung open, more footsteps. "Val?"

Footsteps back down the hall, Sheba barking. Then Deane's door flew in. "Cosita, where's your mother?"

"In her room?"

"She's not." Alex's glasses were lopsided. He looked positively crazed. "Valerie?" His accent was at the forefront of his mouth, Valerie coming out as Balerie.

"I don't—"

"Where's your mother?"

"Dad, I don't know. What's the matter with you?"

"Val," Alex cried, heading back down the hall. Her heart pounding, Deane untangled her legs from the covers and followed him.

"Dad, what's wrong?"

"Valerie," he yelled. "Oh my God, where is she?"

"I'm right here," Val called from the bottom of the stairs. "I was in the basement. What's the matter?"

Alex pushed past Deane and ran down the steps like a thunderstorm. Deane crept after, staring open-mouthed as Alex seized her mother and crushed her against him, folding her up in his arms. Val's hand crept to the back of his head, running through his hair.

"What, what, what," she said. "What's wrong? What is it?"

"Dad?" Deane called, knuckles white on the banister.

"Valerie." Alex's legs buckled. He went right down on the floor, taking Val with him.

"*Dad.*"

"Alejandro, what's wrong?" Val cried as Deane came down the rest of the stairs and fell on her knees by them.

"They called me," Alex said.

"Who called you?"

Alex's hands closed in fists around Val's shirt. He lifted up his face. He was crying. But he was smiling. Tears dripping into his dimples.

"The Medical-Legal Institute in Santiago," he said. "They're sending an email. They found a match. Los encontraron."

"Who?" Deane and Val said as one.

"My parents," Alex sobbed and laughed. "Not the desert, not the ocean. In the ground. A mass grave. Valerie, they *found* them…"

⌒⟋

ALEX SAT AT the computer, Val and Deane on either side, reading the email from the Institute. It came with two attachments: the original report in Spanish, and the director's translation in English, explaining the analysis made on twenty-seven fragments of bone, recovered from a mass grave at a site called Patio 21.

Lot 97-M, sixteen male fragments, matched Alex's Y-DNA markers, indicating a direct paternal ancestor.

Lot 102-F, eleven female bone pieces, matched Alex's mitochondrial DNA, indicating a maternal ancestor.

In a private aside, the director told Alex that no other, individual remains were found with these same Y-DNA or mtDNA matches. In fact, no infant bones had been recovered from the mass grave.

Meaning Alex's brother or sister could still be alive and somewhere in the world.

Or not.

Sometimes not knowing the answer is better, Deane thought.

"Which is harder," she said, sliding arms around her father's shoulders from behind. "The end of hope? Or the truth?"

"They're both hard, cosita," Alex said, stroking her forearms. "Pero al menos no fueron los aviones."

"At least what wasn't the airplanes?"

Alex shook his head. "Nothing."

Deane's eyes filled up, warm and wet. Her mind began to grasp the enormity of her father's life. Staring at the computer screen, she finally understood this indescribable, unresolved loss. The decades of torturous grief that took Alex to Crazytown and back. The miracle within twenty-seven bone fragments dug up from a mass grave.

My grandparents were murdered, she thought. *Thrown into a hole in the ground to be forgotten. Disappeared. Dad was just a little boy. He didn't have a Jav to come rescue him and get him down from the mountain. He flew out of Chile alone. With a backpack, two cardigans and a knife.*

I might have an uncle or aunt somewhere. Maybe alive and still living in Chile, with no idea who they really are. They could've been skiing at Portillo the same time I was. Why not? Ari is my cousin and he was right in front of my face this whole time. I could've stood on the lift line with Dad's brother or sister. One could've been a doctor or nurse taking care of me when I was in the hospital. And none of us knew. How could anyone know? Dad will probably never, never know...

"I'm sorry," she said, tightening her arms. "Dad, I'm so sorry." She slid around his chair, wanting to be both comforting and comforted. She sat in his lap—something she hadn't done in years—and buried her face in his shoulder. "Me duele el corazón, lo siento mucho."

His scarred, tattooed arms were strong around her. He kissed her head, rocked her in his lap and wound her ponytail around his hand. "Thank you," he said softly.

He and Val went to bed early that night. Deane stayed up late, talking to Ari, then reading. She went downstairs for water and passed her parents' bedroom. Sheba was curled up by the closed door. She opened her eyes. Almost seemed to roll them at Deane with a knowing air before returning to rest.

Deane held still a moment, pressed on all sides by the air. Thick and heady. A burgundy red. A core of orange at its center. Through it came a tiny yelp, followed by a shushing hiss. Then soft laughter.

Somebody To Love

*J*AV TEXTED ALEX: **Ari told me about finding your parents' remains. It's unbelievable.**

Alex replied: **I still can't believe it.**

Has to be surreal.

It is. Slowly my mind is getting around it.

It's amazing. I'm really happy you got this closure. What will they do now? I mean, will they bury them in Chile or…?

I'm bringing them here. After 34 years, I want them where I can find them. I want them with me.

Jav smiled, his throat growing tight. **Can't blame you,** he typed. **Really happy for you, Alejo. It's amazing.**

Thanks. How's the book coming?

It's done. Signed off on final edits, final cover, etc. Galleys should be printed soon.

Can't wait to read it. Te extraño.

I miss you.

Jav exhaled, his heart hugging itself. Alex missed him. His absence was noticed. Someone's life had an empty place where he used to be. He echoed in its longing space.

Te echo de menos, he typed back.

He went down to the Hudson that night and stared at the water, thinking *I miss you.*

He told his father, *I miss you.*

I miss you, he said to Gloria.

Ari, his magnificent sister-son. *I miss you.*

Flip, navigating a ship across the skies. *I miss you.*

And Alex. *I miss you.*

Full of empty places, Jav told the truth to the river.

I miss you so much.

He lifted his face to the stars, asking love to be his friend. Admitting out loud, to himself and the world, "I want somebody to love."

"I swear," he whispered. "Give me one more chance and I will make the most of it."

He went home and dug in a desk drawer for an envelope with a flash drive inside. He opened *The Voyages of Trueblood Cay* and read a few chapters.

"A captain who is a king," he said under his breath. Pinky to index, his fingers drummed along the desk. "But the king has no queen."

He stared at the wall, thinking. He picked up the framed picture of him and Naroba. His fingertips touched his sister's face. Then they started to itch.

He opened another drawer and pulled out a file. Encased in plastic was the December 1979 issue of *Cricket,* with his winning story about Naria Nyland. He looked up from the magazine to his computer screen, then down again.

"Nyland," he said. "The land of Nye."

What was Nye?

He drummed his fingers again. *Great was the day when Trueblood Cay sailed into Alondra, the mightiest port of Nyland, where Queen Naria ruled by sword and...*

"Spice," he said, slowly spinning in his chair. A single index finger lifted off the armrest. "Nye is a spice. It only grows in one place. In trees. It comes from a tree. A tree that only grows in this one land. The warrior queens conquered the land for the spice trees."

He put his feet down and stood up. "The land was once ruled by giants. The trees are their abandoned playthings. The trees wonder why no one loves them anymore." He pointed at his reflection in the mirror. "The trees won't make Nye until they're loved again."

He was pacing now, striking matches. "Naria's people are descended from the giants. They took the land back. Became good citizens with beautiful hearts. Built houses in the trees, mined the spice and created Nyland. Nye is valuable. You can't have Nye without love. You put Nye in bottles with rum and it makes a drink. A magic drink. It makes love..."

Arriving back at his desk, he took Flip's hat off the wooden stand and put it on his head. "Trueblood wants the Nye. Because he wants somebody to love"

He sat and made a single spinning revolution.

"Naria Nyland wants Trueblood. She wants *a* Trueblood. An heir to inherit the spice."

Sword and Spice: The Voyages of Trueblood Cay.

Jav hitched the chair closer to the desk and started to type.

A GOOD JOB

SEPTEMBER 11, 2007
GUELISTEN, NEW YORK

*A*MERICAN FLAGS WERE attached to all the lamp posts on Main Street. They fluttered and flapped from poles and storefronts and whiskey barrels of flowers.

Jav parked his car at the gates of the village cemetery and walked the graveled pathways. Coming over a knoll, he found Alex sitting on a bench beneath an oak tree. Elbows on knees and hands laced, staring at the gravestone before him.

"Hey," Jav said.

Alex raised a hand and shifted over on the bench. Jav sat, looked at the silvery granite marker and its chiseled letters.

MARIA CLEMENTINA PENDA 1938-1973
EDUARDO ALEJANDRO GABRIEL PENDA 1936-1973
NOSOTROS DOS

"I was going to bury the knife with him," Alex said. "It seemed the poetic thing to do. But I'd miss having it around."

"He'd want you to keep it."

They leaned back against the bench, arms and ankles crossed. Listening to the wind rustle the leaves.

"It's so peaceful in a cemetery," Jav said. "You think of them as haunted places but to me, it feels...alive."

"I know. I've been coming almost every night after work. Just to sit and tell them about things. Or just sit."

Jav leaned his forearms on his knees, tapping his thumbs and thinking about his father's gravesite in Queens. Wondering if it might be time to go visit it. Sit and tell Rafael about a lot of things.

"So," Alex said. "You find a place that takes pets?"

"Yeah. Nice building on Riverside Drive. I got a neighbor with a twelve-year-old girl who needs pocket money. She's in love with Roman."

"He's easy to love. How's Ari doing?"

"Great. Happy. Busy. Missing Deane."

Alex smiled. "I get the same report from Burlington." He reached to the ground beside him and picked up two small bouquets. He put one on his parents' graves. The other was for Felipe, whose stone stood a foot from Eduardo's name.

"I wanted the brothers next to each other," Alex said, picking a weed out of the ground and tossing it.

"You did a good job," Jav said absently, fixated on the weed. Such a small gesture, but loaded with attentiveness and love and care. Were weeds growing around Rafael's stone? Jav should go dig them out. He needed to go. He'd waited too long.

Alex kissed his fingertips and pressed them to each stone. Then he stuffed both hands in his pockets and headed down the path, Jav following.

"Heading out?" Alex said, turning to walk backward. He wore the light blue sweater that deepened his eyes to pine. He'd had a haircut recently and was growing a goatee.

The beautiful bastard.

"Yeah," Jav said. "I'm all closed up, just have to give the keys back to Trelawney. I wanted to say goodbye."

"To me?" Alex chuckled through his nose. "Good luck."

"Still got my card?"

"The old one and the new one."

At their cars, Jav reached in his passenger seat and drew out a book. "Hot off the press."

"Hey, look at that." Alex took it from him. Looked at all sides, fanned the pages. "That is one handsome book." He hefted it up and down in one hand. "And not a novella."

"I had a lot to say." Jav looked over Alex's shoulder at the glossy cover with its grainy depiction of lower Manhattan.

The Trade, by Gil Rafael.

"When are you going to write under your real name?" Alex said.

"Maybe the next one."

Alex's eyebrows raised. "Really? What's it about?"

"Swords and spices. I'd tell you more, but then I'd have to kill you." He dodged his head as Alex bopped him lightly with the book. "In other news, I've retired."

"From escorting? No way."

"Officially put myself out to pasture. I'll die solely as a starved writer."

"What brought you to the decision?"

Jav shrugged. "Friend of mine said I was worth more."

"You should keep that friend."

"I'm going to try." He cleared his throat. "You know what I realized recently?"

"What?"

"If you take some poetic license, you could say Rog is my brother-in-law. Right?"

"Sure."

"So if you're my brother-in-law's brother-in-law, doesn't that make us kind of…brothers?"

Alex's chin slowly rose and fell and the dimples began to show. "Holy shit."

"My thoughts exactly. Now bring it in, brother, before this gets too cheesy."

Their right palms smacked together and they pulled in hard, pressed chest to chest with their fists on each other's shoulders.

"It felt good," Alex said.

"It felt like me." Jav bussed his mouth against Alex's temple, then grabbed his ass.

"Son of a bitch," Alex said, laughing as he broke away.

"Don't poke the tiger."

Alex opened the driver's side door. With a foot in he stopped. "You know what a group of tigers is called?"

Jav crossed his forearms on the roof of his car. "What?"

"They're typically solitary animals so you don't see them in groups," Alex said. "Sometimes they're called a streak. Or an ambush. Depends who you ask."

"This tiger is making himself a third chance," Jav said. "Third time's the charm, right?"

"A group of finches is called a charm."

Jav put his chin down on his forearms. "I can't tie that back to anything."

Alex slid behind the wheel, slammed the door and leaned an elbow on the window. "What, you're watching me drive away?"

"Yeah. Actually."

"Te quiero, tigre."

"Te quiero, alondra."

⌒

JAVIER PARKED IN front of the Lark building and went into Celeste's.

"You seen Trelawney?" he asked the barista.

"Upstairs in the gallery."

Outside, Jav touched the glossy red door that led to the place he called home for a year and a half.

You walk into my house and I will be on you.

He walked past Lark's, glanced at the window of Deane Fine Tailoring, then went upstairs to the gallery.

Two voices echoed down to him, amplified by the empty room, cleared of its dollhouses and shadowboxes.

I'm having déjà vu.

Trelawney stood in the center of the space with a tall man. "Hey, handsome," she called to Jav.

The man turned around, his arms crossed. A startling flash of blue eyes. Jeans and a black T-shirt. Thick, dark hair easing into silver. A bit of healthy sunburn along his cheekbones and a slowly-spreading smile as his right hand broke free and extended toward Jav. "Hi, I'm Stef."

"Javier. Hi." They shook.

"Jav's my favorite ex-tenant," Trelawney said. "And among other things, a marketing specialist."

"Only free marketing," Jav said. He glanced up at Stef whose eyes glanced away.

"Stef's an art therapist," Trelawney said.

"Really?" Jav said.

"Yeah, I've been doing a program with women and kids at a domestic violence shelter in Poughkeepsie. I'm looking for space to do an exhibit of their work. Raise money for the shelter."

"And awareness," Jav said.

Stef smiled. He had one dimple. "That's right."

"You have a website set up?" Trelawney asked.

Now Stef sighed with a pained expression. "It's on my list of things to avoid."

"You need to talk to this guy," she said, a thumb in Jav's direction.

"You do website design? Seriously?"

"Among other things," Jav said. He had to consciously detach his eyes from Stef's deep blue gaze. Especially the thin scar that cut through one of his eyebrows, telling a story.

The scar was the price for bedding the Queen. He didn't take the cut personally. She kept his eyebrows in a locket around her neck—how many men could say that?

"Come down for a cup of coffee," Trelawney said. She put her hand on Jav's arm. "You, too."

The bookstore was quiet. Only a couple of readers sat by the fireplace. "Holy crap," Stef said, looking around. "I want to be held hostage here."

Jav looked at him. "That's literally what I said the first time I walked in."

"This place with an art gallery upstairs? Dude, I think I just came."

The shop was hot. Jav slipped off his sport jacket.

They sat side by side at the bar and Trelawney served them the house blend. Cupped around the mug, Stef's hands were large, flecks of paint on the knuckles and nails.

He'd painted the one and only portrait of the Queen. It was said he used the blood from his slashed eyebrow to color her lips.

"Who drew all those comic strips?" Stef asked, pointing.

"My nephew," Jav said.

"No shit. Where'd he go to school?"

"He just started at New Paltz."

"Oh, he'll love it there." Stef leaned, blew across the surface of his coffee and took another sip. "They have a great program."

He got up and walked over to the wall where Ari's prints were hung. He sipped and studied. Leaning in. Stepping back. His left forearm, wrist to elbow, was thick with tattoos. The top of another inked design peeked over the edge of his collar.

A tattoo only the Queen had seen.

Trelawney came around from the bar and wiggled back between Jav's knees, pulling his arms around her from behind. Jav put his chin on top of her head.

"If you're my sort of brother-in-law's sister," he said, "does that make you my sort of sister? In law? Ish?"

"Definitely." She leaned further back against him. "Ish."

"Aren't I lucky then."

Stef turned and smiled at them. "I'd say she's lucky."

"He's the best hugger," Trelawney said. "He really should get paid for it."

Jav winked at Stef and mouthed, "I do."

Stef grinned into his cup. The bell on the jamb rang and customers came in. Trelawney went back behind the bar and Stef sat next to Jav. Beneath the counter, their knees bumped.

"You live in town?" Stef said.

"I did. I rented the apartment upstairs from Trelawney. Which reminds me." He reached in his pocket for the keys. He held them a moment, letting the memories jingle in his palm before he pushed them across to Trelawney. "I'm in Manhattan now. Riverside Drive. You?"

"I'm down in Chelsea." Stef checked his watch. "And yikes, my train's in ten minutes. Gotta get." He took a last sip of coffee, then reached for his messenger bag. "Listen, it was good to meet you."

"Same." They shook hands.

"You got a card? I'd like to talk to you about a website."

"Sure. Give me yours?"

Stef set his bag on the stool and dug around. "You can see I'm hopeless at selling myself. I never have a card when I need one. Goddammit..." He took out two marble notebooks and set them on the bar, followed by a paperback with an emerald and black cover.

Client Privilege, by Gil Rafael.

"That's a great book," Trelawney said, leaning her elbows on the counter and not looking at Jav.

"It's fantastic," Stef said. "I'm going to finish it on the train. Ah. Here you go." He slid a card down the counter toward Jav. "Don't lose it."

Jav turned it over.

STEFFEN FINCH
CURATOR & SAILOR

Stef shouldered his bag and tucked the book under his arm. With a last cobalt-blue look, a flicker of one dimple and a wave, he walked out. A jingle of bells. Then silence. It filled Jav's ears as he stared at the card.

A group of finches is called a charm.

He looked up and through the window, watching Stef cross Main Street to the station.

"Jav," Trelawney said sharply. She reached across the bar and whacked the back of his head.

"Ow. What?"

She pointed toward the door. "*Fetch.*"

Jav bolted off the stool and out of Celeste's.

"Hey," he called, running across the street. "Stef." His tongue pushed the name to the roof of his mouth, while his teeth locked against his bottom lip and kept it from escaping.

The finch turned around, his hair and eyes full of the sun.

"I'm actually driving back into Manhattan," Jav said. "Want a ride?"

"So touching purest and so heard
In the brain's reflex of yon bird;
Wherefore their soul in me, or mine,
Through self-forgetfulness divine,
In them, that song aloft maintains,
To fill the sky and thrill the plains
With showerings drawn from human stores,
As he to silence nearer soars,
Extends the world at wings and dome,
More spacious making more our home,
Till lost on his aërial rings
In light, and then the fancy sings."

—George Meredith, *The Lark Ascending*

Acknowledgements

YOU HAVE TO BE CAREFUL what you say and do around me, because it will end up in a book:

As the family legend goes, Aunt Susan was sick in bed with the flu. And Uncle Dave was being impossible, teasing and yanking the covers off her bed. He ran and hid in the bathroom to gloat. Susan backed down the hall and in a fever-induced rage, kicked the bathroom door in. We tell this story every time we get together. These are the stories that make a beautiful life. And not everyone gets one.

When I was about three or four years old, living in Croton-on-Hudson, a family called Trueblood lived next door. They eventually moved away but the name stayed behind, stuck in my head like a beautiful untold story. Until now.

When PJ Geraghty's daughter had mono and insisted she was dying, he told her not to die in the house because he'd have to disclose it when he tried to sell the place. You just can't squander that sort of line.

I forgot who referred to Connie Buono as "often wrong, never in doubt," but it's not a bad way to go through life.

The late, great Jerry Gross told my father about the distinction between walkers and nephews (said information gleaned from a book Jerry was editing at the time). My father didn't believe him until some years later, when he was at the April in Paris ball, and heard a woman behind him shriek, "Cynthia! You have to come meet my nephew, Derek!" True story.

I went straight to Art Harvey for a recommendation on what kind of car Felipe would drive. Without hesitation he told me the 1966 Ford Thunderbird Convertible.

Jen McPartlin found the camel swing coat on a rack at Savers. It wasn't her size but on principle she had to alert her fellow patrons. "Does anyone *realize* this is a *Halston?*"

Bourgeois twit is a nod to Rosamunde Pilcher's *The Shell Seekers*. When told by his daughter she might get involved with an American Ranger, Laurence Stern advises her she is, yes, a married woman, "but not a bourgeois nit-wit."

On 9/11, Krista Rizzo told her husband Will, "Come here *now.*" They are one of my favorite love stories.

The postcard reading *Everyone who knew me before 9/11 believes I'm dead* first appeared on the extraordinary blog *Post Secret* and has never been explained or solved. From the moment I saw it, I thought, "Here's a story…"

My friend Marla Behler has a Nova Scotia Duck Tolling Retriever named Luke. He's beautiful and chill and when I started sketching out Ari, I knew Luke was his dog.

Kevin Smith has the dubious honor of crash-testing Deane's ski accident. Unlike Deane, he got up after the collision, told the U-turner off in no uncertain terms, and did another run on his broken binding. Then he thought maybe he should get himself checked out. Men.

I never met the late George Buffaloe and I know he didn't invent the saying "Here's to those who wish us well, all the rest can go to hell…" But I have fond memories of it from both his daughters' weddings, so he gets credit.

My father, the not-so-saintly Bernie, wrote letters to me at college and ended every one with "con muchos abrazos amor y besos, pero no pesos."

My mother, Carol, taught me to sew clothes and costumes, and built me a dollhouse from the plans in *Better Homes and Gardens*.

Sometimes I ask people to deliberately tell me things so I can put them in a book. I cannot reveal the names of three gentlemen who openly and generously answered my thousand questions about escorting, but without them, Jav would not exist, nor do the excellent job he did.

Sometimes I have to thank strangers. I only know him as Carlos, and he appeared on a segment of Momondo's DNA Journey series. He's Cuban, or so he thought. I watched his face as he looked at his true-blood and discovered he was a man of the world. His smile made me want to tell a story. He became Flip. And everything about *Larks* changed.

Then I have my usual suspects, people without whom I cannot do anything:

My editor, Becky. I do the thing, I give it to her, she does the thing and gives it back to me a better thing.

My designer, Tracy Kopsachilis. I ask for a beautiful thing on the cover, she gives me the beautiful thing.

My formatter Colleen Sheehan. I want a thing to look like this. She makes the thing look like this.

Rach Lawrence of the microscopic eyes. She does a final proofread and picks out all the wrong things.

My assistant and squishy, Jennifer Beach. She makes me pretty things, and then does all the things on my list of things to avoid.

My army of advance readers. I write a lot of things. They read all the things.

Naroba Castillo Lozano, who let her name be a thing.

Elsa Calderón Bornay, who corrected my miserable Spanish things.

My daughter, Julie. My squheeghy little woman-girl. Even in the rough teen years, she always for to take leetle nap with me.

My magnificent, most excellent son, AJ. This kid is going places.

And always, JP, who is happiest on the mountain. You fact-checked the ski chapters. Pointed out Stella Artois wasn't on the market in the 1980s. Didn't question why I had eleven books on the sex trade industry in my Kindle. And endured the synopsis that lasted from New York to Philadelphia (there's the elevator pitch, and then there's the stuck-in- the-elevator pitch). I love being your wife. Our combined bullshit has always been bigger, better and more important than all our individual crap. Thanks, fucky.

Thank You

IF YOU ENJOYED *An Exaltation of Larks,* I'd love to hear about it. Please consider leaving a short review on the platform of your choice. Honest reviews are the tip jar of independent authors and each and every one is treasured.

If you're a Facebooker, join others who enjoyed my books in the Read & Nap Lounge:

LQRWRITES.COM/LOUNGE

Stop by my website

SUANNELAQUEURWRITES.COM

or look for me on Instagram at

@SWAINBLQR

Wherever you find me, all feels are welcome. And I always have coffee.

Also by Suanne Laqueur

A Small Hotel

THE FISH TALES
The Man I Love
Give Me Your Answer True
Here to Stay
The Ones That Got Away
Daisy, Daisy

VENERY
An Exaltation of Larks
A Charm of Finches
A Scarcity of Condors
The Voyages of Trueblood Cay
Tales from Cushman Row
A Plump of Woodcocks

SHORTS
Love & Bravery: Sixteen Stories
An Evening at the Hotel

ANTHOLOGIES
Flesh Fiction

About The Author

A FORMER PROFESSIONAL dancer and teacher, Suanne Laqueur went from choreographing music to choreographing words, writing stories that appeal to the passions of all readers, crossing gender, age and genre. As a devoted mental health advocate, her novels focus on both romantic and familial relationships, as well as psychology, PTSD and generational trauma.

Laqueur's novel *An Exaltation of Larks* was the grand prize winner in the 2017 Writer's Digest Book Awards and took first place in the 2019 North Street Book Prize. Her debut novel *The Man I Love* won a gold medal in the 2015 Readers' Favorite Book Awards and was named Best Debut in the Feathered Quill Book Awards. Her follow-up novel, *Give Me Your Answer True,* was also a gold medal winner at the 2016 RFBA.

Laqueur graduated from Alfred University with a double major in dance and theater. She taught at the Carol Bierman School of Ballet Arts in Croton-on-Hudson for ten years. An avid reader, cook and gardener, she started her blog EatsReadsThinks in 2010.

Suanne lives in Westchester County, New York with her husband and two children.

CPSIA information can be obtained
at www.ICGtesting.com
Printed in the USA
BVHW07082823062
666255BV00014B/1199